THE DEVIL'S TRIANGLE

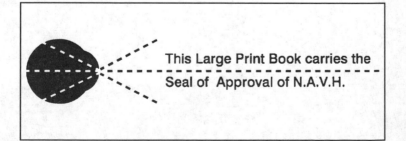

This Large Print Book carries the
Seal of Approval of N.A.V.H.

THE DEVIL'S TRIANGLE

CATHERINE COULTER
AND J.T. ELLISON

THORNDIKE PRESS
A part of Gale, Cengage Learning

Farmington Hills, Mich • San Francisco • New York • Waterville, Maine
Meriden, Conn • Mason, Ohio • Chicago

GALE
CENGAGE Learning®

LIBRARY OF CONGRESS CATALOGING-IN-PUBLICATION DATA

Names: Coulter, Catherine, author. | Ellison, J.T., author.
Title: The devil's triangle / Catherine Coulter and J.T. Ellison.
Description: Large print editlon. | Waterville, Maine : Thorndike Press, a part of Gale, Cengage Learning, 2017. | Series: Thorndike Press large print basic | A Brit in the FBI thriller
Identifiers: LCCN 2017002645 | ISBN 9781410497543 (hardcover) | ISBN 1410497542 (hardcover)
Subjects: LCSH: United States. Federal Bureau of Investigation—Fiction. | Terrorism—Prevention—Fiction. | Intelligence officers—Fiction. | Large type books. | BISAC: FICTION / Suspense. | FICTION / Espionage. | GSAFD: Suspense fiction. | Mystery fiction.
Classification: LCC PS3553.O843 D49 2017b | DDC 813/.54—dc23
LC record available at https://lccn.loc.gov/2017002645

Published in 2017 by arrangement with Gallery Books, an imprint of Simon & Schuster, Inc.

Printed in the United States of America
1 2 3 4 5 6 7 21 20 19 18 17

To all my wonderful writer comrades
who get together at my house for lunch,
laughter (lots of laughter), life/writing
updates, and Dom Pérignon:

Nyree Belleville, Allison Brennan, Josie
Brown, Deborah Coonts, Carol Culver,
J.T. Ellison, Barbara Freethy, Tracy
Grant, Anne Hearn, Brenda Novak,
Veronica Wolff, Jami Worthington
CATHERINE

For Catherine, and this amazing
journey we're on
And, as always, Randy J.T.

ACKNOWLEDGMENTS

To our village, many thanks for putting it all together!

We are indebted to the fine folks at Gallery Books, especially Louise Burke, Jennifer Bergstrom, Lauren McKenna, Elana Cohen, Kristin Dwyer, and all the rest of the team, who are not only doing so much to get these books into the hands of so many, but do it with grace and good humor. And adult beverages. That always helps.

Robert Gottlieb and Scott Miller are verifiably the two best agents in the business. Thank you for always having our backs.

The following were a huge help in the daily creation of this story: Karen Evans, Laura Benedict, Amy Kerr, Ariel Lawhon, Sherrie Saint, Jeff Abbott, Joan and Jerome Tussey, and J.T.'s heart, Randy Ellison, who kindly obliged me with a research trip to Venice, and spent hours upon hours in the Piazza San Marco, shooting bad guys from behind columns and on balconies. Fun, and so helpful!

Also, a special shout-out to Alicia McNeil, who caught the typo of all typos. Trust us when we say you're glad she did.

Lastly, many thanks to the wonderful librarians and booksellers who share these books with their patrons, and our amazing online communities on Facebook and Twitter and Goodreads. We couldn't do it without you!

■ ■ ■ ■

PART ONE

■ ■ ■ ■

He who controls the weather, will control
the world.
He who controls gravity, will control the
universe.
He who controls time, will never be around.
— THOMAS FREY, FUTURIST

PROLOGUE

Clos Lucé
Amboise, France
April 30, 1519

The light was dying, and so was Da Vinci.

Francesco Melzi stood in the window staring out at the gray spires of the Château Amboise. Saying goodbye to his friend, his mentor, his lover, was impossible. But there was no escaping the reality they were facing. Da Vinci had days left to live, and his copious papers were not yet completely sorted.

Melzi's lover lay on the bloodred velvet coverlet, pillows stacked behind him. He was asleep now; there was a peace about him, a gauzy aura that made Melzi realize Da Vinci truly was not long for the world.

Melzi lit more candles against the falling light and stepped to the table. They were down to the last three crates, so old the wood was cracked and stained. He would sort some more before he took a light dinner in the kitchen. Da Vinci was too weak to make the trek himself anymore. A tray would be brought later, and the old master wouldn't eat from it.

Melzi studied the pages, admiring the ingenuity, the genius, not understanding everything he was reading and seeing. A man ahead of his time, was Leonardo.

A voice, weak but warm, came from behind him. "Oh, to be young in the face of death."

Melzi jumped to his feet and went to the bed. "You're awake."

Da Vinci smiled weakly. "Not for long, I am afraid. Are we nearly finished?"

"I'm down to the last few crates. How are you feeling?"

A small twisted smile. "Like I am dying. I am sorry to leave you, my friend."

"Stop, please. I do not wish to hear it. In my mind, you will live forever."

"These are good words for an old man to hear. Now, where were we?"

Melzi went to the table and picked up the folio he'd just opened. The image drawn on the front was easily understood; a monstrous lightning bolt took up the entire page.

Da Vinci whispered, "Ah, my thunderbolt. Bring it to me."

Da Vinci's hands were too weak to hold the folio, so Melzi placed it in his lap and opened it.

Inside were numerals and drawings and more depictions of lightning.

Melzi asked, "What is this?"

There was new urgency in Da Vinci's tone and a sudden fire in his eyes. "Listen to me carefully. This must be destroyed."

"Destroyed? We can't destroy any of your work. Surely you must be joking."

"I am not. These plans, these ideas, they are not of this world. If the wrong person were to see them and try to build this machine, it could be the end of all our days."

"Whatever is it meant to be?"

Da Vinci began to cough, clutching the folio to his chest. The parchment became flecked with small droplets of blood. Melzi rushed to the pitcher, poured doctored wine into a goblet, and brought it to his mentor's side.

"Drink this. It will help."

"I do not want drugs." Da Vinci heaved. "You must swear to me, Francesco, that these pages will be burned. Do it now while I watch."

"Drink some wine, and I promise I will do as you say."

Melzi helped Da Vinci drink, then set the

glass back on the table.

"Now, before I consign it to the ashes, what is this?"

Da Vinci's eyes were still bright. *"La macchina di fulmine."*

"A lightning machine?"

"Si."

The lightning bolt on the cover made more sense now. Melzi looked at the pages in awe.

"You are telling me you have designed a machine that can control the weather?"

"No, no. It was only an idea, born of an ancient myth. A painting I was commissioned for, of Zeus and his thunderbolt. I turned down the commission, but the idea of the power he supposedly held fascinated me. All things are brought forth by nature. Why could one not control nature in return?"

"So you found a way to bring it to life? A way to harness the power of a storm?"

The drugs in the wine had worked quickly, but Da Vinci fought against them, shaking his weary head to clear it. "It is too dangerous to discuss the details of how it could work, even with you, my friend. If someone were ever able to control the weather, they could control the whole world. Fire the pages, now. I insist."

Melzi had no choice. He went to the grate and began feeding the folio into the flames, one page at a time. He glanced over his shoulder and saw Da Vinci had fallen asleep. Sadness overcame him again. He reached for another page, caught himself staring at the sketch. It was beautiful, like so many of Da Vinci's works.

Da Vinci began coughing again, the blood coming to his lips. Melzi set the folio down on the table, went to his friend, his master, wiped his face and held him. There would be time to burn the papers later. For now, he needed to hold the man he loved.

CHAPTER ONE

Venice, Italy
Mid-June
One Week Ago

Kitsune stood on the Rialto Bridge and watched the sun flash against the waves of the lagoon. She enjoyed the early mornings in Venice, before the summer crowds flooded into the city. She watched pigeons peck the ground for yesterday's crumbs, watched a row of tethered gondolas bob in the heavy sea swell. There would be a storm soon — she tasted it in the air. She looked at her watch. It was time to go. Her client had instructed her to take a water taxi to the San Zaccaria dock, then walk to the house.

She should have been on her way before now, but she'd waited there on the bridge to see who was following her. Even though she hadn't seen anyone yet, she'd felt eyes on her, felt them since her plane had landed an hour earlier. At the airport's dock she'd caught a glimpse of one of them: a man — dark sunglasses, a slouchy work jacket. There were probably others, but where were they? She hated being in the open like this — a target — and the large tube in her hand a target as well. She still didn't see anyone.

She bent down to adjust the strap of her sandal. From the corner of her eye she saw him. She was sure it was the same man she'd seen at the Marco Polo airport, still wearing sunglasses and a jacket. He wasn't very good at his job, since she'd spotted him, standing in the alley to the left of the Hotel Danieli, chewing on a toothpick like he didn't have a care in the world. But where were the others? She knew she hadn't been followed to Venice, she was sure of that, so why now? For some reason, her client didn't trust her. She felt a lick of anger. It was an insult to her reputation. Or perhaps someone knew what was inside the large tube and wanted it?

Ah, there he was, the second man, hovering near the dock, a cap pulled low on his head, wearing wrinkled jeans and scuffed boots. Both men were in their thirties, muscled, garbed in everyday working clothes. Thugs. One was tall, the other short. Mutt and Jeff. She saw no one else.

18

Only two of them? Another insult. She took note of the small sign above Mr. Short's head — *Calle de la Rasse.*

Kitsune had learned the complicated layout of the Venetian streets, an integral part of her preparation, since she could run much faster than she could swim.

She checked the men out again. Both cocky, sure of themselves, but she could take them. Easily.

Not yet, though. The time wasn't right.

Their presence bothered her. Why the sudden distrust from her client? Her reputation was built on absolute discretion, always delivering what was commissioned and never asking questions. She had no false modesty. She could steal anything, anywhere — even the Koh-i-Noor diamond, that magnificent bloody stone that had nearly gotten her killed. A pity she'd had to give it up.

This client was paying her a small fortune, and half of it, five million euros, was already deposited in four different accounts in four different banks, as was her custom. She would receive the other five million upon delivery. All of it was straightforward, so why the two thugs following her?

Kitsune had been a thief for too long to ignore the prickle of unease that went down her neck. The tube was heavy, and she hugged it closer.

The breeze picked up between the Venetian buildings, blowing gently down the narrow canal. She continued forward, over the small bridge, up the walkway, past the arriving gondoliers, who watched her and wondered. Grant told her she moved differently, with singular grace and arrogance, and she looked like what she was — strong and dangerous — and then he'd held her close, stroked her long hair, and whispered against her temple that only the very stupid, or the very desperate, would mess with her. She felt a warm punch to her heart thinking of her husband of ten months, how the green of his eyes turned nearly black when he was kissing her. Soon, she would be with him again. She would give the prize to the client, and be gone.

She'd fulfilled the first part of the job three days earlier, when she'd pulled off one of the most fun heists of her career. She'd dyed her hair the deepest black, worn brown contacts, and used a semipermanent stain to make her skin appear two shades deeper, a process she didn't relish, but it helped her blend in beautifully with the population of Istanbul. With her forged credentials, which included a signature from Turkish military leader Hulusi Akar, the palace authorities had followed orders and assigned her to work security at the Topkapi Palace. It had taken her more than three months to work her way out of the harem complex and into special security in the Holy Relics exhibit, where Moses's staff was displayed.

Her arms had gotten tired carrying the H&K MP5 machine gun all day. Even with the strap around her neck and shoulder, the carbine got heavy, and being on alert for twelve hours at a time was exhausting. Despite the heat and grit and the hordes of tourists trooping in and out of the treasure-filled rooms in the palace, her assigned areas gave her a lovely view of the Bosphorus. The sun shined on the water, sprinkling diamonds, the sea breezes cooled her, and the tourists gathered nearby to take photos. She was careful, very careful, never to get in the shots. It wouldn't do to have someone post a photo of her on Facebook accidentally, have some government drone monitoring the Internet run the photos through facial recognition, and blow her cover.

She wondered again: did her unknown client really believe that what she carried in her hands was the very embodiment of power? That what she carried wasn't simply an ancient knob of wood but the actual staff

21

of Moses? Or, as some called it, Aaron's rod? No matter what it was called, this staff was one of the most sought-after and priceless artifacts in the world, and she'd managed to break into the Holy Relics exhibit after hours and take the staff out of its lighted case after cutting the wires to the security alarm, and disappeared. And that brought a smile of satisfaction.

No more inky-black hair, no more dark brown eyes, the stain washed away. She was back to her blue eyes, her white skin, and her own dark hair.

Yes, it had been a clean, perfectly executed job. One of her best, and she, the Fox, had a string of risky, daring jobs behind her.

The international news channels were still leading with the theft. No way was she going to take a chance of being caught in the crosshairs. She'd make the delivery, get her other five million, go home to Capri, and talk Grant into visiting Australia or America, anywhere away from Europe. He was due for a vacation, having spent the last three months in Afghanistan guarding a high-ranking British officer.

The house she was going to was only a drop site. She'd used this protocol many times — empty house, the owners probably on vacation. Clients rarely wanted the Fox to know where they lived. She wondered who would be there to receive the stolen staff.

A winding alleyway took her deeper into the neighborhoods, along the canals. And there it was, a simple, classic Venetian home — red brick, the second and third floors balconied, set between a narrow street and a small canal.

She went up the steps, knocked on the dark green door. Waited a moment before the thick, old wood swung open. An older man in a dark suit and silver tie told her to come in.

Inside, all was silent. She followed him through a small courtyard, a marble fountain at its center. He showed her into a parlor, to the right of the fountain. The door closed behind her.

The room was empty, the silence heavy. She heard voices, a man and a woman, somewhere nearby — above her, probably — speaking rapid Italian. The clients? Although she understood exactly what they were saying, it still made no sense to her.

The woman said clearly, excitement in her voice, "I wish I could see it, the Gobi sands — a tsunami sweeping over Beijing."

"We will see it on video," came a man's matter-of-fact voice. "All the sand, do you

23

think? Could Grandfather be that good?"

"You know he is. And we will see the aftermath for ourselves. We will leave in three days, after things have calmed down."

The man said, marveling, "Can you imagine, we are the ones to drain the Gobi?"

Kitsune stood silently, listening. She shook her head. Drain the Gobi Desert dry? All that sand covering Beijing? By their grandfather? What she'd heard, it was nuts, made no sense. An image of Moses raising his staff, parting the Red Sea so the Israelites could escape the Egyptian army flashed through her mind. It was a famous image, given all the paintings and movies, and there were many who believed that was exactly what happened. But not her.

Kitsune held by her side a gnarly old piece of wood the Turks had stolen when they'd plundered Egypt in 1517, audacious enough or credulous enough to proclaim it to be Moses's staff. She didn't care if it was real or not, it didn't matter. Ten million euros would keep her in bikinis for a long time. She pictured Moses again, only this time she saw him waving his staff to send the sands flying out of the Gobi Desert. Such a strange image.

The voices faded away.

Moments later, the door to the parlor

opened and a man came in. He was short, with dark hair and flat black eyes. This one, in spite of his well-cut dark suit, his perfectly polished boots, couldn't be the client. He looked coarse, crude, a lieutenant playing dress-up. Another thug, only this one with a bit of power, probably running the other who'd followed her. So the man and woman she'd heard talking wanted him to handle the transaction, then bring them the staff. Fine by her. All she wanted was her money.

He crossed the room to the small desk, picked up a silver lighter, and touched it to the end of a cigarette. He blew out a stream of gray smoke and said, in passable English, "I am Antonio Pazzi, and you are the Fox. You have the package?"

"Of course." Kitsune set the tube on the desk and stepped back. Pazzi pulled a stiletto from his coat pocket, slit open the top of the cylinder, and upended it. The well-wrapped staff slid out into his waiting hand. He reverently laid it atop the desk and peeled off the packing. He looked at the staff, motionless, staring, but not touching it. Finally, he looked up at her, smiled widely, showing yellow tobacco-stained teeth. "I did not believe you would be able to steal this precious rod from the Topkapi. Your reputation is deserved. My masters

25

will be pleased."

She saw him press a small button on the desk, and in the next instant she heard a door close, a boat's engine fire to life. So he'd signaled the client that she'd brought the staff? And they'd left. Pazzi handed her a long white envelope. "Five million euros. You will leave now."

As if she wanted to stay, maybe have a drink with this oily cretin with his yellow teeth. She wanted to open the envelope, but he kept smiling, herding her toward the door, and she felt that familiar shiver down her neck and went on red alert, her body flexed and ready to spring. Were the two men outside the door, waiting for her? Pazzi gave her a small salute, and at the last moment, he slipped past her and slammed the door behind him. She heard the key turn in the lock. In the next moment, another door opened, this time behind her. Mutt and Jeff stepped through, and both held guns in their hands.

"What a lovely surprise," she said in Italian, and, quick as a cobra, she dove at Mutt's feet. He had been expecting her to run, and he hesitated a moment. She rolled into him and knocked him backward, his arms flailing for purchase, and he fell against a chair. She popped back to her feet

— Mutt on her left, struggling to get back up, and Jeff on her right, his Beretta aimed at her chest.

Kitsune fell to her knees, whipped out her two Walther PPKs cross-armed, and pulled the triggers almost before she'd squared the sights. Jeff fired at the same time. If she'd stayed standing, she'd be dead. Now he was the one who was dead, sprawled on his back on the floor, blood blooming from his chest. She'd missed Mutt, but his gun had clattered to the floor and slid under a red velvet sofa. He sprang to his feet and came at her, fast and hard, fists up and flying, trying to knock the gun away and kill her with his bare hands. He was fast, she'd give him that, but she was faster. A heartbeat later he was on the floor with a hole in his forehead.

Kitsune had never used guns, but in the past few months, Grant had trained her in them, and trained her well. And when he was satisfied, he'd given her the two Walthers. Almost as if Grant had known she would need them. She sent him a silent thank-you as she pointed the gun in her right hand over her shoulder, toward the locked door, just in case, and walked to the opposite side of the room. She listened but didn't hear anything. The house had gone silent. Too silent. As if someone was listening. She had to get out of there, now.

She heard voices shouting. She yanked open the door and ran down a long hallway ending in a staircase. The house itself was narrow and old, the walls cool gray stone. She had no choice but to run up the stairs.

She heard feet pounding after her, shouts growing closer. Kitsune burst through onto a rooftop terrace. Up this high, she saw that terraces littered the rooftops, and the Venetian houses were crammed cheek by jowl, separated by the small canals that crisscrossed Venice.

She didn't look down at the murky canal below, paid no attention to the shouts from the staircase, as men ran up to the terrace. She leaped across to the neighboring terrace. She felt a bullet whiz by her ear, and she dropped and rolled, was on her feet in a second, running to the next terrace. She heard the man leap after her, moving fast, gaining on her. She raced to the end of the rooftop and leaped again, barely missed a window box overflowing with pink and red geraniums, and skidded along the pebbled roof.

He followed her, shouting, shooting. People screamed through open windows, gondoliers looked at the sight and shouted, tourists stared up in awe as light-footed Kitsune soared over them like a bird in flight. Laundry lines tumbled into the water below. She was careful to avoid the electric lines; she'd be dead and gone before she hit the water if she grabbed one of those by accident.

She looked back, saw that it was Pazzi chasing her. She hadn't expected him to be so fast, but he was reaching his limits, and dropping back. With a yell of frustration, he took another shot. The bullet skimmed her arm, cutting the fabric of her shirt, stinging like mad. Blood began running down, turning her hand red. Not good.

She made a last desperate leap, grabbed a laundry line, swung down and smashed against the wall of a redbrick house, knocking the air out of her lungs, and dropped, hard, onto the deck of a water taxi.

The captain, gap-mouthed, stumbled back, and she pushed him overboard, roared the engine to life and took off. She heard shouts, curses behind her, but didn't look back. She pressed her right hand against the wound in her upper arm.

The boat shot out by the San Zaccaria vaporetto station. She was free now, in the lagoon, and she gunned it.

She was breathing hard, and bleeding, but for the moment, she was upright and safe, cool water splashing her, the wind tearing through her hair. She heard sirens. The police would be after her any minute now. She had to ditch the boat. It was a thirty-minute run to the airport, but that would be suicide; she could never fly out.

Think, Kitsune.

South, she'd go south, to Rimini, dock there, and start her way home.

She checked the gas, excellent, the tank was nearly full. She left the channel and headed into the open seas, leaving behind the wails of the sirens. She remembered she'd stuffed the white envelope Pazzi had given her inside her shirt. At least she'd been paid for the job. Or had she? She ripped the envelope open and inside she saw a folded sheet of paper. She opened it and saw a rough drawing of a dead fox. She felt the tearing pain in her arm as she wadded up the paper and tossed it overboard. Five million euros was that critical to them? But why had they wanted her dead? It didn't matter, she didn't care. There would be hell to pay.

CHAPTER TWO

Venice, Italy

Cassandra Kohath lay back on a chaise, watching her twin brother, Ajax, stare out the window toward the lagoon. Was he thinking about the now-dead thief, carted out to the channel by Pazzi, weighted and tossed into the water? They heard the wail of sirens, rising and falling in time with the lapping of the water against the lower walls of their villa, and both snapped to. What was that all about?

Ajax's phone buzzed. He listened, then punched off and turned to her. "That was Lilith. Two of Pazzi's men are dead, and he couldn't catch the Fox. Don't worry, he has the staff and will be here soon, doubtless full of excuses why he and his men failed to kill the wretched woman."

Cassandra said, "I hate loose ends, Ajax, and she's a big one."

He thought a moment. "We don't want

the *polizia* to catch her, that could prove fatal if our friends aren't the ones who control the situation. Lilith knows everything about the thief, her habits, her disguises, where she lives with her husband. We'll get her, don't worry."

A knock sounded on the door. Cassandra called, "Come in," and Pazzi entered, sweating, his beautiful suit ripped and dirty, his hair wild around his face. He said nothing at all, simply came forward and placed the wrapped staff on the chaise near her feet. He straightened, continued standing silently, waiting for punishment he knew would come. He feared Ajax more than Cassandra, because Ajax was the devil he knew. He'd seen Ajax slip a stiletto into a man's chest, after one small inadvertent insult. He'd watched Ajax pull the stiletto out of the man's chest, swipe off the blood across the man's face, and slip it back in its sheath. And then he'd continued his conversation with Pazzi — over the man's twitching body.

As for his sister, he didn't know if she was as deadly as she was beautiful, but he didn't doubt it. The two of them, side by side, were striking, mirror images of each other — blond, blue-eyed, strong, born of wealth, raised on power. Both deadly. Was the sister smarter than her twin? He didn't know that, either. At first he'd wanted her, as he imagined most men did when they saw her, but that had passed when she'd looked at him as if he were nothing more than a piece of dirt beneath her feet, and he'd known, deep down, this was exactly how she viewed him, a clod of dirt, not to be shaken off so long as he was useful.

Would Ajax slip his stiletto in Pazzi's own heart, wipe his own blood on his face? He wanted to tell them that the woman, the Fox, was beyond anything he'd ever seen, and even now he couldn't believe she'd taken out his men in less than a minute and she'd actually not killed herself flying high over Venice. He'd hit her, he knew he had, but he also knew it would do him no good at all to tell them. He calmed himself. After all, he'd brought them the staff.

His eyes strayed to the frame on the wall above Cassandra's head. Heavy and ornate, it nearly overpowered the small parchment inside — a careful, intricate drawing of a lightning bolt, faded with age, spots of black along the top edge. Such a curious piece. It was rumored to have come from Da Vinci himself, though Pazzi couldn't believe such a thing, but if it was true, his bosses had certainly stolen it. Arranged for it to be stolen, that is. Had they killed the thief who'd managed it?

Maybe his failure was more important at the moment than their precious staff. With this thought, his heart was pounding hard now, bile rising in his throat, and he had to swallow. His wife had never asked him why he chose to live with such fear because she already knew. They paid him very well and he was a venal man.

A lifetime of waiting to Pazzi was only a couple of seconds. Ajax said only, "Well?"

Cassandra wasn't looking at him, all her attention was on that tube that held the staff.

He tried to stand tall and straight. "I did all I could. That woman, the Fox, she killed my men and escaped over the rooftops. I went after her. I know I hit her, but she didn't slow." He could barely get the words out. "She has escaped." He bowed his head, braced himself.

Ajax said quietly, "We pay you a great deal, Pazzi. Yet you have bungled things."

"I am sorry, sir. I did everything I could."

Ajax let the silence grow heavy, then said, "You will have one more chance. The woman is a loose end that could ruin us. Only a fool would trust a thief with such knowledge as she has now. We are not fools.

As I said, we will give you one more chance. If you fail to kill her, then your life is forfeit. Do you understand me, Pazzi?"

His heart gave a leap. *He wasn't going to die — this time.* "Yes, sir, I understand. What do you wish me to do?"

And Ajax told him.

Cassandra added, "Since we have friends in the Carabinieri and the *polizia,* we can add another layer to the plan. That house isn't connected to us, it was only a drop site, nothing more. We left nothing behind. The Rinaldis will not be home until late this afternoon. Murder them, Pazzi, ransack the place, and then let your friends in the *polizia* know the Fox was responsible. If I recall, Signore Rinaldi is a member of the Venetian council. There should be plenty of outrage in finding the killer of such a prominent Venetian citizen."

Murder the Rinaldis? They were good people, but — He didn't want to be dead. Pazzi bowed his head. "Yes, madam. This is a wonderful plan. I will handle it directly."

"See that you do it right, Pazzi," Cassandra said, and smiled at him — a smile so cold it froze him to his bones. "Or it will be your headless body floating in the Grand Canal. Now, off with you. I want to hear nothing more of this but a success story.

Find the Fox, kill her. Now."

Ajax said, that smooth voice low, "Don't fail us again, Pazzi. Lilith wouldn't like it."

Lilith, another demon from hell.

The instant he was out the door, Cassandra lightly touched her fingers to the wrapped staff, Pazzi and the Rinaldis forgotten. Had it really belonged to Moses himself?

Ajax came and stood by her chaise. "Shall we?"

"You know what is supposed to happen when we open it, when you and I together touch it."

Ajax said, "Yes. We will soon see. Are you ready?"

She slowly unwrapped it, so afraid and excited, her fingers shook. She said, "I'll be careful not to touch the staff itself. The prophecies are clear. We must do it together. We are the last twins of the Kohath line. We are the only ones who can bring the power of the staff back to life."

He patted her face, almost a slap, but not quite. "I know. We've spent our whole lives listening to the prophecy."

She continued to reverently remove layer after layer. "If it is the real staff the Turks stole from Egypt, then it means we're probably looking for the Ark in the wrong place."

Ajax said, "We will soon know if the Ark is in Egypt. I believe whatever the outcome, our expenditure of five million euros was worth it."

She carefully peeled away another layer of linen. Pazzi had been careful to rewrap it securely. "I want it to be real, I do, but I cannot believe our mother was led astray by faulty information."

"You're being too slow, Cassandra. Open it now."

She pulled away the last covering, a layer of even softer white linen, and they looked down at a staff made of brown wood — almond wood — their mother had told them, about forty-eight inches long, with a thick knob on the side, near the top of the staff, that gave the impression of a small branch beginning to sprout out the side.

Cassandra reached toward it, her fingers nearly touching it. "It's not singing to me the way I expected, the way Mother told me it would."

"We won't know if it's real until we pick it up."

"Yes. Together." Their hands hovered over the staff. "One, two, three."

They grasped the staff with both hands and stood it upright, their hands stacked upon the other, each fully touching the staff.

According to the prophecy they'd heard since they were old enough to repeat the words, their united hands should instantly make the knob on the staff begin to bud and bloom. But there were no buds, no blooms. There was nothing at all but the old misshapen stick.

Cassandra wanted to weep. "It's a fake."

Ajax said, "Come, you really didn't expect it to be real, now did you? And now we know Mother was on the right track all along." He walked to the desk, pulled out a tape measure, measured the length of the staff. He smiled. "The staff is over three inches too long to fit inside the Ark. The Topkapi had to know it was fake." He picked up the staff, broke it over his knee, and threw the two pieces out the window into the canal.

She heard the wood pieces splash into the water below. She walked to the bar in the corner of the large room, opened the small refrigerator, and popped the cork on a bottle of Veuve Cliquot. She poured two glasses, handed one to Ajax.

"Screw the Topkapi. Serves them right for perpetuating a lie all these years. Now the good news: we now know for sure the Ark isn't in Egypt."

They clicked glasses and drank.

"And to the death of the Fox," Ajax said. "The only thread left to snip in our needful experiment."

They drank deeply.

A moment later, a knock sounded.

"Come," Cassandra called.

The door opened, and a tall, slender woman, with long blond hair curving around her narrow face, stepped into the room.

Ajax went to her, took her arms in his hands, and smiled down at her.

Lilith said, "Don't tell me the staff from the Topkapi is the real deal."

"A fake, as we suspected," he said, his hands moving to her face, lightly stroking. "You're grinning like a loon, Lilith. What is it?"

"The storm will be under way in two days, no longer."

"Excellent news."

It was indeed good news, and it was news that Cassandra should have known before Lilith. She'd planned to call Grandfather that very evening to get the status. She eyed her brother, his arm still around their own private assassin. Lilith Forrester-Clarke was from Roslin, Scotland, the small town made famous by the novel *The Da Vinci Code*. Cassandra found herself wondering yet again how the very bedrock of Christianity could have spawned this devil's seed. Lilith and Ajax had been together for nearly four years now, lovers, confidants, but Cassandra knew he was the one who had the control, she'd never doubted that. He was Lilith's handler, fondly called her his ultimate weapon. Together they formulated plans, and she executed them. As far as Cassandra knew, Lilith had never failed. So why hadn't Ajax assigned Lilith to deal with the Fox instead of that buffoon Pazzi?

Cassandra watched Lilith pour herself a glass of champagne, turn and smile at both of them. Lilith raised her glass.

Ajax said, "To fulfilling our destiny: bringing the Ark back to the Kohaths. To our mother, and may we prove she was right all along." And they all drank. He said, "Lilith, turn on the television, let's see the latest reports on the theft from the Topkapi Palace."

Lilith switched on the television and heard a cardinal talk about what the loss of Moses's staff would mean to the biblical community.

Lilith drank more of her champagne. She loved the taste of it on her tongue, loved the slide of it when she swallowed. She watched Ajax, then his twin. Both were athletes, strong and fit. She knew both believed it critical to keep themselves in perfect condition in the field, and out of it. Of course, they weren't yet thirty, not her thirty-six, and that made a difference, though she'd never admit it.

She knew Cassandra distrusted her, but usually she managed to hide it, at least in front of Ajax. Cassandra probably wouldn't believe it if she knew Lilith admired her more than Ajax, more than any other person on this earth except for Benjie, her young brother, who'd died so very young and so needlessly. The drunk driver had lived only six more days before the life left his body at the bottom of a quarry near Edinburgh.

She drank more, looked toward Cassandra using her hands as she spoke to Ajax, such excitement in her voice when she spoke of bringing the Ark home. Cassandra was the face of the Genesis Group, a flawless face, and her wit and charm were legendary in the archaeological community. Few knew that her charm and beauty hid a coldness so profound it even occasionally gave Lilith pause. The Genesis Group, a perfect name, Lilith had always thought, and what a history. The vast, very wealthy international archaeological firm had been started by the twins' great-great-grandfather Appleton Kohath, back in the 1920s. From the beginning they had sponsored digs across the globe, providing funds when budgets ran short. In the past forty or so years, their financial assistance to the archaeological community had grown exponentially. They were respected, honored in every country.

Cassandra's was a huge responsibility for one so young. As Ajax would remind Lilith in the dark of night, deep inside her, it was her responsibility to ensure his twin remained safe when she stepped in front of the cameras.

She listened to brother and sister crow and laugh as they listened to all the moaning and groaning about the theft of the famous staff. The authorities still had no leads, and no clues.

CHAPTER THREE

Capri, Italy
Present Day

Kitsune only wanted to get home to Grant. When she'd called him on her burner phone, an ironclad rule when they were separated, she knew he was as angry as she was that the client had tried to kill her. They would discover the identity of the client together, and see them punished.

She took the hydrofoil from Sorrento across the bay to the island of Capri, blending in with the tourists. She was in disguise, of course, a blond wig, shorts, flowy top, and flip-flops, a white sweater knotted around her shoulders, and round white sunglasses. Kitsune never arrived on or left the island looking the same, and she never came and went as herself.

At last she reached the villa on the island's eastern hillside, her own glistening white slice of heaven she'd inherited from her mentor, the Ghost. She missed him, sometimes, but her only thought of him now was that he would tear her limb from limb at how badly she'd managed to let this job go south.

She paused only a moment to look out over the glittering water of the Bay of Naples, then back at her home. The house itself had open verandas, all four tiled in black and white. Ancient stone columns rose up, seemingly from the mountain itself, supporting two stories. Inside, it was light and open, windows everywhere. Kitsune remembered how intimidated she'd been when she'd first lunched here with Mulvaney as a teenager. Now the magnificent house was her home. It represented not only safety but also security and love. It meant Grant.

But her sanctuary was empty. The house was trashed, a major battle fought here, and she was too late. Grant was gone.

There was a sheet of paper on the kitchen counter, printed in bold black letters:

COME BACK TO VENICE OR
YOUR HUSBAND DIES.

She wadded up the paper, blind with rage and fear. How had they found this house?

How? Both she and Grant were always so careful. She heard something and looked up to see the television was on, and why was that? Then she couldn't believe what she saw.

Nicholas Drummond's face was on the screen. She quickly turned up the volume.

While she'd been trying to get home, the Iranians had attempted to assassinate both the president and vice president of the United States, and Drummond and Caine — of course it was Drummond and Caine — had brought the Iranians down. Those two, they always seemed to be in the eye of the storm, and from personal experience, they usually won.

The thwarted-assassination story was abruptly suspended to a horrific sight. A mile-high wall of swirling sand was sweeping up from the Gobi Desert, headed directly for Beijing. It was an unreal sight, terrifying, far beyond any previous sandstorms that had plagued Beijing since time began. This was the mother of all storms, the broadcaster said, the desert sand being whipped up by a giant cyclone that no one could explain, and it kept growing and growing, moving faster and faster, miles of thick killing sand bearing down on Beijing.

Kitsune suddenly remembered the strange

45

conversation she'd overheard in Venice. She'd been too busy saving her own skin to think about it, had actually forgotten it, until now that she was witnessing what shouldn't be possible.

The woman: *I wish I could see it, the Gobi sands — a tsunami sweeping over Beijing.*

The man: *We will see it on video. All the sand, do you think? Could Grandfather be that good?*

You know he is. And we will see the aftermath for ourselves. We will leave in three days, after things have calmed down.

Can you imagine, we are the ones to drain the Gobi?

Kitsune didn't believe in coincidences. She'd bet her last euro there was a connection between the Gobi storm and the staff of Moses she'd stolen from the Topkapi — but what? What would tie the two together?

Kitsune suddenly knew she was in over her head. They'd tried to kill her, these clients who predicted the emptying of the Gobi Desert, these same clients who wanted the staff of Moses, a fake, Kitsune was sure of that, because biblical lore stated the staff was inside the Ark of the Covenant, and if the staff was real, the Ark would be in a museum, too.

She had to go back to Venice, immediately.

She had to save Grant. But what to do?

And then she knew.

She pulled out her burner cell and dialed a number she'd long ago committed to memory.

Moments later, she heard a deep male voice with a posh British accent say, "Drummond here."

"Hello, Nicholas. I trust Michaela is nearby?"

"Yes."

"This is Kitsune. I need your help."

CHAPTER FOUR

FBI Headquarters
26 Federal Plaza
22nd Floor, Home of Covert Eyes
New York, New York

Nicholas grabbed Mike's arm, mouthed *Kitsune,* and the two of them stopped, leaving Ben, Louisa, Gray, and Lia to their merriment as they set up their stations, argued over space, plugged in their computers, and settled in. He pressed Speaker.

"Kitsune, we didn't expect to hear from you again. What sort of help could you possibly need from us?"

There was no teasing soft Scottish burr, no smart mouth, only a whoosh of breath, then her frantic voice. "I'm in real trouble, and my husband — they kidnapped Grant to get me back to Venice, to kill me."

Mike met Nicholas's eyes. "Kitsune, it's Mike. Tell us why your husband was kidnapped. Who wants to kill you?"

48

Nicholas said, "You stole something, didn't you? And pissed off your client, right? And here I thought marriage to a straight-up Beefeater would turn you legit. Tell me right now, Kitsune, what did you steal?"

"The line isn't secure. No, don't hang up on me, Nicholas. Grant's not a Beefeater anymore." A pause, then her voice came back again, more under control. "No, I did everything just as I usually do. There's something more, something really big and scary. Quickly, turn on the television."

Mike said, "We're setting up our new offices, it will take a moment. This better be good, Kitsune, or I'll kick your butt if I ever see you again."

Kitsune said, "You could indeed try, Michaela. Hurry, turn on the television."

They went into the conference room just as Louisa plugged in the huge wall television and turned to CNN. What they saw made their jaws drop. It was beyond scary, it was surreal, like a special effect in a movie. They watched as miles of whipped-up sand hurtled madly into Beijing. Everyone was too shocked to speak.

Mike said quietly to the team, "It's Kitsune on Nicholas's cell. Please listen and take notes." Everyone nodded, not looking away from the terrifying real-time mountain of sand, miles wide.

"Okay, Kitsune," Nicholas said, "we're watching the Gobi Desert whip a bloody big sandstorm into Beijing."

"It's not just a bad sandstorm, Nicholas. People are dying, they can't breathe. It doesn't matter if the people are indoors, the sand is forcing itself into their buildings. It's been going on for hours, it came on with no warning. Beijing is being wiped out."

"Kitsune," Mike said, "there's nothing we can do about it. It's a horrible natural disaster —"

Kitsune interrupted her. "That's the thing. I don't believe it is a natural disaster, and that's why you have to come to Venice. You have to figure out how this happened and why. It's not only for Grant and me, you see that, don't you?" She was talking fast, her words tumbling over each other. She was very upset and very frightened. Nicholas raised an eyebrow at Mike. This was not the Kitsune they remembered: no fear, lightning fast reflexes, and a powerful brain.

Mike said, "You said there were no warnings? That hardly seems likely."

Gray Wharton was now on his laptop, one eye on his screen, the other on the television. He rolled his wrist toward Nicholas in a *keep her talking* motion. He was trying to trace her call. *Good luck,* Nicholas thought. He'd bet the bank she was using a burner.

Kitsune said, "You see the extensive satellite imagery, right? You see that the loss of life will be in the thousands. It came on too fast for anyone to escape. People are lost on the roads, dying in their cars."

Nicholas said, "Yes, we are seeing all that. But how can it not be a natural disaster?"

"Because it's an engineered storm."

That brought everyone in the room to a standstill. Brows raised, mouths opened to ask questions, but Nicholas raised his hand. "They have sandstorms in Beijing all the time. Granted, this one seems terrible, but it happens from time to time, right?"

"This one's on a much bigger scale than anything anyone's ever seen before. Eleven provinces in the north are unreachable. They've issued a red-alert warning, but it's come much too late."

Mike said, "But who could engineer a sandstorm? It can't be done."

Nicholas grabbed his tablet and tapped into NASA's Aqua satellite, pushed the content on his tablet to the large screen in front of them, so everyone could see the satellite imagery. The images made Mike's heart go to her throat. The satellite images

51

were more horrific than the ground footage. Walls of sand, hundreds of feet high, battered the edges of the skyscrapers, filled the spaces between buildings, covered the roads and streets twenty feet deep; it was a monstrous, massive tidal wave of sand.

She couldn't imagine being in that storm and prayed for those who were. When Kitsune spoke again, Mike realized she truly was scared, very scared.

"Here's the deal. The delivery I was making to the client wasn't a run-of-the-mill thing. It was an artifact. A historical object."

"What was it?"

"No secure line."

"Okay, who were you working for?"

"I can't tell you because I don't know. But I do know that the clients have something to do with the sandstorm. I'm positive it was engineered. No matter our differences in the past —"

"Our differences? You mean the times you tried to kill us?"

She went on, speaking faster. "Remember I gave you the Koh-i-Noor and the pages of proof, just as I promised I would. I kept my word. You've got to help me, you've got to find out who's doing this."

Nicholas switched screens, typed in "stolen artifact." The Topkapi Palace Museum in Istanbul was first on the list, with multiple stories dating back a week.

Mike whistled. "Only you could have stolen the staff of Moses from the Topkapi. That place is guarded by Turkish military. How in the world did you pull it off?"

Silence from Kitsune, which said it all.

Nicholas said, "Tell me more about the client, Kitsune. Even if you don't know who it is, there must be a trace of some sort, a way for you to figure out who is behind this."

"I can't contact them. You know I have rules — all correspondence was in timed email accounts, destroyed now. I can give you the account numbers and phones we used, but I checked, they've been wiped clean. The note they left in our house — I'm to come back to Venice or they'll kill Grant. So I know they're in Venice. Listen, it's not so much about what I stole, it's about what it might mean."

"Explain," Nicholas said.

"What do you two know about the Ark of the Covenant?"

CHAPTER FIVE

Nicholas watched Mike pace. She was talking to herself, waving her hands when she made a point. Their first disagreement about an assignment of Covert Eyes was under way.

"Come now, Mike, why not?"

"I believe this is all about Kitsune's rescue —"

"— and her husband's rescue."

"So you want to fly to Venice, Italy, where I've never been, spend thousands of dollars to rescue a thief?"

"— and her husband, the former big-gun Beefeater. I've never met a Beefeater I didn't like."

She was shaking her head. "I know, another Brit, but you know Zachery will have a cow. As for Dillon, he'd probably laugh his head off. We are not riding to Kitsune's rescue —"

"— and her husband's."

"Yeah, neither are American citizens, there's simply no way to justify it. And how can you seriously believe this sandstorm in the Gobi was engineered, and probably by her clients? Get real, Nicholas."

"There's the Ark of the Covenant," he said, voice mild. "Do you believe it exists, Mike?"

Mike stopped in her tracks. "No, well, who knows? It's a myth, a legend, and a screenwriter's dream for Indiana Jones."

"That's certainly true, but personally, I've always believed it does exist, that it's been lost over the eons."

"Nicholas, it's an allegory from the Bible. There are dozens of legends of magical artifacts, but that's what they are, legends, myths, like I said, simple tales to tell and retell, since they didn't have television for millennia."

Nicholas smiled at her. He loved watching her get worked up. Truth be told, watching her, listening to her, turned him on, but still, he knew her well enough to go carefully. He wouldn't tell her just yet that he was already mentally packed for their flight to Venice in their brand-new airplane. He knew she'd love Venice.

"Don't most legends have some basis in fact, even ones from so long ago? Think of it, Mike. For the first time, we have permission from on high to go off-book, to take chances, to fight for truth, justice, and the American — and British — way, without the bureaucracy weighing us down. Imagine: the Ark of the Covenant, the staff of Moses, an engineered sandstorm. What more could you possibly ask for? This could be a groundbreaking case for our new team."

"Are you forgetting that Kitsune is dangerous? She almost got us killed. She lied and cheated and —"

"Well, maybe a little bit, but Mike, she did keep her promises."

"Yeah, yeah, you've always had a soft spot for her."

"Not a soft spot. Professional respect. She came through the last time. Well, maybe something of a semi–soft spot."

"Well, okay, she did, but Zachery will sit on us, probably handcuff us, before he'll approve our going to Venice."

"Not if he believes it's possible the Gobi sandstorm was engineered. He'll drive us to our plane himself." He grinned. "Time's a-wastin'. Let's go see how far our new powers stretch."

Nicholas and Mike walked up the stairs to their boss's office, Mike still arguing all the way, more to herself than with him.

Before they stepped into Zachery's office, Mike turned, looked up at Nicholas, and asked, "Do you believe Kitsune is telling the truth? About all of it?"

Nicholas framed her face with his hands and said, without hesitation, "Yes."

He watched her come to a decision, watched her finally nod. "All right, then. Let me think. This calls for some discreet strategy."

Milo Zachery and Dillon Savich were in Zachery's conference room, working out some of the last-minute details of Nicholas and Mike's new group. The wall television was on CNN, showing the destruction in Beijing.

Nicholas knocked on the doorframe.

"Back so soon?" Savich waved them in.

Zachery frowned. "The space won't work for you?"

Mike said, "The space is perfect. That's not why we're here. We have it from a reliable source that this monstrous sandstorm from the Gobi Desert that is hitting Beijing isn't a natural disaster." She drew a deep breath. "It was engineered."

That stopped the two men in their tracks.

Zachery started shaking his head. "You're kidding me, right?"

"No, sir," Nicholas said.

Savich sat forward on the sofa, his full attention on them. "Engineered? Admittedly, there have been plenty of scientists over the years who've tried to manipulate the weather. Cloud seeding for rain is a multibillion-dollar industry right now. There was a story only last week about cloud seeding in California as a way to help them get out of their drought. They can create a fog, cool things down, which will help save the trees. Weather manipulation isn't unheard of, in fact, it's readily available, and worldwide."

Zachery said, "But to create a dust storm big enough to kill thousands of people in Beijing? You heard the broadcasts — they're describing it as an inland hurricane of sorts, only made up of sand instead of rain and tornadoes. Who would want to do that, even if they could? It makes no sense."

Savich studied them a moment, then asked, "You said you got this engineered-storm business from a reliable source? Who is it?"

Nicholas said, "Kitsune."

Zachery said, "Victoire Couverel, the Fox, that Kitsune? The Kitsune who nearly blew up the Met? The Kitsune who tried to kill you? That one?"

Mike said, "The one and only. Actually,

58

she nearly blew Nicholas up in Geneva, too. The Met was just a small bomb, easily defused. She's offered us a sort of trade. She'll help us find out who's engineering this sandstorm and we'll save her bacon."

"— and her husband's."

"All right," Savich said, "enough playing around. What did Kitsune steal this time that's gotten her into trouble?"

"She stole the staff of Moses from the Topkapi Palace."

"You're kidding me," Zachery said.

Mike said, "No, sir. This is by far the highest-profile case of artifact theft since the Koh-i-Noor. We believe our team can recover the staff, just as we recovered the Koh-i-Noor. Imagine how great that would make the FBI look. Think of all the goodwill we'd engender if we can return it to the Topkapi. Plus, maybe, just maybe, we'll find the Ark of the Covenant on the way. The staff is supposed to be with the Ark. Who knows?"

Zachery shook his head. "You're FBI, not Indiana Jones."

Nicholas said, "Here's our chance to be both."

Savich called up the theft on his laptop MAX. "It's a pity Kitsune's a criminal, she is remarkably talented. What happened? The deal went south? Why?"

Nicholas said, "She told us she didn't know who her clients were, but that didn't matter. She said everything went shipshape until they tried their best to kill her. She has no idea why. Then they kidnapped her husband. For leverage."

Zachery rubbed his chin, thinking. Finally, he said, "All right, find out who paid the Fox to steal the staff, and why, and what it all has to do with the Ark of the Covenant. And how all of it ties up with engineering a freaking sandstorm in the Gobi Desert. This is your first assignment. Make it count. You don't need the entire team to go with you to Venice, it would be too unwieldy. I need both Gray and Ben here in New York. If you need their expertise, you can tap into the secure video con.

"Now, I know you'll want to rescue her —"

Mike said, only a quiver in her voice, "— and her husband — who happens to be a Brit."

Savich laughed. "Right. To make this legit, let's plan on you bringing her back here for a nice long stretch in jail, if you can manage to keep your hands on her, which could be a bigger challenge than engineering the weather." He nodded at Nicholas and Mike.

"Good luck with that."

Nicholas said, "I'd like to take Adam Pearce, our young über hacker. He's staying with his sister here in New York, so it won't be a problem getting him to the plane. Lia and Louisa should come, too." Actually, he'd already texted Adam. He'd meet them at Teterboro.

Zachery said, "Fine. I see this as a quick in-and-out. Keep it simple."

When the door closed, Zachery said to Savich, "Those two are like puppies. If they don't have something death-defying to do they'll chew up all the shoes and tear the stuffing out of the couches."

Savich laughed. "I'd say this assignment could qualify."

"As for the Fox, this Kitsune, I think they'll do what's right in the end. I'd better call Callan Sloan to get her approval. The vice president's agreement will mean we're all covered."

Savich looked at his Mickey Mouse watch. "It's time I headed out." The two men shook hands.

Zachery said, "Have a good flight back to Disneyland East. Savich, do you think they told us everything?"

"Of course not." Savich paused. "But I'd trust Nicholas Drummond and Mike Caine with my life. If anyone can get to the bottom of this, it's them. Also, I have a feeling that if we want to know what they're up to all we'll have to do is turn on the TV for the news bulletins."

CHAPTER SIX

At Teterboro, there were three Gulfstreams on the tarmac, two painted white with blue stomachs, the American flag on the tail, and UNITED STATES GOVERNMENT printed along the side above the windows. Mike knew one of the blue-and-whites was meant for Savich to travel back to D.C.

They walked past the fancy ones to the Covert Eyes plane.

Mike said, "I like ours, it's more down and dirty. Look at the white with the red racing stripes — gets me all revved up."

"At least it doesn't look like a cargo plane."

Their FBI pilot was standing by the stairs, Adam grinning at them over his shoulder. The pilot was several years older than Nicholas and looked like a fireplug with a big smile. Nicholas didn't think he'd like to go three rounds with him.

"Greetings, Agent Drummond, Agent

63

Caine. I'm Agent Robert Clancy, your new pilot, call me Clancy. I come to the FBI by way of the Air Force. I flew sorties over the Middle East for ten years until I mustered out and came on board with the FBI."

He patted the fuselage like a proud papa. "This puppy isn't quite Raptor status, but she can barrel-roll if I need to wake you up from time to time. Welcome aboard."

Nicholas saw another pilot coming around the edge of the plane, running her hands along the hull — a tall, lean woman with short dark hair. Clancy gave a loud whistle, and she turned. "That's my copilot, Agent Kimberley Trident, doing a final check."

She called out, "Call me Trident or Poseidon, makes me feel superior."

"She's been with the FBI longer than I have," Clancy said. "The director believes she could fly in and out of a teacup in a pinch. We're both excited to take on this detail. I hear we're headed to Venice today?"

"That's right," Nicholas said. "How long is the flight?"

Clancy was bouncing on the balls of his feet to get going. "About eight hours, unless you're in a rush, then I can shave off thirty minutes or so. Let Trident and me show you the plane. Ah, I see the rest of your team is here. Why don't we all go inside for introductions?"

The inside wasn't Raptor status, either. Mike took in the dark brown leather seats, the rounded windows and natural wood. It looked pretty swank to her. She gave Nicholas a grin. "Slumming it, are we?"

Trident, along with Lia and Louisa, go-bags in hand, joined Mike and Nicholas and Adam in the cabin. They all shook hands.

Nicholas said, "Good to meet you, Agent Trident. Welcome to Covert Eyes."

She had a touch of a Southern accent, not nearly as heavy as Clancy's. "That was a hell of a save with the president, Agent Drummond, Agent Caine. When Mr. Zachery put out the call, Clancy and I were first in line to request the duty."

Clancy said, "You'll see this baby has all the bells and whistles. The onboard equipment is nearly as good as what's in the director's plane, but don't tell him I said that. The comms system is completely encrypted, so don't worry about taking or making calls, and the Wi-Fi is bouncing off a couple of NSA satellites configured for our own use, so that's totally secure as well. Food and drink are in the galley. No attendant for you, hope you can fend for yourselves."

"We'll be fine," Nicholas said. "Let me

introduce you to the team going to Venice. This is Special Agent Louisa Barry, our forensics expert. She's been known to pull DNA off a toothpick. She's a marathon runner and has to chow down carbs so she won't disappear into a shadow."

Louisa said, "Trident, you're a runner, too, right? I recognize a fellow asphalt-slapper."

Trident nodded. "Big-time, though I hear it's tough to run in Venice, unless you're being chased."

Mike said, "This is Special Agent Lia Scott, in charge of communications. You want to communicate to Sergei in Siberia with no bars on his cell, don't worry, Lia will figure out a way. She'll want to check out your encryption system. If she likes you she might loan you one of her earrings." Today Lia wore six studs going up the shell of each ear. No nose ring today, never when she was on duty, but Nicholas wouldn't be surprised if she had a belly button ring. He admired Zachery for not caring about a dress code when an agent was as valuable as punk rocker Lia Scott.

Trident said to Lia, "I was admiring your T-shirt. I recognized the double helix on the back, but who's Rosalind Franklin?"

"Don't ask her until you've got a couple

66

of free hours," Mike said.

"And this is Adam Pearce," Nicholas said, "our own private guided missile and computer expert. He doesn't have piercings and he doesn't run, but he could hack into the Bank of England and leave a crumpet so all would know he'd been there."

Trident looked at the lanky youth, with his dirty-blond hair and sharp brown eyes. "You could be my kid," she said, and shook Adam's hand.

"He turned twenty last week," Lia said. "We're all grateful he's no longer a teenager." She gave Adam a pop on the arm.

Nicholas said, "Adam's not an agent yet, but we're hoping he'll take the plunge one of these years. Hey, Adam, you look taller than the last time I saw you."

Adam said, "It's the boredom. I've had nothing to do but grow. Are we really going after the Fox?"

Now how did Adam know that? "The Fox is only the tip of this iceberg. I'll tell you everything. Now, buckle up, everyone. Clancy, Trident, let's get this bird flying east."

CHAPTER SEVEN

The Genesis Group Headquarters
Rome, Italy

Cassandra stood on the podium, composed, charmingly patient, as the media sorted themselves out. Not once did she blink against the flashbulbs. She'd been trained by the best. She knew media meetings were important because she was the face and spokesperson of the Genesis Group. It didn't hurt that the cameras loved her face.

Ajax stood by her right elbow. He was looking restless and bored, and that would never do. She pinched the back of his arm, and he shot her a smile that wasn't at all friendly. But he straightened, even managed a smile, of sorts. Women thought he was sexy and dangerous. They weren't wrong about that. Men believed he was smart and ruthless, and they weren't wrong about that, either.

The beautiful Roman sun beat through

glass walls of the media room. At last Cassandra waved a hand to quiet the horde and looked down a last time at her notes. She stood for a moment, looking out at all the faces, making eye contact with each one of them, no matter how brief, as she'd been trained to do. She cleared her throat and said in her cultured, elegant voice into the microphone, "Ladies and gentlemen, thank you for coming today. We're here to honor the memory of the founder of Genesis, a man with a great vision, our great-great-grandfather Appleton Kohath. On this day nearly one hundred years ago, he established the Genesis Group. I'm very proud to say that we continue to carry on his mission all over the world.

"I'd also like to announce today that we continue in his vision. We're granting ten million euros to Nezabylice in the Czech Republic, the site of the Marcomanni tombs, to further the excavations of ancient Germanic artifacts that will provide us an invaluable look into these long-ago civilizations.

"The Genesis Group is first and foremost focused on unearthing the past." Cassandra leaned close, her lips nearly touching the microphone, again, making eye contact. "We are all one earth, all one people. We will not allow those cultures that came before us to remained buried and forgotten. We want to understand how we've come to be here, and understanding our forebears, no matter who they fought with, or for, is the only way to do so.

"The science of archaeology must continue to be married to the other sciences if we want to make these discoveries. I am thrilled today to announce this joint venture with our Polish counterparts, and give the microphone over to Agnieszka Půlpánová-Reszczyńska, who will give you a brief history of the project. But first —"

A young man dressed in all black handed her a bottle of champagne and two glasses. She uncorked it, poured out two flutes, and handed one to Půlpánová-Reszczyńska, a weather-beaten older man who looked out of place on the stage beside her. She smiled at him. "To the past," she said, "and the present, and to our future," and drank deeply. Her Polish counterpart smiled and followed suit.

She walked offstage to applause, tuning out the Pole even before he started to talk. Ajax joined her, and together they disappeared into the hallway behind the conference room.

Ajax said, "You are so antisocial, and yet,

put you in front of cameras and you dazzle the world. Mother trained you well. The press loves you."

"We'll see how much they love me if they ever find out what we've been up to."

A trill sounded, and Ajax checked his text message. "Lilith is waiting for us. She has news."

"It better be good news."

Cassandra looked out at the rounded edge of the Pantheon dome outside the bank of windows as she walked the long hallway to their offices. The sky was a bright, clean blue today, unlike Beijing's, which was choking under an ocean of sand. Some were calling it a prelude to the end of days; some believed it retribution, but against whom, no one ventured a guess, at least in China.

She was surprised at an unexpected stab of conscience. So many thousands dead in Beijing, suffocated. She quashed it for the moment. A large portion of the Gobi Desert now resided in Beijing, exactly what they'd needed to happen. And now they would find the Ark, with the real staff of Moses, and all its power, inside.

She'd believed as a child that her mother would find the Ark, but Helen Kohath had died in the effort. That was a pain deep in Cassandra's heart she knew would never go away. She and Ajax had their grandfather, but he was outliving his usefulness. He would die soon, and that would leave them alone, with no more family, unless, of course, if one of them married and had a child. It was strange, but she knew, deep down where fears resided, and knowledge, that she would never birth a child, nor would Ajax father one.

And that meant she had to accept whatever casualties happened. Did Ajax even care about all the deaths in Beijing? She looked briefly at his profile. Outwardly, he seemed well controlled — but not always. He was, however, a computer genius like their grandfather. She was her mother's daughter — focused, resolute, committed. Neither of them were anything like their worthless, greedy father.

Lilith was waiting in Ajax's office, seated on the edge of a white leather sofa. She stood when they came into the room.

Cassandra saw the smile bloom on her brother's face at the excitement in Lilith's eyes. "You've done it?"

Lilith pointed to a small satellite phone in the middle of the glass coffee table. "Dr. Gregory and his team are on-site. There's news."

The twins sat down side by side. "We're ready."

Lilith keyed in the microphone on the sat phone, and the screen popped up. A man's face swam into focus, a face that looked older than his thirty-four years, seamed and lined from years spent outdoors, in all weather. His thinning dark hair looked gray from the swirling sand.

"Vincent Gregory here, Mysore Base. Ajax? Cassandra? We are at the site, and we've uncovered a treasure trove of material — two tents, a couple of bags of tools, all with the old *G* we used to have in the logo on the outside. We thought it was sterile soil and we'd missed the right location, but something told me to do a shovel test pit, and boom, I found the mother lode." He paused, drew in a deep breath. "I know we've found your mother's lost dig site."

Cassandra didn't think she could speak. They'd finally found the last known whereabouts of her mother. The last place on earth Helen had been. She saw the pulse pounding in Ajax's neck, heard the excitement in his voice.

"Send me photos, Gregory."

"Photos should be in your secure email now."

Lilith handed Ajax a laptop. He opened it

so quickly he nearly broke the hinge. Such a small thing, but it proved to Cassandra how deeply he felt about locating their mother's last dig site. The email was waiting, and he took a deep breath before he clicked it open.

The scene was just as Gregory had described: dark blue bags half-buried in sand, the sun shining on the tools left out, a cable wire from a tent.

The phone crackled to life again. "Ajax, I'm sending a second photo now — we uncovered some bones. No way to tell who they might belong to. We're going to have to excavate the site, and fast. We've done our best to create a stable platform here, but I don't know how long we'll have. You know these sands like to blow around."

All Cassandra heard was "bones." She took her twin's hand, squeezed his fingers until they were white.

The second photo came, so many bones, all jumbled together, impossible to sort out what was what. Or who.

Please not Mother, please not Mother.

Another email came through. Gregory said, "You should be receiving a live feed right now."

Cassandra was so afraid of what that live feed would show, she could scarcely speak.

She swallowed. "Yes, Dr. Gregory, let's see everything."

They'd been searching for their mother's last known dig site in the Gobi for nearly a dozen years now. Would she recognize her mother's skull? No, it wouldn't do to think about that. Stay focused on the prize, on what their mother had died for. The Ark. Was it still buried in the sand, waiting to be found, the staff of Moses inside?

The site was awash in sunlight, the bare rock exposed, the last remnants of sand that remained from their mega storm swirling in the air behind them. The camera slowly moved over the flags they'd hammered into the ground to mark where each artifact had been found.

There wasn't much to see except — the camera panned right, and suddenly there it all was, a pit opening into the earth. It looked organized, a grid meticulously set up. Their mother had done that, Cassandra was sure of it. Was their mother buried in that pit? Her mother's bones. Cassandra didn't know if she could bear the reality of finding proof of her mother's death.

The camera focused on a large skull, clearly a man's. Her mother had been delicate, beautiful and fine-boned. Cassandra closed her eyes and gave a thank-you to a god she wasn't sure she believed existed.

"Show me the bags, Dr. Gregory," she said, pleased she sounded strong, in control.

Gregory shifted the view to a stained burlap sack. "See, here's the old *G*, and here are the orange tents, we moved to yellow five years ago. This is the site, I'm sure of it."

Ajax met his twin's eyes as he said, "Excavate it, Gregory. Don't leave a grain of sand unturned. Our plane is standing by. We'll be there tomorrow morning."

"I'll report back later tonight with more footage of our progress. Congratulations!"

The camera feed ended abruptly and with it, Dr. Vincent Gregory's face.

Lilith was amazed at how calm the twins appeared. She knew what a great force their mother had been in their lives, yet they'd just seen the place where she'd probably died.

Ajax finally spoke, and Lilith heard wonder, not sadness, in his voice. "This is our mother's lost site. And the Ark could be there. Imagine what this will mean to the foundation. Think of it, Cassandra, when we find the Ark, everything will change. Think of the power it holds, and it can only be ignited by our family. A century of work, a century of effort."

Ajax sat back on the couch. "I admit I doubted we'd find it. This is a banner day." His mood changed on a dime. He rose and walked to Lilith. He took her hands in his. "Tell me you also have word of the Fox?"

"Sadly, no. The Venetian police are looking for her. Interpol has a red notice out for her, their highest level. She can't go far or stay hidden. Add to that, we have her precious husband. I understand there is great love between them —"

"To be expected," Cassandra said, "given they've only been married for a matter of months."

"There is that," Lilith agreed. "It required five highly trained men to restrain him. He's been drugged and taken to your palazzo in Castel Rigone. He can be easily disposed of after we kill the Fox."

He gave her a hard fast kiss, rubbed his knuckles on her cheek. Lilith flinched; Cassandra saw it. "See to it, my beautiful Lilith. Now."

When she'd left the room, Ajax held out his hand to his sister. "Come, let's pack. We need to go to the Gobi."

"But first, we need to call Grandfather. He will be overwhelmed by the news of what his magnificent sandstorm has brought us."

CHAPTER EIGHT

1908: A massive explosion over Tunguska, Siberia, leveled sixty to eighty million trees over 2,150 square kilometers. Blamed on an asteroid or comet, or Nikola Tesla's Coil.

The Bermuda Triangle

Jason Kohath was drinking a cup of the finest coffee the world had to offer, Black Ivory, which he imported directly from northern Thailand to Cuba. The boys brought it to the island once a month, and he was careful to ration it out, one cup a day — more, and his heart seemed to jump into his throat.

He looked at the line of clocks that gave him local time anywhere in the world, and fixed on Italy. The twins should have called by now.

He took another sip of his coffee, surveyed the screens that surrounded him, some ten feet tall, some only twelve inches. Some showed the oceans, others the sky, others the cities across the globe, others the atmosphere above the earth. Still more held calculations, ran computer models, showed weather patterns spreading across the globe.

They took up nearly all the wall space, and he sat in the center in front of them at his solitary command post, his comfortable chair on wheels so he could easily scoot across to any of the screens he wished. He was proud of his control center, a huge cavern set directly in the center of the island, over a now-defunct volcano. From there, he ran the family business. From here he decided where the next storm would occur. The Gobi sandstorm was his masterpiece, its purpose not to make more millions for the Kohath coffers but to find his precious Helen's last dig, and he'd bowed to the fact that it had to be done. Now he had to wait to hear if his calculations had been on target.

Why hadn't the twins called him? He could call them, of course — after all, he owned the satellites, could move them into any place he wished across the planet. No, he wouldn't call them, that wasn't the protocol he'd established when they'd turned sixteen.

Jason Kohath sat back in his comfortable chair, sipped the rest of his coffee. From his uncharted island, deep in what was called the Bermuda Triangle, he controlled the skies, the clouds, the oceans.

And he controlled the weather.

He'd once dreamed about controlling the gravitational forces of the moon, but he knew he'd be dead before that could be possible. In the twins' lifetime, maybe. Ah, the twins. Both were gifted, no doubt about that, but he knew he would have to accept what his beloved daughter, Helen, had finally realized so long ago. The twins had no understanding of humanity and what it meant, and what was worse, they had no desire to gain the understanding. He'd never forget when they'd been seventeen and sent by their mother for two weeks to a dig in Ankara, Turkey, their job to assist the team leader, Dr. Demir, a good friend of Helen's, an estimable man of excellent character, to learn the ropes and do whatever they were told. They hadn't wanted to go.

One morning, Dr. Demir had been found dead in his tent, bitten by a black viper. Helen had known they'd put the snake in his tent, she'd known even before she'd spoken to other team members and verified the twins' uncooperative attitude. The twins had returned to England on the next flight, overflowing with respectful sadness about Demir, and back to Oxford and, Helen suspected, their supply of cocaine.

Now, ten years after their mother had disappeared, he had to accept that they never would become what either their mother nor he had hoped. He thought they saw the world through crazy eyes, something even their respective genius IQs couldn't fix. They saw the world as theirs to control, to kill without remorse for something they wanted. They would decide on something they wanted, use their clever brains to rationalize it, and then be willing to move the earth to get it, no matter that it wasn't important, or it was a bad idea, or that people could get hurt, or die. They were very rich and they had a great deal of power, too much of both. For them, that combination was poison, and yet, he still desperately hoped they would somehow change, that they would see themselves as a power for good. But then he'd remember the young Oxford student, dead in an alley, stabbed in her heart with a stiletto. The local police knew Ajax had slept with her for more than six months, but had he killed her? Nothing could be proven. Cassandra had provided his alibi, along with a young man Cassandra had been sleeping with. Odd, but he, too, had died in an accident three months later. Helen knew what Ajax had done, knew Cassandra was complicit, and she'd wept as she'd told her father of the blackness in their souls — such darkness — no remorse, no guilt for what they'd done, only pleasure they'd escaped. She had no more hope, but she knew he did.

If only he could change the past, he would try harder to convince Helen not to marry that crazy David Maynes. But she hadn't listened. He knew before she'd left for her last dig in the Gobi Desert, she'd finally accepted that her faithless husband had injected madness into the family through his children.

A proximity sensor lit up, flashing red. A boat was nearby. He immediately made sure the electromagnetic net he'd designed was tight around the island. It wouldn't do for someone to happen upon him. His cloaking device was magnificent, yes, but over the years, a few planes and boats had ventured too close, and he'd been forced to take them down. He'd refined the cloak every time and now had an excellent pop-up storm system programmed into the computers. He launched the storm protocol, saw the lightning strike the water, watched as the seas around the island began to churn and the sky began to darken. The small pleasure craft that had drifted too close was faced with sudden waves too large for it to handle, and so it turned tail and shot away.

He allowed the storm to play itself out; it would look suspicious to have it come up suddenly then disappear with no warning. Besides, he rather enjoyed watching a good storm right outside his front door. Whenever he looked upon a storm he'd created, he thought of England and how he missed the cold, drizzling weather, and the thick gray fog that swirled around the ankles.

He eyed the small maelstrom surrounding his island, wild and beautiful, his own creation. His grandfather, Appleton Kohath, had been undoubtedly brilliant, as was his friend and partner, Nikola Tesla. Jason's own father, Alexander, and his mother, Babette, had been quite clever, too. But Jason was the genetic masterpiece, and a good thing, too, given what he'd had to do.

But the genetic masterpiece, namely himself, was getting old, and couldn't be restored. He had to accept the sore joints, the pains in his heart, arthritis in his hands, unlike the twins, not yet thirty, brimming with good health. The twins — always the twins — and what was he to do? Their selfishness amazed him. They'd focused on finding the Ark for the simple reason that they wanted the power to rule the world. It made him shudder. Had any of his predecessors been as ruthless as these two?

Earlier, on his closed-circuit TV, he'd seen Cassandra present ten million euros to some Polish archaeologists. Knowing her as well as he did, he still found himself admiring her show of sincerity, admiring her charm, her obvious popularity with the press. He knew that many believed the twins to be brilliant archaeologists, they had the pedigree and the schooling and the experience, but he knew differently. He'd seen firsthand what was in their hearts, in their souls.

In objective moments, Jason had to admit his own motives weren't all that pure. He'd lusted after the Ark since he'd been a young man, known if he could only touch it, forever would be his. No sore joints, no pills for his failing heart. Holding God's hand, he'd have accomplished anything he wished. The technology assembled before him would be considered child's play, antiquated. Every storm he'd ever created, all the money he'd put to good use from the storms' disasters, all was in pursuit of the Ark of the Covenant. He'd always believed if he were the one to possess the Ark, he would govern and shepherd this world, and the people would love him for it.

The phone buzzed and a small hologram popped up above it. His assistant was calling, not the twins. Jason pressed the button for the speaker. At least he'd married the technology to video and created the hologram. It wasn't quite as distant.

"Yes, Burnley?"

"Sir, there is a shipment coming in thirty minutes. Will the storm have cleared in time for a soft landing?"

"Yes. Tell them to come the southerly route, I had to chase someone away earlier, and the seas are still rough on the leeward side of the island."

"Yes, sir. Also, your grandchildren have requested an audience. Shall I put them through?"

"Yes, of course."

Their beautiful faces appeared. They greeted him, and Cassandra began talking. By the time she'd shut her mouth, Jason had managed to get control of his disbelief, his rage, at what they'd done. "You're telling me that you had the staff stolen from the Topkapi? You never thought to discuss it with me?"

Ajax said, "We wanted to surprise you

with it, Grandfather. We thought —"

"No, you did not think. Stealing that ridiculous staff, what good did it do you? You say you wanted to verify that the staff of Moses in the Topkapi was fraudulent? Of course it was. I could have assured you of that if you'd only asked me. And now you're telling me you've actually kidnapped the thief's husband to lure her back to Venice to be killed?" He wanted to scream at them, but he managed to remain calm and in control, to be the voice of reason.

Cassandra's lovely clipped voice said, "I think what we did was smart. We only had some bad luck, that's all. We used some men who proved incompetent. We are not stupid, Grandfather, nor are we children. We will take care of the thief." She paused, then gave him a big smile. "Congratulations on your magnificent storm in the Gobi. Dr. Gregory believes he's found Mother's last dig site."

As he'd hoped it would. "Why didn't you tell me this immediately?"

Ajax said, "Because you've always preached that we're to inform you of our actions in their proper order, and I was complying." Jason heard the smirk in his voice, knowing he'd scored a point on him. "Cassandra and I are on our way to the

Gobi now. And we'll be in touch as soon as we can to tell you what we find."

"Go, then," Jason said, picturing it all in his mind. "I will be watching."

The hologram ended, and he turned away from the screens. Only now did he allow tears to gather and run down his face at the succession of memories flooding his mind. He felt his heart fluttering like a bird in a cage. "Not now," he whispered, swallowing a pill to stop the palpitations. He closed his eyes and breathed deeply, willing the medicine to work.

CHAPTER NINE

Over the Atlantic

Once they'd cleared New York airspace, Nicholas rose and clapped his hands. "Our flight is about eight hours, so we have plenty of time to develop a plan for how we're going to save Kitsune, her husband, and find out if the Gobi storm was engineered."

Lia fingered one of the studs in her left ear. "Is that all you want us to do?"

Laughter, then Mike said, "Beware, people. I predict that within thirty minutes of landing, we're going to break rules. 'Breaking Rules' is Nicholas's middle name, right after Desmond."

"You're kidding," Adam said. "Desmond is one of your names?"

There were looks all around, then grins.

"Moving right along," Nicholas said.

Adam said, "I thought that's why they created Covert Eyes in the first place, no worries about breaking rules."

Mike took her glasses off to clean them. "Within reason. Adam, we need you to find out everything Kitsune's been up to in the past four months, including her marriage to Grant Thornton, and where the clients might have taken him."

Nicholas said, "I don't think they'd stash him in Venice. Adam, I did a quick search on Thornton earlier, after he left the Beef-eaters — doubtless because he'd married a criminal — he became a freelancer. He works for a company called Blue Mountain. They specialize in close protection and security, employ mostly ex–Special Forces."

Adam said, "Are we supposed to arrest Kitsune?"

"We'll see," Mike said.

"Dude, I don't want to throw her in jail, I want to marry her, let her have my babies. Can you begin to imagine how smart they'd be? They'd rule the fricking world."

"That could work until there was some-thing you had that she wanted," Lia said. "Then you'd be toast."

"Adam, don't romanticize Kitsune. Actu-ally, she'd hate that. Okay, people, let's set up the secure videocon with Ben so he can give us a rundown of the history behind the Ark of the Covenant and the staff of Moses. We all need to be on the same page."

Adam tapped on his computer for a moment, then Ben's face filled the video screen.

Louisa said, "Hey, Ben, bet you were sitting there, all down in the mouth, just waiting around for us to call, right? Hey, do you know your hair isn't as red from thirty-five thousand feet?"

Lia laughed. "You said the last time you raced Ben, Louisa, you lost only because you had a sprained ankle and his hair blinded you."

More laughter, then Nicholas said, "Ben, tell us about the Ark and the staff. Start at the beginning."

"I'm going to give you the CliffsNotes version. After God gave the Ten Commandments to Moses, he instructed Moses and his brother, Aaron, to craft the Ark of the Covenant to hold the tablets. God also gave Moses a jar of manna to keep in the ark, then instructed him to leave his staff in the Ark as well."

"Wait, what's manna?" Adam asked.

"It's a special kind of bread. I guess you'd have to say it's magic because it never runs out, always perpetuates itself, which means no matter how much you take, it replenishes instantly."

"Now there's a bread with colossal mojo," Mike said.

"Good one, Mike. Okay, the count on the Israelites escaping from Egypt is more than six hundred thousand people. A jar of manna would feed this many people — in what time frame? Never mind, let's stick with the myth and the magic and drop the logic. So while they wandered around in the desert, it's written the manna is what kept them alive.

"And they carried the Ark, which was basically an acacia wood box that had all this incredible ornate gold work on it — cherubs and sundials and the like. It was more than a talisman to them, it literally held the power of God. The Israelites went into battle with it, and always won. Interesting factoid: in 1070 BC, the Philistines stole the Ark and took it to their territories. Soon after, they suffered an attack of what they called the 'golden rats.' "

Louisa said, "The plague, most likely."

Ben nodded. "They wrote that anyone who got near the Ark got sick and died. They lost battles, lost lands, lost crops. They finally decided the Ark wasn't worth all the misery, so they tied it to a cart and sent it back.

"Now here's the best part. There's an Ark prophecy that clearly states that only members of Moses's family — the Kohaths, also called the Levites — can handle the Ark without dying. The Kohaths are the direct descendants of Moses."

"So where is the Ark supposed to be?" Mike asked.

"Good question. There are long stretches of history when there is no mention of the Ark. It's last known address was Solomon's Temple. King David — of David-and-Goliath fame — is said to have brought it to Jerusalem, and it resided in the temple for many years. Jerusalem was sacked in 892 BC, and the Ark vanished. Many historians believe the Egyptians got their hands on it, but no one really knows."

Lia said, "But wouldn't the Egyptians have had the golden rats show up and kill them?"

"Good point. I don't know," Ben said.

Adam said, "Why is it called an Ark? Wasn't that Noah's boat?"

Ben said, "Just a second, let me check that out." He typed for a minute, then said, "Says here an ark is technically anything that holds something. A box or a ship, an ark is essentially a container. This ark contained something holy."

Nicholas said, "Calling it the Box of the Covenant just didn't have the same ring to it."

A few groans. Mike threw a pencil at him. Nicholas caught it, tucked it behind his ear. "Okay, Ben, tell us about the staff."

"Moses received the staff directly from God. Moses and his brother, Aaron, used it to perform the miracles that ended in the Jews' exodus. They used it to turn rocks into water, although how that would work I can't imagine, and one legend has the staff devouring snakes. But the staff, too, was lost as well as the Ark."

"Now we get to move to the modern era. As I said, the Ark was in Solomon's Temple, the last place it was ever seen. In 1519, when the sultan Selim conquered Egypt, he supposedly got his hands only on the staff of Moses and took it back to Istanbul, where it stayed in the Topkapi Palace until they put it on display with the Holy Relics thirty years ago."

"It didn't start a plague there, either?" Adam asked.

"Evidently not."

Mike said, "Does any reputable historian believe it's real, Ben?"

"Of course the Turks claim it is. They don't have an explanation why it would be separated from the Ark, though. Is it the real deal?" Ben shrugged.

Louisa said, "Tell us about the museum

where the staff has been all this time."

"Looking, looking. Okay, the Topkapi was the palace for the sultans of Turkey until the Ottoman Empire abandoned it in the mid-nineteenth century. It was turned into a museum in 1924 and opened to the public. It's reputed to have layers upon layers of security, all guarded by the Turkish military. The staff has been in the Holy Relics area of the museum since the seventies, which is even more highly guarded. So if Kitsune really did steal it, she is really good."

"If there's one thing we've learned about Kitsune," Nicholas said, "it's to never underestimate her. I have a feeling I know how she did it, given her tactics at the Met."

"She got hired as a guard?" Lia said.

"Yes."

Ben said, "Well, whatever she did, it was amazing, given the legendary Topkapi security."

Adam said, "No doubt in my mind now, I want to marry her."

Ben laughed. "You haven't had the joy of meeting her before, Adam. We have. She's a master of disguise, and she's perfectly willing and able to stick to a role for a long time. She's focused, single-minded when she's on a job. I agree with Lia, she infiltrated the museum staff, probably as a guard."

Mike said, "She's not a shock-and-awe kind of thief. She'd have studied the Topkapi as she would a puzzle. She doesn't give up. And that's why she's the best of the best."

"And still free," Nicholas added.

Adam said, "So who hired her?"

"I have some ideas about that." Nicholas glanced at his watch. "We have seven hours left before we land in Venice. Take half an hour to think, then we'll brief. Then everyone needs to sleep. We don't know what we're walking into, and if we're going to be operational for a few days, rest is paramount now. So get moving. Thanks, Ben. If you want, you can take a nap, too."

Ben sighed. "I've always wanted to go to Venice."

CHAPTER TEN

Mysore Base Camp
Gobi Desert

When Cassandra and Ajax arrived in the Gobi, the dig had halted. Their team was watching for them, standing in a row like a group of household servants, so excited they could barely contain themselves.

Their site lead, Dr. Vincent Gregory, rushed to open the car door. He practically pulled Cassandra out.

"We have good news. We didn't want to tell you in the air. And we stopped the moment we saw it. We have to hurry, there's a storm coming, but you must see this."

Cassandra's heart began to pound. When she and Ajax were nearly nineteen years old, their mother's last transmission had come in from this exact location, her voice crackling across the cell phone lines, her words not understandable, but her face, her beautiful face, glowing. They heard her say something about a storm bearing down. Then, nothing more for the next decade. When they'd gotten to the site after the horrendous storm had subsided, the dig had been swallowed by the desert, then under hundreds of feet of sand. The Genesis Group had been trying to uncover the site ever since.

The western edge of the dig was roped off. The skies in the distance were red with the oncoming storm. But there was sun for now, and when they grew closer, Cassandra could see something flashing.

"Is that —"

Vincent Gregory was grinning from ear to ear. "The moment we saw gold, we stopped and marked it off. There's something big down there. The scanners show a rectangular structure. It's the right size."

So long, so long — could it be real? She whispered, "The Ark?"

Gregory handed her a brush.

She dropped to her knees and heard it: bees, hundreds of bees, buzzing there from beneath the dirt. She brushed gently and uncovered a curved edge of gold. The bees buzzed louder. She continued to brush, even more gently.

Ajax dropped to his knees beside her. "It's

a wing," he whispered. "It's a cherubim's wing."

She looked up. "Don't you hear that, the bees?"

Gregory said, "Hear what?"

Ajax lightly touched the wing. "It feels warm and it's sending the warmth into me."

She continued to brush off the remaining sand. "Ajax, it's buzzing loudly now."

"The warmth is stronger, but I hear no buzzing."

Of course he couldn't hear the buzzing, it was meant only for her. "I can't believe it." She slipped her fingers under the wing and slowly lifted it, gathering it to her chest. "Oh no."

"What is it? What's wrong?" But he could already see. The gold wing wasn't attached to anything.

"Then the Ark is still down there. Hurry, shift the earth away. Cassandra, move away."

The team got to work immediately.

They stood, Cassandra still holding the wing. "I heard it calling to me and you felt its warmth. I'm sorry, Ajax, but whatever is below us isn't the Ark."

Gregory looked up, as did two other archaeologists digging with their small plastic scoops. "How do you know? How could a chunk of gold break off?"

"I don't know," she said, and held the golden wing close. "Feel, Ajax, touch it and feel the warmth coming off of the gold. For you. And it sings for me. It's definitely a part of the Ark. It was here, I'm sure of it. It's not here anymore, though. We'd feel it."

Ajax said, "The wing broke off from the Ark. We know it was here. Keep searching."

The archaeologists finally uncovered a large crate. When they eased it from the ground, they saw the stylized *G* for *Genesis* on the rotting wood.

Gregory sat back on his heels. "I thought, I'd hoped . . . I must tell you, we uncovered the bodies of all the members of your mother's team. But the count is off. We are missing one female. Based on the evidence we've gathered from the bodies, remnants of clothing and jewelry, your mother is not here."

Cassandra felt a bolt of excitement but it quickly faded. "But how is that possible? You must be wrong, Dr. Gregory. Where are Mother's bones?"

"I don't know. I do know they aren't here, with the others. Another thing — the skeletons are mostly intact. We didn't see anything that speaks to a cause of death. No bullet holes, no broken bones. Yet all the team members were somehow killed. Not only are your mother's bones not here, neither is the Ark."

Ajax said, "It must mean she took the Ark. But where would she have gone? Why wouldn't she have contacted us? And why would she leave behind the wing, and all the team members, dead?"

Cassandra had no answer. She felt numb.

For an instant, Ajax wanted to slit Gregory's throat, but he gained control, shrugged. "Someone double-crossed them — perhaps they were poisoned, it's a decent explanation, a very fast-acting poison — and they simply dropped where they'd stood. And whoever it was stole the Ark from the site and took Mother captive, someone who knew the prophecy, knew they couldn't open the Ark without her. She could still be alive."

"She could, yes," Gregory said, but he didn't believe it for an instant. "Whatever happened here — it's a mystery. I'm so sorry."

One of the technicians, Maccio, rose, dusted his hands on his trousers. "There's nothing else here, only the crate."

The sandstorm struck and they ran for their tents, the assistants dragging the crate with them.

Cassandra watched Ajax stalk around their

small tent, knew he was cursing, but she couldn't hear him over the shrieking winds. She knew without looking that the skies were dark red.

Once Ajax had gotten a hold of himself, he said again, "Mother isn't here, and neither is the Ark. All of our work has been for nothing. Nothing!" He flung a canteen against the tent wall. Cassandra calmly picked it up, unscrewed the lid, and took a long drink. Even safe inside the tent, the sand still somehow managed to get into everything. She handed the canteen to Ajax.

She said, "We have to believe Mother made it out of the Gobi, either on her own or she was forced by someone who took her, someone who killed the team. So there is more work to do and we will do it. We will contact Grandfather and start the search again."

Ajax cursed, then threw himself onto the camp cot. "Fine. Call Jason. Tell him we failed, and listen to him moan about the thousands of people dying for nothing. And just where do we tell him to look now?"

"We didn't fail, Ajax. We've discovered a piece of the Ark." She picked up the gold wing and held it close, rocking, like a mother would a babe. "We know someone took the Ark by force and murdered the team. Without Grandfather's storm, we never would have found this. Grandfather will be pleased."

"The old bastard will blame us, you know he will. Anything happens that's not to his liking, he blames us."

Cassandra said, "Then we won't tell him."

There was a knock on the tent pole, and Gregory came in, his eyes wild. "Quickly, come with me."

They tied heavy cotton scarves around their faces and stepped out into the storm. They followed him along a rope line. Three tents away, Maccio was standing over the crate.

He said, "Dr. Gregory wanted to x-ray the crate before we opened it."

Gregory spoke over him. "There's something inside, but we can't tell what it is. We didn't want to open it without you." He held up a tablet, showed them the screen of the x-rayed crate. They saw something that looked like a cross wedged against a side of the crate.

Ajax took Cassandra's hand. "Open it. Now."

The wood was old, very old, and came apart easily. Cassandra saw the flash of metal. Maccio lifted an object out of the shifting sands that nearly filled the crate.

Gregory examined it. "It's nothing but an old soil core, to collect soil samples." He started to throw it away.

Ajax said, "Wait, careful, Gregory. There's something inside of it."

Maccio set the soil core on a table, and Ajax teased out a piece of paper.

"Hurry, Ajax, hurry."

He carefully unrolled it, looked at her, eyes gleaming. "It's a map. It's Mother's handwriting."

She looked down to see the map was covered with topographic images, with dozens of circular wavy lines radiating from the center. Ajax said, "The concentric lines keep getting smaller and that indicates altitude. It's a mountain. Turn it over, Cassandra, carefully now."

On the back was a handwritten note. It, too, was in her mother's writing, but the letters looked somehow strange, curved and looped, unlike her mother's spare, straight cursive, and the words looked somehow ancient, which was ridiculous. Still, her hands trembled as she read aloud:

The answers to the true resting place of the Ark are in the pope's letters. My beloved children, use this knowledge wisely.

"But where is it?" Dr. Gregory asked.

Smiling, Cassandra carefully turned the map back over and pointed to the legend in the corner. "Longitude and latitude. Ajax, it's Castel Rigone. The Ark is at home."

CHAPTER ELEVEN

Venice, Italy

Kitsune walked through the Piazza San Marco wearing a cream-colored straw hat over a long blond wig, shorts, and sandals, and following the tail end of a tour group. The guide stopped in front of the basilica and began droning on about Saint Mark. Kitsune watched the pigeons congregate in the square, flocking about tourists throwing bread for them.

Children ran screaming into the flocks of birds, making them scatter.

Drummond and Caine were due in an hour, which meant backup in the shape of the Carabinieri should be there soon. Michaela the rule follower would have it all set up.

Kitsune had arrived early, as always, in order to scope out the square, locate possible escapes. And there were multiple ways out of the piazza. After she was satisfied she'd found an appropriate bolt-hole, she sat down at a café in the middle of the piazza, at a table in the shade, near one of the many mini-orchestras playing Italian music for the tourists.

She would wait. She took off her sunglasses and began her watch.

She would make sure Drummond and Caine were safe, even if Kitsune herself was not. She owed it to them.

CHAPTER TWELVE

Mike wasn't much impressed with Venice until their water taxi went around a promontory and into a world of sprawling estates with brick walls and small paths leading from the individual docks. Then their driver motored into the heart of the city and Mike didn't think she'd ever seen anything so utterly surreal, like a movie set with too many extras roaming everywhere. Everything was so very old, so precariously situated, yet this incredible place had endured.

And it sure wasn't Omaha. Mike laughed at that thought and raised her face to the hazy sky, and breathed in the lovely smell, the smell of magic. Nicholas smiled, took her hand. "This is your second trip to Europe, but alas, you're still not here as a tourist. When this is done, Mike, we'll come back."

"You promise?"

"Oh yes," he said. He'd also told her the

magic smell was gone in August, when the weather was hot and ripe, but she didn't think she'd mind it. Everything was like an impressionist painting and she'd been plunked into it.

Adam was hunkered down, his laptop out. He looked up. "Kitsune was right to tell us not to take the airport vaporetto — it would take an hour to get to the hotel. At least this way, we're going fast."

Nicholas's hair was blown back from his face, and he was grinning like a maniac. "The water taxis are much more fun, anyway. The vaporetti are too slow."

Lia said, "It was nice of Kitsune to send a boat for us."

Mike pulled herself away from the glory of Venice and opened her gun case, took out her Glock. She slipped it into its leather holster and attached it to her belt on her right hip. Nicholas raised a brow. "Don't you think it's a bit early to arm yourself, Mike?"

Mike said, "This is Kitsune we're meeting. Bad guys are after her, they could be in a gondola coming right at us. They could be waiting for us on the dock. Nope, I think all of us should be armed. Now."

"You're right." Nicholas stepped from the prow of the boat, sat on the interior bench, and followed suit. He put his Glock into its stiff leather holster and affixed it to his belt, then shrugged back into his soft leather jacket. Everyone followed suit, except Adam, who had no training. Nicholas knew he'd have to address that sooner rather than later. He couldn't have Adam helpless.

Louisa joined Mike at the prow. "I've always loved the smell of Venice. It's the smell of the sea overlaid with gasoline from the boats' engines."

"You've been here before?"

"My dad's a diplomat. We traveled everywhere." She pointed. "There's our hotel coming up, the Savoia and Jolanda. We never stayed there, Mom always preferred the Danieli. So many tourists wandering around, having fun, admiring everything. It's hard to think there could be real danger here."

The taxi was slowing, approaching the shallower lane that would take them to the dock near their hotel.

Mike said, "Okay, everybody, stick together. We don't know what's to come today, and I don't want anyone getting hurt."

Adam elbowed her in the ribs. "Gosh, Mom, do you want us to have a buddy, too?"

She punched his arm. "I'm serious."

Adam said, "We're on alert, don't worry."

"I am worried. You're green, Adam, sort of like an avocado."

Louisa laughed. "He'll be fine once he's on land, right, Adam?"

"I like avocadoes," Adam said, and swallowed.

Nicholas scanned the San Zaccaria dock. "I wish we weren't all arriving at once. Should have thought of that," he said to Mike, who stood at his shoulder.

"Too late now. Besides, if someone's watching, we'd have been nailed coming in anyway, even two at a time."

Nicholas said, louder, so they could all hear, "Here we are."

The boat's captain, doubtless handpicked by Kitsune because he'd keep his mouth shut, fiddled with the mooring ropes. When Mike stepped onto the dock, she saw him speaking into a walkie-talkie. Nicholas said, "I do hope he's talking to Kitsune, telling her we're here. Everyone, stay alert. We have no idea what's going to happen."

The hotel was dark stucco, old, warm and inviting. Inside, it was as advertised — wood and glass and comfortable. A blonde behind the counter greeted them, her eyes never leaving Nicholas's face. He leaned close and

111

spoke to her in rapid-fire Italian.

The rest of them stood back, scanning the lobby. Mike saw a group of people start to come in, then pull up short, turn around, and leave. Some things were always the same. No matter if they were on the moon, they still looked like cops.

Nicholas began passing out keys and instructions.

"Lia, set up our comms, I want to know everything's working. Adam, get online, build a router repeater to get a decent signal, and scramble it six ways to Sunday. There are far too many open Wi-Fis in the area. Louisa, until there's forensics, you'll keep your eyes on Kitsune — when we find her — and on us." He paused, frowned, "Our receptionist put Mike on the third floor, everyone else is on the second. Drop your things and come to my room in fifteen. The receptionist is having coffee sent up. We'll down some caffeine, and get this over with."

Everyone straggled toward the bank of elevators. Mike and Nicholas rode up together. "I hope you don't mind separate rooms."

"No, this isn't fun time, it's work," she said. "The jet lag, it's really getting to me. I want to wash my face and fall on the bed.

You said fifteen minutes, plenty of time."

He cupped her chin, gave her a quick kiss. "It is indeed. I could help you unpack your go-bag. It looks pretty heavy to me."

She kissed him back, patted his face. "It's obvious you weren't thinking ahead. You're into details, Nicholas, and fifteen minutes isn't enough time for you."

He cursed under his breath. She was right. He particularly loved all her details. Mike read him perfectly, laughed. "I'll drop my bag and come down to your room before we meet up with the others, and head out to meet Kitsune." She waggled her fingers at him as the doors slid closed.

She went up another floor and opened the door to her room. Dark brown walls, a minuscule balcony that faced the hotel next door, and a tiny bathroom she prayed had some hot water. "Well, thank you, Ms. Blonde Receptionist, for my fine accommodation and the lovely view of Venice."

She dropped her bag, washed her face, and put her hair back in a ponytail. She sat on the bed. Hard as a rock. So much for a nap. Mike cleaned off her glasses, grabbed her briefcase, and took the stairs down to Nicholas's room.

He opened the door with a grin. She stepped in, and nearly fainted. It was a huge suite, with two balconies opening onto the lagoon, gorgeous gray marble walls with white trim, sheer white curtains moving lazily in the breeze. The two bedrooms with their own en suite bath were almost bigger than her apartment in New York.

She went to the balcony, stepped out to admire the view. "You know we're on government per diem, right? We're not going to be able to put this room on the expense reports."

He mumbled something, and she turned, her elbows resting on the balcony railing. "What was that?"

"Free upgrade."

"Ah, Ms. Blonde at the front desk. Did she slip you her phone number with your key card?"

She had, but Nicholas only shook his head. He joined her on the balcony, pointed to the right. "Look, Mike, the Piazza San Marco, Saint Mark's Square, is right down there. There will be tourists and pigeons thick on the ground. Not good."

"I agree, but what else can we do?"

He didn't say anything, merely studied the entrance to the square.

Mike said, "My room may be a dump, but at least it's secure. You're too exposed here, out front, for the world to see."

He moved closer, pulled her in. She smelled like saltwater and lilacs.

Mike rested her head on his shoulder. "This whole thing, Nicholas — we have no idea what we're stepping into. So many people . . . I know, to be expected, since this is tourist season, but any of them could have a gun or a knife. We don't know the face of Kitsune's enemies. I'm relieved you asked Lia to call the Carabinieri. If there's trouble, they'll already know it's coming."

"I called the Carabinieri, too. They're not happy to have the FBI running around their city, but they'll back us up, if needed."

Mike pointed. "Look at him."

Nicholas edged to the glass and saw a man standing by the Hotel Danieli gondola stop, staring directly at their window. When Nicholas made eye contact, the man shoved a toothpick in his mouth and strolled away.

"Yes, they're watching," Nicholas said.

"Kitsune's people?"

"No. I think we're Kitsune's people."

"That's irony for you."

"It is indeed." He gave her a blazing smile. "Time, Agent Caine, to have ourselves an adventure."

CHAPTER THIRTEEN

Venice was even more crowded than the last time Nicholas had visited, only a year ago. He stood at the door of the hotel, staring out at the crowds. It was an operational nightmare. He understood why Kitsune had picked Piazza San Marco to meet, the crowds were also protection from enemies neither of them knew, but any of them could be used as a hostage, or taken out as a target.

He checked his watch, turned to the team behind him. "Adam will stay here, but the rest of us should get going. We're supposed to meet Kitsune in forty-five minutes, enough time to do a full sweep of the piazza and get each of us into position."

Mike said, "We're going to stand out, since we're not in tank tops and shorts. Even with our jeans and shirts, we have to wear jackets to hide our weapons, and believe me, in the middle of the day, in this

116

heat, that's odd. There's nothing we can do about it, so try to look like this is normal to you. Everyone ready?"

Lia said, "Here are your comms."

They inserted tiny earwigs and tested tiny mics hooked under their shirt collars.

Mike said, "Testing, one two."

Lia nodded, tested Nicholas's and Louisa's. "Good, all of you are clear as a bell. I'll be monitoring your frequency."

Nicholas said, "I spoke to Major Salvadore Russo at the Carabinieri. He said his men would be here, so our backup's in place. I sent him our photos, so they're watching for us. I hope he was smart enough to keep his men in uniform. That would discourage anyone after Kitsune."

Lia said, "I'll be up on the balcony of the Doge's Palace and have a great view of the piazza and all of you."

"I'll hang back a bit," Louisa said, "follow you into the piazza, cover you."

Nicholas said, "Louisa, once I've spotted the soldiers and they've spotted me and Mike, and we're as certain as we can be that the scene is clear, we'll do the meet with Kitsune. Everyone has their vests on, right?"

Everyone nodded. Lia said, "Don't fret, no one is taking any chances." She looked at her watch. "You need to go, find Kitsune." She gave them a salute and stepped out the door, quickly blending into the crowds of tourists.

A minute later the three of them left the hotel, too, turned right, and walked over the bridge. The Hotel Danieli was on their right. Up and over one more bridge, dodging immigrants selling selfie sticks and people abruptly stopping to take pictures of the Bridge of Sighs, and then they were at the entrance of the Doge's Palace. A few more steps and they were at the eastern edge of the Piazza San Marco.

The piazza was huge, magnificent; the buildings a testament to Venetian wealth from her heyday. The Doge's Palace on their right was like something out of a fairy tale. There was color and noise and too many people.

"Even though we don't look like tourists," Nicholas said against Mike's ear, "no one's paying any attention to us."

She snapped to attention. "He is."

Nicholas looked to his right. The man he'd seen from his hotel room balcony was standing at the corner of the palace, in the shade, still chewing on a toothpick.

"And to your left," Mike said.

Nicholas looked left, saw another man sitting at a small round table, alone, wearing dark-tinted sunglasses. Even with his eyes hidden, it was clear he was staring at them. They kept walking.

"Any more?"

"There are men at every corner," she said. "Are they Kitsune's people, or the guys after her?"

Nicholas stopped abruptly, knelt down, and retied the laces on his right boot. He took in the men following them, the two ahead of them. They were all armed.

He stood back up. "I don't know. Go carefully, Mike."

"We should have met her in the hotel."

"You know she had to have a crowd to hide in. In her shoes, I'd have picked the piazza as well."

They kept walking, past the stalls selling tourist T-shirts and oven mitts and harlequin masks.

The bells of Saint Mark's Basilica began to ring. In her ear, Mike heard Lia say, "Ugh, that's so loud. I'll never be able to hear you over it. Stay away from the bells."

"Roger that," Mike said.

They turned left into the main piazza, crowded with more people than she could count, and children and pigeons. Scores of people sat at the outdoor café tables, six cafés by Nicholas's count, drinking espresso and prosecco and nibbling potato chips. The lines from the basilica tours extended out into the piazza. *So many people,* Mike thought. *We can't control the scene.*

"Over there, Nicholas, the blonde with long hair, and big straw hat sitting. It's Kitsune and she just signaled me."

The woman at the table didn't look anything like the Kitsune he remembered. She looked like the rest of the hordes in the piazza, all casual and relaxed, sipping a glass of wine. Then she straightened and started shaking her head.

"Crap." Nicholas spoke rapidly into his mic. "We're compromised. Abort. No way to control this scene. Abort, I repeat, Louisa, Lia, abort."

Kitsune looked straight at Nicholas, and he saw the fear an instant before the piazza erupted in gunfire.

CHAPTER FOURTEEN

Nicholas dove to the right, knocking Mike off her feet.

Screams filled the air as bullets started to fly through the piazza.

Lia was shouting in their ears. "I see some of the shooters. Louisa, move to your left, two columns, the man in jeans and black T-shirt."

Nicholas yelled into his mic. "Lia, we're blind. Where are the shots coming from?"

"I can't tell, too many people are running. I've lost them. Louisa got one of the shooters."

Mike shouted, "Kitsune's gone!"

"I see her," Louisa yelled, "about one hundred feet to my right, leaving the piazza. I'm right on her tail, and she hasn't seen me yet."

Lia continued in her calm voice, "Two more shooters on the balconies, one right above you guys and the other directly across the square. Both have dark hair, thirties, jeans and black T-shirts, no body armor."

A shot hit the plaster column that protected Mike and Nicholas, showering sharp chips down on their arms, thankfully covered.

More shots, more screams. Tourists ran in all directions, fleeing into the shops and cafés that lined the square. Mike heard the European sirens, but she didn't see any Carabinieri or police. Major Russo had assured Nicholas that they'd be here to back them up. Where were they?

Nicholas's voice sounded in Mike's ear. "Mike, we need to get free from the columns, get those two shooters. You break left on my mark, I'll cover you. Ready?"

"Yes."

"Good. Get across the western edge of the piazza to the alley, it's forty feet from your spot. Three, two, one, go left."

Mike exploded out of the small space, gun pointed, Nicholas laying down cover fire. A shot grazed her shoulder and she returned fire. She missed, but reached the alley. She had a much better view of the piazza from this vantage point.

Lia said, "Mike, balcony, shooter at your ten o'clock."

Mike turned and fired, all in one motion.

A man fell from the balcony, landed ten feet from where she stood.

"Lia, Nicholas is still stuck behind a column, down by the white grand piano. Can you free him up?"

"I can. Nicholas, a shooter's directly above you, and I see another one across the piazza. I'll hit the one above you if you get the guy across the way. This one's blond, dark sunglasses."

Nicholas shouted, "Where the bloody hell are the Carabinieri?"

"I don't see a single one," Lia said. "They're coming, though, hear the sirens?"

"That's the *polizia,* not the Carabinieri. Okay. Lia, take him out."

Nicholas heard Lia's shot, saw a man sprawl onto the ground. Nicholas rolled from behind the column, shooting up at the balcony as he went. A man screamed, his gun flying, and fell at his feet.

"Five down — there are probably more. Nicholas, we need another aerial view, I need someone else up here to spot them. Can you get on the balcony?"

"Yes." Nicholas yelled at Mike, "Cover me, I'm going up."

He burst out into the piazza, running hard. He stepped on a table and used it to catapult himself up to the balcony where

123

the shooters had originally been grouped. His hands hit stone, scraping his palms, but he held on, managed to pull himself to the small parapet. He swiveled to look back at the piazza. Now he could see everything that was happening. He saw a sixth shooter, long black hair, stationed right above Mike, saw the edge of his weapon. He aimed and squeezed the trigger. The man yelled curses as he grabbed his wrist and watched his gun clatter to the ground.

Nicholas caught a glimpse of a furious face, then the man was off and running. Nicholas had no idea where he was going, but he took off after him, running on the narrow balcony, south along the piazza. At least the balcony ran the length of the piazza. He caught sight of Mr. Long Hair and he had another weapon in his hand. He was running parallel to Nicholas, down the balcony on the other side of the square, shooting at Nicholas when he could.

Nicholas shouted as he ran, "Mike, the balcony opposite me. Do you see him? Black hair, long? Do you have a shot?"

"I don't, but if I come out into the piazza, I will."

"Lia, cover her. Louisa, where are you?"

A breathless voice said, "I'm still tracking Kitsune. I've lost sight of her. Maybe she got into a boat. Do you want me to keep looking for her?"

"Yes. We'll deal with this."

Nicholas heard shots, looked over the edge of the narrow balcony to see Mike, her arms pointed at the balcony opposite, where Mr. Long Hair was crumpled half on, half off the edge. He looked quite dead.

Nicholas stopped. He counted six shooters. How many more?

A moan came over their comms.

"Who's hit, who's hit?"

Mike screamed, "Lia!"

Nicholas saw her, slumped against a pillar, her hand pressing again her shoulder. Even from fifty feet away he could see Lia was deathly pale.

"Man, this hurts, Mike, a bullet got me right above my Kevlar. I'm —" Lia slid to her right, facedown, and stopped moving.

Nicholas shouted, "I'm coming —"

A fist slammed into his jaw. He heard Mike yell as he staggered back. The same fist got him in the belly, and his momentum took him backward over the edge of the balcony. He clutched the rough stone, heard Mike shouting again. Whoever had hit him was running away. Another shooter.

The local *polizia* rushed into the square, and behind them, Carabinieri soldiers.

He had to get to Lia. Nicholas started to pull himself up, but the rough edge had scored his hand, the blood making his fingers slip. He dangled a moment before swinging back to grab the ledge. The fall was about thirty feet, certainly far enough to hurt.

He heard a gunshot and jerked his head around to see another shooter fall to the ground below, right off the balcony beside him. This one had been only ten feet away, sneaking up on him.

Someone had just saved his life, and it couldn't have been either Louisa or Mike.

He felt a hand on his back. "Take my arm," a voice said. He recognized the soft Scottish burr.

He looked up into Kitsune's light blue eyes, like chips of ocean glass.

"Kitsune. Fancy meeting you here."

"Take my arm, or you will fall, Nicholas."

He let go of the rough stone and grabbed her forearm. The extra leverage had him up and over the balcony in a second. He landed in an ungraceful heap. By the time he got to his feet, he was alone.

Like smoke in a breeze, Kitsune was gone.

CHAPTER FIFTEEN

"Get to Lia," Nicholas shouted in his comms to Mike. He clattered down the stairs into the piazza, ignoring the people gathering around him, and ran with her to the Doge's Palace.

"I lost her, I lost Kitsune," Louisa shouted over the comms.

"Yes, I know. Go back to the hotel, Louisa, right now," he replied. "Make sure Adam is safe, tell him to hack into the Carabinieri, find a Major Salvadore Russo. To stand us up like this, let us get shot at — they sacrificed us. I want to know why and how deep this goes. Tell him to check who Russo's been talking to. I have a bad feeling about this. Go."

Piazza San Marco was chaos, a babble of noise, cries, shouts. People were coming back outside, camera phones and iPads filming everything.

A second later, Nicholas was shoved up

against a stone pillar, soldiers surrounding him, guns aimed at his chest, shouting at him in Italian. Nicholas put his hands up.

"American FBI," Nicholas yelled back in Italian. "My credentials are in my left breast pocket, and one of my teammates is shot. Where the bloody hell were you when we needed you? You were supposed to be here."

Rapid-fire Italian, and a young lieutenant stepped forward, roughly grabbed the creds from Nicholas's jacket.

He flipped open the leather case, studied it closely, then handed it back.

"I am Lieutenant Marco Caldoni. We were told the meet wasn't for another hour. But then we heard the gunfire and came immediately."

"And I was told by Major Salvadore Russo that he and his men would already be here. Can I put my hands down now?"

At Caldoni's nod, Nicholas said, "So where is your bloody major?"

"I don't know, sir. You and your people have killed many men, and I hope none of them were tourists, or there will be hell to pay. Tell me what happened."

"We were doing recon of the piazza when we were shot at. We took measures to keep ourselves safe." He looked up at Mike waving frantically from the balcony. "I have a wounded agent."

"I see EMS is climbing up the stairs as we speak. Someone called 118 when the shooting began. Is any other agent hurt?"

"Not on my team. I lost count of the number of shooters, but at least seven, maybe eight. Did we kill them all? I certainly hope so."

Nicholas heard a quiet voice in his ear. "It's Louisa, Adam is fine. Is Lia okay?"

Nicholas said, "She's being attended to." And to the lieutenant, "Where will she be taken?"

"*Ospedale San Giovanni e Paolo.* It is five minutes away."

Nicholas repeated the info to Louisa. "Mike and I will meet you there. Louisa, tell Adam to stay put and keep pulling information. You'll need to come back and assist the Carabinieri to figure out what just happened."

Caldoni said, "Who are you talking to?"

"A brilliant forensics specialist, FBI. Her name is Special Agent Louisa Berry. She will help you. Take me to the hospital, right now."

Caldoni drew himself up, all stiff and commanding. "I regret to tell you, *signore,* that we will need statements from everyone on your team who was involved, and we will have to re-create the scene —"

"Let me rephrase, Caldoni. I am going to the hospital with my colleagues. Your boss can speak to me there." Then he turned and walked toward the palace, leaving Caldoni cursing behind him.

He said into his comms, "Mike, is she all right?"

"It looks bad, Nicholas. As she said, the bullet hit her high on her chest, just missed the body armor. They are taking her away now. She's unconscious."

"Come down. We're going to the hospital."

The lieutenant appeared at his elbow. "And I will take you there. You are not going to just walk away from this mess, Agent Drummond. My superiors want answers."

"Fine. You mean Major Russo?"

Caldoni nodded.

"He can give me answers as well. Let's go, you can get us there even faster."

Mike jogged up to him, rubbing her bloody hands together, like Lady Macbeth.

"Lieutenant Caldoni, Special Agent Michaela Caine."

Mike got in his face. "This shouldn't have happened. Where were you, Lieutenant?"

Caldoni said in credible English, "*Signorina,* we came when we were supposed to come."

"That's Special Agent Signorina." She waved her hand around. "This should not have happened."

"No," Caldoni said, "it shouldn't have happened. It will harm tourism."

It was close, but Mike didn't punch him.

"Let's go," Nicholas said. Caldoni led them around the corner, across a bridge, and into a speedboat. "It is faster than walking," he said, and they roared off.

CHAPTER SIXTEEN

Ospedale San Giovanni e Paolo
Venice, Italy

When they raced into the emergency center, Lia was already being taken to surgery.

Lieutenant Caldoni guided them to a small waiting room and asked them to stay there while he called Major Russo. There was a small Nespresso machine on a side table. While Mike watched numbly, Nicholas made shots of espresso for both of them. Usually Mike drank her coffee black, but after one look at her, Nicholas poured three sugar packets in hers.

They drank silently. Nicholas set down his paper cup and put his head in his hands.

Mike knew he was mentally replaying what had happened at the piazza and beating himself up, par for the course.

She said very precisely, "Listen to me, Nicholas, what happened was not your fault. It was the freaking Carabinieri's no-show, this Major Russo's doing, no doubt. I'm thinking, too, that Kitsune should have known the shooters were there, and warned us. If we spotted some of them, why didn't she? You know what? I say let's blame her. Yes, that makes me feel better."

He raised his head, gave her a twisted grin. "Yes, all right, we'll blame Kitsune. I can't believe we aren't all dead. If Lia doesn't make it —"

She kept her voice matter of fact. "She will make it. She's young, she's strong, she's in excellent shape, and they got her here and into surgery quickly. Lia will be fine."

"Do you think they'll take all the earrings out of her ears?"

She laughed, couldn't help it. "I hope they leave in her belly button ring." She hiccupped, and her breath hitched. "She lost a lot of blood, Nicholas. It was all over the marble floor on the balcony."

And on your hands, too, from trying to stanch the flow of blood. He looked at her hands, now scrubbed clean of Lia's blood. "All right, she'll make it. We were lucky."

They sat quietly for a moment, the shock of one of their own being shot, the possibility of Lia's dying, it was too scary to talk about anymore.

She said, "It's no big mystery. The Carabinieri knew we'd be there and they let the shooters go for us. They wanted all of us, particularly Kitsune."

"This time she's made herself some powerful enemies."

"Do you think it will make her reconsider her career choice?"

"No."

She said, "It isn't supposed to be like this, Nicholas. As Covert Eyes, we're supposed to be covert. That's the whole idea. Whoever set this up knew we were coming, they were waiting for us to come. They didn't care if tourists got hurt or killed. Too many shooters, too many."

"Kitsune killed one who was about to take off my head. Then she helped me up onto the balcony and disappeared."

Mike whistled. "So that's why Louisa lost her. She doubled back." She studied his impossibly handsome face. "Know what I think? She saved you because she likes that dent in your chin."

Nicholas rolled his eyes. "She saved me because we're all she's got."

"Do you think Adam will find anything useful? Like the identity of Kitsune's client?"

"If Adam can't, then no one on this earth can."

"Oh yes there is. You."

"Your faith in me is grossly overrated —"

She shushed him, pulled out her phone. "It's time to break the news to New York."

But before she could dial, the phone rang in her palm with the familiar 212 area code. Mike picked up, said, "Sir, I was just going to call you."

Zachery said only. "Tell me it wasn't you."

"Sir?"

"Have you not seen a television? Or Twitter? 'Breaking news: the Piazza San Marco overrun with a gun battle'? Seven believed dead, one transported to a local hospital. No tourists hurt."

"Yes, sir, I'm afraid it was us. We were ambushed."

"All right, I know you've all sorts of justification, but more important, is anyone of ours hurt?"

"Lia was shot, the bullet hit her just above her body armor. She's in surgery right now. Nicholas and I are here at the hospital, waiting for Louisa."

A long pause from Zachery, then, "Gray was monitoring you, then everything went dead. We had no way to contact you. I trust you kept young Adam safe?"

"Yes, he's fine, working at the hotel."

She turned on the speaker.

"A moment, sir," Nicholas said. "You were monitoring us and we went dead?"

"Completely. Satellite went down, all the comms went offline. This happened before the shooting, mind."

"That makes no sense. Our team comms have been working fine the whole time."

"Gray doesn't have an explanation. All I know is I haven't been able to reach you until now, which means the satellites are up again."

Nicholas said, "Someone must have used a jamming device. Someone intentionally blocked us from your view. And who could that be other than Kitsune's clients, who want her dead, and apparently want us dead, too?"

Both Nicholas and Mike heard Zachery draw a deep breath. Mike looked up when Louisa came running into the waiting room, Adam right behind her. She held up a hand, mouthed, "Zachery."

Zachery said, "Do I believe you, Drummond? Or did you personally go offline to black us out?"

"No, sir. I would never do that."

Mike said, "Sir, we did not black you out. Nicholas told you we were ambushed. As you know, the Carabinieri was supposed to watch our backs, be on-site in the square,

136

but they weren't. We're checking into it."

Nicholas said, "Which means we've got a very powerful enemy. They took you offline, removed our backup, and tried to take us out. This isn't good, sir. The only people who knew we were coming were Carabinieri and Kitsune. And she didn't engineer this."

Louisa said, "When the Carabinieri finally showed up, it was over. They didn't want to let Nicholas go."

Zachery said, "I'll make some calls. You won't be detained or hassled again."

Ben came on. "Will Lia be all right?"

Mike said firmly, "She will be fine, Ben, but I won't lie to you. It was close."

Zachery said, "I'm calling her dad. He'll want to come over to be with her. Keep me posted on her condition. Look, guys, you're always telling me Adam Pearce could call the moon if only there were someone there to pick up the phone. I don't care if another satellite goes down, you stay in communication with me."

CHAPTER SEVENTEEN

1989: Hurricane Hugo made landfall in South Carolina. The 162 mph winds caused 61 fatalities and resulted in $10 billion in damages.

The Bermuda Triangle

Jason opened his notebook to an empty page and began his daily journal entry, a family tradition he valued. It was his hope that in the future, someone would read his journals, perhaps even understand what he had created and why.

He recorded the events of the day, closed the fine leather cover, and stared at the North Star satellite system. He was tired, he admitted it.

A subtle beep.

Jason opened his eyes — he'd just been resting them for a minute — not really been napping.

His longtime assistant said, "The twins

are on the line, sir."

"Put them on the screen, Burnley."

Two identical faces stared out at him.

Cassandra said, "Hello, Grandfather."

Ajax said, "Sir."

"Yes? What did you find?"

"We found the site, the materiel, even a gold cherubim wing, looked like it was broken off the Ark." Cassandra paused, then, wonder in her voice, "Grandfather, I hear it buzzing at me, and Ajax feels its warmth. It is real, it is amazing."

Jason asked carefully, "Your mother? And the rest of her team?"

Cassandra's eyes filmed with tears. "Mother's bones aren't here, but all the rest of the teams' are. We couldn't tell what killed them. It was as if they'd simply fallen down dead. We're thinking someone poisoned them but we don't know who.

"Sir, even though the Ark isn't here, we have the cherubim's wing."

"Any clues to what happened to your mother and the Ark?"

Cassandra swiped her hand over her eyes. "Yes, Dr. Gregory dug up an old crate and inside we found a map. In Mother's handwriting." She held up a sheet of paper. "We hope it's the location of the Ark, but she doesn't say. I've scanned it and you should have it now."

Jason pressed a button and the page appeared before him.

Ajax said, "As you can see, it's a map of a mountain, not just any mountain, sir. It's our mountain."

"Castel Rigone?"

"Yes."

"But it's been excavated," Jason said, "and searched and searched —"

Ajax said, "Then we haven't searched hard enough. Mother left this for us to find, she knew we were the only ones who could. We pray she somehow managed to avoid being killed and got the Ark out of the Gobi and back to Italy. We are heading back home today, to Castel Rigone."

Cassandra was shaking her head. "I'm not convinced. How could Mother have gotten the Ark back and buried without anyone's knowledge? All we know is that the Ark was stolen from the palazzo and lost in a sandstorm in the Gobi. I have the proof — the cherubim's wing, broken off the Ark. Grandfather, as I told you, I can feel its energy, it's welcoming me. Do you think the letters from Pope Gregory X are accurate?"

Jason said, "Our family has operated all these years under the assumption that yes, they are, that the Polo brothers stole the

Ark from the pope, his plan to present it to Genghis Khan. It would seem you've found the evidence to prove that. Despite the idiotic move of stealing the staff from the Topkapi, you did manage to find the cherubim's wing."

Ajax lurched back, fury on his face. He felt Cassandra's hand on his arm and regained control of himself. "I wouldn't say it's proof. For all we know, this piece was simply broken off the Ark and buried here. Why? I don't know. None of this makes much sense. Do you understand any of this, Grandfather?"

Jason said, "I will accept that the Ark did reside in the Gobi — for a very long time. Didn't you find anything useful, some evidence of why the entire team died? Where your mother possibly could have gone?"

Cassandra said, "No. And we don't understand this. As I said, if Mother somehow made it out of the Gobi alive, why didn't she contact us? We're her children. We could have gone to her."

Ajax said, "It's possible someone followed Mother, poisoned the team, but who knows? Fact is, I don't know what to believe, Grandfather. All we know is she's gone, the Ark is gone as well, and all her team is dead.

She left us a map, and it intimates that the Ark is at Castel Rigone."

Cassandra said, "Grandfather, remember the storm you engineered ten years ago to clear her specific site? Well, it makes no sense Mother would have wandered out of the safe zone. So maybe she's still somewhere out here in the Gobi, with the Ark, still hiding, or captured, unable to contact us. Maybe another storm —"

Jason shook his head. "Listen, you two, there will be no more storms, not in the Gobi. We've done too many lately in search of her camp, we can't run the risk of someone taking too close a look, especially considering the magnitude of the most recent event."

Ajax said. "I know you didn't think it necessary to go so large, but if you hadn't, I doubt we would have discovered Mother's site. Surely it was worth it. If we have one more we can search farther away —"

"The magnitude of this storm left over three thousand dead in Beijing, and that's only the latest count. You never weigh the chances of success or the likely destruction and loss of life before you want to take action. I see no upside to creating another storm. And our next incursion is already in play, and it will wreak enough havoc."

"But —"

"Cassandra, you showed me the Genesis balance sheet. To survive we need more money, and quickly, particularly after your lavish grant to that Polish archaeologist."

Ajax said, "This is the hurricane heading for the gulf? Oil futures are down, I take it?"

Jason said, "Everything is in motion. There will be plenty of warning, so people can evacuate. You will both go to Castel Rigone as you planned."

Ajax said, "What worries me, Grandfather, is that the Ark might not have ever made it to Italy."

"Go back to the palazzo. Search again. And I want you to bring me the cherubim's wing. I must see it for myself."

Jason tapped off the hologram and sat back in his chair. Tangled visions of his beloved Helen flashed through his mind — then one final vision. He leaned back in his chair and closed his eyes. So many more steps to take.

He thought of all his and Helen's efforts to keep the Genesis Group's true purpose a secret, and they'd succeeded, beyond their wildest hopes. But the twins could ruin it all — he couldn't believe they'd actually had the wretched fake staff of Moses stolen from the Topkapi — how could he have foreseen their doing that? Even if he had foreseen it, what could he have done to stop them?

Even now, people as powerful as they were could be asking questions, getting close. And the thief who'd actually stolen the staff? What had happened to the thief? He'd forgotten to ask them.

He looked at the latest weather service assessment of the storm he was building. No one was concerned, everyone predicted it would move from the coast into the Atlantic and out to sea, never touching the United States.

They were wrong.

Jason decided to hold off on the hurricane in the Gulf, since he couldn't predict what catastrophe the twins might spawn next. Best reprogram the storm, make a bit of a diversion for the world's eyes.

Finally, he was done. He sat back in his chair, rubbed his hand over his eyes. He was tired, beyond tired, and depressed. Three thousand lives lost and he still didn't know where Helen was. He wondered if he'd ever know.

CHAPTER EIGHTEEN

Ospedale San Giovanni e Paolo
Venice, Italy

Lieutenant Caldoni came into the waiting room, accompanied by another soldier, clearly his superior.

Nicholas looked at the face of the man behind Caldoni and knew it was Major Russo.

Russo stood at attention and said in excellent English, "I am Maggiore Salvadore Russo. I know you are upset that we were not in the piazza at the scheduled moment. We were unavoidably detained by a civil emergency, and we were called away by our superiors."

Nicholas said, "I trust the civil emergency was satisfactorily resolved?"

"Of course. We are looking into the situation at San Marco. I apologize for the inconvenience. We are all greatly relieved that no civilians were hurt."

Mike stood, ripped off her jacket, and showed them where a bullet had ripped through her jacket and shirt beneath, barely missing her. "One of our agents is in surgery. And see this? *This* was too close."

Russo gave her an impatient look, and his voice was cold. "Did you not understand me, *signorina*? I explained to you what happened." Then he had the gall to shrug. "It is regrettable."

Mike shrugged back into her jacket. "We're finished here. I'm going to go check on Lia." She paused at the doorway. "Major Russo, our superior, President Bradley, will not be pleased about your supposed civil emergency." Then she stalked out.

It was an excellent shot. Major Russo drew back, and finally, he nodded.

So Major Russo could be intimidated. Nicholas took a step closer. "Agent Caine is right. You failed us, Major Russo, and I ask myself why this happened."

"Do I really need to repeat myself, Agent Drummond? This incident is very disturbing. This Fox, this thief, it is obvious to me that she set you up. She is obviously very dangerous indeed, to you and to everyone in the piazza."

"The Fox wasn't behind this."

Russo said, a sneer in full bloom, "Surely

you do not believe what you say. This woman is a dangerous criminal. She is wanted here in Venice for the vicious murder of a member of our city council and his wife. It would be a coup for me — for our country — to apprehend her. There is no one else who could be behind this attack."

Nicholas remembered Kitsune's elegant Italian curses when she'd told him they'd even framed her for the murder of the owners of the "drop" house. He didn't say anything.

Russo continued, and now his hands were fists. "Attend me, Agent. We have counted seven dead Italians, no dead Americans. It is we who have suffered violent death, not you. If there are questions about culpability, you must address them."

Nicholas said, "The way I see it, we've helped you eliminate seven of your lowest criminals with great risk to our own lives. You're welcome."

Russo drew himself up to his full height, all those medals on his chest glinting in the light, the pompous little toff. "I am detaining you, Agent Drummond, until the particulars are sorted out. You will give me your weapons for ballistics analysis." He nodded to Caldoni, who looked from Russo's face to Nicholas's. He didn't look happy. He took a small step forward.

Nicholas laughed. "No, you won't be detaining us, Major Russo, and we will not hand over our weapons. There is an active threat against us, and we will not go unarmed. Especially when we can't count on your people to provide assistance."

"You will do as I say, Agent Drummond, I am in charge here, not you. Who are you calling?"

"My boss, the president of the United States."

Russo turned to stone. "How can a lowly policeman like you know the president?"

"I saved his life. Didn't you read about it?"

Nicholas knew Russo would like to shoot him here and now but he couldn't be sure if Nicholas was bluffing. Nicholas saw rage in his eyes, at being challenged, at being thwarted. Russo backed down, cleared his throat. "There is no need to do that."

Nicholas studied his face. Good, he was afraid of what his superiors would say if he caused an international incident. Nicholas punched off his cell. "I am happy to meet with you again once I have determined there is no more threat against us. We will do ballistics tests then. This is Agent Louisa Barry, one of the finest forensics technicians in the

FBI. As a courtesy from our government to yours, if you ask her very nicely to help your people work the crime scene, she can assist you."

"My pleasure," Louisa said.

Nicholas said, "You know how to reach us." He and Louisa started again for the door.

"Agent Drummond, clearly you do not understand. We have our orders."

Nicholas looked coldly over his shoulder. "Orders from whom, I'd like to know."

Russo's anger was once again very clear, then he tried to mask it, nodded. "You may leave — for the moment. Let me add that you and your team did a piss-poor job of being covert today."

Nicholas shrugged. "Feel free to take that up with the president. I'm sure he will appreciate hearing how you were too busy attending to a 'civil matter' to back up his lead investigative team their first time on Italian soil. You want a diplomatic nightmare, feel free to get on the phone. As for me, I'm going to check on my wounded agent. Good day, gentlemen."

Mike was in the hallway with Adam, grinning. "Well done. So we're not to be arrested?"

"Russo would love to clap us in irons,

well, he'd rather shoot me dead, but he has a healthy fear of what his superiors would do to him if our president got involved. Adam, I'm glad they didn't try for you at the hotel."

Adam looked pale. He only nodded.

Mike gave him a hug. "Lia will be all right, you'll see. What's amazing to me, Nicholas, is that you didn't punch that arrogant jerk. The president really would get involved, and personally."

"So what's next?" Louisa asked. "We sit here and wait to hear about Lia, obviously, but then what?"

"We must find Kitsune," Mike said. "She's still here, somewhere in Venice."

"Given what you've told me about her," Adam said, "she'll contact us."

Nicholas checked his watch. "You're right, she will. So let's go check on Lia."

Mike said, "Zachery called to tell me Lia's dad is on his way to Venice."

"Good," Louisa said. "Once we see how Lia's doing, let's get some coffee before jet lag knocks us on our butts."

They were met by a nurse, smiling. She gave them a thumbs-up, spoke in rapid Italian.

Nicholas thanked her, said, "Lia is going to make it."

CHAPTER NINETEEN

Lia was very pale. She had a large pressure dressing across her chest and shoulder, her left arm in a sling. Her short blond hair was spiked up, and a dark bruise was creeping up her neck. She brightened when she saw Nicholas and Mike walk through her door, Adam and Louisa behind them.

Nicholas smiled, seeing her earrings still marched up her ears.

"Hey," she whispered, throat scratchy from the anesthesia.

"Hey, yourself," Mike said, sitting in the chair next to the bed. She took Lia's right hand in hers. "What were you thinking, jumping in front of a bullet?"

"Maybe that I wanted to spend the next six weeks in a sling, having all of you wait on me? Broke my collarbone, and they said the bullet nicked the lung. Hit me right on top of my vest, went down instead of through. Funny angle. Doc said a shot like that couldn't happen again in a million years."

Nicholas leaned over and kissed her forehead. "Mike and I would probably be dead if you hadn't spotted the shooters for us. Good job."

Mike said, "You're going to have to stay here for a couple more days, but I have a surprise for you. Your dad's coming. He'll be with you early tomorrow morning."

Lia whispered, "You really did that for me?"

"Zachery did," Nicholas said. He leaned down, took her hand, studied her face. "Louisa tells me you and your father are great chess competitors. Cutthroat games should keep you occupied." Nicholas lightly touched a finger to one of the sterling silver studs on her left ear. "What does your daddy think of these fashion statements?"

Louisa said from behind Mike, "Her dad, who, let me add, is a Lutheran minister, says he wouldn't have minded if she'd rebelled when she was a teenager, gotten it over with, piercings included — but not his Lia, she had to wait to adulthood."

Lia whispered, "I figured I'd have more money, buy better accessories."

A nurse came in. "*Mi scusi,* you need to leave now. She needs rest."

Nicholas paused a moment. "Adam, you and Louisa go back to the hotel. Mike and I need to speak to Zachery again about the local Carabinieri and this Major Russo. No reason for you to stay and hear the fireworks."

Louisa leaned down, kissed Lia on the cheek. "You sleep. I'll see you in the morning."

Adam said, "I'll find you some good websites for accessories."

Lia's voice was fading out. "Maybe I can put it on my expense account."

Louisa and Adam left, Louisa saying, "I'm so tired I could fall asleep right here."

Nicholas knew he had to give Zachery a heads-up about Russo, and called him on his private cell. He got Zachery's voice mail: "Piper is a princess in her school play this year, and not a tree. She makes progress in her acting career."

He grinned. "A bit of whimsy from Zachery. Who would have thought?"

She punched his shoulder. "I met his wife. She told me he is a real jokester, drives her and the kids crazy with his stunts."

They stepped out of the hospital into a dark Venice night, the air soft against their faces. It was quiet, stores closed down, restaurants finally empty, tourists tucked into their beds.

"It feels good to be outside. I want to clear my head." She stopped a moment, looked around the deserted square. "It's so quiet, Nicholas."

She could see multiple alleys extending like arms from the piazza, and the water flowed heavily beside them in the canal and back into the lagoon.

From the corner of her eyes, she saw a shadow. It didn't move. Her hand went to her Glock.

He was close in an instant, whispering, "What is it? What did you see?"

"Not sure, a shadow, but the thing is, it's not moving. I think someone's standing there, watching us. I don't like it, Nicholas."

And the sky lit up in front of them.

They were in the open. He grabbed her hand and they ran toward the passageway next to the canal and ducked under an overhang. Bullets whizzed by them. "I can't tell the angle," Mike said, but she returned fire, then ducked back under the overhang. "I only have one extra magazine, how about you?"

"Same here," Nicholas said. "Shoot in short bursts, pray for accuracy."

They were on their own, no comms, no backup, facing an unknown number of thugs shooting at them. She took two fast shots, didn't hear any yells, only more gunfire. "You'd think someone in the hospital would be yelling their heads off. Where are the *polizia*? Nicholas, I gotta say it, I'd sort of hoped we'd mowed down all the bad guys in the piazza today."

"Have you ever heard of a shortage of criminals and guns?"

More shots, bullets striking the wall and the overhang, too close. They went down on their haunches, backs pressed against the wall. "I hate this bloody town, everyone wants to kill us."

Nicholas pointed. "There's one."

She sighted and pulled the trigger once. The man who'd been crouched atop a building twenty feet from them fell silently, splashing into the canal.

He squeezed her shoulder. "Good shot. How many more? I wonder."

The piazza was deadly silent, as if Venice were holding her breath. So were Mike and Nicholas. Nicholas let his breath out slowly, centering, eyes roaming. "There can't be only one shooter. I mean, confidence is one thing, but there are two of us and we are FBI."

She had to laugh; he sounded so insulted. "I know, and we're the toughest dudes in

155

the universe. There are more, don't worry."

"Cover me, I've got to be able to see more of the area." Nicholas inched forward, crouched low, toward a small bridge arching over the canal. He saw another shooter, this one sneaking up behind Mike, taking sight. He raised his gun, smoothly pulled the trigger. The shot echoed, and the man disappeared, not shot; he'd melted back into the shadows. *Well, bloody hell.*

Where were the *polizia*?

Movement, he saw it, off to the north side of the piazza. He saw two men running past, taking up new positions, flanking him and Mike. So four shooters at least.

He needed to move some twenty feet to his left for a better position. He was about to make the dash when five shots came from his right, smooth, fast, from two guns. Small caliber, sounded like a Walther PPK, a British gun. But why would Italian thugs have British weapons?

He saw one of the shooters rise up to fire, and the British gun fired, and he went down.

He looked across at Mike. Her Glock was up, she was sweeping the area, like he was.

"Go," a female voice shouted. He knew it was Kitsune. She slipped out of the darkness and was rapidly firing across the piazza. He took off back to Mike, grabbed her hand, and the two of them ran along the edge of the canal. Bullets sounded behind them, some striking the walkway, some splashing into the canal. They heard a man scream. A body fell in front of them and they leaped over it, not missing a stride, and went around a corner.

Adrenaline was flowing hot and heavy and Mike was blazing with fight. "Nicholas, who shot that man? Who was shooting back in the piazza?"

"Kitsune."

"You're kidding. What is she? Our guardian angel?"

"You'd think. This is the second time today she's saved my hide."

"What are we going to do? We can't leave her to face the rest of the shooters and I'm nearly out of bullets."

"I've only a few shots left myself."

Another six shots from the British gun, then it was utterly silent, only the sound of the water lapping against the walkway. They heard footsteps, light as a feather, coming closer. It had to be Kitsune.

A quiet voice said, "Take the water taxi. I left it for you. I'll come to you at the hotel. And Nicholas? Mike? Try not to get yourselves killed on the way."

And she was gone.

They heard the wail of a siren. At last, the *polizia.*

He was glad the cops had finally showed up, but he didn't want to talk to them. It would be too much. He grabbed Mike's hand and they ran for the water taxi bobbing in the canal. They were on board; the driver, without a word, took off into the night, spray churning up like wings.

Nicholas glanced back once to see Kitsune standing on the pylon where the boat had been tied, covering their escape.

He said again, "That's twice in one day."

The boat made a sharp fast turn and spray hit her in the face. Mike swiped the water out of her eyes, laughed. "What is one to do with a criminal who rescues you?"

"Let's start with finding out what she's gotten herself into."

CHAPTER TWENTY

Louisa met them in the lobby, candy from a vending machine in her hand. She did a double take. "What on earth happened to you?"

"More bad guys tried to kill us," Mike said. "It was exciting there for a while, then Kitsune showed up, saved us yet again. No *polizia,* no Carabinieri, and that really pisses me off."

"After the no-show in the piazza," Louisa said, "I've got to think Kitsune's clients paid them to stay away."

Nicholas thought of Major Russo. "It's reasonable to assume there are certainly a couple of high-ups who are doubtless on the clients' payroll."

Mike said, "Given someone's tried to kill us twice today, and not a soul from the Italians' side was around to help, I think we need to accept that we're on our own."

Louisa punched the elevator button.

"Thank goodness Kitsune was there. She's turning into Wonder Woman."

Mike said, "I figure she has to save us, since she got us into this mess, whatever this mess turns out to be. Hey, Nicholas, you okay?"

He'd gone white. He was looking at a new tear in Mike's jacket on her other shoulder. He felt a wave of panic, gently pushed her jacket and shirt down and examined her upper arm. "Not bad," he said, and let out a breath. "I'll fix you up when we get to the suite."

Mike looked down at her ripped jacket. "I didn't feel a thing." She looked up at him. "It hurts now. Isn't that something?"

Louisa said, "It doesn't look bad, Mike, thank goodness."

Nicholas pulled Mike's shirt back up, closed her jacket. "You are not sleeping in that room our lovely receptionist assigned you on the third floor. My suite has two bedrooms. The living room is good-sized, so we can use it for business. Don't even think of arguing, Agent Caine, I can't protect you if you're half a hotel away. Louisa, would you please bring your first-aid kit? I need to clean up Agent Caine's wound."

Ten minutes later, the four of them were congregated in Nicholas's suite, room service ordered, everyone settled in. Mike filled in Adam and Louisa on the shoot-out near the hospital while Nicholas cleaned up her arm. She wasn't going to make a sound. She talked fast, through gritted teeth.

"There, all done," he said what seemed like two years later, but she knew was only a couple of minutes. "The steri strips are fine. You'll be good to go in a couple of days. Here, take the aspirin. I'll have the nurse give you a lollipop on your way out."

"Har-har."

Adam handed her a glass of Coke Light and she got the aspirin down. "While we were waiting to hear about Lia's surgery, I called Gray to ask him about the coverage drop in New York. He said he was still working on it, but it appeared the satellite they were using got off course and lost its signal. It's totally down. It might have been tampered with, it might have been hit by space debris, don't know yet."

The pain in Mike's arm was down to a dull throbbing, thank heavens. "But that doesn't explain the inability to call us. Cellular shouldn't have been affected."

"That's right," Adam said. "Gray told me they went dark on all the screens for almost forty minutes. He said he'd get back to me when he had more information.

"Now, I've been searching for the drop in the system, myself, Nicholas, but so far, nothing. It's gone. The data from that time has been erased. If our comms had gone down I'd be inclined to say it was a small EMP — an electromagnetic pulse — and that still might be the case, if there's someone out there who's developed a directional EMP. But at this rate, we might never know what happened. There aren't any bugs in the system, none that I can see, at least. It's like someone unplugged the coffeepot for a while, then remembered it hadn't brewed totally and plugged it back in."

"Keep on it, Adam, and your contacting Gray was a good idea. Keep in touch with him. If it was done on purpose, to cut communication to us, I'm betting there'll be a trace. I have a hard time believing it was an accident, though."

"Sounds coordinated to me," Louisa said. "Adam, tell Mike and Nicholas about keeping track of Kitsune."

Adam said, "Since she's keeping an eye on us, we'll see her again."

"Sorry," Mike said, "I forgot to tell you. Kitsune said she'd be coming here later."

"Good. When she gets here I can tag her with a GPS tracker. Lia brought a couple of our new ingestables. It's in her best interest for us to know where she is. Then we give her some tasty pasta, and pow! — she's covered for seventy-two hours, give or take, and we always know where she is."

"I think she will come," Mike said. "But then I think about all the cock-ups today. She might be reconsidering our value to her as we speak."

There was a knock at the door. A female voice called out in strongly accented English, "Room service."

All eyes went to the door.

The knock sounded again, the voice more urgent, this time in Italian, *"Apri la porta, per favore."*

"Not again. Wait, Nicholas, something isn't right here." Mike pulled out her Glock. Nicholas took one side of the door, Mike the other. Louisa had her weapon out as well, standing in front of Adam.

Nicholas opened the door, his Glock pointed at the server.

It was Kitsune, dressed in the hotel's service outfit. She smiled, said, *"Grazie,"* and walked into the room.

"So where's our dinner?" Nicholas said, slipping his Glock back into its holster.

"When I checked, I was told there was a twenty-minute wait. I hope you don't mind, but I added an order of my own to yours."

Mike said, "Well, no more long blond hair. But you still aren't you."

"No. To visit the hotel, I decided to go Italian native, no more tourist." Kitsune patted her dark wig. "I am very sorry about your agent. Will she be all right?"

"Yes," Mike said. "Thank you, Kitsune, for keeping a watch on us, for keeping us safe." She paused. "You're not a bad shot, either. I thought you hated guns."

"I did. I do, but Grant — my husband — said I would occasionally find them useful and that meant I had to learn how to shoot. When he was satisfied, he gave me two Walther PPKs. I like them."

Nicholas said. "I want to meet Grant and shake his hand. He taught you well. Sit down, Kitsune, and tell us what's going on here."

She sat forward. "Listen, time is of the essence. They have Grant, they kidnapped my husband." Her voice cracked, just a bit, then she shook her head at herself, got it together. "I was told to set up a contact email account. My only message from his kidnappers was to be in the Piazza San Marco on the time and date — today. Nothing else."

Nicholas looked at her closely, saw the fear in her eyes, not for herself, no, for her husband. And he knew without question

164

that she would trade herself for him.

"Somehow they found out I'd called you, how, I don't know, but they knew. They knew everything. And that's why they were there in the piazza, waiting and watching for us to hook up and take care of all of us. I don't think they have Grant here, I don't even know if he's still alive." Kitsune hated saying those words aloud, hated how they sounded so stark, so final. She wanted to fold in on herself, but knew she had to keep it together, she had to move forward. It's what Grant would expect of her. It's what she expected of herself.

Mike said, "You realize, of course, that your clients have buddies in the Carabinieri, probably on their payroll?"

"I didn't, not until the shooting started and they were nowhere to be seen."

Another knock on the door, and Nicholas covered Mike as she went to open it. This time, it was their dinner. Mike gave the server a big tip and wheeled the cart inside, wincing only slightly at the pulling pain in her arm. She'd been lucky — this was nothing.

She set the tray on the table. "Everyone, dig in."

Nicholas took a bite of carbonara, then another. It tasted nearly as good as Pietro's on East 43rd in Midtown.

"Kitsune, let's start at the Topkapi. I want to hear how you managed to steal the staff of Moses, a priceless artifact. Just like you stole another priceless artifact, I might add, from another well-guarded museum."

Kitsune chewed on a bite of gnocchi. "Suffice it to say the orders to give me a slot with the palace guards came from the very top. I look good in green and carrying an M5."

Mike said, "So you were a guard. You watched and you waited, learned everyone's routines, the timetables. When you were ready, you put the security feed on a loop, turned off the infrared and bypassed the alarms, and did a weighted replacement for the staff."

Kitsune smiled. "You should get into the business, Mike. You think like a thief."

"Why, thank you," Mike said.

"Wait a minute," Nicholas said. "The Top-kapi is guarded by the Turkish military. How in the world did you get around them?"

"I will say only that General Akar's signature is remarkably easy to duplicate. How I stole the staff is irrelevant. The Topkapi's security has many holes, as any museum does. We need to talk about Grant and how we're going to find him. And save him."

"First, Kitsune," Nicholas said, "we want you to tell us about how the sandstorm in Beijing wasn't a natural disaster."

CHAPTER TWENTY-ONE

Kitsune nodded. "Very well. I've been doing some research on recent storms in the Gobi. I discovered a pattern. There have been a spate of sandstorms, always starting from the same quadrant, every few months for the past three years. If you check your email, Nicholas, I sent you a report before I came here."

Nicholas pulled his mobile from his pocket, opened it to his private, secure FBI mail app. "I won't even ask how you got my secure email address."

"Truly, Nicholas, if the Americans have any hope of remaining at the top of the world food chain, they need to realize that giving every agent the same-patterned email address isn't a safe road to security, no matter the level of encryption."

He tossed the phone to Adam. "Adam, please offload it."

Louisa asked, "But why would someone

want to be causing sandstorms in the Gobi? Why would someone want to control the weather at all? And how is that even possible? You think someone's figured out how to damage their competition one storm at a time? It's all about money?"

Kitsune said, "It usually is. But now I believe the systematic sandstorms are about something bigger than money. I believe whoever hired me to steal the staff of Moses in the Topkapi has something to do with these sandstorms."

"The Gobi is a big place," Mike said. "I assume there are many lost treasures."

Kitsune nodded. "The Mongolian Empire was quite large. Whole cities were lost along with their treasures, their gold. As I told you on the phone, Nicholas, I think they're looking for the Ark of the Covenant in the Gobi Desert."

"The Gobi Desert?" Adam looked confused. "How can that be possible? I mean, Indiana Jones was nowhere near the Gobi."

Mike said, "Adam's right, tell us more, so we'll understand. Why is your client looking for the Ark of the Covenant? And why in the Gobi Desert?"

Kitsune said simply, "I believe they want the power the Ark holds. God's power. You see, the staff of Moses belongs inside the

169

Ark. I've read the Ark's power is inconceivable. With it, they'd be unstoppable. If I'm right about this, they've already found a way to control the weather."

Adam looked up from his laptop. "Kitsune's right. There is a pattern to the sandstorms. It's hard to see if you didn't go in already expecting to find it. Their inceptions concentrate in a single area."

"How can you possibly know that?"

Kitsune said slowly, "I can't prove it, but I believe it to my soul. If you wish, call it intuition.

"I stole the staff of Moses for them, and they tried to kill me. Why? I know you don't consider my profession to be particularly noble, but there is a code of conduct. They broke it. I could see no reason why, certainly not to save themselves five million euros. I did my job and did it cleanly, no chance of any blowback on them. So why do they want me dead?"

Mike said, "Because you're a loose thread."

Kitsune nodded. "Yes, that is true, but surely —"

Adam raised his head. "Why do you believe these sandstorms tie directly into finding the Ark? Do you have any proof?"

"The only thing I have is this. When I was

in Turkey, standing around guarding the palace, a woman came for a VIP tour, and with the director of the museum, no less — very unusual. She was tall, fit, blond. I didn't see her face, nor was I close enough to hear her talk, but she was treated with the utmost respect by the museum's director. I remember he fell all over himself to get her inside as quickly as possible. I heard she spent most of the time she was there in front of the staff of Moses. She left less than thirty minutes later. The guards were talking about her, how they'd like to get her into bed, you know how men can be. I heard several of them call her *hazine avcisi,* some sort of professional treasure hunter, but more, they said she was an expert on the Ark of the Covenant. I looked up the visitor records later that night. All references to her being there had been deleted. Gone. Completely.

"I couldn't ask about it, clearly, but there was something to her visit that felt wrong to me. I never found out who she was. But I know it has something to do with the Ark, perhaps why they're trying to kill me.

"It's said it takes one to know one. I think she's a criminal, a pro, there to check out the staff."

"Did you see enough to sketch her?"

"I told you, I wasn't able to see her face. But there was something about her that alarmed me. She must be well connected, probably very rich and powerful, given how the director fawned over her.

"Is she the client? I don't know. You have to help me figure this out." She drew a deep breath. "But the most important thing is what I heard the man and woman speaking about when I went to the drop site to deliver the staff, what I told you, Nicholas."

Nicholas drew a small notebook from his jacket pocket and read aloud: " *'I wish I could see it, the Gobi sands — a tsunami sweeping over Beijing.' 'We will see it all on video. All the sand . . . Could Grandfather be that good?' 'You know he is. And we will see the aftermath . . . leave in three days after things . . . imagine, we are the ones to drain the Gobi?'* "

Nicholas looked at Kitsune. "And you believe they drained the Gobi to find the Ark of the Covenant?"

"Well, they already have the staff of Moses," Kitsune said. "But you see, as I said, the staff is supposed to be inside the Ark of the Covenant. So what does it mean?"

CHAPTER TWENTY-TWO

Adam thought about it. Build the code himself, encrypt it, and build a special back door so the Italians would never know he'd broken into their CCTV feed for Piazza San Marco? He knew they'd be able to identify the shooters, and maybe connect them to Kitsune's client. Or, turn to Istanbul and find the blonde? Adam knew she had to be the key. He heard Kitsune say, "It was certainly a man and a woman speaking about the storm in the Gobi. Now that I think about it, their voices sounded young."

Adam went on the DarkNet. Here, he was Dark Leaf. His former name, Eternal Patrol, had been well buried when he'd come on board with the FBI. He and Nicholas had regularly pulled white-hat jobs together to establish the credentials of the new hacker name on the block. Dark Leaf was a dissident, a hacker with multiple website takedowns and proxy raids, and now a popular member of the online world of anonymous. As a result, Dark Leaf had a growing reputation and was known in all the wrong circles. No one would ever guess it was all a fabrication.

A message window opened, four other hackers popped up and greeted him in their own special language.

Hellop!
Foo?
WYB?

Adam started to type, using his own peculiar hacking shorthand, not Dark Leaf, simply DL. Were someone to look over his shoulder, they'd see what at first glance looked like nonsense, strings of letters and characters and numbers. But to Adam, this was his world, the place he was most comfortable.

The conversation was general for a few minutes, catch-ups and bragging, then he singled out a hacker named Ham for a private-messaging session. The window opened on the top right, yellow words on a black background, graying out the rest of his screen.

DL: Has anyone had contact with GR8T
lately?
Ham: He went to join ISIS.
DL: Please, that's not true.
Ham: Of course not, haha. Last I heard
he was still in Constantinople. But
flaky.
DL: I need a pipe in. Can you help?
Ham: 5

Ham logged out of the chat. Adam bit a
thumbnail. Five minutes later Ham's handle
popped up again, and a second name appeared.

Ham: DL, here's your genie.

And he disappeared before Adam had a
chance to thank him. He knew Ham would
be back soon enough with a request or
requirement of his own. That was fine. This
was the price of doing business in the
hacker world.
Adam addressed the new chat mate.

DL: Good to see you. Can you help with
a project?
GR8T: What do you need, and how
much are you paying?
DL: Enough. I need a feed for the
cameras surrounding the Topkapi.

GR8T: Military-grade, dude. Gonna cost ya.
DL: Sky's the limit. Bring it.

GR8T disappeared from the chat. A long string of numbers appeared. Adam used it to wire transfer five thousand dollars. Good-faith money. Moments later a file appeared, floating in lazy circles in the middle of his screen. Adam scanned it, found exactly what he needed, then downloaded it. With two more clicks, he transferred another twenty-five thousand dollars, then logged out of the chat.

Hackers were predictable, thankfully. Wave some cash and you could get whatever you wanted. Adam appreciated the fact that Nicholas had created the "bank," as they liked to call it, and given Adam approval for up to $100,000 in transaction fees without extraneous approval. It made working the DarkNet so much easier. Plus, the hackers knew when Dark Leaf asked for help, they got paid. It was a win-win for everyone.

Opening the file GR8T had sent him, Adam disguised himself further, coded open a slick back door through the museum's firewall, and tapped directly into the ultra-secure video feed at the Topkapi Palace.

He worked quickly, fingers crossed this

ploy would work, that he hadn't just wasted a quarter of his bank on nothing. So many museums recycled their feed at the end of the day, or the end of the week. From what Kitsune had said, he'd need the feed from about two weeks earlier.

He was in luck. The Topkapi didn't recycle their feeds weekly. They kept them all, bless their paranoid little souls.

He saw the feed appear for the time frame in question.

He made a quick copy of it, exited out the back door, closed it thoroughly so no one would know he'd been in the system, wiped all his tracks, and shut down the link.

All in all, it had taken him less than five minutes to make the grab.

Should he tell Nicholas now what he'd done? No, better to wait, see if he could identify the blonde who'd visited the Topkapi before he said anything. He heard their voices; he really liked Kitsune's voice, the Scottish lilt. He started running the feed from the Topkapi against the FBI's NGI facial recognition databases.

If the woman Kitsune had seen was a criminal, Adam would find her.

While that was running, Adam decided to open a fresh window and tap into the Venice CCTV video feed. He wasn't interested in the shooters in Piazza San Marco today. He wanted to zero in on what happened the day Kitsune had nearly been killed.

The Venice CCTV did recycle daily, but he quickly found the archive where they dumped their old files. He pulled twenty-four hours of feed, downloaded them, released the cameras, and started his search. He combed through hours of footage quickly, running the feed at ten-times speed, looking for Kitsune jumping from rooftop to rooftop.

He was about to give up when he caught sight of her, leaping through the air like an inky blackbird. He stopped the video, ran it back, and watched in total awe as the woman flew off the edge of the building, soared in an arc fifty feet wide, and landed in a boat below. Switching cameras, he saw her shoot out of the canal into the lagoon, bullets smashing into the water behind her. Adam whistled, low. He thought at first she'd been really lucky, then changed his mind. She was that good.

And it occurred to him. What he really needed to see was the man chasing her. He rewound the video and changed the camera angle, looked closely toward the area he assumed the bullets had come from. Sure enough, a face appeared at the edge of the building, watching Kitsune escape unscathed. Taking a screen grab of the face, Adam sent it to Gray to run, while he searched through the NGI database for the blonde.

It was a half an hour before the computer dinged. A match. But it wasn't what he expected.

He'd struck gold.

CHAPTER TWENTY-THREE

Adam walked into the living room, a huge grin on his face. "Hey, kids, gather around. Daddy's got a nice surprise."

Some laughter, then Mike said, "What do you have for us kids, Daddy?"

"I found the blond woman Kitsune saw at the Topkapi. Nicholas, I'm sure glad you got your buddies in MI-5 to sync with us, because that's where I found her — the MI5's facial recognition database. Her name's Lilith Forrester-Clarke." He handed Kitsune a printed screen grab. "Is this the woman?"

Kitsune frowned as she touched her fingertips to the woman's face.

Nicholas said, "Do you recognize her?"

"Yes, from somewhere, maybe a long time ago. It's going to take some thought for me to remember. But that name — Lilith — unusual name and it's familiar."

Mike hugged Adam, kissed him full on

the mouth. "I'm so glad I talked Nicholas into bringing you on board."

"Wow! Wait, wait —" There was another ding from his computer. "Hey, look at this, guys, I've got another hit. Kitsune, I got footage and saw you flying over rooftops, and that made me see if I could find the guy chasing you. Yep, here he is, name's Antonio Pazzi. He's got a sheet, minor stuff mostly, lots of charges, but he seems to have a Teflon coating. He's Venetian, and we should be able to find him here. The local cops will have him on their radar for sure. Unless he's one of the dead shooters in the piazza. In which case, he'll be even easier to find."

The two grainy shots were passed around.

Kitsune stared down at Pazzi, looked over at Adam. She rose slowly, walked to him, and took his face between her hands. "You are remarkable. If I were not already married to the very best man in the whole world, I would marry you, young Adam." And like Mike, she kissed him. "You're a genius. Thank you."

"I'm not going to kiss you," Nicholas said.

"I will," Louisa said. "But later. Maybe, depending on what you do for me."

Adam was grinning from ear to ear. "Louisa, you've got a ways to go to beat Mike."

"That's why we pay Adam the big bucks." Nicholas punched Adam on the arm.

Adam said, "Hey, is there any food? I'm starving, my brain's starving."

"You just ate." Mike laughed. "Forgive me, I forgot. You're still growing. There are potato chips in the minibar." She turned back to Kitsune, pointed to the photo. "You're sure this is the man you made the delivery to? The man who chased you, tried to kill you?"

Kitsune nodded. "He's the one, all right. Antonio Pazzi. Adam, wait a moment. The blond woman at the Topkapi . . . oh yes, I remember her now. But it's so hard to believe it could really be her.

"It was a long time ago, when I was very young. She was a bit younger than I, and I remember she had lots of dark brown hair, and she was pudgy, but then again, many kids are."

"In Roslin, Scotland?"

"Yes. I'm surprised you remember that, Nicholas."

Nicholas simply raised an eyebrow.

"Never mind, of course you remember. Lilith and I lived close to each other. She went to my school." She frowned over the photo. "Maybe not, how can it be? This is simply too big of a coincidence."

"Let me see what I can find out about her." Adam dusted the potato chips from his hands, sat down, and started typing. "Bingo. Lilith Leigh Forrester-Clarke, age thirty-six, from Roslin, Scotland. Attended Cambridge, majored in archaeology — copied you in her studies, Kitsune. What's this? She joined MI5, was with them for four years. Her current address is in London, and she works for the Genesis Group, headquartered in Rome."

"What's the Genesis Group?" Mike asked.

Kitsune still clutched both photos in her hands. "The Genesis Group is one of the leading archaeology firms in the world right now, very powerful, very wealthy. They fund digs all over the world.

"Yes, they are headquartered in Rome, but they got their start in London, more than a hundred years ago, under a man named Appleton Kohath. He founded the firm around the turn of the century and it's been passed down through the generations, has always been run by family members. They are well regarded in the archaeology community." She paused. "And now everything makes sense."

Adam had the Genesis Group website up. He turned the computer around to show everyone the slick, well-designed page, then began to read from the About section.

He read, "The Genesis Group is the preeminent archaeology firm in the world, with an annual endowment of over a billion dollars."

Kitsune said, "The accepted wisdom in the antiquities world is Appleton Kohath founded the Genesis Group to go after the Ark of the Covenant. And that's how he got his start. He was a contemporary of Howard Carter of King Tut fame. Kohath was there, at the dig. And he was a part of every major dig thereafter during his lifetime. Again, most of them centered on discovering possible sites of the Ark of the Covenant. I read Kohath's biography, written by Elizabeth St. Germaine, an English writer."

Nicholas was shaking his head. "Elizabeth St. Germaine. Her family and mine have been friends forever. Elizabeth died quite suddenly a couple of weeks ago. It came as a shock to everyone." He paused, then, "So, Kitsune, you think the search for the Ark continues, and you think the Kohaths running the Genesis Group today hired you to steal the staff of Moses. Why? Perhaps it would hold some clues to the location of the Ark?"

Kitsune shook her head. "No, if they indeed are the clients, I think they hired me to steal the staff of Moses because they wanted to know for certain it was a fake, then they would know the staff is still inside the Ark. Wherever it is.

"That's another reason this is so puzzling. It was a professional job, one of dozens I've completed successfully over the years. I simply do not understand why they would risk trying to kill me. They want me dead so much they even kidnapped Grant to get to me? And look what it got them." And she waved her hands around at the group.

Nicholas shrugged. "I don't think it's such a mystery, Kitsune. Secrecy is very important to them and you could talk. They didn't want to take that chance. They wanted anonymity, and you being dead is the only way to guarantee it."

Adam ate the last potato chip, tipped up the bag to get the crumbs, then swiped his mouth. "Okay, reenergized. Who do you want me to hack now?"

"You'll see what we need right on the website. Who currently runs the Genesis Group?"

Kitsune said, "No need to look it up. I know. It's Cassandra and Ajax Kohath-Maynes. They're twins, late twenties, very smart, very photogenic."

Mike looked up from studying the website.

"They're evidently very good at fundraising, given how wealthy they are. Have you met them?"

"Once, in London, a while ago — six, eight years. Both are trained archaeologists, Ajax is a computer whiz, helps to search out where there is probable payoff for a dig. They are usually together, although I seem to remember that Cassandra was married for about ten minutes when she was very young. I don't know what happened to her husband.

"Although now I'm more on the edges of the archaeology community, I still hear rumors."

"Rumors about what?" Mike sat forward in her chair.

"Rumors of instability, I guess you could say."

"These twins — you mean they're nuts?" Adam said.

Kitsune shrugged. "More that they're mercurial, unpredictable, fast to anger — particularly Ajax — but still brilliant, both of them. Could they be my clients? Yes, I think they could. They have not only a house here in Venice, they also have other holdings as well."

"All right," Mike said, "let's say the Kohaths didn't want to show themselves to you because you would know who they were and why they wanted the staff of Moses."

Adam said, "Their working budget appears tremendous. But their continuous financial outlay is staggering. My question is, where do they get the money to continue year after year? All from fund-raising? Even the best politicians at home couldn't fund-raise like they have, for decades."

Mike said, "And what about the weather? The devastating sandstorm in the Gobi? How does that tie in? Why would they want to devastate Beijing?"

Nicholas paced to the window, turned back to the group. "Have they actually figured out how to start a sandstorm or any other kind of storm, for that matter, from a specific place? If so, there would be no stopping them. They could hold the earth for ransom."

"Usurping the power of God," Louisa said. "That's beyond frightening."

"These people are supposed to be the descendants of Moses," Kitsune said. "Kohaths, Levites. The Ark of the Covenant is central to their family history. Their family's mission has always been to find the Ark, it's never been a secret. And now that we've reached an era of remarkable scientific innovation —"

Nicholas said quietly, "Perhaps the power of God and the brilliance of science have merged at last."

CHAPTER TWENTY-FOUR

"What are we going to do now?" Adam asked.

"First things first," Nicholas said, "Louisa, if you would bring a tracker and a glass of water to Kitsune."

Kitsune looked at what appeared to be an oversize vitamin pill and nearly rose straight out of her chair. "I am not going to run. Where would I go? You are my best hope of staying alive and finding Grant. What is this?"

"We call it an ingestible," Louisa said, and handed it to her. "Now we can keep you safe. We will never lose sight of you. It lasts about seventy-two hours."

Kitsune stared at her a moment. "Keep me safe? You want to keep me safe?"

"Of course," Nicholas said. "You're our bait."

"Yes, of course," Kitsune said, and smiled.

"I want to talk to Cassandra and Ajax Kohath."

Louisa said, "Bottoms up. And be sure to wash it down. It can give you heartburn if you don't."

Adam looked up. "The twins live on the Grand Canal." And he gave them the exact address and preened.

Kitsune said, "If they're not here, they're in Rome, at the headquarters of the Genesis Group. Six hours if we drive."

"It would be faster to fly."

"Your own plane, Nicholas? I am impressed. Imagine, now you're officially in the American FBI. Amazing step for you to take. Just look what you and Mike have done in such a short time."

Nicholas raised an eyebrow.

"Nicholas, you must understand that people are watching you and Michaela's every move. You didn't save just anyone's life, you saved the president of the United States' life, brought down Zahir Damari, no mean feat. You've become an active threat to a number of people, especially now that you've been given more power, and that's exactly what we're going to need if we're going up against the Genesis Group. Their money, their influence, the number of bad guys on their payroll — we're going to have

190

to be very careful."

Mike said, "We should hit them now, here at their home. Maybe we'll get lucky."

Kitsune stopped cold. "Wait, wait. I just remembered. Okay, the cataclysmic sandstorm in the Gobi — the twins' mother went missing in the Gobi Desert a decade ago. She was on a dig and was caught in a sandstorm. The site was never found, and word was the twins were devastated. The entire company shuts down every year on the anniversary."

"And who was their mother?"

"Helen Kohath-Maynes. Brilliant archaeologist, an amazing woman. I studied her in school. She was a leading Ark scholar, and led the foundation for a short time but allowed her husband, David Maynes, to handle the day-to-day running of the foundation's business so she could be out on digs, searching for the Ark.

"Rumor also has it that the twins kicked their father out of running the Genesis Group when they turned twenty-one and took control. They also dropped his name, which has to tell you how much they distrusted and disliked him. Now they're only called Cassandra and Ajax Kohath. I believe he died a short while ago."

Mike said, "Well, if David Maynes is dead,

he isn't a player in all of this. Here's what I don't understand: Why would the world's leading expert on the Ark of the Covenant believe it was buried in the Gobi Desert? It makes no sense."

"And that, I believe," Louisa said, "brings us right back to the huge sandstorm and controlling weather."

Kitsune said, "It does. And it makes no sense to me, either."

Nicholas said, "At least we're finally starting to see a pattern emerge. Adam, get us everything you can find on Cassandra and Ajax Kohath. We don't want to trot up to their front door unless we know what to expect. If they are behind this, they've already tried to kill us and Kitsune, twice now. They even want her so badly, they took her husband."

Adam said, "The Genesis Group has an extensive online presence, pretty typical for a company these days. They're an open book — all aboveboard, so far as the public can tell. I'm searching through their files, so far nothing at all alarming. Their holdings are all over the globe, and they appear incredibly flush with cash. I'll have to get inside to see about their actual cash flow. On the surface, I don't think I've ever seen a healthier balance sheet. We're talking billions of dollars. Ah, listen to this. Lilith Forrester-Clarke is listed as their chief of operations."

"Interesting," Kitsune said. "I'd also suggest taking a historical look at the Kohaths as well. There's only so much to be gleaned online."

Louisa said, "I'll call Ben, ask him to take the lead on that angle."

Nicholas said, "Louisa, also ask Ben to get in touch with Melinda St. Germaine in London. Since her mother, Elizabeth St. Germaine, was the biographer of Appleton Kohath, the creator of the Genesis Group, perhaps there is information there that will help us. Hopefully Melinda will agree to let Ben look at her mother's materials. Tell him to use my name."

"Got it," Louisa said, and turned away to dial Ben in New York.

Nicholas stretched. "Now, this Lilith character. Tell me about her, Kitsune."

"I remember she always seemed to be hanging around me, always wanted my attention. I didn't like her much, tried to ignore her, lose her when I could, but she always managed to find me. But she was a little kid then — I can't imagine she'd even remember me."

"Oh, she knows exactly who you are,"

Nicholas said. "And I'll wager she recommended the Kohaths hire you to steal the staff because she's followed your every step through the years. She was MI5, remember? She would have had complete access to everything known about you and your world. She doubtless followed your exploits. Did she envy you? Probably so.

"I'll also wager she managed to find the location of your home. Did she know about your marriage to Grant Thornton, and his leaving the Beefeaters? Sure she did. And I'll bet she was at the Topkapi to check on you."

"To see if I was there?"

"If her bosses were your client? It makes sense. When we see her, we'll be sure to ask about her visit. And about her fascination with you."

Mike shrugged, drank some water. "If Nicholas is right, it means she's been watching you for years from the shadows. Maybe that's why she also studied archaeology. Because you did. As Adam said, she copied you."

Kitsune was silent, trying to take it all in. She said, "We still don't have a definitive link from the Kohaths to the Genesis Group to me, and we need that."

Nicholas said, "We'll get it. Now, you guys

carry on. I need to talk to Savich. I have an idea."

CHAPTER TWENTY-FIVE

While Mike called Zachery to give him an update, and Louisa talked to Ben, Nicholas walked into his bedroom and punched in Savich's number. It was just short of 2:00 a.m. in Venice, so that would make it dinnertime at the Savich house.

Savich answered on the first ring. "Nicholas — how is Lia?"

"She'll be fine, her dad will be here in the morning. Another couple of days in the hospital and he'll take her home."

"I've had several calls from Zachery. Both he and I have seen how you shot up Saint Mark's Square and made a big-time enemy of a higher-up in the Carabinieri."

Nicholas laughed. "His name is Major Russo. We're looking at his files, checking to see if he was really detained, or purposefully called off. Or called himself off. We'll see."

"Nicholas? Sherlock here. Your shoot-out

at Saint Mark's Square is all over the news. Unfortunately, yours and Mike's names were given out, the Italian government raised a ruckus, and yes, I believe the vice president got involved. Dillon, tell them what she said to you."

Savich said, "The vice president was still fired up when she called me. She spoke to the Italian president, currently, Giorgio Grasso, but she mentioned he probably wasn't long for the office, which was sad because she rather liked him, said Grasso voiced all the proper apologies. She also said she trusted you and Mike implicitly and hoped you would save the world from destruction one more time. Do you have Kitsune?"

"Yes, she's here, working with us."

"Hmm," said Sherlock. "We see she's now wanted for murder in Venice."

"She was set up," Nicholas said. "If what's going on is as serious as we believe, then Kitsune's a heroine for alerting us."

Savich said, "I hope you're only fifty percent serious about possible world destruction."

"It's all very complicated, Savich, and to be honest, I'm still not sure, but we have an excellent lead now. I need a favor."

"Tell me."

"Can you program MAX to explore possible past ventures into controlling weather?"

"Yes. MAX will enjoy that."

Adam came into the room, and Nicholas put the phone on speaker. "Hi, Agent Savich. Don't have MAX go much earlier than the turn of the twentieth century."

"Adam, glad to hear your voice. You're still operating under the assumption the massive sandstorm in the Gobi was somehow engineered, and not a natural disaster?"

Adam said, "Yes, sir. We've already verified several storms hit nearly the same spot in the Gobi over the past decade."

Nicholas picked it up. "None of us think nature could be so precise, and this feels very precise. So I got to thinking, has there been any work done along this line in the past that might have been used as a building block, that might give us some clues? Some understanding into how controlling the weather could actually be accomplished.

"And one other thing, Savich. If MAX could also have a hard look at those who made great profits from Hurricane Katrina. The oil companies, for example — the price of oil went through the roof. If someone knew about the severity of Katrina beforehand, shorted the stock, bought oil futures, they made millions."

Savich whistled. "For argument's sake, let's say an outside force can control the weather, that this outside force has built upon earlier work, and has managed to create disasters and reap the profits. Do you know who're the most likely candidates?"

"The Genesis Group is at the top of our list, privately owned by the Kohath family. Both Adam and Gray are deep into their files as we speak."

"There's a lot more to this, isn't there, Nicholas?"

"Yes. If you have two minutes, I'll boil it down for you as best I can."

"Let's hear it."

"It all goes back to the Ark of the Covenant and why Kitsune called me." And Nicholas filled him in quickly on what had happened since they arrived in Venice.

When he finally came up for air, Savich said, "This is the stuff of nightmares."

"Yes. The world would be scared if it knew."

"All right, I'll have MAX look into past efforts in weather control, the results, the protocols, as well as the big winners with Katrina, which I suppose you want me to try to connect up to huge profits for the Genesis Group."

"Exactly. As fast as you can find something useful the better. Thank you, Savich."

When Nicholas hung up, Adam said, "I'd sure like to get my hands on MAX. Yeah, yeah, like that would ever happen. I'll keep searching."

Nicholas did some quick research on his own computer. Nothing popped. He wished he had the mainframe at MI5 at his disposal again.

It was nearly 3:00 a.m. when he walked back into the living room to see Adam slouched over his laptop, asleep. Everyone else was dragging. Time to hang it up. He sent Kitsune with Louisa to bunk down with her. "Be back here in the suite at nine. We'll have breakfast and decide our next step."

He looked over at Mike, who was headed toward the second bedroom. "Mike."

She turned, leaned against the door of the second bedroom, as if she needed to prop herself up, and gave him a silly grin. "Sure was a long day, Nicholas," and she yawned. Her hair was ratty, half out of its ponytail, her clothes wrinkled, and she was lightly rubbing her wounded arm. She looked ready to fall over.

He raised a brow. "Yes. It's time to fold down your angel wings. Don't you think it would be safer for both of us if we slept in one room? There's only the two of us now, no more safety in numbers."

Mike kept rubbing her arm, aware of only a low throbbing pain now. She stared at the man she'd give her life for, his clothes as wrinkled as hers. He badly needed a shave, although she liked the beard scruff. His shirt was half hanging out of his pants, and he looked so perfect to her she wanted to leap on him and kiss him until her mouth went numb.

Instead, she took off her glasses and started polishing them on the edge of her shirt. "You've had lots of good ideas today, Nicholas, but you want to know what?"

"What?"

She slipped her glasses back on. "This one's the best. I'll race you."

She dashed past him, into his bedroom, and jumped on the bed, bounced a few times, then looked around the bedroom. "Now, this is pretty fancy. I'll have to thank your blond admirer for treating you so well. You should give her a call, Nicholas, it'd be a great reward."

"Hold that thought," he said. "You want the bathroom first?"

"Nope, you go on."

When he came out, all the lights were still

on and he saw Mike sprawled on her back in the middle of the bed, fully clothed, deeply asleep.

"Well, bloody hell." He pulled off her biker boots, slipped her Glock out of its clip at her waist, started to unbutton her blouse, then yawned and plugged in their cell phones. He carefully laid her glasses next to them. He crawled in next to her, pulled the covers to their chins, and was asleep beside her in under a minute.

Savich called Nicholas at 7:00 a.m. Venice time. It was Mike who answered after four rings.

"If this is God, I swear I didn't do it."

Savich laughed. "Good morning, Mike. Give me Nicholas."

Nicholas was immediately alert, synapses firing. He put his cell phone on speaker. "Please tell me I'm not bonkers and MAX has banned me."

"No and no. Hurricane Katrina first. There were many very big winners, from the oil companies to contractors hired to repair and replace hundreds of houses and businesses in New Orleans. You were right, the Genesis Group cashed in to the tune of one hundred million dollars, give or take. Even though their buys were diverse, you'd see the pattern if you were looking at them specifically. It's all there — oil stocks, gas stocks, a number of publicly owned contractor firms, furniture and appliances chains, medical equipment, just to name a few — whatever was critical to rebuilding New Orleans, they invested in the public companies and made a killing."

"But the profits weren't out of line with other profiteers from Katrina?"

"Only if examined closely, then, as I said, the pattern is clear. Someone studied this extensively, then bought huge blocks of shares in the key industries."

"Better and better."

"As for people building machines to try to control the weather, MAX found nothing of any legitimacy, though there is plenty of scientific research work being done, and weather control for creating rain — cloud seeding and such — has been around for decades. However, I did find information that sparked my imagination. What do you know about Nikola Tesla?"

"About the same as anyone, I suppose. He was a genius, way ahead of his time, what we'd now call a futurist, with his uses of electromagnetic forces, briefly worked with Thomas Edison. Some weird explosion he was blamed for, that's about it."

"That's a good start. What drew me was Tesla's Coil. As you said, he worked with electromagnetic force and resonance. What caught me was how his Coil was said to shoot lightning bolts and create electron winds.

"In 1908, during experiments with electromagnetic force in the ionosphere, there was a sudden horrific explosion in the Tunguska region of Siberia. It destroyed everything within hundreds of miles, flattened thousands of trees. Many blamed Tesla's Coil for the explosion. Does this have anything to do with possible attempts to influence weather conditions? I don't know, but he was toying with forces that could certainly influence the weather."

"And perhaps someone took that technology and has privately engineered it."

"Nicholas, weather manipulation at that level is the stuff of science fiction. I hope. But the Gobi storm — you'll find out. Now, speaking practically, you already have more than enough enemies — hiding in the shadows, even in the Carabinieri itself. Be very careful. If I can offer any other help, let me know. Ah, I suppose you're bringing Kitsune in, aren't you?"

"Oh, absolutely. The moment we track all this down, we're on the plane, the Fox in handcuffs."

Mike rolled her eyes at him and imagined Dillon doing the same thing.

CHAPTER TWENTY-SIX

Cassandra woke after a solid eight hours of wonderful dreams — her mother standing in front of the tunnel in Castel Rigone, a hand on the Ark, and she'd looked luminous. She felt the quiet steady sound of the airplane engine. Cassandra stretched, yawned, and smiled over at Ajax as he made coffee.

At her first sip, she felt caffeine send a lovely zing to her brain. And she felt the movement of the plane. "Where are we?"

"We'll be home in an hour."

"Has there been any news on the thief?"

"Lilith called me to tell me our people missed again, but I'd already seen what happened for myself. I told her I would have to punish her." Ajax smiled. Then he pulled out his iPad. "You can always count on tourists and their cell phones to record everything. Take a look."

Cassandra watched the scene unfold.

When it was over, she said, "I never saw the thief."

"Lilith said she never spotted her, either, but she already told me she was a genius at disguise. The FBI team killed all Pazzi's men."

"And Major Russo? What does he have to say about this?"

"Lilith says Russo is very angry. Apparently this FBI agent, Nicholas Drummond, got in his face, humiliated him, blamed him. Then she laughed, said Russo was primed and ready for payback, that she believed he could be the answer to all our problems."

"Nicholas Drummond," Cassandra said slowly. "Isn't he the British FBI agent who saved the American president's life?"

"The very one."

"But however did this Drummond get hooked up with the thief? I mean, he brings a team to Venice to save her, save a criminal?"

"Lilith told me she believed there was some sort of bond created between them, even though Drummond bested her and brought the Koh-i-Noor back to New York. Lilith thinks they might have struck some sort of deal, but she doesn't know what it is and doesn't know how to find out."

Ajax sat down beside her, crossed his legs.

He took a sip of his coffee. "Lilith also told me Pazzi's men are in the Venice morgue and Pazzi is babbling, he's that scared, and, she thinks, ready to run. She has calmed him and also made it clear to Major Russo that there will never be a connection made to Pazzi or to us, or the good major will never again sleep with his new mistress. Lilith would personally see to it. Evidently he believed her, which means he's not altogether stupid."

Cassandra tapped her fingertips together. "We're still at risk, grave risk, despite Lilith's assurances. Listen, Grandfather already has a storm queued in the Atlantic, this one is meant to go to the Gulf of Mexico — drive down oil futures with another Katrina, provide us needed funds. This would take the focus off what happened today in the Gobi Desert, and possible tie-ins to us. Maybe we should have Grandfather release it now."

Ajax said slowly, "I don't think we can count on Grandfather to do anything we want. I don't think he trusts us any longer, Cassandra, nor does he approve of our methods. You know he expects all his minions to do his bidding, bow before him. He expects no less of us."

She clutched his arm. "The old fool's

crazy. He's been isolated for too long, I doubt he'd even know what do in the real world. He lives in his own fantasy, a world of his own creation where he's an omnipotent god. I don't think the real world — our world — even exists for him any longer. So sanctimonious about all the deaths in Beijing, makes me sick. I mean, do you think he cared about the loss of life before the Gobi? No, all those deaths over the decades were outside and apart from him, like deaths on the movie screen. The misery never touched him."

Ajax said, "Well, it's never touched us much, either. That's why I'm worried he no longer trusts us. He's grown a conscience."

His sister shrugged. "Who cares? Listen, Ajax, we can't allow it to touch us, because we're gods of a different sort."

He liked that. He leaned over and kissed her cheek. "It is unfortunate we have to pander to him." He shrugged. "But we have no choice. We want to achieve a particular result, then we have to go to the island, hat in hand, love and admiration for the old coot oozing out of our mouths."

Cassandra sat back, wrapped her arms around her bent knees. "I remember he wasn't always like this, not until Mother went missing in the Gobi." She smashed her fist against her thigh. "I miss her, Ajax, every single day."

He looked out the window. They were encased in clouds. He felt anger at his grandfather boiling up again. "The old man admired our mother, even worshipped her, she was his lodestone, his guiding star. We've never been anything to him. Even with the cherubim's wing and mother's map hinting the Ark might be under the mountain at Castel Rigone, still it's not enough for him. I wonder what direction he will turn? What will he do?"

Cassandra said, her voice vicious, "If we could only talk him into giving us his formula locked away in his precious vault, then we could simply kill him and take over." She stopped talking, and Ajax knew she was deep in thought.

"Yes," she said at last. "There has to be a way." She rose and began to pace up and down the aisle. She paused, looked out the window. "Not long now. Where is the thief's husband?"

"Lilith had him taken to the dungeons beneath Castel Rigone. He's strong, tough, trained Special Forces, so I told her to keep him drugged so we wouldn't have to worry about him escaping.

"I also told Lilith she has to get a message

to the thief — since the debacle in San Marco. Tell her Grant Thornton is a dead man if she doesn't present herself to Pazzi in Venice."

"I have a better idea," Cassandra said, and she was smiling. "I no longer trust Pazzi to get the job done. We need to find a way to get the thief to Castel Rigone. Let her know if she doesn't come, then her husband's minutes on this earth are numbered."

He frowned, then slowly nodded. "All right. I'll have Lilith put up a message board that will connect to this Agent Nicholas Drummond. I have no doubt the FBI will escort the thief, and they'll all be together. Kill two birds with one stone."

CHAPTER TWENTY-SEVEN

Venice, Italy

After breakfast and a gallon of coffee, Kitsune said, "Adam, I have an idea — came to me in the shower this morning. I have video surveillance of Grant's kidnapping at our house. I already accessed it, but naturally I didn't recognize any of the men who took Grant and I didn't have access to a facial-recognition database. You do. Also, if you can get Major Russo to give us photos of the shooters in the piazza yesterday we can compare them to the men who took Grant. We get matches, we get IDs, then that will settle it, right? We'll have a definitive link."

Mike said, "Louisa, can we get photos?"

Louisa gave a huge grin and waved her cell phone. "We don't even have to take the chance of Russo trying to arrest us, Nicholas, I've already got photos of all the dead bad guys."

This time, Kitsune walked to Louisa and kissed her. "Trust the forensics expert. Thank you."

Because she wasn't stupid, nor completely trusting, Kitsune drew Adam and his laptop away into the second bedroom Mike hadn't yet used. They sat down side by side. Kitsune laid her hand on his arm. "I would appreciate your keeping this private. All right?"

Adam thought about Nicholas holding him up by his heels, but he approved of dodging Big Brother whenever possible. "Hey, so long as you don't screw Nicholas or Mike, you're golden with me."

She rewarded him a smile. "I promise I will do nothing to jeopardize you, or them. Do we have a deal?"

Adam nodded.

"Okay then. I have an extensive video surveillance system. There are cameras around my house, all egress and ingress points, and on the neighboring estates."

He raised an eyebrow.

"One can never be too careful. The camera feed backs up to a secure server farm in Ohio, in the States. It is very discreet. I would prefer you allow me to enter the information and access the feed, without you monitoring my keystrokes."

Adam handed her the computer. Three

minutes later, she'd pulled the feed. She knew it had geolocating tags in it, but she trusted Adam not to access them.

He saw the tension in her shoulders, knew she was afraid her husband was already dead. He said nothing, accessed the video feed.

"There." She pointed.

He studied the screen. Four men, a team, all with dark hair, sand-colored pants and shirts with vests — clothes too heavy for such a warm day — walked down the long drive toward an incredible white house on the cliffs.

He froze the screen, tapped the keyboard, said, "Operators, no question." He hit play again.

The men looked neither right nor left. When they hit the bottom of the drive, they fanned out, coming at the house from four directions.

"Can you get their faces?"

"Already grabbed them."

She watched as his computer screen changed. The four men were sectioned into four quadrants. Adam had downloaded Louisa's photos of the eight dead shooters lying where they died in the square. The matches happened quickly — the four at Kitsune's house matched four of the dead shooters.

"Bingo. Now, let's see who the rest of these gentlemen are." Adam called up the FBI's facial-recognition system. Red lines began running down each face from forehead to chin to create a baseline, then reconstructing it into gridded lines that the computer would run for a match.

"You want to watch what happens next?"

"No," she said, "I've already looked at it a dozen times, looking for clues, anything. They were careful. There are no cameras inside the house, so all there is to see is fifteen minutes after they enter, when they come out the front door, dragging my husband. I'd love to know how they incapacitated him, it must have been drugs of some kind. We need to find out how they got on and off the island."

"This is Capri, isn't it?"

She nodded slowly.

"Don't worry, I'm not going to say anything. My dad used to work with a rare book dealer on the island of Anacapri. They were great friends. We visited when my sister, Sophie, and I were kids. I remember the little boats we had to get on and the rope the guy used to pull us into the Blue Grotto."

Adam typed a few commands and a new

segment of screen popped up. "How many public and private cameras are there on Capri?"

"Quite a few of both kinds. There are thousands of tourists each year who must be protected. And many wealthier people have homes there, so security is considered very important. I have a number of them myself as well."

"That's good. I'll pull feeds from every camera I can access. Where are the entrance and exit points?"

"The ferry landing is the main one, and there are a few private boat docks in the same area, plus several around the island itself. Capri is accessible by helicopter as well."

"I am going to bet they didn't come by public transport. It wouldn't do to carry an unconscious man into a crowd. Let me look at the private boat docks, then I'll check the helipads."

Kitsune marveled. It took Adam less than ten minutes to access the cameras he needed.

He started a sweep around the island, a geographical mapping of the coastline. There were a number of coves where boats were docked. He could see pleasure boats and tourist boats roaring through the waters circumnavigating the island.

"Look, this must be the spot. It's right down from your place, and there's a boat waiting. Duh, I should have looked there first thing."

The boat was a large Codecasa yacht, about forty meters, bobbing gently in the waves of the cove. They watched the four men in a Zodiac with a small outboard motor, zooming toward the yacht.

Adam fiddled with the cameras and was able to focus on the center of the Zodiac, where Grant Thornton lay, still unmoving.

Kitsune's voice was urgent. "Get the name of that yacht. Please."

"I'm working on it. I can only look at three angles at a time. I'll have to drop one."

"Drop the wide shot. We know what happened up top."

He narrowed the focus onto the yacht. "They're pointed the wrong direction. We have to wait for them to leave. I have to say, I am incredibly impressed by your setup."

"We're not getting facial matches yet on our other bad guys, and that's weird. They're thugs, probably career criminals, just like the other four, but why aren't they popping right up?"

Kitsune said, "Let's run their faces against

transportation feeds, private airports, especially."

He thought for a minute. "I can do that. I have access to those databases now. I think I can reconstruct the analytics to see if we can match them that way, might be faster. It's going to take a while, though. Hey, look. Boat's leaving. Okay, they're one-eighty now." He zoomed in. "*Elysian Fields.* That's the boat's name. Should be easy enough to track them down."

He flipped open another database, fingers flying. "Got it. Look, Kitsune, here's our absolute one hundred percent proof." He pointed to the screen. "Gray found this information earlier, it's all right here. Black Diamond is a financial entity created by the Genesis Group through a New York holding company. Looks like this arm holds all their western assets for both North and South America, plus the Caribbean. Here, Kitsune, read this."

Adam pushed the laptop toward her, let her read the financial report he'd just pulled.

Kitsune said, "They bought the boat six years ago from a company in Saudi Arabia, and it's docked in Bermuda. They really are global, aren't they?"

She gave him a blazing smile, grabbed his

face, and kissed him again. "You have my gratitude forever, Adam. Forever."

"What's this, more kisses? What'd you do now, Adam?" Nicholas stepped into the room.

Adam gave Nicholas a cocky grin. "The people who kidnapped Grant Thornton hauled him away in a boat belonging to the Genesis Group. *Elysian Fields.*"

CHAPTER TWENTY-EIGHT

Mike was rubbing her hands together. "A splinter arm called Black Diamond." She wanted to hoot and holler until she saw Kitsune's still face. She said with total conviction, "Your husband is alive, Kitsune. They're not stupid enough to kill him until they have you. We will find him and then we'll nail these power-mongering — Hey, Nicholas, why are you grinning like an idiot?"

"Kitsune, I've confirmed Lilith Forrester-Clarke has been your shadow, for years now. And, not surprising, her interest and focus have intensified the last few months."

"How do you know this?"

"I called Gray, asked him to look through Lilith's financials. He accessed photos of you and Grant in the Genesis Group computer assigned to Lilith. The photos date back to when you were playing the role of the young artist in London, prior to your

Koh-i-Noor engagement. She's responsible for bringing you into this, without a doubt."

"Was it her personally, or do you think she was under instruction to vet me for the Topkapi job?"

Nicholas handed her the sheaf of papers. "See for yourself. Gray sent us everything he could find — it looks like she wanted to know even more, and so she paid a private investigator, an expensive one, out of her own pocket. Because she knew you, admired you and your skills, she recommended you to the Kohaths. She knew you were one of the very few thieves in the world who could steal the staff of Moses from the Topkapi." He paused a moment. "As you know, the other one died in a fire."

Kitsune swallowed. "Yes, Mulvaney."

"Your old mentor."

Nicholas scraped a hand against his face. He needed a shave badly. "She upped her surveillance on you for the last six months, then hired you to pull off a nearly impossible heist, which you did, and instead of handing you the second half of your payment, she tried to have you killed."

Mike said slowly, "Maybe it wasn't Lilith's decision to kill you. Maybe the Kohaths saw you as a loose thread and wanted you dead."

Louisa wandered into the small bedroom,

eating a banana. "We need to find out where they took Kitsune's husband."

Adam didn't look up from his computer. "I'm looking now. I have a lot of irons in the fire. I've been trying to hack Russo's email and haven't had any luck, either. Can you guys leave me alone for a while and let me sort through everything? As soon as facial recognition comes through on the dead shooters we don't already know, I'll holler." He did look up then. "Kitsune, I'll find Grant. Just give me a little time. I've got an idea."

Nicholas said to everyone, "Let's go back into the living room. I'll tell you about some interesting abnormalities Gray has found in the Genesis Group's financials."

"Like what?" Kitsune asked.

He didn't answer, pointed at Adam, whose brow was furrowed as he stared at the screen. They followed Nicholas into the suite living room, set themselves at their stations. Kitsune stood by the window, looking out every few moments. A well-ingrained habit, Mike imagined.

Nicholas said, "Now, we need to run some other data as well, try to match it to the financials —"

Mike stopped, put her hands on her hips. "Stop, right there. Listen, Nicholas, as soon

222

as Adam finds where the Kohaths are holding Grant, we need to move. We have everything we need. I'll even wager the Kohaths will be wherever Grant is being kept. We can't just sit around gathering more data."

Louisa said, "I agree with Mike, Nicholas. I think we should go at them hard, and do it now, before they have a chance to cover anything up. Or before Major Russo comes here with a platoon of soldiers and tosses all of us in his Italian hoosegow."

They heard a whoop, then Adam came running into the living room, waving his laptop. "I found Grant. You're smart, Kitsune, the private airports were the key. I found where the yacht docked, traced them to a plane at a small airport outside of Naples. Yesterday, a plane with the same tail number landed in Perugia, that's about four hours southwest of here, toward Rome. There are several security cameras placed around the hangars, and they still hadn't recycled the feeds."

He had the video queued up, hit play. There was Grant, handcuffed, his arms held by two men. It was obvious he was deeply drugged. They dragged him to a small hangar and the screen shot changed.

Kitsune couldn't help it, she blew out a shaky breath. "Those bastards. But he's alive, he's alive."

"I pulled satellite footage from the area. Got lucky, there's a U.S. Army base north of here, Aviano, and they do regular flyovers. Otherwise I would have had to ask the Italian government for help, and I assume after we banged up their piazza, they wouldn't be so hot to lend a hand.

"So, look here. They're getting into a Peugeot, driving west. Sorry, I lost them after that."

Nicholas clapped Adam on his shoulder. "Fine work, Adam, and no, I'm still not going to kiss you. Do the Kohaths have holdings near Perugia?"

"Let me see." He typed for a second. "Yes, here it is. The Kohaths have a house in a town called Castel Rigone, near a big lake called Lake Trasimeno. It's only thirty minutes from the airport in Perugia. Huge place, too. Practically a castle."

Kitsune was already heading toward the door. "That's where they are. Mike's right — since Grant is there, the Kohaths must be, too. We have to go now."

Nicholas shook his head. "Look, I agree with all of you. We will go get Grant. But think about this logically. Interviewing these two in Rome at their headquarters is one thing, confronting them in their own personal castle is quite another. We need a plan."

The room phone rang. Nicholas answered, "Major Russo?" then listened. He hung up and looked at Louisa. "I guess we're going to have to find another castle for you to storm, Louisa. Major Russo has respectfully requested your forensics assistance. It seems his team is not performing as he expected."

"But —"

He raised a hand. "This is important and I figure it's the only way we can try to smooth over some of the chaos we caused. Plus we need all the evidence you can gather, more nails for the Kohath coffin, and I want eyes on Russo. I don't trust him. You're the only one who can do this, Louisa, and see that it's done right."

Louisa didn't look happy. "All right. But you know, guys, sometimes it isn't all that wonderful to be the greatest forensics expert on the planet." She turned at the doorway. "You were supposed to laugh. That was a joke. Keep me posted. I'll join you as soon as I can take care of Russo's mess."

Nicholas turned to Adam, but before he could speak, Adam said, "I know, you want me to stay here with Louisa, keep an eye on her, and gather more evidence."

"Yes, thank you, Adam," Mike said.

"While we get ourselves together, pull everything you can on the Kohaths' house." She paused a moment. "They could be moving him around, Kitsune. It's possible he's no longer even there."

Kitsune was still standing by the door, shoulder tense. "He's there. I know it. It makes the most sense."

Adam said, "I've got the tail number of the Kohaths' private plane — a Citation CJ3 Plus, really swanky. I'll see where they are, what flight plans are recorded."

"Good," Nicholas said. "If we're going to storm the castle, all the information you can muster is welcome."

CHAPTER TWENTY-NINE

2005: Category 5 Hurricane Katrina made landfall in New Orleans. Levees failed, 1,245 were killed, and damages were estimated at $108 billion.

The Bermuda Triangle

Jason watched the news every night. It was an old habit, ingrained from childhood, when having a television was something rare and exciting, and a nightly news report was, with the exception of the movies, the only way to know what was happening outside of his backyard.

He could have watched on the computers, but he had a small theater, with comfortable chairs and a monstrous television. He sat back and tuned into another showing of the footage from Beijing. He watched the sand sweeping through the enormous city, choking the air and the people, suffocating thousands. He knew it had to happen in exactly this way, but still, the loss, the waste of it all, made him hurt deep, it hurt his soul. And in the end, what had been the point? For some predestined future to play itself out?

But then the evening news turned to the shootout in Saint Mark's Square in Venice. Details were sketchy, but it was said that an American government operation had gone badly wrong, and an American federal agent was in the hospital. There was footage of the shooting, filmed by tourists, and most of it was shaky. But all the violence, the bloody deaths, the panic, were crystal clear to see. He stared, unable to believe what he was seeing. Unlike his own disasters, this one involved characters he knew very well, they were of his blood, and he knew in his gut the twins were tied to this mess — more, he imagined, they were responsible for it. The thoughtless, uncaring young idiots. So unworthy of their proud name, of their mother's name. He was so angry, so despairing. He felt nausea and dizziness and quickly placed a nitroglycerin pill under his tongue. Slowly, he felt his heart calm, his body right itself.

All those men killed in the square had worked for the Kohaths; he didn't need anyone to tell him that. Well, it was done, over with, and the chips would fall where they would fall, and he didn't doubt for a minute that where they fell would spell disaster. And all because of yet another poor decision by Cassandra and Ajax. The waste of it all, he thought again, the sheer waste.

No more, he thought, he simply couldn't do it. There would be no more arguments; there would be no more orders from him they ignored, no more acting on their own.

He knew time was flowing like a river into a desert. He wondered how many more people would have to die before time ran out.

He returned to his control room and sat in front of his bank of computers. Once calm, he flipped one of the screens to a weather station he liked, out of Atlanta. Naturally, the topic there was the out-of-season hurricane currently off the coast of Puerto Rico. There was no real concern; the storm was predicted to weaken, that if anything at all, there would be only heavy rains before the storm moved back out into the Atlantic.

He sucked hard on the sliver of nitroglycerin under his tongue. He would do what he had to do, no choice. He would call attention away from that disastrous incident in Venice and he would do it now. He had already stirred up the atmosphere in the Gulf of Mexico, warming the waters with the Coil's laser.

He had a choice, certainly, of letting the hurricane simply peter out, but he thought of the millions and millions of dollars the Genesis Group needed to continue their exemplary archaeological work, he thought of the police tracking down Ajax and Cassandra. No, he didn't really have a choice.

In the past he'd always managed to do a superb job of rationalizing, witnessing the influx of cash from Katrina and their other ventures. This storm was also needful and he knew exactly where to aim it.

Ten minutes later, the storm was reprogrammed, strengthening. It felt wrong, using a storm to cover his grandchildren's tracks. He knew he was blackening his own soul to protect them. And should something happen, well, he could turn the storm and have it dissipate with the push of a button.

While he watched the endless variety of weather around the globe, storms causing untold destruction, violent hurricanes, snowstorms, and tornadoes he hadn't caused, he picked up the folio he kept on his counter. In it were all his personal letters from Helen. He pulled one written nearly twenty years ago to the day. Helen's hope, her excitement, all but leaped from the page. The paper was creased and worn from so many readings. He ran his gnarled finger along Helen's rounded letters, still girlish despite her age. It hurt to read her words, yet he did, over and over again, always feeling close to her, for a brief time. The letter was addressed to her children. He'd read it to them, then put it away to keep it safe.

His hand shook as he read his daughter's words.

Mysore
Base Gobi Desert
1996

Cassandra and Ajax:
Soon I hope to announce that your mother is the best archaeologist in the world. And this is why:

You two have always loved to play with our people as they excavated the tunnels beneath our home in Castel Rigone. You always knew we were looking for something important, heard the word *Ark* over and over, and when you were little, we told you it was a box, but a special box.

Now you know it is the Ark of the

Covenant we've sought for all these years. We never found it and I couldn't understand why. After all, I had Pope Gregory's letter stating he sanctioned the Knights Templar to hide the Ark beneath our mountain — then their mountain of course — which I know they did, along with their own immense treasures. We have found much of their treasure, but the Ark isn't there and at long last, I have found out why.

Today, I found another letter written by Pope Gregory. He writes of how his plans hadn't materialized because the Polo family devised a plan to steal the Ark and present it to Genghis Khan in Zhongdu (now called Beijing), China. The pope doesn't write how the Polo family learned of the Ark's hiding place in his own vaults, and now it hardly matters. The Ark never got into the Templars' hands.

I know the path the Polos took — it's called the Silk Road. I know they were drawn off course, and were hit by a tremendous sandstorm near Dunghuang that lasted for days. And when they made it to Beijing, they did not have the Ark.

So, my darlings, it is time for me to

follow their route, and dig where we think they were waylaid in a storm. Our only hope is that the storm was so severe they lost the Ark, and it is still there, buried in the sand. Every sign points to a certain spot. I am sure it is there.

Since they were not Kohaths, they had no right to the Ark and they were punished for their thievery. It will not punish me, it will embrace me.

So I write to you as I wait in Dunghuang for yet another sandstorm to end and the skies to turn crystal blue and make the air clear and crisp. I hope to set out for the site at noon.

Your grandfather will guide you. As you know he is a magician when it comes to storms, and you will come to understand this when you are older.

Ajax and Cassandra, it is my dearest wish that you study with your grandfather, so you may understand how to continue our family's honorable profession. Do not ever forget your magnificent calling, a calling that demands honor, obedience, and goodness.

I devoutly pray both of you will follow in my footsteps and become archaeologists. Also, you must study hard to understand the business of the Genesis

Group. The Ark will be mine — ours — and the company will need a steady hand to lead once I'm gone: your hands.

Pray for my success. Your grandfather knows exactly where and when to strike to maximize our profits.

I must sleep now. I love you both with all my heart. Wish me luck!

Always,
Your mother

Jason folded the letter, gently placed it back in its folder. He started going through the stacks of old letters. He pulled one out from his father, a letter Alexander had written to his wife, Jason's mother, Babette. Like Helen's letter, he never tired of reading the words that had given him this life.

Cuba
1961

Darling Babette,
Forgive me for the shortness of my letter, but Jason and I have made a grand discovery. Not Atlantis, like I believed, but there is an island here, about one hundred miles north and west of our Cuban base, that is perfect — perfect! — for our experiments with Father's

Coil, and I suppose I must add Tesla's name as well. There is a volcano, and a beach, the island is small enough to walk across in an hour.

We were sailing toward the base when our instruments went haywire. We got off course, and that's when we found it. There is an electromagnetic signature here, coming from the center of the island itself. Jason — our brilliant young man — thinks he can harness it and use it to make the Coil stronger.

We laid claim to this small piece of land and found the most curious things — a decrepit dock and tunnels dug through the mountain. Perhaps the Russians set up a base here, trying to get weapons aimed at America, since it does have the feel of an abandoned military base. We think the electromagnetic interruptions must have been too much for their tools, and they gave up and left. We may never know who founded this place, but it is perfect for our plans. We will develop the island, bring in the necessary equipment. Jason will return to England for more schooling, but I will stay here to oversee the implementation.

Just think, a single place from which we can work. No more hiding. We will be hidden by nature itself.

Your husband,
Alexander

Jason folded this letter, as carefully as he had Helen's. His father had died here. He himself had found him dead among the rocks on the beach one afternoon, having suffered a heart attack on his daily walk. By then, they'd built one of the most sophisticated weather-tracking stations in the world, with the beginnings of an electromagnetic field that would hide them from prying eyes. They were controlling the weather by balloon launches, but they soon bought their first satellite, and Jason took the Kohaths to the next level, developing the laser that was their bread and butter, the Coil's most sophisticated iteration yet.

And then he had decided to stay.

No choice really. The moment his father died, it was up to Jason, the future of the Kohaths was his burden to carry. By the time he'd developed the Coil to its current incredibly powerful incarnation, he'd lost his own wife in childbirth. Diana, who'd loved Jason despite his idiosyncrasies, left him alone with a small girl babe he'd named Helen.

Helen hadn't turned out to be a scientist

— no, she was much more; she was an adventurer, more fire in her gut than even their creator, their founder, Appleton Kohath. Helen was the one who truly understood the importance of finding the Ark, of what it could bring the family, and the world. Most of all, Helen was filled with goodness. And, he remembered, smiling, she'd always loved discovering long-ago secrets buried for millennia.

The day she'd left on her first dig, Jason had moved permanently to the island and isolated himself from the world in order to protect their family's technology, and created himself a home in the island bunker. To keep her safe, to keep the family in money, to keep the Genesis Group at the top, he sacrificed his freedom.

CHAPTER THIRTY

FBI Headquarters
26 Federal Plaza
22nd Floor, Home of Covert Eyes
New York, New York

Ben looked over his notes again, then pulled out his cell, punched in the number Louisa had given him for Melinda St. Germaine in London. Of all things, she was a member of Parliament — did Nicholas know all the muckety-mucks in England? It was a pity her mother, the biographer herself, had died. And so recently, too.

Melinda St. Germaine answered on the first ring. Lovely, no-nonsense voice, with Nicholas's crisp enunciation. Ben smiled as he said, "Ms. St. Germaine, my colleague Agent Nicholas Drummond gave me your number. He wanted me to ask you if I could come to London to consult your mother's papers."

"Nicholas! He sent me a note, and his

family sent lovely flowers to Mother's funeral. And you say you want to come here to look at my mother's papers?"

"Yes, if I could."

She was silent a moment, then, "I'm in the middle of something myself. But what papers do you wish to examine?"

"Your mother wrote a biography of a man named Appleton Kohath."

"Goodness, yes, she did. The book came out three years ago, I believe. Unlike my brilliant mother, I couldn't be bothered with anything historical but Churchill. Sorry, I can see her now, looking over the top of her glasses disapprovingly while I played with model tanks." He heard her breath hitch. "Her death, it came as such a shock."

Ben said, "She sounds like a very fine woman. I'm sorry, Ms. St. Germaine."

"Forgive me, I suppose I'm still reeling. Now what is all this about the Appleton Kohath biography?"

Ben said, "We know Appleton Kohath was an Ark of the Covenant enthusiast, and the creator of the Genesis Group, but now we've run into a bit of a wall on a case. Nicholas hoped your mother kept her papers, her research, notes, anything that might quickly help us gain more insight into this man and his family. We need a shortcut into his world."

"Oh, yes, I see. The entire shed in back of the house is crammed to the ceiling with her notes. You're welcome to them. I need to sort them, her publisher has been after me. . . . Oh, I guess you don't know. Mother was finishing an updated edition of the biography, far more in-depth, this one about Kohath and his family." She sighed. "Her publisher wants the draft to see if it's workable. I simply haven't had the time to dig in. If you have the manpower, they're yours."

"Thank you, ma'am. I'm leaving from New York. I'll be there as soon as I can."

"Don't call me ma'am."

"Yes, ma' — Okay."

"Call me Melinda."

He smiled as he said her name, and disconnected. Ben then called Nicholas, told him he was on his way to London.

Nicholas said, "You'll like Melinda. She's very savvy, well on her way to leading our country. Thank you, Ben. We'll keep you posted and please, return the favor."

Forty-five minutes later, Nicholas, Mike, and Kitsune said goodbye to Adam and Louisa, who complained that her Spanish wasn't Italian, and the going was tough working the scene's forensics. Clancy and Trident had the plane in the air in ten minutes flat. It was obvious they were bursting with questions but knew they'd have to wait for answers when everything was resolved, over beers.

A rental car waited for them, a gray Škoda Octavia, practically new, manual transmission, midsize, so the three of them fit comfortably. Nicholas liked the car; it was game and had enough power to keep driving interesting. He had the map to Castel Rigone open on his phone.

Mike looked thoughtful as he pulled out onto the highway. "We've got to figure out how to rescue Grant without getting all of us dead. I don't think knocking on their front door and asking to see him will work."

Kitsune said, "It's me they want." And she looked at Nicholas. "I have my two PPKs."

Nicholas said, "Given what happened in Saint Mark's Square yesterday, they want to kill all of us. I know you're an excellent shot, Kitsune, but even with your Walthers, there's no way we're going to let you sacrifice yourself. Mike's right, we need a plan, a way to sneak in."

As they drove into the countryside, there was less and less traffic. Nicholas looked in his rearview and noticed a black sedan with dark tinted windows staying several cars behind them.

Mike said, "Nicholas, I don't like the looks of that black car, can you see it? About fifty feet behind us."

He smiled. "Yes, I see him and I don't like it, either. Let's see if they're up to no good." He pressed the Škoda's accelerator. The sedan sped up, too, drawing closer.

Kitsune said, "Take a right, here, now! I know this road."

Nicholas pulled the wheel to the right and the car skidded onto a small dirt road, deeply rutted from tractor wheels, and he soon saw why. There were olive groves to the left and right.

The sedan behind them nearly missed the turn. The driver was good, managed to straighten the car, accelerating as he did so, coming fast.

Mike saw the passenger window drop, saw a gun pointed at her. A man fired three times, in rapid succession. Kitsune fired back. Her second shot tore the side-view mirror off.

"Get away from them, Nicholas!"

"I'm trying." Nicholas was weaving the car to the left then right, in and out of the ruts, making aiming hard. He called, "Get the Glock off my hip, Mike. There's a second magazine in my pocket. Hurry, they're coming back for more."

She took his Glock and another magazine, dove into the back, started shooting out the side window.

"Nicholas, the driver looks like one of the thugs in the piazza outside the hospital last night. Whoa, watch out!"

Nicholas almost didn't make the sharp right curve, barely managed to get the Škoda back into the rutted path. The sedan behind wasn't so lucky. It hit one of the olive trees but slipped around the edge of the grove and caught up to them.

A bullet struck the back window, splintering the glass. Kitsune, a Walther in each hand, shouted, "That's it, that's enough!" She sent a barrage of bullets into the sedan. The windshield splintered, both headlights exploded, and the car swerved sharply left before straightening. She shouted, "Nicholas, the road will intersect with a two-lane paved road. It winds back down the hill. Be careful, it's a popular tourist drive, and there are some hairy turns."

Nicholas pulled onto the road, tires squealing, right into the path of three cars. All three managed to swerve around him, horns honking, shouts, curses flying. He saw the sedan sideswipe a red Alfa, then start gaining again. He gunned it, nearly hit a motorcycle as he rounded a curve, then slammed the brakes before crashing into a small knot of oncoming traffic. Mike and Kitsune slammed against the seat.

Mike grabbed Kitsune's arm to hold her steady. "Hey, Nicholas, don't get us killed."

He shot her a grin in the rearview.

They screamed down the mountain road, bullets flying as the Škoda juked and jived.

Kitsune was firing both Walthers smoothly, rhythmically, the way Grant had taught her. She hit the windshield three times in succession. The third shot shattered the glass completely, and the sedan swerved drunkenly as its windshield collapsed inside the car and onto the driver.

"That will slow them down."

"Good shot, but they're still coming," Mike said. "Take out the front tires. We've got to stop them dead in their tracks."

Nicholas heard Kitsune slam in a new magazine into each PPK. He saw Mike's face in the rearview, focused, getting ready to fire again.

He yelled, "Are you running low on ammo?"

"Yes, so keep the car straight so I can hit them. Nicholas, they're gaining on us. Kitsune, aim for the tires, the engine block,

244

whatever will stop them."

His heart nearly stopped to see another black sedan coming down a narrow rutted mountain road to their left. They were going to crash. "Hang on!"

The second sedan came straight at them, not hesitating as it hurtled down the mountain. At the last second, Nicholas rammed the accelerator to the floor and they shot past the sedan by a nose. It hit the Škoda's back quarter panel and they spun out, wheels screaming. Nicholas went into the zone, as his driving instructor had taught him so many years before in Special Forces. He gently rotated the wheel, slowly, slowly, pressing the brake for a fraction of time, easing off, bringing the fishtailing car back under control.

The two cars ran side by side for a moment. Nicholas shouted, "Hold on!" and wrenched the wheel to the left, plowing the Škoda into the sedan. There was the horrendous sound of shearing metal and they watched the sedan slide off the edge of the road, straighten once again, and jerk back behind them.

It was a good try. But there were now two sedans chasing them, at least four men. Both Kitsune and Mike took turns, shooting hard and fast out the windows, ducking shots that came toward the car.

Mike shouted, "I got one of them, didn't kill him, but he's not going to be that good a shot now. Come on, Kitsune, show me what you can do."

"The driver," Kitsune said. "I want the driver."

She got him on the third bullet, watched him fall against the steering wheel, and the sedan did a spectacular pirouette off the side of the rode, nose first into a ditch, then spun twice more and landed upside down in a mess of olive trees.

A bullet came through the back windshield, shattered it, barely missed Kitsune.

Both women dove down.

He heard Kitsune say, "That one nearly parted my hair."

"Hang on. Curve." Nicholas downshifted hard, hugging the side of the road. He saw a vineyard ahead, and a line of cars waiting to make the turn.

"Take out the second car now or we're going to be in bad trouble!"

This time Mike was the one to hit the driver. His foot must have hit the accelerator because the sedan sped up, and the shooter was so desperate to get him off the steering wheel he didn't even see the shot Mike took at him. The bullet got him in the neck. Kitsune and Mike watched the sedan weave off the road and down a steep embankment, and disappeared from sight, one hundred yards before it would have slammed into the line of wine-tasting tourists.

Nicholas slowed both the Škoda and his heart. He called out, "Thank you. Now keep an eye out for any more thugs."

They drove the rest of the way down the mountain, then Nicholas pulled over, cut the engine. His heart was still kettle-drumming in his chest. Close, way too close. He turned in the seat. "Well done, ladies, well done."

Kitsune laughed. "Not bad driving, mate. Nearly as good as Grant."

"That's Special Agent Lady to you." Mike smacked his arm.

He grinned at her, windblown hair, tangled around her head, her eyes tearing from the wind, so high on adrenaline he bet she could fly. Kitsune's eyes were dilated with stress and excitement, her skin flushed from the wind, and she looked like she could take wing with Mike. His own fear, mostly for Mike, he knew, was slowly falling away. They would all want to fall over when the adrenaline high crashed. But not now.

Mike said, "We better check in with

Adam. He's probably wondering why we're driving all over the back roads of Italy at the speed of light."

Nicholas held up a hand, passed back bottles of water that had survived. "Drink." He did as well, drew in a deep breath. "Don't call Adam just yet."

"Why not?"

"How did they know we were coming here, Mike? How did the Carabinieri know where we'd be in time to get two teams in place?

Kitsune said, "They're bugging us somehow. They're listening. The Italians would have the power to monitor you. It's not polite, but it's done."

Mike smacked her palm against her head. "Call me an idiot for not realizing — it's that witch at the front desk of the hotel. Nicholas, that's why she upgraded you to the big suite, not because she wanted to sleep with you. No, they wanted to listen to what we had to say, and they prepped that suite for us. Well, maybe she wanted to sleep with you too, the slut."

Nicholas said, "But the Carabinieri already knew we were coming, we'd asked for them to meet us and back us up. Which they didn't do."

Mike said, "It wasn't that. They wanted to

know what we knew about Kitsune, where we'd be, what we'd planned to do. They jammed the signal earlier. Someone high up to manage all this, someone like Major Russo. No doubt now, he's on the Kohaths' payroll."

She fiddled with her cell. "I've encrypted my phone, I'm sending a message to Adam that we're compromised. I wish we had Lia with us, she could jam their signal in a heartbeat."

"Tell Adam we'll need tighter oversight when we get to Castel Rigone. I want him watching and listening to every move we make from now on."

"Okay," Mike said, "for all the good it will do us."

Kitsune said, "Listen, I think I might have a plan. Castel Rigone is very old. I remember there are tunnels all over the place — Etruscan excavations. There are very likely tunnels under the palazzo. We need to see if Adam can hack the plans and send them as quickly as possible."

CHAPTER THIRTY-ONE

Kohath Palazzo
Castel Rigone, Italy

Cassandra stood on one of the balconies of the palazzo that stood high atop a hill overlooking the small town of Castel Rigone, looking out over the beautiful Umbrian countryside, then down at Lake Trasimeno, shimmering beneath the noonday sun. She and Ajax had grown up here, knew every corner of each of the seventy rooms in the ancient fortress that had strided this magnificent hill since the fourteenth century. The palazzo even housed the town bells in one of the towers. As children, she and Ajax had nearly made themselves deaf ringing them.

And how she loved the tales of the Knights Templar, basked in the fact that they'd once called this home, this town, their sanctuary during their persecution.

When asked her favorite flower, she'd

always said without hesitation it was the Templar rose, and here in Castel Rigone, it was everywhere — carved into door lintels, around fireplaces, on stone fences, throughout the town, and at the palazzo.

As a child she'd pictured the Knights Templar gathered around one of the great fireplaces, knowing the end was coming, and yet they'd remained loyal and strong in their faith, until their deaths.

Their grandfather had deeded the palazzo to her mother and father on their wedding day, but they hadn't loved the house as she and Ajax did, only what lay beneath the mountain. Restoration had been up to the twins.

Ajax joined her, breathed in the sweet Umbrian air. "I've always wondered if the Knights Templar ever took lovers. I like to think many of them did, some warmth, some comfort."

"Like you and Lilith?"

He shook his head at her. "Let's focus on where the Ark could be." He pulled out his mother's map. "I wish she could have been more specific. Only identifying the mountain, it's not much use to us."

"We have to believe that somehow she got it back here. We have to believe it's buried here, otherwise why go on?"

He asked the question that had been making him crazy. "If Mother got the Ark out of the Gobi, then where do you think she is? Why would she leave the Ark behind?"

"I think she's afraid to contact us, for fear of discovery. I think she left the Ark for us to find. We'll hire more workers, Ajax, have them focus on finding the Ark, not more Templar treasure."

"So many digs over the past thirty years, even under the town itself. And we don't know how many more secret tunnels the Templars excavated. I think about our private museum, it's full to overflowing with their treasures." He sighed. "But where is our crown jewel? Where is the Ark?"

Ten minutes later, Cassandra sat at her cypress desk, shining with the rubbed-in oil the housekeepers used that smelled of sweet oranges. It was her private office, her own sanctuary, restored by her with warm woods and very old medieval tapestries she loved.

She'd placed the cherubim's wing in the center of her desk. She would prove its provenance, but for her and Ajax, not the archaeological community. No one would ever know of this amazing find in the Gobi.

She studied it as she was certain her mother had, and touched it lovingly, awe-struck. She imagined if she looked at it closely enough, the wing would allow her to see visions of her mother.

But she had work to do. She wanted to see the new track of the storm her grandfather was moving from Bermuda into the Caribbean.

She pressed a button on the underside of her desk and a large paper-thin screen rose from the surface. It took up almost the entire width of the polished cypress and was oddly translucent, enabling her to see someone should they come into the room, but they wouldn't be able to see what was on the screen. Grandfather had designed it, making it similar to a Teleprompter, with a beam-splitting mirror that gave the impression the images and words on the screen were floating in midair. The screen was divided into four quadrants, two for Cassandra's work with the foundation, the others tied directly to her grandfather's control center in the Caribbean, so she could monitor the weather he was creating in real time. She could see the storms in play and could also see the status of the satellites.

As she watched the satellites spin, she marveled at the power of the technology their grandfather had created. All based on a weather machine developed early in the last century by Nikola Tesla and Appleton

Kohath, using an early application of Tesla's famous Coil. She'd read in the family letters that when Appleton had shown Tesla the papers and drawings Da Vinci had made of a weather machine, *La Macchina,* Tesla had exploded with ideas, and together they'd tried a number of approaches to creating a working model, and they'd known success, of a sort.

Their first method was to send a large, unregulated weather balloon into the air to spray out a crystal cloud accelerant they had heated in a powerful electric field. They were able to create a spectrum of weather events, often by enhancing the processes that would naturally occur in nature. But they couldn't control the results to the degree Appleton wanted.

But now, with his satellites and lasers in place, her grandfather could energize the atmosphere more precisely, and with pinpoint accuracy create a windstorm or thunderstorm, depending on conditions in a fifty-mile prearranged radius. Cassandra knew his genius was the only reason they'd been able to refine their ideas using the newer technology. He'd tried to explain it to her, and she did understand some of it. She knew building storms involved creating a massive electric charge in midair by focusing the laser beams of three satellites into the lower atmosphere, and this caused a chain reaction among the charged particles, ending in a massive discharge, like a great ball of lightning, a sort of firestorm in the sky. She believed that somehow, the swirling pattern of combustion Grandfather created caused a massive downdraft of air, and updrafts all around it. If there was moisture in the air, massive clouds quickly formed. If not, the wind itself would rip up the ground below. Over water, the growing disturbance quickly spun into a powerful hurricane.

She'd seen it happen, watched a small cloud form in a pure blue sky, almost in the blink of an eye, with a center like a blinding golden ball with lobes that would start to spin in the clouds formed around it. Then it would spin upward, like a rising tornado, the fiercely glowing firestorm still inside it, and the massive winds would follow. The storm would move in the winds it created and make landfall as a controlled and intense weather event. It was fascinating to watch. Ajax understood enough, and soon now, he would take Grandfather's place, and they would have the control, make the important decisions, not Grandfather.

It was amazing, really. Over the years, Grandfather had gotten more and more precise, and the Genesis Group coffers were kept full on the backs of the localized disasters, buying and shorting stocks of the insurance, construction, and supply companies most affected, sometimes buying and selling them wholesale. Their spiderweb of finances was run out of Singapore by a brilliant analyst, Landry Rodgers, a Brit, whose soul had been suitably corrupted years before. Landry was a man as skilled at manipulating investments as Grandfather was at controlling barometric pressure.

Appleton and Nikola Tesla would have been proud. Their concept — Da Vinci's concept — had been perfected in fewer than one hundred years.

She sat back in her chair and watched the screens. Suddenly, a spear of sun caught the golden edge of the cherubim's wing, making it shimmer. She reached out a finger and traced the long line of the wing's edge. What she and Ajax had believed were grooves carved in the gold to create the illusion of feathers, were now more visible in the bright light. Not grooves — there were glyphs carved into the gold.

She pulled a magnifying sheet out of her drawer and looked more closely. The markings weren't unfamiliar to her, but she couldn't read them. Had they been made in the beginning, when the Ark was built, or were they a more recent addition?

She looked up to see Ajax come into her office.

"What are you doing?"

She gestured toward the phone. "I need you. Come here and look. There are some markings on the edge of the wing, runes or glyphs, I can't tell which. Nor can I tell when they were made."

She handed him the magnifying sheet, and he bent low over the wing fragment. He looked up, his eyes shining as bright as the cherubim's wing.

"They look like Cuneiform, and that predates Moses by a few thousand years."

"Shouldn't markings from his era be in Hebrew?"

"That would be the most logical language, yes. Give me a sheet of paper and a pencil. Let me see if I can decipher this."

She did, and he bent his head over the gold, scribbling on the paper. "It will take me some time to translate. But a few I can pick out — Oh, I'm wrong. It's Phoenician. Makes more sense, and makes things easier. See, here's the glyph for door, and here's . . ." He stopped.

"What? What is it?"

"Weapon."

Cassandra stared.

He scribbled for a few more minutes, then met his twin's eyes. "It's a warning. It reads: *Through this door lies a weapon of great power. Open it, and it will indeed kill.*"

"What does that mean?"

"Something to do with the power of the Ark, surely a warning to those who aren't Levites or Kohaths, so it doesn't apply to us. Still, it doesn't get us any closer to finding the Ark itself. Unless" — he paused, studied the cherubim's wing — "unless the wing will somehow guide us to the rest of the Ark."

"As in divine magic of some sort? As in it gave you warmth and I heard its buzzing? You really think it could search out the rest of the cherubim itself?"

He shrugged. "Who knows? I came to tell you I've instructed the crew to start a fresh dig in the southeast quadrant. It's one of the few spots we haven't searched extensively."

"Good idea. But first things first. We must alert Grandfather." She picked up the encrypted satellite phone and started the detailed process of calling the Genesis Group's true headquarters in the Caribbean. Before she could finish dialing, there was a knock at her office door.

"Come."

Lilith entered. At the look on her face, Ajax jumped to his feet.

"What is it?"

"We have a problem. A very big problem. Major Russo failed. They're on their way here — the FBI agents and the Fox."

CHAPTER THIRTY-TWO

Ajax cocked his head at her and said, his voice soft, "I don't understand this, Lilith. How could they even know about us?"

"I don't know," Lilith said, and took a step back at the look on his face.

Again, that soft voice. "You *should* know, Lilith. You should know everything about this mess. You were MI5, you know all the players, all their skills, their resources. You've had control, always carried through. But this time you've screwed up royally."

"It is not my fault. Major Russo's men should have killed them. But now they're all dead. I was following, and I found them. One of Russo's men wasn't dead yet, he told me Drummond was still alive, and the fool died without telling me anything else. I came here to alert you."

Cassandra slowly rose, splayed her hands on her desk. Unlike her brother's, her voice was hard as chipped ice. "Lilith, it is you

260

who has failed. You were in charge of everything — the thief, the plan to kill her, and when that failed, the plan to capture her husband to draw her out. And now you're saying it was Russo who couldn't get the job done?"

Lilith wanted to leave now, run out that door and keep running. She ran her tongue over her lips. "Drummond is better than anyone could have expected."

"Cassandra is right," Ajax said. "It is you who are always preaching accountability, Lilith, that one must always take the blame as well as the praise. Isn't that true?"

"Yes, of course, but Ajax, these FBI, the Drummond agent, I couldn't have imagined they'd manage to beat Russo's men. He's very proud of the killers he's trained, and you have to admit, he's performed admirably for us for years."

He pulled her against him, put his arms around her, held her close, and Lilith eased. He ran his fingers through her hair, whispered against her temple, "I begin to believe this Drummond must be a magician. Perhaps he waved his wand and destroyed Russo's men." He kissed her, leaned back, and before she knew what was happening, a stiletto buried itself in her chest, up to the hilt. "Goodbye, Lilith." She heard his soft voice as if from a great distance, but there was no regret. No regret. She died in his arms, his voice chiming in her head, soft, so very soft.

Ajax eased her to the floor. He pulled his knife from her breast and wiped it off on Lilith's black slacks.

He looked up at Cassandra, who hadn't moved. "I will miss her," he said.

Cassandra said, "They're coming here."

He leaned down, picked Lilith up, and threw her over his shoulder. "I'll be back. I'll bury her in one of the tunnels. And, Cassandra, crash the public server for Genesis, put up a 404 message that we've been hacked and we'll be back online very soon. We can't run the risk of this Drummond and his team getting into our servers."

She nodded.

He paused at the doorway. "We will find a way to stop this FBI agent. He and his team have been smart enough to find out about us, then we must assume he also has an idea of what we can do with the weather."

"I know what we'll do," Cassandra said, and her eyes sparked with excitement. "We will have Grandfather wipe out Washington, D.C. Flatten them with a hurricane, maybe a tsunami. The United States government will fall, the headquarters for the FBI will fall — it will be chaos. We will be the last thing on the FBI's mind."

Ajax stared at her. "That's brilliant. But they're coming here right now. We must find out exactly what they know. Then we will have Grandfather act, if it is necessary." He frowned, shifted Lilith's weight to his other shoulder. "I wish I could be certain we will be able to convince Grandfather to flatten the U.S. capital, even if it is necessary to save us."

"If Grandfather refuses, you know how to reprogram a storm that's already in the making, like the current one."

"Yes, I can do that, but I can't program directionality myself without his formula."

"Yes, the precious formula in his bloody vault." She smiled. "Don't worry, we'll figure it out. Can you imagine, you and I will bring an entire country to its knees. And then we'll be safe."

Chapter Thirty-Three

Castel Rigone, Italy

Both Nicholas's and Mike's phones buzzed as the Škoda sped along the highway toward Castel Rigone.

Mike said, "You're going to want to pull off. Adam was fast. Here are the plans for the Kohath palazzo. This place is huge."

Nicholas pulled the car off the edge of the road, into the driveway of a small abandoned farmhouse, and he, Mike, and Kitsune studied the four pages of architectural plans on Nicholas's tablet.

Mike whistled. "Congratulations to Adam for getting his hands on the plans. Look at this place, it's three thousand square meters. That's a lot of real estate for us to cover. And what's all this?"

There was another page attached to the documents. "It's from Ben," Mike said, scrolling down, "He sent it to Adam, and Adam forwarded it. It's the palazzo's history prior to the Kohaths' buying it in 1905. Way back, the whole town was supposed to be a secret Knights Templar stronghold. Plus twenty more pages to keep us entertained." She laughed. "He's even marked all his conjectures in red type so we don't get confused."

Kitsune said, "There has to be another way in than by the front door. Given the palazzo is so old, I know there are dungeons or an ancient basement, and I'm betting that's where they've got Grant stashed. With Lilith running the show, they know all about him, how dangerous he can be, so they wouldn't simply put him in a guest room." She pushed her hair off her face. "He's probably drugged."

Nicholas pointed to the screen. "The main entrance is on the square, smack-dab in the middle of town, and the others are down the hill, here and here. I don't know if they're guarded, but it stands to reason there are at least a few armed men around."

Kitsune said, "Wait, look — there are the tunnels I remembered. There are so many of them, under the mountain, connecting to the palazzo, crisscrossing under the town. All over the place. As I told you, this was Etruscan territory — there have been lots of archaeological digs going on around here for many years. All I need is to find a tunnel entrance and I can go in that way, find Grant."

Mike said, "All right, it only makes sense that the tunnels connect to the house, but, Kitsune, didn't you say it's been years since they had archaeological digs here? So they're probably blocked off, the tunnels caved in."

Nicholas raised a brow. "You're thinking of Paris and our lovely evening in the crypts, aren't you?"

Mike shuddered. "I am. I'm not anxious to go for a walk under a mountain, that's for sure. And I don't know if it would be safe enough for Kitsune alone."

Kitsune said, "Let me key up Ben's diagrams of the tunnels. See? I can tell this is an abandoned Etruscan dig site. You can bet the Italian government will have assured it was preserved. It runs right up to the wall of the house, directly into the back. Looks like basements to me. If Mike can get to the door, I can come up through the tunnel, and she can let me in."

Mike was nodding her head. "It's a good plan, Nicholas, if the tunnels are still workable. Will our comms work that far underground? It looks like about a mile from the entrance here" — she pointed at a spot on the map — "to here, the city wall, and the back of the palazzo."

"I can't guarantee they will," he said. "I have an amplifier. It shouldn't be an issue for Mike and me, but I don't know if we'd be able to follow Kitsune through the tunnels. Kitsune, once you're close enough to the house it should work. Assuming you can get close to the house."

Mike said, "But there's another problem."

"What?"

"How are we going to deal with their security? If they have any brains at all, they aren't alone up there. You won't be able to waltz through the back door, and into the house, you know they'll be watching our every move. We know men brought Grant here, and they are more than likely guarding him. Add in whatever staff they have at the house, cameras, sensors —"

"I'm already on it," Nicholas said. "Let's see what Adam's come up with."

The call connected, Nicholas hit speaker.

"Adam, we're in place and ready to go. The house in Castel Rigone — I don't know how you got hold of the plans and I don't want to know. Well done. Have you figured out the security specs yet?"

"Give me a minute, I'm finishing running the reports. By the way, we had a quick visit with Lia. She's feeling better, they're going to discharge her tomorrow. Her dad is pretty cool. He waltzed right into the administrator's office in the Doge's Palace, asked the man to lunch, and off they went, had a big time, Lia told us. I think they've got a flight home tomorrow."

"Good. Everything else okay there?"

"We found three listening devices planted throughout the suite. They've been taken care of. And we're making progress. Louisa is crashed in her room, they finally finished processing the piazza but not a single thank-you from Major Russo for all her help, nor an apology to us for their missing the shoot-out." He snorted. "I think Louisa probably gave him what for. I asked Gray for help piecing together the financials. No irregularities so far, but we're still searching. Okay, here we go, I've got their plans." He whistled. "You're screwed. The house has full-on security. Everything from thermal sensors to motion detectors to on-air live surveillance. They have to have a whole team to run this, it's pretty extensive."

"Awful lot of security for a private home."

"It is. There's something going on there, that's for sure."

"So how do we get around it? We need to send Kitsune in the back through the tunnels while Mike and I go in the front."

"You'll have to find a way to turn it off. Cutting off the electricity won't work, they'll have plenty of generators. I bet the power goes off around that area a lot."

Nicholas said, "Well, if we can't turn it off —"

They could practically see Adam grinning over the phone. "There is one way. You do have that Faraday bag in your kit, right?"

"Yes I do, and I like the way you think. Thank you for reminding me. We'll be in touch. Keep monitoring us, please. I don't want to get into trouble and not have someone to call in the cavalry."

"Do you want me to contact the local Carabinieri?"

"No," Nicholas said. "Let's hold that in reserve. Who knows how many people are on the Kohaths' payroll."

"Good luck getting the security system down."

"Thanks." He hung up and grinned at Mike. "I've been wanting to try this."

Mike said, "I know you have. You and Adam both, not to mention Gray. He is going to be bummed when he finds out we used it without him. If it works," she added.

"I looked it over. I'm about ninety percent sure. We tested it in New York, but under controlled circumstances. I think it's worth a shot."

"Try what?" Kitsune asked.

"I have a micro electromagnetic pulse — EMP."

She gave him a high five. "I like a man who's always prepared. You think a small electromagnetic pulse will knock out their security system. But what about —"

"— I'm three steps ahead of you. I have a Faraday bag to go with my micro EMP. We'll have to put all our comms, mobiles, earwigs, everything electronic we'll need from here on out in here."

He dug in his leather briefcase and pulled out what looked like a large Ziploc bag, but it was opaque silver.

"All electronics in here."

Kitsune said, "I take it this is homemade?"

"Yes, it is," Nicholas said. "Mobile, please?"

Kitsune said, "May I see it? The device?"

Nicholas dug into his briefcase and handed her a small black box the size of a deck of cards, with a thick coil of metal around it and a small switch.

"The EMP is simple, really. We found the designs on an earlier case and made modifications. Upped the wattage, basically, so it can take out more than the closest electronics. It should work fine against an internal security system. I flip the switch and it will send out a pulse that will take everything within a hundred-yard radius offline. Be careful — you don't want to shock your socks off."

Kitsune said, "Sorry, I don't have anything to put in the bag. You know I only use disposables."

"Not a problem. You've still got the ingestible tracker in you, so if anything does happen to you, we'll know where you are."

"You do come up with elegant solutions, Nicholas."

Mike snorted.

Kitsune watched them, smiled. "When did you two start sleeping together?"

Dead silence.

"Please, you two were already circling each other when we had our little adventure with the Koh-i-Noor. It's good, and I mean that. Life is too short, too fragile, to only look to the future. A lesson it took me long enough to learn. While you guys are in the house taming the lion and lioness, I'll find Grant and get him out. You ready?"

"How do you plan to get him out?"

"Back the way I came in, through the tunnels."

Mike nodded. "We'll keep them busy and

occupied long enough for you to get in and get out. I don't think we'll be able to buy you more than an hour. I'll figure out some way to get to the basement door and let you in."

Nicholas turned in his seat. "In case you do get lost, or we can't get to you, we need a plan for getting you out of there."

"I will leave you a trail of bread crumbs. You set off your EMP, talk to the crazy twins, try not to let them kill you. And, Mike, I'll expect you at the basement door."

CHAPTER THIRTY-FOUR

The Bermuda Triangle

Jason was horrified, but he wasn't surprised, nothing the twins did since their sixteenth birthdays would surprise him. He watched their faces, listened to the words coming from their mouths, telling him Lilith had convinced them that they should kill the thief, that the men she'd hired had failed, and how she'd had the thief's husband, Grant Thornton, kidnapped, to make an exchange. Lilith had assured them it was necessary, had to be done, both of them killed and disposed of.

He looked into those faces, listened to all the lies. But his voice remained calm. "Where is this man, this Grant Thornton, the thief's husband Lilith had kidnapped?"

Ajax said, "She wanted to make the exchange in Venice, but that didn't work out."

Jason said, "I saw how that didn't go well for your men. The world saw. It was a

273

disaster."

"Lilith's men, Grandfather," Cassandra said.

Ajax said, "So she brought him here, to the dungeons beneath the palazzo. She convinced us the thief would come here and we'd have both of them."

"And what makes Lilith believe the thief will come to Castel Rigone?"

Cassandra said, "Lilith told us the thief was desperately in love with her husband and would do anything to save him. Once we have both of them, there will be no more problems."

"And the FBI agents I saw in the Piazza San Marco?"

"They won't be a problem, either," Cassandra said. "If they come to us making accusations, we will tell them about Lilith — we will convince them she was the one who engineered the theft of the staff from the Topkapi. All will be well, Grandfather."

"But you are the ones who wanted the staff of Moses stolen."

"We are Kohaths," Cassandra said. "It was our responsibility to ensure the staff was a fake."

"I see, and what did you do with the fake staff?"

"We destroyed it," Ajax said, and

shrugged.

"I still don't understand why you simply didn't pay the thief and be done with it."

Only a slight pause, then Ajax said, "Again, it was Lilith who made that decision. She said loose ends always came back to cause trouble. And now we have no choice. Lilith has left us, returned to Scotland, she told us, so now we have to act even though we don't wish to. We will remove the thief and her husband. Then the FBI will have nothing."

"You could tell the FBI that Lilith went to Scotland."

Another telling pause, then Ajax said, "I think that Lilith lied to us, Grandfather. She's committed heinous crimes and she is probably in hiding. We couldn't very well order her to stay."

"It is a pity she is not available to be arrested for her crimes."

"Yes, it is," Ajax said, "but she is gone. Probably forever."

Cassandra said, "Grandfather, Lilith isn't important. What is important, urgent, really, is that you prepare to move the Atlantic storm, just in case things don't work out."

Here it comes. Jason said, his voice emotionless, "And where would you like this storm to hit?"

Ajax said, "Washington, D.C. You always told us you didn't like the place, too full of men and women who thought too much of themselves, braying asses, you called the politicians. Think of it as an opportunity. Should the FBI not be convinced of our innocence, we'll wipe them off the map — their White House, their government, all their FBI agents. Then no one will have time to give us a single thought."

Cassandra said, "Ajax is right, Grandfather. You already have plans to have the storm hit the Gulf. You can simply change its trajectory and let it slam into the eastern seaboard instead."

Jason wanted to weep, looking at what his precious Helen had birthed — two beautiful young people, identical faces, smart as whips, both of them, yet they weren't even competent liars, at least to him. Nor did they have a shred of conscience between them. What he did was always for a greater purpose, always to gain money to further the search for the Ark, to keep the Genesis Group at the forefront of archaeological discoveries, at least that was always his justification.

But these two — they didn't want to get caught for the senseless and stupid mistakes they made, the misery they'd caused, and now, they wanted to bring down a nation, needlessly murder thousands of innocent people, and for nothing, not a single noble goal. It was all to try to save themselves, no one else.

What am I to do with your progeny, Helen? But it wasn't your fault, you were always noble, pure. No, it was that insane husband of yours, David Maynes, a man who is finally dead, only weeks ago, and I did rejoice, I drank an entire bottle of champagne. But he passed his madness to his children, you know he did.

For Helen's sake, he would try reason. "Cassandra, Ajax, think about destruction of this magnitude. It is not New Orleans we're talking about here, although Katrina wouldn't have wreaked such havoc if the levees had held as they were supposed to.

"But Washington, D.C.? It is a nation's capital. It goes against everything we believe. It does nothing to further the family's goals, Genesis's goals. The Coil is not meant to cover your mistakes."

"It was Lilith's mistakes, Grandfather," Cassandra said. "Hers, not ours."

It was no use. What could he do?

"I will think about it," he said, and punched a key to turn off their faces from his computer screen.

CHAPTER THIRTY-FIVE

Castel Rigone

Nicholas and Mike dropped Kitsune halfway up the hill with a flashlight, water, and her two guns, then drove the rest of the way up to the town square.

Nicholas saw a jumble of stone buildings, winding paths with trees and flowers. As he parked, he saw the town was beautiful, small, all the ancient buildings like glittering diamonds around a magnificent stone at its center, the Kohath palazzo.

The palazzo had been beautifully restored. Nicholas could see where small chunks of newer stone had been inserted to mend the original. The flagstones gleamed. Above the palazzo's entrance, the flags of Italy, the U.K., and the province of Umbria snapped in the breeze. There was a war statue dedicated to the local soldiers lost in the world wars, a common sight throughout Italy. A café with three empty outdoor metal tables, four attached stone houses, and a medieval Gothic church rounded out the large square.

Across the piazza, two older Italian women came to their doors to watch the strangers, faces suspicious and wary.

Mike breathed in the soft Italian air. "It's beautiful here, Nicholas. Can you imagine relaxing over in that small café, sitting and drinking a glass of wine, watching the world go by? Maybe not today. It's easy to see we're not welcome. Do you think the Kohaths already know we're here?"

"Of course they do. When this is all over, perhaps you and I can come back here and have that wine and watch this small world go about its business. . . . You ready?"

"I am. When we split up, promise me you'll be careful. And try to buy me enough time to get Kitsune into the house."

"I will. Don't forget, in three-minute intervals I want to hear your voice, otherwise, I'm coming after you."

"You have my Faraday bag?"

He reached into his go-bag. "For you, Agent Caine, I have a smaller one. It should fit into your pants but I could be wrong."

Mike studied the small silver bag, about the size of a sandwich Ziploc. "Are you saying my jeans are too tight?"

"Oh, no. They're quite perfect. As is what

goes in them. Put your phone and earwig in it, stuff it down the front of your drawers, and let's go."

"Is there a reason why I can't put this in my jacket pocket?"

"If they frisk us, we might end up with guns to our heads."

He watched her slip the bag down the front of her jeans as he clicked the button on his comms. "Gray, do you have us?"

"I do," Gray said. "From New York to Italy, amazing. You're going to go offline shortly?"

"Yes. I'll be back up and running in about thirty minutes. With luck, I'll get a couple of bugs in place so we can hear what the Kohaths decide to do after we leave." And Nicholas hoped that would be the case.

"Don't forget, the transportable parabolic only has a range of about fifty yards. If you're sure they're going to stay in a room, plant it on the furniture. But if you think they'll move around, try to get it on clothing.

"Nicholas, what worries me is that if the walls are too thick, it might not work at all."

"You're good, Gray. It'll work."

"From your mouth to God's ear. Good luck."

Mike and Nicholas got out of the car and

walked to the palazzo's front door, aware of being watched and studied. Mike realized to sneak into this place would be impossible, even in the dead of night.

There was no bell, but the double wooden door had twin brass lion-head knockers, a ring through the extended tongues. Nicholas rapped a tongue against the door three times.

Moments later, a small, dark-haired woman in a white silk blouse and black pants opened the door. A maid, but a very stylish one.

"*Si?*"

Nicholas and Mike already had their credentials out. Mike said, "Good afternoon. Do you speak English?"

"*Si,* yes."

"I'm Special Agent Michaela Caine, with the American Federal Bureau of Investigation. This is Special Agent Nicholas Drummond. We need to speak with Cassandra and Ajax Kohath."

The woman didn't look surprised to see two American federal agents on her doorstep, nor did she look surprised to hear English. She merely nodded and gestured for them to come inside, and closed the heavy wooden door behind them.

"You will come with me. I will announce

you." Her English was heavily accented but clear enough.

Mike's first impression of the Kohath palazzo was one of great wealth. They stood in a long foyer that led into an open square interior garden. Of all things, the white-washed walls were dominated with can-vasses of modern art, eight large pieces, all with unrelenting white backgrounds, each bisected by a wide, thick paint slash of red or black. Like the artist had taken a large paintbrush, dipped it into the paint color of his choice, and swiped it across the white canvas. The pictures were so very much at odds with what she knew the Kohaths revered and treasured, it was jarring. She imagined these paintings were originals, and probably worth thousands, go figure that. She also imagined the artist was laughing all the way to the bank.

The maid stopped at the end of the foyer, waved for them to join her. As they entered the interior courtyard, Mike saw the Ko-haths had turned the open space into a garden filled with marble sculptures — each representative of a different culture — prob-ably from their digs. Some were very old, missing feet, or hands, or heads. She saw beautiful Ionic columns connecting great marble arches that held up the higher stories of the palazzo. She remembered the Joslyn Art Museum in Omaha had a garden similar to this. It was a feast for the eyes.

Nicholas did not appear to be either amazed or impressed. He looked annoyed. Then she saw why. Three security guards had stepped forward from the outer edges of the garden, all wearing black, all armed, all watching them closely, looking ready to shoot them where they stood.

She saw two more guards standing at the far end of the garden. The maid stopped beside them.

A big guard with a blond buzz cut stepped forward. "Your weapons," he said, and he held out his hand. He was a Brit and a bruiser, heavily muscled, his eyes flat and hard. Could she take him down? She flexed her hands, felt a shot of adrenaline. She was ready.

"I don't think so," Nicholas said. "Where you from? Bristol?"

Buzz Cut kept his hand out. "If you want to speak to the Kohaths, you do it unarmed. No, not Bristol."

Nicholas said, "Close, though, right? You'll only take my gun when I'm dead, mate."

"Very well. No gun, no talk. Escort them out, Chiara."

The maid appeared by Mike's right elbow,

283

gesturing toward the front door at the end of the long foyer. But before Nicholas could decide what to do, a cultured female British voice said, "That won't be necessary, Harry. See my guests to the Blue Room, please."

The bruiser's name was Harry?

"But, ma'am —"

Mike and Nicholas got their first look at Cassandra Kohath. *Tall, fit, striking, and somehow off,* were Mike's first thoughts. Maybe it was her eyes, Mike couldn't be sure.

Lethal was Nicholas's.

"The Blue Room," she said again, and without another look or word, walked back down the hallway that led off the garden.

Buzz-cut Harry only shook his head.

"I guess that's Cassandra Kohath," Mike said.

"Yes, follow me." And Harry set off.

After two right turns, putting them at the back of the palazzo, Harry stopped in front of an ancient open door.

"You're really off," he said to Nicholas. "I'm from Oxford." He moved to stand against the wall, arms crossed.

"Not that far off," Nicholas said.

Mike said, "May I use your restroom, Harry?"

Harry didn't say anything, but he must

have made some sort of sign because the maid appeared from the shadows.

"Through there, *signora*," she said, and she pointed through an archway.

Harry started to follow her. Nicholas said, "Hey, Harry, I doubt she needs help. Why don't you stay here and guard me and my gun? We can discuss which pubs you liked best in Oxford. Ever toss down a pint at the *Swan and Castle*? No, how about the *Lamb and Flag*?"

Harry looked like he wanted to punch Nicholas, but instead, he pulled a walkie-talkie out of his jacket, giving Nicholas a glimpse of a shoulder harness and a Beretta 92. He spoke to another guard who stood at attention some twenty feet away, now watching Mike like a hawk. Nicholas saw the guard nod.

Harry called after Mike. "You stay with Adcock. Do not leave his sight, do you understand?"

"Your British English is very clear," Mike said. And nodded to Nicholas.

How many more guards for a couple of harmless archaeologists? Were the guards all Brits? Hard to be afraid of a short, pit bull of a guard named Adcock until you saw the Ka-Bar strapped to his side, and the look on his face that promised mayhem as he watched Mike approach.

Mike was going to need some luck to get out of Adcock's sight long enough to slip away and let Kitsune into the house.

When Nicholas saw Mike follow Adcock around a corner, he reached into his pocket and pressed the button on the micro EMP.

Time to get started.

CHAPTER THIRTY-SIX

Kitsune was shrouded in darkness the moment she stepped into the ancient Etruscan tunnel. She'd cut the orange service tape across the door and found the door was unlocked. She saw no guards.

She set off, torch in her left hand, a PPK in her right. She fancied she heard echoes of ancient history as she moved slowly through the impenetrable darkness, making no noise on the packed dirt floor, carved out by the Etruscans so long ago, then later, the path of the Knights Templar.

Even though the tunnel hadn't been used recently, the path was clear, the walls and ceilings reinforced with handmade wooden arches, like huge ribs, the walls coated with cement on top of the wood.

She was making excellent progress, but it couldn't last for much longer. She assumed she'd soon reach the spot where the tunnels would be blocked off for safety reasons, since there were no more archaeological digs.

Deeper and deeper she went, upward now, the climb steep. Thirty minutes later, the main tunnel turned sharply and she saw there were six different paths to choose from. None were blocked off. These paths were not on the plans.

She studied her compass. The middle tunnel was heading north, the right direction to continue under the house, but it didn't feel right, and then she smelled something — freshly turned dirt. She walked into the fourth tunnel, saw that it shot off to the right at a forty-five-degree angle. The smell of dirt was stronger. Who was digging down here? And why?

She walked forward, aiming her torch down at her feet so no one would see her light.

She saw lights ahead, heard voices. She listened carefully, heard two men speaking Italian. One was a native speaker, the other spoke well, but with a faint British accent. The Italian spoke the local dialect, but the Brit was speaking the Roman, more common internationally. What was a Brit doing down here?

Were they guards? She edged closer, listening to the conversation.

"Why did you kill her?" the Italian asked. "I thought you were sleeping with her."

The Brit paused only a moment at the impertinence before saying indifferently, "There was no choice. I will miss her, but her failures, they were too great. Giovanni, make sure you bury her deep so no one will ever find her. Then get back to digging. My sister is anxious to unearth this section of the mountain as quickly as possible."

Giovanni's voice grew excited. "It is true, then? You truly found a piece of the Ark in the Gobi Desert?"

The Brit paused. "Where did you hear that?"

Kitsune imagined Giovanni shrugging. "You know gossip, it spreads like wild fire. The whole crew has been buzzing about it. You and the *signorina* found a piece of a cherubim's wing at the Mysore Base, and you have brought it home."

The Brit spoke, his voice cold. "These walls seem to ooze gossip. Now finish the job."

Kitsune heard footsteps coming toward her. She ran back toward the center point where the six tunnels branched off and eased into the smallest of the tunnels. The Brit was soon in the center point — it had been close, too close. She fell to her knees, looked out, and saw him turn into the main tunnel, the one that went north. She didn't see his face, but his hair was blond and curly. Was it Ajax Kohath? He'd killed his lover? A moment later, she heard an engine turn over. It sounded like a motorcycle.

Smart, she thought. Small, portable, easy to maneuver underground. The tunnels were extensive, she'd seen that much on the map, but now she was wondering just how extensive they actually were, if the diggers moved around on motorbikes.

If the Kohaths were resorting to murder in their own house, something was going badly wrong in their world.

Kitsune couldn't help but wonder about Giovanni's other comment — the cherubim's golden wing, a piece of the Ark? Found in the Gobi Desert? Incredible to imagine.

A piece of a cherubim's wing — for a brief moment, she wondered if she could steal it after she'd rescued Grant. The thought of how much money such an archaeological prize would bring — Kitsune laughed at herself.

When she was sure the motorbike was far enough away, she again started up the center tunnel, north, toward the house.

A pity she couldn't grab a motorcycle, too,

but she was moving pretty fast now, and soon, she stepped into a large, hollowed-out cavern at least fifty feet wide, the ceiling too high for her to see. The huge space was lit with soda vapor lights, focused on the ground. And there were people working, all men, five by her count, moving boxes and crates. She saw four motorbikes parked on their kickstands near the wall. Then she saw it, behind the motorbikes, what had to be the basement door.

But how to get past the workers? Suddenly, two of them turned and started coming toward her. Nowhere to hide. She looked up, saw reinforced beams above her head. She stashed her PPK and torch, leaped up, and grabbed on to a burnished two-by-four. She dragged her legs up and over, flattened herself against the beam. It was a tight fit. She held her breath as the two workers walked under her, unaware she was above them.

She waited. The lights went off in the tunnel. At last Nicholas had activated his EMP. She had to hurry, she didn't want Mike to have to wait, it would be too dangerous.

She heard the workers groan, curse, saw the beams from torches being turned on. The men who'd walked below her were coming back. Neither had had a torch on them, they were using the walls to guide them.

"What happened?" one of them shouted in Italian.

"Everything's gone offline," another yelled back. "Might as well take a break until we get it fixed. Unless you want to light the lamps?"

"No, let's not bother. By the time we get them all lit the power will be back on. I could use a break. Last one to the break room makes the espresso."

The men walked beneath her again, talking, joking about their unexpected break, back into the cavern. She watched as one by one they disappeared into the open door, torches bobbing.

Nicholas's EMP had worked perfectly. The lighting in the tunnels must be run off a computerized system rather than straight electrical circuits. More to their advantage than she could have hoped.

When she saw the last of the crew disappear through the door, she dropped down and started toward the entrance. If she was right, this passage would lead to the basement.

It was strange, this ongoing dig under the mountain. What could they be looking for? Surely not more Etruscan artifacts? The activity was so clearly regulated, something else was going on. It was a huge undertaking, shoring up tunnels, digging new ones, the cost alone must be staggering.

Then it hit her. The cherubim's wing — could they possibly think the Ark was buried here? How could that be possible?

Kitsune walked through the door and saw a long hallway stretch out in front of her. It was eerie down there in the darkness, with no lights, too cool for comfort, and damp. She shivered.

She didn't risk turning on her torch. She stood quietly for a moment, hoping her eyes would adjust, but the darkness was profound. She listened but couldn't hear any voices or footsteps. The floor was rough concrete, as were the walls. This tunnel was more recent than the others.

She started up the hallway, walking carefully, slowly, one hand on the wall so she didn't trip and lose her balance. After a turn, she thought she could see light up ahead, and walked faster. This door had to be the one that directly connected the tunnel system to the basement. Mike could already be there to let her in. Then she'd return to Nicholas, and Kitsune would find Grant and they would leave through the tunnels.

She shielded her arm with her gun and pressed the button for the digital display. It flashed blue in the dark, and in that eerie light, she saw a row of doors, doors that had no handles, only small indentations to slide them open. Storage rooms, most likely, for the excavation equipment. Considering the age of the palazzo, and the many wars that had been fought in the area, maybe they were there to hold prisoners.

Like Grant.

She went to the closest door and fit her fingers into the indentations, and pulled. It didn't move. It was locked, as was the next and the next. Whatever was behind these doors had been sealed off. She wanted to yell with frustration.

With no hope, she fit her fingers into the indentation on the fourth door. It opened easily. It was as dark as a pit in hell. She heard a person breathing.

She turned on the torch and stared into the blinking eyes of her husband.

His beloved face was dirty, and she saw blood matting his hair over his temple.

"Who is it?" His voice sounded slurred.

She realized he couldn't see her. She whispered, "It's me, Grant, Kitsune." She dropped to her knees by his side, and pulled him into her arms. She kissed his bloody hair, his filthy face, his mouth, hugged him, rocked him. "You're alive, you're alive. I'm going to get you out of here. Can you stand?"

Grant smelled her familiar scent, breathed her in. She was here, but that was impossible, which meant he was out of it on the drugs, hallucinating now. In his saner moments, he'd known he should accept that she had to be dead. That damned last job, that impossible stunt she pulled, and for what? His brain looped back. She was here, with him, and he let her hold him while he tried to clear his head, bring himself back into focus. He felt her tears on his cheek. Tears, Kitsune's tears. She was here, she was here, to rescue him.

"What day is it?"

"What? Oh, it's Tuesday."

"Three days. They've kept me drugged for three days." And he breathed her in again. "Give me another minute to get my brain together."

"What have they been giving you?"

"Ketamine, I think."

"Do you remember what happened?"

He thought, shook his head. "No, but maybe it will all come back once my head is clear."

She'd tell him later of the video of his

kidnapping, but not now.

"I remember I saw the news about the stolen staff from the Topkapi. Well done, a good, clean job."

"Yes, it was, and I got away clean, too, but it was the clients who tried to kill me in Venice. Then they took you for leverage after I escaped."

Leverage, such a bloodless word. He knew she'd planned to give herself up for him, her life for his. He felt fury and pain, in equal measures. But now wasn't the time. "Where are we?"

"Castel Rigone, a small town north of Castiglione del Lago. It's a huge old palazzo owned by the Kohaths, the people who hired me to steal the staff."

His brain latched on to that. They were in the middle of Italy. "But why would they try to kill you? You did your job. Why?"

"I'll tell you everything, but later, Grant. We've got to move."

"I know, they'll be coming back to pump more ketamine into me. Okay, let's try."

She put a shoulder beneath his and tried to haul him to his feet, but his coordination wasn't back yet. He sagged against her. "Don't tell me you managed to break in here alone?"

"I called Drummond for help. It's not just

help for you and me, Grant, there's big trouble and now they're in the middle of it. We're in a very old store room beneath the palazzo. There are excavation tunnels leading to the outside. We have to be careful, but we can make it. Come on, you can do it."

He wanted to laugh at the irony of it but couldn't find the energy. He had to move. If there was one guard coming with a needle then he knew Kitsune could take him down, but more than one? He said, "I wish we had my team here rather than Drummond. They'd tear this place to the ground."

"I think Drummond notified them, but I don't know anything more. Let's try again. Come on, soldier, you can do it. You have to do it."

But it was too late. There were no warning footsteps. A large man suddenly appeared in the doorway, a Maglite attached to the nose of the M4 strapped across his chest, his finger ready on the trigger.

"Now what have we here?" Another Brit. A light shined in her face. "Who are you, cutie? How did you even get in here?"

Kitsune let go of Grant, jerked out her Walther, and pointed it at him. "Go to hell!"

She heard an echo of a laugh as his leg lashed out and her gun went flying. Fast, he was very fast, but she knew she could take him, even if she was in close quarters, no choice, and so she spun to the side and kicked out. He grabbed her ankle, twisted, and sent her flying into the wall. Kitsune had the breath knocked out of her, but she leaped up and ran out of the small room. He was Special-Forces skilled and she needed more space to maneuver to have a chance against him. He came at her again, eyes focused, ready, poised. She waved her Ka-Bar, cutting a wide swath in front of her.

Again he laughed. "I like women like you," he said, and lunged for her, ducking when she slashed at him, spinning on his feet. She got him once in the shoulder, not all that deep, but it had to hurt and he cursed, called her a bitch, whipped around, and slammed his fist into her jaw. Fast, he was so very fast. She saw stars, but still she fought him even as he kicked the knife from her hand. She fought until he threw her again against the wall, headfirst, and everything went black.

Grant leaped on his back and slammed his fists against his ears, once and again, but he didn't have the strength to pulverize his brain. The guard threw him onto his back, and kicked him until his head was swimming, his body screaming with pain, and he knew he was going to pass out. He saw Kitsune, his brave girl, lying motionless on the ground. He saw a syringe in the guard's hand. And knew it was all over. For both of them.

CHAPTER THIRTY-SEVEN

Nicholas stepped into the Blue Room. It was quite empty. Harry had stayed outside. Nicholas quickly moved out of sight of the door, placed his earwig. He heard Mike's voice: "Perfect timing, Nicholas. The EMP is working. I'm in the stairwell. It's very dark."

He answered her with one tap, as a portion of the wall across the room opened with a soft click, and Cassandra Kohath stepped into the room. What? The queen staging her magic? "Agent Drummond? I'm Cassandra Kohath. Do join me."

He gave her a nod. "Ms. Kohath." Her beautiful face was politely composed, her eyes faintly inquiring, a perfect eyebrow arched.

"And what may I do for you this beautiful day?"

"Only answer a few questions. Why do you have so many guards? Aren't you and your brother archaeologists? You're hardly in need of protection, are you?"

"We run a large international company, Agent Drummond, with extremely valuable artifacts at our disposal. We are always careful. As for my guards here at the palazzo, I will admit, they tend to be overprotective." She stuck out her hand. He shook it. "How nice to finally meet you, at last. Yours is now a household name. I've been told you were attacked during a tourist event in Saint Mark's Square while visiting Venice. How terrible."

"Yes, it was. You have quite a name in archaeological circles, I understand."

"You've heard of me? How lovely."

"It's impossible not to know all about you. In Venice, we were attacked, yes, by trained operatives who did all they could to kill us. But I'm sure you know all about it. What part of England are you from?"

He saw a glimmer of amusement in her eyes before she turned it off.

"I'm from East Sheen, you know, in Richmond. It's an old hunting lodge originally built for the Earl of Northumberland. My great-great-grandfather Appleton Kohath bought it in 1905, I believe, a wedding present for his wife. Alas, neither my twin nor I have spent much time there. We were always on digs with our mother, though Ajax and I visit whenever we get a chance. Don't you agree it's always nice to go home?"

"Who lives in the hunting lodge now?"

She shrugged. "Oh, our father was the only resident. He died, you know, a short time ago actually. We haven't decided what to do with the pile yet. I believe the National Trust wants it, but we'll see."

"My condolences. When did your father die?"

"You are full of questions, aren't you? My father died two weeks ago, a heart attack, we were told. We weren't close. He left the business nearly ten years ago. I suppose you could say he was eccentric, a man who liked his parties and conspiracy theories. But of course, your family's history is much more illustrious than mine. I've seen photos of the Drummond estate in Farrow-on-Gray as well as photos of the gardens — and your labyrinth is famous. I'd love to visit sometime. And you'll be a peer soon enough, won't you?"

"Not for a very long time. You've learned a lot in the past day and a half."

She laughed. "Come now, Agent Drummond. You were all over the news last week. You're famous, the man who saved the lives

302

of the president and vice president of the United States. And now you're here, killing off Italians."

Nicholas smiled at her.

She gestured toward a sofa in front of the fire. "Please, have a seat. Can I get you a drink? Scotch? With water?"

"No, I prefer it straight."

"Of course you do. You have that nice straightforward air about you." Cassandra handed him a crystal lowball and he took a sip of the Scotch, nodded.

He wondered as he clicked his glass to Cassandra Kohath's if she would still be standing if Mike were here instead of him. Maybe not, maybe Mike would have already slugged her.

"It's excellent."

"My brother, Ajax, is quite the liquor con-noisseur. Now, enough questions. Tell me, what really brings you to my house, Agent Drummond?"

Before he could answer, she reached for a lamp cord, pulled it. Nothing happened. "Oh, bugger," she said. "We'll have to speak by firelight. Don't be concerned, the lights go out here all the time. It's being so high on the mountain, you see, and the circuits are old. The generators will kick in shortly."

He wondered how long he had until the

generator powered the house back up and her people realized all their computers were down. He heard Mike's voice in his ear again. "Checking in. She's not here yet, I'm going in farther to see if there's another door."

He said, "I see you've done extensive work to the palazzo. You've done a nice job."

"Thank you. It took us over ten years. The palazzo was a wedding gift from my grandfather to my parents. My brother and I have always loved the house, so filled with Templar history. We wanted it to be beautiful again. I was wondering, Agent Drummond, why did you join the FBI? I mean, for someone like you, with your background, your experiences, the FBI seems rather confining."

Nicholas took another sip of Scotch. "No, as it turns out, I'm free to do pretty much what I want and that's why I'm here in Italy. To catch a thief."

"A thief? What did the thief steal?"

"The staff of Moses, from the Topkapi. Surely you know all about this, being an archaeologist."

"Of course. My brother and I found it somewhat amusing."

"And why is that?"

"All archaeologists know the purported

staff of Moses at the Topkapi is a fake. So who cares if it was stolen? It doesn't matter at all." She raised her Scotch glass to his again. "Still, if you want so desperately to find the thief who stole something quite worthless, then good luck, Agent Drummond."

"Thank you. We believe you and your brother had the staff stolen. Since you are a Kohath, you would doubtless want to verify that it was indeed a fake. After all, isn't the staff of Moses supposed to be inside the Ark of the Covenant?"

"Such is the accepted wisdom."

"But you weren't one hundred percent certain it was fake, so you had it stolen. How did you prove it wasn't the real staff?"

She laughed. "I'll say it again, Agent Drummond, neither Ajax nor I would have any reason to want that absurd fake staff. We were told from the cradle it was fake, so, you see, I fear you will have to look elsewhere for the mastermind behind your thief."

Nicholas stretched his arm across the back of the sofa. "May I speak to your chief of Operations? Lilith Forrester-Clarke?"

"Lilith? Whatever for?"

"I believe Ms. Forrester-Clark was involved in obtaining the services of a particular thief, even traveled herself to the Top-kapi to verify the thief was there, in place, ready to execute the theft."

She said, "If Lilith traveled to Istanbul it would be to discuss something with the museum director, Haluk Dursun. Haluk is a consultant for the Genesis Group. Feel free to contact him, of course."

He nodded. "I shall. Tell me, where do you think the staff is?"

She paused, smiled at him. "Perhaps it now resides at the bottom of a lake, or is being sold on eBay. Some people are so credulous."

"Still, I would like to speak with Ms. Forrester-Clarke. Is she here with you now?"

"No, she is in Rome, doing the foundation's work."

"Ah, now that's strange. We called there, looking for her. We were told she was here with you."

"Whoever you spoke to was clearly mistaken."

"When might I have the pleasure of meeting your brother?"

"Soon, I expect. Perhaps he'll run into your partner and bring her back with him. Does Agent Caine enjoy Scotch?"

"She's more of a wine drinker." Nicholas knew he needed to buy Mike and Kitsune more time. "The Genesis Group is quite renowned. You and your brother are young to be running such a large foundation."

She shrugged again. "I was raised to run the Genesis Group, it's the family business. I'm surprised you aren't running yours."

"Perhaps I will one day, but for now, I'd rather track down criminals."

He set the drink on the marble table beside him, looked closely at that beautiful, lethal face. "Tell me, Ms. Kohath, what have you done to further your search for the Ark of the Covenant?"

Chapter Thirty-Eight

She smoothed a hand over her sleeve, and he saw a slight tremor, but when she spoke it was in a teacher's voice, "I cannot tell you about the scope of our searches for the Ark. That we keep close, but I will say that our search has continued throughout many years, since the Ark ties to our family all the way back to Moses, a Levite. Also, the Ark's discovery would be, indisputably, the most important archaeological find in history. The Genesis Group wants to be the one to discover it. No, I want to be the one to discover it. As I said, it is my family's duty to find it, to be reunited with it. I'm very determined, Agent Drummond."

"So determined that you will allow nothing to stand in your way? Stealing the staff from the Topkapi to prove it's a fake? Manipulating the weather to empty the Gobi Desert of sand to uncover your mother's lost site, killing thousands of people in

Beijing in the process? Don't you believe that is a bit over the top, Ms. Kohath? A bit extreme? A bit crazy?"

Calling her crazy, it had simply come out of his mouth. But it had triggered her. He saw the sudden wildness in her eyes, like rolling fog, gathering speed, momentum. Would she try to kill him now? Right in this room? Then the madness died and she was once again in perfect control of herself, and that, he'd learned over the years, was what happened when madness melded with brilliance. She even laughed.

"Controlling the weather? Surely that belongs in the realm of science fiction. And blow all the sand out of the Gobi Desert? A romantic and terrifying notion."

"Terrifying, yes, but romantic? I strongly doubt it if you were one of the thousands who choked to death on the sand. That does not include the missing." He tapped on his ear three times.

"It is tragic, of course, but when there are huge storms such as the one that buried parts of Beijing, I suppose it natural to weave all sorts of conspiracy theories as to its genesis. This is a very odd idea you've got, Agent Drummond. May I inquire where and how you dreamed this up?"

He'd met only one other criminal in his

life like her — very smart, utterly focused, perfectly presented, and greatly talented at manipulation. A true psychopath. If he didn't know what Cassandra Kohath had done, and he'd simply met her, would he still believe her crazy?

Nicholas smiled, took another sip of Scotch, let the peat scent rise up his throat. He said mildly, "You're a very good liar."

"Me? A liar? I'm not lying, Agent Drummond, I have no need to. I have no earthly idea what you're talking about." She looked at her watch, a lovely thin rose gold band that circled her wrist three times, like a small golden snake. "This house is vast. I hope your partner isn't lost. Or perhaps looking in places that are not safe."

"I'm sure she's fine, probably being escorted back by a dozen or so of your guards. Bulgari, is it?"

Cassandra moved her wrist this way and that. "Why, yes, it is. You have a good eye." She rose with a smile and took his glass from the side table. "Let me freshen your drink."

"Thank you." Nicholas rose at the same time and brushed against her. She looked up at him and gave him a slow smile. As she turned to the drinks cart, Nicholas took the opportunity to signal Mike again; he tapped his ear three times. She needed to get back, and quickly.

"Kitsune's here, but there's a problem."

He tapped again three times.

What had happened to Kitsune?

CHAPTER THIRTY-NINE

Mike couldn't believe her luck. When the palazzo had been renovated, the bathroom was given two doors, one to the main hallway and the second that opened onto a passageway to the interior of the house. She wouldn't have to get rid of Adcock. He couldn't cover both doors. She went out quietly through the interior door and hurried down the deserted hallway, this one similar to the front foyer, with white plaster walls covered in discreetly lit art, all of it starkly modern. She went to the end of the hall to a door she knew from the plans led to stairs to the lower levels. As she went through the door, the lights went out around her.

Mike stepped into complete darkness. She pulled the bag out of the front of her jeans, put in the earwig, clicked it on. She pressed the flashlight button on her cell phone. It glowed, giving off enough light to get down the stairs.

"Perfect timing, Nicholas. The EMP is working. I'm in the stairwell. It's very dark."

He acknowledged her with one tap. He would only signal back if there was a problem. When the door closed behind her, she walked carefully down the pitted, worn stone stairs, thankful for the grip on her boot soles.

She made it to the basement quickly and found herself stepping into a large room with four identical doors, not the single one she was expecting. Which door was the right one? She pictured the blueprint of the basements; yes, only the one door, and it was on her far left, facing the interior of the mountain. She walked quickly to the door and quietly turned the knob. It was alarmed, she knew; there were cameras in the corridor, but without the power, there were no lights, no Klaxon wailing. Nicholas's micro-EMP had worked perfectly. She'd give him a big hug for that one.

She said quietly into her collar, "Checking in. She's not here yet, I'm going in farther to see if there's another door."

The smell of dirt and must were ancient, but there was a newer smell as well, human sweat. Someone had come through here minutes before her for the scent to linger

like this. Thank heavens she'd missed whoever it was. She moved carefully, pausing
every few steps, wondering where Kitsune
was. Had she chosen the wrong door?

She stepped into a large storage space that
was between the basement proper and the
actual tunnel. For art storage perhaps. No,
that wasn't right; it was far too damp and
musty down here to store anything valuable.

There had to be another door, another
way out of this space.

She followed her cell phone light another
few steps, saw a corner up ahead. She
pressed the phone hard against her leg,
blacking out the light, and turned into the
new corridor. Three steps in, she froze.

There was a fight going on, she could hear
the noises clearly, amplified in the dark
enclosed space.

It had to be Kitsune, and she was in
trouble.

Mike's first instinct was to rush forward,
but she stopped herself when she heard
three taps in her ear — a warning from
Nicholas to get out and get back to him.
Now.

Then, silence. Mike risked a quick look.
She made out the figure of a man coming
toward her with what looked like a small

sack over his shoulder. She backed up, ran back into the corridor where she'd found the four doors, and ducked into the stairwell just as the man walked by. He was carrying Kitsune, and she was clearly unconscious. Or dead. As they passed, Mike heard a moan and breathed again.

But now both Kitsune and Grant were prisoners. Mike wanted to follow, but there came three more taps in her ear. She whispered, "Kitsune's here, but there's a problem."

Three taps again. Crap.

At the top of the stairs she listened carefully and heard nothing, so she opened the door. The hallway was still empty. She started back toward the bathroom, paused. Which was the bathroom door? She was so brilliant she'd forgotten to count, and now she was faced with a long series of closed doors.

She'd walked halfway up the hall, pulling open doors, when a man came around a corner. He wasn't a guard in black. He wore khakis and a polo shirt, black boots. He was tall, fit, young, quite handsome. Her hand hovered over her gun. Then she recognized him from his photos.

A British voice said, "What are you doing? Are you lost?"

315

Mike relaxed her hand and turned on a high-wattage smile.

"I am lost, how did you know? I went to the bathroom and I think I must have come out the wrong side. I'm supposed to be meeting my partner in the Blue Room, but I can't figure out which door leads back. Can you help?"

"Partner?" the man asked.

"I'm Special Agent Michaela Caine, FBI. We're here to speak to Cassandra and Ajax Kohath."

He inclined his head. "Then you're in luck. I'm Ajax Kohath, Agent Caine." Up close, he was even more handsome, curling blond hair, chiseled features, like his twin sister's. Her perfect counterpoint.

Mike nodded. "I'm very glad you came and not one of your guards."

Her voice was friendly; his was not. "Let me get you to the Blue Room. It's through here."

Adcock and another guard came around the corner. "Found her, Adcock," Ajax called. "She'd gotten lost in the dark. When will you have the lights back on?"

"Sir, we're working on it. The generators are on, but there's something wrong with the computers — they won't reboot."

"Get it figured out." They started up the hallway.

Mike said, "I hope Ms. Lilith Forrester-Clarke is in the Blue Room with Agent Drummond and Ms. Kohath."

"Lilith? No, she's in Florence today, I believe. She's hard to keep track of, always on the go. Now, Agent Caine, the Blue Room is through here. Let's go meet your partner."

He turned a knob and the door opened directly into the room. Nicholas rose when he saw her. "Got lost, did you?"

"I did. Thankfully I ran into Mr. Kohath and he kindly showed me the way."

Ajax shook Nicholas's hand, nodded to his sister, studied her face for a moment, before saying, "Forgive my tardiness. I was in the basement, attending to some of our newest stock."

Cassandra said, "How lovely to meet you, Agent Caine. May I offer you a drink? Wine, perhaps, or Scotch, like your partner?"

"Thank you, no, nothing for me. I apologize for taking so long. I got very turned around on my way back."

Ajax walked to the cart and poured himself a vodka rocks. He turned, gave them both a salute, and drank it down.

Mike said, "Nicholas, have you explained

to Ms. Kohath why we're here?"

Cassandra said, "Not entirely. I will say that he has many curious ideas about the staff of Moses and the Gobi Desert. He even wanted to speak to Lilith, to accuse her, I believe, of hiring the thief who stole the staff from the Topkapi. But he cannot since Lilith is in Rome."

Mike said, "But Mr. Kohath said she was in Florence."

"Wherever," Cassandra said. "I'm sure if you look long enough, you will track her down."

Nicholas leaned forward. "You could phone her. I don't happen to have her number."

Ajax shrugged, said very quietly to his sister, "Tell them."

Cassandra stared at Ajax. "Tell them what exactly?"

Ajax took his sister's arm, as if to steady her. "There is no use trying to pretend. We might as well tell them the truth and be done with it."

"I don't know, Ajax, I'm not certain —"

Ajax said to Nicholas and Mike, "Lilith is no longer in our employ."

"Ajax, really —"

He shook his head at Cassandra, faced the FBI agents again. "Look, I apologize for the deception. It's been a bit embarrassing, really. We don't want it to reflect poorly on the foundation, or the family. We've been considering coming forward, but it's been a busy time and to be honest, we've been torn.

"The truth is, we had to dismiss Lilith earlier in the week, and it's not something we take lightly. She's been with us for a very long time, is almost as familiar to the industry as a part of our company as Cassandra and myself. You mentioned the stolen staff of Moses, taken from the Topkapi last week?"

Cassandra said, "Agent Drummond believes we hired the thief to steal the staff."

Ajax said, "Well, now they'll know the truth. As I'm sure you know, our family's legacy is deeply rooted in the search for the Ark of the Covenant. Lilith, acting on her own initiative, decided to help us along by hiring someone to steal the staff of Moses, or the rod of Aaron, whichever you wish to call it.

"Once we realized what she'd done, what a horrible position she put us all in, we asked Lilith to turn herself in. Instead, she ran. So honestly, we don't know if she's in Rome, or Florence, or Timbuktu. But if there's anything we can do to help you find her, the foundation — and my sister and I

— are at your service."

Nicholas took an easy sip of his Scotch, then clapped slowly, once, twice, three times. "Well done, and all on the spur of the moment. Or was it? Did you practice it? An excellent tale. I don't even know where to start."

"I do," Mike said. "Where's the staff of Moses?"

CHAPTER FORTY

Ajax shook his head. "We don't know, we never saw it. Lilith came to us and admitted what she'd done. She said the thief she'd hired refused to give it to her, and so she refused further payment."

Mike said, "I see, this all came as a great surprise, and neither you nor Ms. Kohath had anything to do with the theft."

"Of course not. The staff at the Topkapi is a fake, everyone knows this. There was no reason to steal it. When Lilith admitted what she'd done, we told her how badly she'd compromised our company's values, and severed her from service." He shrugged. "Stealing isn't how the Genesis Group works."

"Lovely sculptures you have in your garden," Mike said. "All acquired through digs you've sponsored, yes?"

Cassandra looked ready to slap her. *Oh yes, sister, come on, try it.*

Instead, Cassandra stood. "I'm afraid I am terribly behind schedule, and as you can tell, there's a problem with our electricity, so I must attend to it before my next appointment. I hope your concerns have been answered. Ajax, could you see our guests out?"

"Of course."

Nicholas said, "I fear we will need affidavits from you."

Mike said quickly, "However, we cannot do it now, we will need to hire a stenographer. Would tomorrow morning suit you?"

"Let me check my schedule." Cassandra pulled out her cell phone. It had to be dead, no way it had survived Nicholas's micro EMP. Mike caught Nicholas's eye, made a small gesture toward the door. He finally stood.

Cassandra frowned. "Ajax, may I have your phone, please? My battery seems to have died."

Ajax pulled his from his pocket.

"Strange. My battery is dead, too."

Cassandra looked at Nicholas. "I don't suppose your cell phone is working, Agent Drummond?"

He pulled it out of his pocket. "Yes. Not sure what your problem is. Perhaps the Italian mobile service has gone down."

"Perhaps. Well then," she said. "Seeing as I have twice as much work to do, I would ask that you call before you arrive in the morning."

As they walked to their car, Mike said, "Nicholas, sorry to rush you out of there, but Kitsune was captured. I saw a man carrying her over his shoulder down in the tunnels. I don't know if her husband is down there, but it looked like a bunch of storage rooms, perfect for hiding people. Or bodies."

"Now we have to rescue her and Grant."

"And we need to plan it better. I'm very glad we got out of there alive, it was close there for a moment. I saw blood on Ajax's shirt cuff, and I'm willing to bet he didn't cut himself shaving. You don't think —"

"That Lilith is the sacrificial goat? That she's dead? Wouldn't surprise me."

"I just hope they don't hurt Kitsune before we can get to her."

Why was nothing ever easy? Nicholas wondered. But as Mike said, at least they were still alive.

CHAPTER FORTY-ONE

Eyes followed them all the way to their car. Nicholas got inside before calling Adam in Venice.

"You hear all that?"

"Yes, I did. They were fast, Nicholas, throwing the blame immediately on Lilith."

"Adam, let's treat her as a missing person. Look for a cell phone, credit card usage, the works. Maybe you'll find her. Maybe she's still alive."

"Or not," Mike said.

"Will do."

"Adam, what else have you discovered?" Nicholas asked.

"Gray is running a complete forensics analysis of the Kohaths' investment port-folios. He'll have a report ready shortly." He yawned, mumbled, "Sorry."

"You need sleep, Adam," Mike said. "Or a Snickers bar."

"No, I don't. We've been having heaping

plates of carbonara — you know Louisa never stops eating — and expensive bottles of wine and charging it to your suite. Well, okay, one thing I did see that was interesting, the Genesis Group owns an insurance index. You have any relatives at Lloyd's of London?"

"Sorry, no relatives, but my dad knows one of the directors. What about them?"

"Well, in addition to providing insurance for large-cap stock companies, I discovered the Kohaths are using the markets to trade on other insurance companies. Lloyd's is one of them. It's very risky, very speculative stuff, since you never know when a disaster is going to hit and an insurance company is going to go out of business and take your whole investment down with you. Right now, they are making a lot of money on it."

"Is it illegal?"

"No. Not at all, if you're playing it straight and assuming the risks. I've not seen anything so far that isn't completely aboveboard, but that doesn't mean anything. The best Wall Street thieves know how to hide their tracks. Like I said, it's going to take more than a couple of hours to dig through everything we pulled."

"Mike and I are going in the tunnels beneath the palazzo to rescue Kitsune and

Grant. We're not notifying the local cops. The Kohaths could have some control there, and no calling the Carabinieri, either, for the same reason."

Adam said, "One more issue, Nicholas. It might not happen, but if you're taken, what do we do?"

An excellent question, but he said aloud, "We won't be. Turn on Kitsune's tracker, it will help us locate her quickly."

"I see," Adam said. "So you and Mike will pop in, grab her, locate Grant, and pop back out."

"That's right. On with the tracker, Adam, and thank you. Keep plugged in, all right?"

Mike said when he'd punched off, "You know they've very likely doubled their guard count?"

He grinned down at her. "Entirely possible, but I have a plan." And he dialed up Adam again.

"Adam, one more thing. Agent Caine rightfully pointed out they've probably beefed up security, so get together with the folks at Aviano and have them retask whatever satellite is closest. I want you watching every move they make."

"And how do I convince them to do that?"

"Simply tell them the American FBI is in trouble, remind them about the shootout in

Venice, and they'll move fast, you can count on it."

"All right, I'm on it. I'll be watching. Be careful. And find Kitsune."

Nicholas punched off the cell, arched his brow at Mike. "I find myself wondering if Adam cares more about Kitsune than us."

Mike said, "Yes, of course he does. She told him if she weren't married, she'd marry him. Now, we need to get moving." She pointed to the palazzo. He looked up and saw a flash of curly blond hair in the second-floor window.

"Ajax."

"Yes. He's watching. Tell me you were able to plant the bug on one of them."

"Yes, indeed, I managed to bump into Cassandra, stuck a very tiny mic under her collar." He turned it on, listened. "Yes, it's already up and working fine. My, my, in addition to being barking mad, it appears Ms. Kohath is mightily pissed off."

CHAPTER FORTY-TWO

Nicholas said, "Let's take a walk, go over to that café, let the locals see how harmless we are, and we'll listen to our two psychopaths."

They sat down at a small table outside the café, ordered espresso from a suspicious waiter. Nicholas handed Mike an earwig, watched her discreetly place it. And they listened.

Cassandra: It's time to move the storm. It's time to get the FBI agents out of here, and this will do it. You know Drummond didn't buy for an instant Lilith was behind all of this. It was a good idea, but he looked like he wanted to laugh, didn't buy it for a minute.

Ajax: You're right. It's time to move. I'll kill the thief and her husband.

Cassandra: No, I'll do it. You handle the storm and our transport. You told me there was only so much you could do from here and that means we have to go to the island and face Grandfather down.

She paused, and Nicholas heard the vicious excitement in her voice.

Cassandra: We'll make the old fool move the storm to hit Washington. If he doesn't, we'll kill him and do it ourselves.

They heard a manic laugh.

Cassandra: It'll be fun. Imagine the destruction we will bring to D.C., their precious FBI headquarters, and the White House. They thought Beijing was hard hit? That was nothing compared to what we will do. We need to move fast. You know they'll be back, and probably before tomorrow morning.

Ajax: If they come, Harry and his men will kill them. They're not like those idiots in Venice.

Cassandra: I wish I could believe that, but I doubt it, because . . .

Nicholas said, "Sorry, Mike, no more,

they're out of range." He threw some euros on the table and they headed back toward the car.

They drove away, past the square and the palazzo, back down the mountain road.

Mike said, "Nicholas, she's going to kill Kitsune. We need to go in and get her."

"We will."

"I hope your plan is good. You heard them — they're going to position a storm to wipe out Washington, too." Mike felt equal parts fear and anger. "But first they're going to have to go to this 'island' where their grandfather is. Is he the mastermind? He's the one who controls the storms? Evidently so. He's turned against them?"

"Possibly. Whatever. Now they hate him and they're going to kill him."

"Nicholas, where are you going? Oh, I see, we're going into the palazzo the same way Kitsune did."

"We have her tracker. We'll find her. Now, it took less than half an hour for her to get into place before you heard the fight and saw her captured."

"Right. So all we have to do is get in there, grab her and Grant, and get out before they realize we're even there. We can do it."

He cupped her face in his hand, kissed her fast and hard. "You're my grand girl, you know that? Now we need to hide the car, it's too open here, and we don't want anyone coming down the mountain to see it."

While Nicholas drove, Mike pulled her vest and tactical gear from her go-bag, started getting into them. "You and Adam deserve a medal for the way the Faraday bag worked. We're going to have to remember that little trick. It's very convenient."

She watched him as he turned a hairpin corner. The last of the sun shined briefly on his face. He needed a shave. She laid her palm on his thigh, felt the muscles tighten. "You're pretty grand yourself. Wait, Nicholas, you just passed a small dirt road, looks like it leads into an olive grove. It might work for the car."

He backed up and turned onto a dirt path rather than a road. "Yes, perfect. Good eye." The car rumbled over the small track until he was sure they were in far enough not to be seen from the road. Unless, of course, someone was looking for them. He looked over his shoulder and nodded, satisfied.

The sun was setting as they climbed out. Nicholas put on his tactical gear and hit his comms.

"Adam, are you ready? You have eyes on us?"

"It takes more than five minutes to redirect a satellite," Adam said. "Hang on, we almost have it."

"Kitsune's in imminent danger. We have to go in now. Do it as fast as you can."

Adam's excited voice came across the comms. "We've got Kitsune's tracker live, I'm sending the coordinates to your phone. She hasn't moved since we turned it on. She's definitely still in there. You should be able to use the phone to locate her."

There was a moment's silence, then Adam said, "We'll be online in one minute, watching from the sky."

"Good. Shout when you're ready for us to move in."

They set off at a jog, through the brush of the olive grove, angling up the hill, back toward the tunnel.

CHAPTER FORTY-THREE

Cassandra left Ajax at the computer screen, talking to himself as he tried to figure out how to move the storm's trajectory. She went to Lilith's rooms and grabbed her laptop. She already had her cell phone. She'd get rid of them, then she and Ajax had a long flight ahead of them. They'd depose the old king. Her mother would approve, she would, Cassandra knew it to her soul. She knew Grandfather wouldn't be willing to do what was necessary. He was old; he was fearful. She and Ajax would right the ship.

After the storm had flattened Washington, D.C., she and Ajax would come back to Italy. They'd find the Ark. And then what? Then, they would own the world.

She was humming when she went to her room to pack. She buzzed Harry on her cell as she walked down the back stairs, through the storage area, to the basement. The lights were back on, thankfully.

Harry met her at the basement door. "This way," he said. She kicked off her stilettos and stepped into a pair of Wellies.

They went into a small tunnel off the main cavern. Only the workers' foreman, Giovanni, was waiting for her.

"She's in there." He pointed toward his office. "She's not going anywhere. You want me to put her with the other one again?"

"Not yet. I want to talk to her first."

"At last we have lights again, but the computers are not functional, *signorina.*"

"Yes, I know, and what are you doing about it?"

Giovanni shrugged. The witch was in a temper, something he was used to. Occasionally he wanted to break her neck, but not with Harry standing right there. "We have new routers and new computers being driven in from Perugia, but it will be another forty minutes or so before we can get them in place and online. We don't know what happened to them. It is like someone hooked them up to an electrical charge and they all shorted at once."

"I know what happened. Now leave me. I need to talk to the prisoner alone."

Harry and Giovanni left. Both knew she was going to kill the woman.

Kitsune was tied to a set of metal lockers in the corner of the office. Her face was bruised, her nose and jaw bloodied. Her eyes were shut.

Cassandra kicked her hip. "Stop faking, wake up."

The pain from the kick was nothing compared to the pain in Kitsune's head. She managed to stay silent.

"Come on, you bitch, open your eyes and talk to me, or I'll have your precious husband killed while you watch, then you, and we'll bury you along with Lilith. What a loss that one was."

Kitsune stared up at Cassandra Kohath. She'd seen photos of her, so beautiful, perfect, really, except for her eyes. Her eyes were as mad as a hatter's. "Those Wellies look pretty stupid against that Dior dress you're wearing."

Cassandra kicked her again.

Kitsune didn't make a sound.

"Now you will tell me what the FBI plans to do next. I mean Drummond and Caine, of course."

Kitsune studied her face. She said very precisely. "I'll be glad to tell you. They will come back very soon and blast your palazzo into small bits of stone and bury you beneath it."

Kitsune watched Cassandra's face as she spoke. She didn't see any fear, but she did see rage, and it was building. Would she kill her right now? She closed her eyes.

Cassandra came down on her knees beside her. "Drummond doesn't have proof of anything. Besides, soon it won't matter what he believes or what he knows and can prove. Won't matter at all." And she snapped her fingers. "All gone."

What did she mean, all gone? Kitsune opened her eyes again. Cassandra's face was close to hers. She whispered, "Be afraid, Cassandra, be very afraid. Drummond will snap your neck like a chicken's. Even if you and your mad twin run, he'll find you. And Agent Caine? That one never gives up, she'll keep coming and coming until she puts a bullet in your brain."

Cassandra slapped Kitsune. Another hit of pain, enough to make her eyes water. She wanted to kill this insane woman herself.

"Drummond and Caine? They left, defeated because they know they have nothing at all. They're like toothless hounds, all rules and regulations. Our friends in the Carabinieri will protect us."

"You mean like that incompetent idiot, Major Russo? I doubt he was in one of the cars he sent after us, but he was listening, wasn't he? Do you think he's coming to help you now? I doubt it, Cassandra. I'll bet he's already on a plane out of Italy."

"You have a cat's nine lives, don't you? But soon, you'll have none left." Cassandra rose, dusted off her skirt. "I suggest you tell me what they're planning now or I will have Harry and Giovanni drag your husband in here and let you watch them torture him."

Kitsune whispered, "I'll tell you, but not until you release Grant."

Cassandra sneered down at her. "You want to negotiate with me? You can't. Tell me or he's a dead man."

Kitsune closed her eyes, leaned her head back.

"Very well. Say goodbye to your precious husband." She opened the office door and started to walk away. "Kill the man," she said to Giovanni.

"Wait!"

Cassandra turned back, slowly, a brow raised, arms across her chest. She repeated, "Tell me what you know and I will spare his life."

Kitsune knew this woman would kill Grant with less thought than she'd give to her dinner, but she had to buy time. She knew Nicholas and Mike would come, if they could. "How can I believe you?"

Cassandra eyed her, said coolly, "I don't enjoy killing, but I've found it sometimes necessary. I am not a psychopath." She lurched back. Why had she said it aloud? Saying the word made something deep inside her hot and eager. No, no, not eager. She wasn't mad, she wasn't. She remembered Drummond had called her crazy, remembered how she'd wanted to rip his heart out.

She got hold of herself. "Tell you what, you talk to me, tell me what they're planning to do now, tell me what they know, and I'll let your husband go and call in my own private doctor to see to you."

Yeah, like that would ever happen. Kitsune looked directly into her eyes. "They are studying your private financials. They know about your broker, Rodgers, in Singapore, how he invests the money you make profiting from the storms you create. As for what they will do, I have no idea. How could I?"

Cassandra was shaking her head, she couldn't believe it. How could they know about Landry Rodgers? If she'd had any doubts about destroying Washington, she had none now. She heard herself ask, "Do they know about my mother?" Where had that come from? She didn't believe for an instant the FBI could find her mother.

"I know there's an FBI agent in London right now, reading all St. Germaine's notes from her second book on Appleton Kohath. Your great-great-whatever — the mastermind of all this, right?"

Cassandra kicked Kitsune in the ribs again. Kitsune held herself perfectly still, let the pain settle, accepting it, dealing with it. At least she hadn't broken a rib with that kick. The Wellies weren't hard enough.

Cassandra closed her eyes a moment, cursed. How had they found out about that bloody biographer? She shrugged. "It doesn't matter."

"Drummond and Caine think it does."

Cassandra tapped her fingers along the desk. "Do you know my idiot father gave that woman my great-great-grandfather's journal? When the original biography came, he read it, saw he wasn't in it, and so he went back to St. Germaine and gave her our private papers, the sick, vengeful bastard. He was so excited someone was going to write about *his* contributions, *his* achievements, but what he really wanted was cash and fame. He even called himself the Kohath heir.

"You want to talk about crazy? My worthless immoral father is certifiable. When we heard what he did —" She broke off, panting now, rage pouring through her. This time she banged her fist into one of the file cabinets. It had to hurt, but she didn't seem to notice. "I'm glad he's dead, and now Ajax and I won't ever have to worry about what he'll say, never have to see his face again, hear his whining voice. Who could blame us for kicking him out of Genesis? Who could blame us for taking care of him?"

Kitsune didn't move, watched Cassandra Kohath spin out of control. The woman was shaking now, pacing the small space, hitting her fist against her palm. "If only my mother hadn't trusted him, if only she hadn't given him access to the Kohath papers! And look at what he did! He betrayed our family, he betrayed my mother!"

Suddenly, Cassandra became perfectly still. She stared into the distance at something Kitsune couldn't see. A tear streaked down her cheek. Then she whispered, "If only my mother were here, I know she would have killed him herself." She was mumbling to herself now, pacing. "At least Lilith took care of that ridiculous biographer and my bastard of a father. But now it's up to me to get all those papers back. They're mine, do you hear me? They're mine."

She stopped talking, rubbed her hand over her forehead.

Kitsune took it all in. They'd had their own father murdered? And the biographer? And Lilith? At this moment, it didn't matter. Reality became a red pinpoint light for Kitsune. Cassandra was looking at her, death in her eyes, and Kitsune knew it was all over for her. Still, she had to try.

"So Lilith murdered both your father and the biographer?"

Cassandra smiled down at Kitsune. "You've learned a valuable lesson now, haven't you? No one crosses me or my brother."

Kitsune said nothing more, what was there to say?

She watched Cassandra's face change. She braced herself, mentally, said goodbye to Grant.

The idea came to Cassandra in a flash. So clear, so perfect, she now knew exactly what to do. Both she and Ajax knew their grandfather would die before he'd hand over the formula. But now they wouldn't have to torture him to get him to tell them the combination to his precious vault.

At her feet lay a master thief, that's what Lilith had called the Fox in a worshipful voice, and she'd sworn this pitiful woman was the best in the world. She remembered now Lilith had been devastated when they'd

341

told her the thief had to die, it was too dangerous to allow her to live, but Ajax had finally talked her around and she'd given the order to Pazzi. But the thief, this Fox, had proved her worth, her skill — she'd actually managed to steal the staff out of the Topkapi museum. So why couldn't the Fox open her grandfather's vault?

Kitsune could nearly taste Cassandra's sudden excitement. What was going on here? Cassandra leaned down and patted Kitsune's face, then, she jumped to her feet and nearly danced out of the small office. "Don't go anywhere," she sang out over her shoulder. And without another word, she was gone. She heard Cassandra say to Giovanni, "We're leaving now. Bring her. Leave the man."

"Shall I kill him?"

"No, it's a waste of a good bullet. Leave him for the rats."

Kitsune closed her eyes. Why had the crazy woman kept her alive? What did she want? It didn't matter. All she cared about was Grant, and she knew he'd be okay, Nicholas and Mike would find him, free him.

It was Harry who came into the office, and in his hand was a syringe. She saw some marks on her face from her blows and a bandage on his arm where she'd gotten him with her Ka-Bar. Even though he'd beaten the crap out of her, in that moment she didn't care.

He came down on his knees beside her. "Don't move or it'll be worse." And he rammed the needle into her arm and pressed the plunger. She was unconscious in under three seconds.

She didn't hear Cassandra say, "On second thought, bring the man, too. We may need him for leverage."

CHAPTER FORTY-FOUR

Nicholas and Mike hiked in silence until the sun was down, the sky a faint pink. Mike turned and caught a glimpse of the lake below among the thick olive trees, the water now a deep purple. She heard crickets singing, saw a few bats swooping overhead.

"There," Mike said quietly, and touched Nicholas's shoulder lightly. "There's the entrance." A guard was standing in front of the orange tape. "Is that an L85 he's carrying?"

Nicholas pulled out a monocular. "Good eye, Mike, yes, it is. New model, too. Cassandra and Ajax are quick, aren't they? And he's another Brit, I'd wager — the L85 is the favored assault model for our Special Forces. They aren't messing around, not that I ever thought they would. But still, it's only one guard."

"Does he have night vision?"

"Maybe, though he doesn't have his goggles out right now or we would have a serious problem. Sloppy of him."

Mike readied her Glock. "You want me to take him, or will you?"

He stashed the monocular. "You don't have a suppresser and we don't want the noise. We don't want him to have a chance to get on his radio. Give me time to get around to the other side, then distract him, let him see you." He grabbed her arms. "Do not get shot, do you understand me? Just get in his line of vision, give him a glimpse, and I'll take him from behind."

"That goes for you, too."

Their steps were silent, cushioned by the new growth of buttercups edging the grove. Branches of flowering borage and the deepening darkness gave them cover. They moved to within twenty feet of the entrance, then Nicholas signaled for her to get ready and started tracking off to the east to circle around.

Mike had counted to twenty when Nicholas hit his comms, gave her a tap in the ear. She shook an olive branch beside her, darted away, quick as a rabbit, twenty feet to another small grove.

The guard immediately went on alert, walked ten steps from the tunnel entrance toward her. He didn't call out or get on his radio because it was dark and he knew there was a good chance he'd heard an animal prowling around. But his finger was on the trigger guard.

Mike moved again, drawing the guard's attention to the right, Nicholas came silently around the edge of the tunnel entrance and hit the guard on the head with a rock. He went down without a sound and lay unmoving on his side, the rock, smeared with blood, beside him.

"Is he dead?"

"Nah." Nicholas pulled rope from his backpack, tied the guard's hands and feet, gagged him. Then he dragged him into the grove, covered him with branches of borage.

Without another word, they entered the tunnel. The lights from their flashlights barely cut through the darkness. Mike shivered.

Nicholas whispered, "I see the light fixtures, but the lights aren't on and why not? The power came back on over an hour ago. Maybe they don't use the lights unless needed."

"I'm going to vote for unused. Nicholas, look. You can see two sets of footprints in the dust — one small going in, one large heading out. Kitsune and the guard are the only people who've been in this tunnel recently."

She touched his sleeve. "This worries me. Why would the Kohaths allow such easy access to their house? They're so security-conscious, it seems odd they'd leave a perfect tunnel in place for someone to waltz through the back door. And only one guard."

"Think back, Mike, isn't this how the Knights Templar would have gotten out when there was trouble? Don't forget, not many people have access to the detailed plans Adam was able to find, plus it is private property. Watch your step there, we're heading uphill."

He grabbed her by the waist and swung her over a stake in the ground. He stopped and aimed his light on it. It was a piece of branch, sharpened to a point. "Kitsune's trail of bread crumbs?"

Mike knelt down, examined the branch. "I'm thinking it's a weapon she made if she had to get out quickly and needed something fast." She stood, wiped her hands on her pants. "Whatever, she didn't have a chance to use it. They got her farther up the tunnel."

"Kitsune is very skilled, very dangerous.

Do you think she allowed herself to get taken?"

Mike shook her head. "I honestly think she wanted to get in, rescue her husband, and get out as quietly as possible. From the noises I heard, someone bigger and faster surprised her and beat her. She was unconscious when I saw the guard walk by with her thrown over his shoulder, and I doubt she allowed that to happen. I only got a glimpse of him, but I think it was Harry. Oh, now what? This is all we need — the tunnel splits ahead."

They pulled up short. Nicholas ran his Maglite over four different tunnel branches. "From the plans, we know to go north. That way." He pointed to the center tunnel.

"What are they doing down here? This looks modern and we know the Etruscan excavations ended years ago."

"Ben sent me a theory from St. Germaine's first book on Appleton Kohath. One of the Ark legends has the Templars guarding the Ark for the Church. In the pages he sent, he pointed out the nearby church, San Bevignate, that temporarily housed the Templars on the orders of Pope Gregory. Maybe they stashed their treasure here instead of burying it under the church, thinking it safer to have it farther away. And the Kohaths came across that information."

Nicholas said, "So Pope Gregory somehow got his hands on the Ark and gave it over to the Knights Templar to protect? Well, this is a seriously out-of-the-way place, but maybe that would be the pope's reasoning. Safer in an unknown location than where his knights were housed."

"It's possible. And the Kohaths, knowing this, have been searching for the Ark here ever since. Explains why they bought the place, and modernized the tunnel reinforcements."

"Makes a sick kind of sense." Nicholas stopped, shined his Maglite on two more branching tunnels. "Okay, these weren't on the plans. Which tunnel do you choose?"

"Whenever we have a choice, we have to continue inward and that means north."

They moved deeper into the tunnel and into the mountain. A few minutes later, Nicholas put up his hand. "Do you hear that?"

Loud voices arguing, coming toward them.

They ran back to the tunnel junction and into another passageway. The voices grew closer, then faded away as the two arguing men disappeared down another tunnel.

They started off again into the north tunnel. Mike smelled dirt and damp, and blood, a copper smell like none other. She stopped, leaned into him, and whispered, "Do you smell something off here?"

Nicholas stopped. "I do." He shined his Maglite around. "Mike, there's a body here, poorly buried."

He knelt down, began brushing away loose mounds of dirt.

"A woman," he said.

Oh no, oh no. "Kitsune?"

"I don't know yet." Nicholas kept brushing away the dirt from the face.

A light and shadow suddenly appeared, and a man's voice shouted, "Hey! What are you doing?"

Mike flashed her Maglite toward the voice, effectively blinding the man. She caught a brief glimpse of him — large, muscled, buzz-cut hair, shouting at them in a British accent — it was Harry.

He moved fast. Mike's gun was in her hand, Nicholas by her side, his Glock up as well, shouting, "Back off, mate. You don't want to tangle with us."

"Drummond, you bastard — you took down Joey, tied him up and left him outside to rot? I've been tracking you. Ms. Kohath thought you two were long gone, but I didn't. I've worked with your sort, knew

350

you'd come back. I've been tracking you and now you're going to die down here. No one will ever know what happened to you two."

He had guns in both hands, but Nicholas was faster, he brought up his arm and fired, all in one smooth motion and shot Harry twice in the chest. Mike, a millisecond behind him, shot him in the forehead. The shots reverberated through the tunnel, echoing loudly. Harry looked at them, shock on his face, and then he fell, a gun landing on each side of him.

Mike grabbed Nicholas's arm. "Everyone down here is going to be on us in a few seconds." She looked toward the shallow grave. "Is it Kitsune?"

"It's not Kitsune. It's Lilith. Come on."

They started off in a slight crouch, their Glocks at the ready, Nicholas's Maglite lighting the way.

"I'm praying that Kitsune and Grant are together, and they're still alive."

Nicholas was praying the same thing.

They hurried deeper and deeper, until Mike grabbed Nicholas's wrist, whispered in his ear. "There are lights up ahead."

They turned a corner onto a large fully lighted cavern. It was a full-fledged underground operation. Nicholas saw a row of

351

ten or so motorbikes by the doors, steel storage units, an array of tools. Half a dozen men were working. No one seemed to have heard the gunshots.

"I think they're pulling up stakes," Mike whispered. "Nicholas, look over there."

They watched Kitsune being dragged from a small tunnel offshoot by a small man with gray hair, and ahead of them was Cassandra Kohath, calling out orders. "Be ready to leave within the hour. And don't forget the man."

They were alive. Mike said, "They're going to run for it. Can we take them down from here, do you think? Before they miss Harry and the guard at the tunnel entrance?"

He nodded and pointed his Glock toward the cavern. "On my mark. Three, two —"

But Mike yanked him back against the tunnel wall, out of sight. "No, no, someone's coming."

They heard shouts, in Italian and English, accompanied by running steps. Too many, too many. She leaned up. "Either they found Harry or they saw us. We can't get to Kitsune and Grant now. I hate this, but there are too many of them. We have to go back the way we came, and fast."

They scrambled back down the tunnel,

past Lilith's body, into the darkness.

They heard shouts behind them.

"Can you understand what they're shouting?"

"They're on radios, calling for reinforcements."

"Let's duck in here." They ran into a side tunnel, this one smaller, darker than a tomb.

Nicholas grabbed her arm. "Wait, stop. Do you hear that?"

"I thought I heard an engine. Like a motorbike." They listened for a moment, but Mike could hear nothing but voices.

"I saw motorbikes in the central cavern. Now I hear them, they're calling for someone to cut us off, to drive us back. Nicholas, this tunnel goes somewhere, it doesn't dead-end. Come on."

They ran into the offshoot tunnel. Without warning, a high-pitched motor revved, close to them, and they were blinded by the single headlamp.

A man started yelling, "They're here, I've found them."

And the motorbike raced toward them.

CHAPTER FORTY-FIVE

"Mike, this way." They turned and ran back toward the main junction, the motorbike right behind them, the engine whine echoing off the walls.

"More engines, more bikes. Run or make a stand?"

He flashed her a grin. "Sorry, sweetheart, but we're definitely outnumbered. We'll circle back around and surprise them on the other side of the cavern."

"Where do we go?"

"Follow me." He sprinted away and she was after him, running hard. Shouts, yells, in Italian and English, loud, closer than they'd like. A bullet whizzed past Mike's head, slamming in the dirt wall.

Nicholas pulled up and threw himself in front of her, pushing her up against the dirt wall, protecting her as he started shooting toward the man on the motorbike. He shot three times and the bike's headlight spun crazily, then the bike slid onto its side, the engine whining, grabbing dirt into the exhaust.

"Hurry."

He grabbed Mike's hand again, and together they ran toward the bike, the rider dead three feet beyond it. Nicholas righted the bike and threw a leg over. "Climb aboard." He sent her a manic grin. "Sorry, no helmets."

She swallowed a laugh and pressed against his back. "I hope Russo doesn't show up to give us tickets. Go, Nicholas!"

Nicholas whipped the bike around and headed back into the smaller offshoot tunnel. The engine revved hard once, twice, nearly bucking them off the bike. Then it caught and they were moving into the darkness fast, only the headlight showing them the way. Mike's pulse pounded, her heart leaped. She held on tight, the air whipping her hair, and she yelled, "Go, go, go!"

Nicholas grinned, couldn't help it.

The smaller tunnel had offshoots, several paths in and out. Mike had no idea which direction they were headed now. Over the noise of the engine she could hear another bike coming fast behind them.

"Company," she shouted, as a second man on a bike tailed the first, both of them shouting and waving guns.

Mike shot one, Nicholas twisted around, shot the other. Mike's target dropped, his bike skidding into the tunnel wall, but Nicholas's kept coming. He wasn't shooting now, he was crouched low, speeding up. He was going to run them down. The instant before the bike hit them, Nicholas turned their bike down another tunnel. Mike nearly fell off, but managed to grab his arm. He pulled her back on. She held on to his jacket with one hand and started shooting behind her with the other.

"There's more, they're coming."

The tunnels were full of the echoes of bikes and gunshots and shouts. Two more bikes appeared behind them, their riders low to the handlebars, guns raised. Mike caught one in the hand, saw his gun go flying. He tried to keep coming one-handed, but he couldn't control the bike and finally dropped it on its side and started running after them. The other ducked off another tunnel and disappeared.

"They're going to cut us off, Nicholas."

"Hold on, let's have some fun."

He slowed, planted his foot in the dirt, whirled the bike around and roared toward the oncoming bike. Mike shot the guard center mass.

More shouts now. Another bike came up from around the curve behind them. Nicholas started again down into the darkness. "They're bloody hydras, every time we take one out three more pop up."

Mike was twisting around in the seat, trying to look behind them and not fall off. "There's three more behind us. They're gaining. I need to reload. Can you circle back around?"

A fourth bike appeared ahead of them, speeding toward them.

"Down there, down there," Mike shouted, and Nicholas took a hard left, so sharply they both hit the wall with their right shoulders before he could plant a foot and straighten the bike out. He gunned it and they flew down the tunnel into the darkness.

This tunnel was very old. It had a deep rut down the middle that wasn't dirt, it was ancient stone. Etruscans had walked down this path.

The bikes behind them were gaining, and Mike could have sworn she heard one of the men laughing. And then she saw why. There was a wall ahead. A solid wooden wall. They were finally trapped.

Nicholas shouted, "Hold on, Mike, hang on tight! Keep your arms around my waist."

Nicholas was shooting at the wall, emptying his entire magazine. She held on for dear life, felt the heat of the bullets from the men behind them pass close to her head. Her heart caught in her throat as Nicholas revved the engine and drove directly toward the wall. His bullets had splintered the ancient wood.

Nicholas slammed the bike into the wall, and through it.

She felt a cold rush of air, they were flying through the dark sky, but they were falling, falling fast, and Nicholas was shouting, "Jump! Jump!" in her ear. She saw a shimmer of water in the moonlight, then she was twisting in the air. She had a moment of clarity, realized they'd burst out of the side of the mountain over the lake, then something hard smacked her head. She saw stars, felt wetness, a sickening dizziness, and then she hit the water, hard. She didn't feel anything more.

CHAPTER FORTY-SIX

Nicholas took a huge breath in before he hit the water. He went deeper than he'd expected, the momentum of the dive off the cliff driving him farther down. He thought his lungs were going to burst before his face finally broke the surface.

He dragged in as much oxygen as he could, treading water. The water was cold, dark. Where was Mike? She was an ace swimmer. "Mike?"

No answer. He shouted her name again, once, twice. "Where are you? Answer me!"

Silence.

"Mike!"

He started to swim, looking for her, but there was nothing around him. The bike was gone, sunk to the bottom. He grabbed the Maglite from his pocket — he couldn't believe it hadn't fallen out — and shined it over the water, looking for her.

Nothing. No blond ponytail, nothing. She

was still under.

He dove, blindly, searching for her, coming up for breath only when he thought he might die if he didn't. One minute passed. Two. Three. He was getting frantic, she was nowhere to be found.

Four minutes now.

Adrenaline pumped hard and fast, kept him together, kept him moving. Impossible to imagine Mike dead, drowned, and all because of him. He dove again and again, and he knew he was crying but it didn't matter, all that mattered was finding her.

Finally, his hand brushed up against something that felt like hair. He closed his fist tight and started to rise, heaving with relief when her weight nearly dragged him down.

He got her to the surface and supported her so she floated on her back. She wasn't breathing. Her face was covered in blood from a nasty wound in her scalp. Her skin was pale gray in the moonlight, her lips blue.

He swam to the closest bit of land, counting the seconds, taking the breaths she couldn't.

It had been five minutes since they burst out of the mountain and off the cliff into the lake before he got her on dry land.

Nicholas started chest compressions,

counted to thirty, checked for a pulse, got nothing. Her legs lay still and relaxed in the water, her hands palm up. He started again. At thirty, he checked once more. Nothing. He tilted her head back, pinched her nose and gave her two deep breaths. He felt her chest rise, willed it to do so again, but there was nothing.

He kept going, silently yelling at her to live, to breathe, cringing when he felt a rib give under the pressure of his hands. He drew her up and began pounding on her back, then shoved her back down and pushed again against her breastbone, again and again and again. He tilted her head back and breathed for her. On and on it went. Panic, fear, the impossible began creeping in, but he didn't give up. He knew it had been too long, she'd been under too long, and then he felt it.

A deep shiver moved through her, and she started to cough, spitting up water. He jerked her upright again and pounded her back. Water poured from her mouth, and she was heaving with the effort.

He pulled her onto her side, wrapped his arms around her while she spit up more lake water. Finally she stopped heaving out water and began shuddering. He felt her pulse — slow and faint, but there. He closed his eyes a moment, giving thanks, holding her tightly against him. She was alive.

She wasn't conscious, but she was breathing, though it was shallow. He needed to warm her up, the water had been very cold. What he knew about hypothermia gave him hope — cold water preserved brain function.

Nicholas pulled his jacket off and wrapped it tightly around her. He checked her eyes with his Maglite, swore he could see the pupils change, though one seemed bigger than the other. She had a concussion. Probably from the nasty cut on her head. And how had she gotten that? She'd struck something when she hit the water, a branch maybe.

He gathered her to his chest and rocked her. He kissed her cold mouth, her forehead, her wet hair, said into her mouth, "Mike, you're going to be all right, no thanks to me. Come on, do you want me to stroke out? Open your beautiful eyes and look at me. You're warming up, sweetheart, that's it."

Even after this night passed, Nicholas knew he would always believe this a miracle. He heard a young man's voice — an angel's — calling from the top of the bank in musical Italian, "Are you okay, do you need help?"

Nicholas called back in Italian, "We need a doctor and an ambulance. Now!"

Time passed, then shouts, calls, and people swarmed over the bank. He was suddenly surrounded by Italians, all barking instructions. He heard the sirens start immediately, and then the ambulance was there, the two EMTs racing down the bank with their equipment. One started questioning him in Italian.

"What happened? Why in the world did you go swimming in this weather?"

"Not swimming. It was an accident. We drove off the mountain, into the lake. She hit her head. She was underwater for several minutes."

They already had Mike on a stretcher, wrapped in a silver blanket, and the other EMT had an IV line started and an oxygen mask in place. "She needs the hospital, immediately. It will be very close. You come with us. The *polizia* will want to speak with you about the accident."

So long as it wasn't more of the Kohaths' guards or Major Russo's thugs in the Carabinieri, he was fine with it.

Through the interminable ride, he held her hand, talked to her nonstop, and thankfully, finally, he felt her begin to warm.

■ ■ ■ ■

PART TWO

■ ■ ■ ■

Whence, then, does it come? Who
knows? Who can assign limits to the
subtlety of nature's influences?
— NIKOLA TESLA

CHAPTER FORTY-SEVEN

The Kohath Letters
Venice, Italy
September 18, 1901

Dear Nikola,
I have made a discovery that might change the course of history.

I was having dinner in a small café when I heard the cook telling his brother that there was a new shipment from the Orient for the *Collezionista* — the Collector.

You know me, I had to see what the man had, and so I went immediately to his shop, which, at first glance, was a jumbled mess. His name is Melzi. He's ancient, at lease ninety-eight years old, but thankfully, with all his faculties intact.

He had no idea what most of the pieces were in his rooms. Most was rubbish, but I spotted a few terra-cotta statues that might have Etruscan roots.

I found the folio while searching through a stack of old dispatches from the Franco-Austrian War. A thick parchment, very old, and on the cover was a large, hand-drawn lightning bolt. Then I saw small black stains along the top edge — I'm certain it is a blood froth. I undid the twine and very nearly passed out from excitement. You will never imagine what I was holding.

Drawings, from the great man himself, Leonardo da Vinci. I asked Melzi where he got them, and he said they were in a trunk of family papers. Then of course I remembered why the name Melzi was familiar to me. It seems he had an ancestor who was a painter, and lived for a time with Da Vinci. The Melzi from that period, as I knew, was Francesco Melzi, and not only was he a painter himself, he was Da Vinci's lover and was with him when he was dying. I assume he was archiving Da Vinci's work.

Melzi took the folio probably because he could not stand having nothing left but memories of his master. I would have done the same had I been in his shoes. After Da Vinci's death, Melzi returned home to Italy and evidently hid them with his most precious things. No one in the Melzi family are scientists, and the papers had been stored in the family trunks for centuries. So I knew this was no forgery, for Melzi was a direct descendant.

There was a warning that came with the papers — and this teases the mind — *the power that could be derived is incalculable.* And what exactly does that mean?

What I've seen so far is mind-boggling. Not only have I discovered a lost trove of Da Vinci drawings, there is more, as you will see in the enclosed Da Vinci papers. You will know what to do with this incredible invention. Do you feel my excitement? Does your amazing brain already envision possibilities?

Appleton

CHAPTER FORTY-EIGHT

London, England
Present Day

After his mad scramble to JFK to make the British Airways flight from New York to London, Agent Ben Houston was happy to arrive the following morning at the beautiful home of the late Elizabeth St. Germaine. The house was on Westbury Road in Ealing, West London. It was a lovely old red brick, with a balcony over the front door and a turret to the left. It was as British as Ben could have imagined.

He was let into the house by a soft-spoken woman named Annalise and shown into a bright, sunny conservatory and brought a cup of tea. Ben knew this was urgent, and he asked when Ms. St. Germaine was coming. Annalise said, with a smile, "The earth is not falling off its axis, I hope. Agent Houston, I assure you, Madam is coming. Drink your tea." Then she disappeared. To keep himself from pacing the beautiful Tabriz, Ben checked his email — nothing new from Nicholas or Gray or any of the rest of the team. He was about to call Nicholas when Melinda St. Germaine came in.

Ben stood immediately, without thinking, and held out his credentials.

She smiled at him, and he found himself smiling back. "That won't be necessary. I believe you're the only American law enforcement gentleman I'm expecting today. So sorry to keep you waiting, traffic was beastly. Why Mother wanted to live so far away from central London I have no idea."

Melinda St. Germaine was small, compact, with an athletic body and an angel's face, a pointed chin and clear gray eyes. Black heels put her only at his chin. She was a redhead, just like him, her hair in a high ponytail. He appreciated her well-fitted black suit. Probably made for her.

"It's fine, really, I've only been here for a few minutes. I'm Ben, Ben Houston, Agent Houston, I mean. FBI." He shut his mouth, he was being a git, as Nicholas would say.

She nodded. "Yes, I imagine you're jet-lagged. I know I always want to fall over when I fly home from the States. You told me you wanted to look at my mother's papers. Annalise told me you looked like you were going to jump out of your skin, so I suppose you're in an all-fire rush to get into my mother's shed, aren't you?" As she spoke, she fixed herself a cup of tea, two sugars and milk, and watched him, holding the saucer in one hand and the cup in the other. She took a sip and set the cup in the saucer with a gentle clink.

"Annalise is right," Ben said. "We're on a case that's breaking quickly and we think there may be some answers in your mother's files. I'm so sorry for your loss. I was told your mother died of a heart attack?"

Melinda buried her nose in her cup. "Yes, two weeks ago. I still can't believe it. I thought, we all thought, her doctor included, that she was in wonderful shape, she'd been steeple-chasing the day before she died. But the postmortem showed cardiac arrest. At her age, I suppose it's common enough."

Her eyes filled with tears. "She died alone. Out in the shed. I suppose it's how she'd want to go, surrounded by her books and papers."

"I'm truly sorry."

She brushed away the tears. "Yes, well. Since we all thought she was in good health and she was alone when she died, and I'm in bloody Parliament, the coroner opened an inquest, did an autopsy and ran a toxicology screen. They're still waiting on the toxicology results, but he's ruled the preliminary cause of her death was, as I said, cardiac arrest.

"The police took a number of her things for testing. It's all been very disturbing. But the biggest thing, I'm afraid I'm not all accustomed to the idea I'll never see her again."

Ben said, "I lost my dad last year, and I don't know that I'll ever get over it."

"So you understand. You keep waiting for them to come into the room, or the phone to ring, and realizing it won't happen — well, it's heartbreaking, isn't it?"

Ben nodded. "I still pick up the phone to call him. Maybe we aren't supposed to get over it. Maybe we're supposed to remember them always and appreciate what we had."

She was quiet for a moment, then. "Just so. If you're finished your tea, follow me. Mother's shed is a bit of a train wreck, I haven't had the heart to go in there. The lawyers have been squawking at me, so you will find everything as she left it."

"Her estate is still being worked out?"

"Oh, you don't know?" Melinda stopped in a long hallway and took a left, out double glass French doors into the gardens. "I thought you called because of the lawsuit."

"What lawsuit?"

"The Kohaths are suing my mother — now my mother's estate — for defamation and theft. David Maynes, the father of the deadly duo, as I call them — Cassandra and Ajax Kohath — approached my mother after the original biography released, with 'new information' as he called it. Mr. Maynes happily cooperated with my mother to draft a second volume. She'd always been fascinated with Appleton Kohath — not only was he a great archaeologist, he was also a scientist, spent time with all the brightest minds of the day. This was around the turn of the last century. He was the one who created the Genesis Group.

"David Maynes showed up with note-books and letters he claimed were from the family archive. Mother read them and was keen to write a new book, a sort of companion to the first biography of Kohath. One of the new things she'd discovered was Appleton Kohath and Nikola Tesla were great friends and worked together on several major projects before having a falling-out. Mother was interested in what drove the two apart and what their major projects were. The publisher was thrilled with the idea — the original book did very well indeed, and they thought another volume, adding in the Tesla connection and their projects, would make for more in-depth treatment, a second bite at the apple."

While she talked, Ben hanging on every word, they'd crossed a lovely English garden, brimming with early spring flowers, white and purple and yellow, and were now hiking up a small rise toward a stone cottage.

He paused a moment, looking around. "Fabulous gardens."

"Yes, they are, aren't they? I used to hide under that stone bench over there and Mother would pretend she couldn't see me, would wander the garden calling my name." Her voice was thick with tears, and Ben reached out and squeezed her shoulder. A few moments later, she gathered herself. "Ah, here we are."

Ben supposed he'd been expecting what she'd said — a shed. But not this. The "shed" was a charming white cottage with black shutters and a stone fireplace.

"It's practically falling down around our ears. I think it was originally used to store grain or something. Mother took it over, added a fireplace, and made it her office. She couldn't work in the house, said it was too distracting. She liked having a completely private space of her own."

Ben was amused, seeing as the St. Germaines' house was nearly as big as his apartment building in New York, and the "shed" was large enough to comfortably shelter a family of four. Nicholas's friends and their British money was something he was going to have to get used to.

Melinda took a deep breath and pushed open the wooden door.

The inside of the cottage was simple. A tiny efficiency kitchen with tea service in one corner, floor-to-ceiling bookshelves all around, holding both books and small treasures, a few pieces of art, a fireplace, and a beautiful white wood desk the size of a door in the middle of the room, perfectly situated to see both the fire and the gardens outside the windows. There was a table behind the desk made from the same wood, and on this, stacked three-feet-deep, were books and notebooks and papers of all shapes and colors and sizes. It was a huge amount of material, but it was in clearly delineated piles.

A small staircase wound up to a second level. "The loft," Melinda said, "in case she needed a lie-down while she was working, or was up late and didn't want to disturb my father coming back to the house."

"It's a nice space."

Melinda said, "She loved it. And don't let the piles scare you. She was a horizontal filer. It might look a right mess, but she knew where every piece of paper was in those stacks. They are organized by subject, person, and date. You shouldn't have any trouble finding your way through to whatever you need. You're welcome to muck about through everything. What the Kohaths don't know won't hurt them. I hope you find what you're looking for."

"So the Kohath family sued over the book?"

"No, they're up in arms because they're claiming their father was coerced into giving my mother the Kohath materials. They've demanded to read all Mother's notes, her draft, and insist all the source materials be returned. They are trying to discredit her, to prove her dishonesty, and they have good lawyers who have tried everything to shut the whole book down.

"They've cited family privacy, but they're off their rockers. David Maynes was the one who approached my mother. He was the one who sat down and gave interviews and turned over the notebooks and letters. According to our lawyers, he was completely within his rights to do so. However, the deadly duo forced an injunction, delayed the release, bad-mouthed Mother in the press, said she was a hack who conned their father, who, they insisted, was not mentally well.

"I wanted to tell them to bugger off — as if my mother would do anything not completely aboveboard."

"So what happens to the book now?"

"The million-dollar question." Melinda toyed with the ends of her ponytail. "Technically, it's still tied up in the courts. The publisher wants to go ahead with it, the family wants it pulled. We've only just buried her, and as I said, I haven't been ready to tackle the business. The publisher has been very kind, understands I need some time to sort things out." She waved her hand around her. "I simply haven't had the heart to get started."

"I understand," Ben said. "Absolutely."

She gave him a smile. "You are very kind. Now, let me warn you. I wouldn't do this for anyone but Nicholas, so I'm trusting you to keep it to yourself if at all possible. Despite what we've told the lawyers and the publisher, Mother was very close to finishing the draft. The manuscript will be in there, most likely in the top drawer of her desk, where she keeps a running version.

You can't take it with you, I'm not willing to defy the lawyers that much. But if you want to read it, I'm fine with that."

"I promise, this is all between us. I'm simply looking for information that will help us solve this case. I'm not looking to exploit your mother or get you in trouble."

She hesitated a moment, a small smile on her lips, watching him. Finally, she said, "Cheers," and turned to the door. "Duty calls, as always. Since I've left my duties and come out to the godforsaken countryside, we're throwing a small dinner party tonight, a few friends I haven't had a chance to see for a while. I'd love for you to join us, if you can."

Ben had the idea that Melinda's idea of a small dinner party was going to be slightly different than his.

"I appreciate the offer. We'll see how I'm doing out here."

Melinda grinned, and the smile took her from serious to ethereal fairy in a heartbeat. "I'm sure you're about to either find everything you need or drive yourself batty. I'll send Annalise with more tea, and a sandwich for lunch. Good luck."

"Thank you."

When the door closed, Ben could have sworn some of the light went from the room. He pulled out his notebook and approached the table behind the desk. He'd read large portions of Appleton Kohath's initial biography on the plane, so he was familiar with the background of the Kohaths, at least. He hoped he'd know what was unique when he saw it.

Since he couldn't take anything with him, he pulled out his phone and opened the camera. He documented everything he could see. With a sigh, he sat down and waded in. He opened the drawer, and the manuscript was there, as promised.

He pulled it out and placed it on the table in front of him, started to read, and his jaw dropped.

CHAPTER FORTY-NINE

INTRODUCTION TO THE SECOND VOLUME ON APPLETON KOHATH (DRAFT ONE)

It isn't rare for a historian to revisit a biography, but there are times when it becomes clear that not all of a story has been told, and I am the first to admit the Kohaths are a family who don't easily let go of the imagination. I was recently approached by a member of the family who wanted to tell me a story. His name is David Maynes. He is a professor of antiquities, a man about town in London, and husband to the famed archaeologist Helen Kohath, who was lost on a dig in the Gobi Desert in 2006. Helen is one of a long line of Kohaths who dedicated their lives to searching for the ultimate treasure: the Ark of the Covenant.

David Maynes came bearing letters, notebooks, an entire cache of Kohath family lore that quickly showed this biographer she had barely scratched the surface of this amazing and obsessive family.

In my first volume on Appleton Kohath, I was fascinated by his dedication to finding the Ark. His dogged, unrelenting obsession imbued his entire family with the desire, more madness, really, for this ongoing quest. And quest it is.

Legends and prophecies abound about when the Ark was last seen, but there is no actual documentation. That has only enhanced its historical fascination, primarily because of its promised power. What I have learned is that the Kohaths believe they alone are destined to find the Ark and control its power.

It is a mad obsession, though one can hardly blame them. Imagine, ultimate power over the world. And more? How far does the power of God reach?

My first biography was solely about Appleton Kohath. With the advent of the letters, notebooks, journals, and other paraphernalia now in my possession, I am able to build a fuller picture of the entire Kohath family, from Appleton to the current day. Five generations of Kohaths, all with a singular focus.

Finding the Ark of the Covenant.

And I now know the secret behind the Kohath family's search.

It began in Egypt and has spanned the globe. As a hint of what's to come, allow me to pique your interest here.

For a decade, young Appleton Kohath was fully convinced the Ark resided in the Valley of the Kings. His contemporary, Howard Carter, so focused on the ancient Egyptians, dismissed Kohath's ideas that the Ark would be discovered inside King Tut's tomb, and the idea that the curse of the pharaoh was actually the curse of the Ark itself. Kohath hung on to the belief despite his friend's disbelief.

I have written before about Kohath's sudden change of focus in the early 1900s. In the previous manuscript, I was not privy to the incident that altered his belief about the whereabouts of the Ark. I now know why Kohath suddenly broke from Carter and began seeking the company of another young genius, Nikola Tesla.

By the time Kohath and Tesla became good friends, Tesla was out of favor with New York society and the scientific community. Why? Because Thomas Edison's people did everything they could to discredit the young genius. In the end, Tesla's funding dried up and he was left with almost nothing — no money, no recognition, and no way to continue his scientific discoveries.

Then Appleton Kohath appeared. The two men became inseparable for several years before they suddenly went their own ways, never to communicate again, the reasons still a mystery.

The project they were working on during those years involved the drawings of a machine — found in a dusty Italian junk shop — which Appleton Kohath believed came from Leonardo da Vinci himself. The diagrams and formulas allowed Kohath and Tesla to develop a machine that could control the weather.

Simply imagine: two excited, innovative geniuses, influenced by Da Vinci, determined to create weather. Did they indeed strip God of this power?

I hope you enjoy this fresh look into the mind of a genius, and the ways his obsession shaped future generations.

Elizabeth St. Germaine
London, 2016

CHAPTER FIFTY

Castiglione del Lago, Italy

Nicholas told them he was Mike's husband so he could keep close. It didn't matter, the emergency room doctors quickly wheeled her away, directing Nicholas to an empty waiting room, where he sat alone, replaying the past hour.

He dropped his head into his hands. He was tired, scared, his brain mush. But over and over he asked himself, how had it come to this? His fault, all of it, his fault; it was always the answer.

He knew he wasn't helping her, wasn't helping himself or anybody else. He got some coffee from a vending machine and reached for his mobile, realized, of course, it was at the bottom of Lake Trasimeno. His laptop and his comms and another mobile were in his car, halfway up the mountain.

He needed to call in, needed to get in touch with Adam and Louisa, but he wasn't about to move from the hospital until he saw Mike and knew she would be all right.

He paced the small room, playing back every move he and Mike had made in the tunnels. And Lilith's body, killed by one of the Kohath twins. The sheer barbarity of it, the utter disregard, made his blood cold.

At least Kitsune and Grant Thornton were still alive. But why hadn't Cassandra Kohath killed them?

His mind circled back, and none of it mattered. What if Mike died? What if she'd been in the water too long, what if —

A young doctor came into the room. She looked tired and grim. She held out a hand to shake, then gestured toward the chairs.

"Sit."

He did, and she sat beside him. "I am Dr. Teresa Sienza. I am a neurologist. Your wife is in serious but stable condition. How long was she underwater before you started CPR?"

"Four minutes, maybe closer to five minutes. I was trying to count off, but it was hard to keep track. Maybe she wasn't under quite that long. But she was definitely not breathing for several minutes."

Dr. Sienza patted his arm. "You'll be happy to know she was conscious when I spoke to her, so this is a very good sign. In these situations, we are always concerned about the impact on brain function. She has a cut on her head that is being sutured now. The cold water helped slow the progression of hypoxia, which was very lucky for us."

His heart wouldn't slow. "Tell me, swear to me, she's okay. She's going to be herself again?"

"Your wife has cardiac arrhythmia, and she is confused, though as I mentioned, she is awake. I believe the confusion is from the concussion, but it could be from the near-drowning. She will be here for a few days while she heals, but I think she will make a full recovery."

"A few days? We — I —" He dragged in a breath, and she patted his arm again.

"It is hard, sometimes, with near-drowning, for the diagnosis to be known right away. We must keep an eye on her to make sure there isn't a secondary event. Her lungs were full of water, so she could get pneumonia if they don't drain properly. She was lucky you were there and knew how to perform CPR. You saved her. Now, how did you get into Lake Trasimeno?"

"We drove off the cliff. It was an accident."

"Yes, of course it had to be an accident. You do not strike me as the suicidal type."

She smiled, then said, "You need some dry clothes and some warm food. I will send someone when your wife is moved to a room."

She stood, and Nicholas did, too. "Forgive me, Dr. Sienza. I will be honest with you. Mike is not my wife. She is my partner. We're American FBI. We're here on a case, and she is in danger. Especially now, when she's not able to defend herself. I need to be with her."

The young doctor stared up at him, her head cocked to the side. "You have proof of this?"

It took him a second to get the water-logged leather out of his jeans, but finally he was able to pull his credentials from his pocket and hand them over. "Special Agent Nicholas Drummond. You're treating Special Agent Michaela Caine. And I need to see her, right away."

CHAPTER FIFTY-ONE

Nicholas stood in the door to the hospital room, heart pounding hard and fast. Why wouldn't his heart believe the news that Mike would be all right?

Her hair was a mass of damp tangles all over her head. She was still slightly blue around the lips, but she had some color in her cheeks. She looked at him come into her room. She reached out a hand, and smiled.

"Nicholas."

Relief poured through him. He sat on the side of her bed, leaned down, and lightly stroked his fingers over her pale cheeks. Her flesh was warm. He brushed the hair back from her forehead, pulling out tangles. He leaned down and kissed her cold mouth, then laid his forehead against hers. "To have you whole again, here with me, smiling at me — I've promised more good works than I can do in a lifetime. But I'm going to try."

He felt her hand stroking through his hair, felt her warm breath whisper against his face. "We're okay." Her voice was lower than usual, her speech slightly slurred. He leaned down, kissed her again, looked into her eyes.

"You and I are a pair."

She whispered, "I can still picture you firing your magazine into that old wall, wood splinters flying, and then we were the ones flying. Do you see the stitches in my head?"

He looked at the small square bandage over her right temple, and it made his heart stumble again. "You hit something solid when you landed on the water."

"I don't know what. The water was so dark, Nicholas. How did you find me?"

She sounded like she was barely hanging on. He said quietly, "It took me too long."

"You lamebrain, you saved me. They told me if you'd given up, I would have died. Completely. Thank you for my life." She leaned against him, her face against his, and closed her eyes.

She felt the wet of his tears on her face. Mike knew she couldn't stay awake much longer, the meds they'd given her were too strong. He was so valiant, she wanted to tell him, but the words floated out of her brain.

Her head hurt, the wound was starting to throb despite the pain medications. She

390

reached up, rubbed her forehead. "I can't remember hitting the water, I can't remember anything. And then I woke up here."

He was glad of it.

He regained control, straightened over her now. "Your doctor Sienza says you should stay for a few days."

"No. I can't stay here. Nicholas, help me get up and get dressed. We have too much to do."

He gently pushed her back down. "You very nearly drowned. There's a danger you could get pneumonia. You have a concussion. At least until tomorrow, let the doctor have her way. Besides, you don't have any clothes. Rest, okay?"

She tried to struggle up again. This time Nicholas took her shoulders in his hands and pressed her down. "Lie still, and that's an order from your partner. Kitsune and Grant are alive, we have the tracker inside her, so we'll know where she is. I'll call Adam, make sure he's watching for it. I'll call Zachery and Savich, warn them about the storm coming to D.C. We both lost our mobiles and our comms in the lake.

"I'm going to have someone give me a ride back to the car. I'll get our go-bags. Thankfully, I have another mobile stashed in there."

He kissed her again, tucked the covers around her neck.

"Nicholas?" Her voice was only a whisper of a sound.

He leaned over her.

"Please, don't leave me behind."

And she was asleep in the next moment, her breathing steady. He touched the pulse in her throat, to reassure himself, he supposed. She was alive, and she would recover, and he thought about all the good works he'd be performing over his lifetime. It wasn't even a partial payment for her life. He kissed her, straightened the covers, and stepped into the hall where the doctor was waiting. "Dr. Sienza, may I have a word?"

"Yes, of course."

"I've lost my mobile and I need to make a call."

"Use mine." She handed over a small cell phone. He looked at it with a smile.

"I know, it is a dinosaur. My son dropped my smartphone off the balcony last night and shattered the screen. At least this one still works."

"It's fine, thank you."

"I will check on your wife — sorry, your partner — while you make your call."

"She's sleeping."

"Ah. Good," Dr. Sienza said, and went

back to reviewing a chart.

He stepped away and dialed Adam's mobile. Adam answered on the first ring, a little out of breath.

Nicholas said, "It's me."

"Where have you been? What happened to you? You've been offline for over an hour, we've been trying to call. Louisa and I were getting ready to find a plane to fly us to you —"

Nicholas managed to stem the tide. "Adam, I apologize. It's a very long story. There's been an accident and Mike was hurt. We're at the hospital in Castiglione Del Lago. Have the Kohaths left yet?"

"No. No one's been in or out since you disappeared off my radar. Wait, Mike's hurt?"

"She'll be okay. Is Kitsune's tracker working?"

"It still hasn't moved, and I'm wondering if the electromagnetic pulse affected it somehow. This long with no movement — stop stalling, tell me what happened."

"We sort of flew out of a tunnel on a motorcycle high above Lake Trasimeno and she smacked her head on a log or something when she hit the water."

Adam said, "Louisa, don't pull the phone out of my hand! Okay, okay, I'm putting him on speaker."

Nicholas filled in Adam and Louisa, but only the highlights.

When he'd finished, Louisa said, "Lots of nice detail at the beginning, then we have CliffsNotes. You're obviously leaving out massive amounts of info, but we'll get it out of you later. You promise Mike's okay?"

"I do."

Adam said, "What do you want us to do now? We've been on hold here, running numbers and watching satellite footage."

"We need to talk more, but first I've got to go to the car. All my backups are in our go-bags in the boot. Oh, yes, Mike and I found Lilith Forrester-Clarke buried in the tunnel. We need to get back into that palazzo."

"You're not going in alone," Louisa said flatly, and it wasn't a question.

"Absolutely not. It's time to get the cops involved. I'll rustle up a couple from the police station across from the hospital. You two pray the locals aren't on the Kohaths' payroll. Give me a couple of hours, then I'll check in again. Still nothing from Ben in London or from Savich?"

"Not yet," Adam said. "I don't suppose you're going to call Zachery, tell him Mike's laid up?"

394

"Maybe, after I tell him the Kohath twins' next plan."

"And that is?" Adam asked.

Nicholas took a deep breath. "Here's the deal, Louisa, Adam. The Kohaths are planning a massive weather attack on D.C. I heard them talking about a hurricane in the Atlantic, whipping it up, sending it to land, destroying Washington."

"What?" Both Adam and Louisa yelled into the phone. "Destroy the capital? Impossible, isn't it?"

Nicholas explained, leaving them in frozen silence.

"No," Louisa finally said. "It's not possible. That's science fiction. The Kohaths are nutcases."

Adam said, "I'm with Louisa. I still can't believe weather control at this level is possible." He paused. "But then again, look what they did in the Gobi Desert . . . and now they want to destroy Washington?"

"I can't imagine how people will take that news," Louisa said. "You and Mike will stop it, won't you?"

Ah, such faith. "We're going to try. You'll know more when I do. Keep doing what you're doing, Adam. Thanks, guys."

When he'd punched off, Nicholas opted to call Savich and explain what he and Mike had heard, let him deal with the powers that be. And Zachery.

After ten minutes of grilling, Nicholas was aware of a headache pounding over his right eyebrow. He knew Savich would speak to the vice president, explain the inexplicable, and then Zachery. *Thank you, Savich.*

He found Dr. Sienza in Mike's room, checking her vitals. He handed back the phone.

She said, "All signs are good for our patient. The *polizia* are here, my brother with them. I have explained she could be in danger. He will stand guard over Agent Caine."

"I also need to report a murder on the mountain."

"A murder? Why did you not tell me this?"

"Doctor, I'm still wrapping my head around everything that's happened over the past two hours. I want you focused on Agent Caine. I should also tell you she will demand to be released tomorrow. If you refuse, she will simply walk out of here, in a hospital gown, if necessary, so patch her up as best you can."

"Well then, you can tell the *polizia* all about this murder and they will get you back to your car. As for Agent Caine, I will get her well enough."

396

CHAPTER FIFTY-TWO

Venice, Italy

The computer dinged, and Adam jolted awake. "I'm up, I'm up. What is it?"

He turned in his chair and saw Louisa stretched on the couch, asleep. In the next second, she jerked up, wide-awake. "Is it room service?"

Adam laughed at her. "You and room service. You were out for almost a full hour."

Louisa rubbed her eyes and yawned. "Better than nothing. Did you hear any more from Nicholas while I was under?"

"Not a word. But my computer just came through. Take a look."

Adam handed her his laptop. To the average person, it would look like nothing more than strings of numbers and letters, total nonsense. Louisa, on the other hand, was computer savvy and she saw it was sophisticated code, even though she couldn't read it.

"Yeah, so what is it?"

"It's designed to break Landry Rodgers's financial history and download it to our servers. Remember? He's the Genesis Group's crooked wizard broker out of Singapore."

"I don't suppose what you're doing is anywhere close to legal?"

"Nope," he said cheerfully. "We're Covert Eyes, remember? I like Nicholas's motto: it's easier to ask forgiveness than to get permission."

"I wonder if Nicholas is a bad influence on you, or vice versa. Will this give us enough ammunition to sink them?"

"Hopefully."

"And can you cut off their money supply?"

He merely grinned at her.

"Go for it, launch it. Let's see what you can find."

"Hold on, I have a few lines of code left to write."

He tapped away while Louisa got herself a shot of espresso. "I've got to joggle my nervous system awake."

"Don't drown it in cream and sugar, and use triple the espresso."

"It's too small for triple the amount." Louisa turned the small ceramic cup over

398

in her hands, then set it under the spout of the Nespresso machine and pressed the button. "Are you about ready to nail this Rodgers dude?"

There was a second of furious tapping, then, "Yes. It's launched. Can we order some food? I'm starving. Sitting around typing drains away the carbs, that, and watching you eat everything in sight."

Louisa patted her flat stomach. "Gotta keep this fine machine in top working order. Lots of carbs or I lose my RPMs. Room service's the greatest, give them a call. How long will the program take to work?"

"An hour at most. All we need is for someone at Rodgers's firm to open the email and it will launch automatically. They'll never even know we're in."

"How does it work?"

"It will download all the transactional data. Which is a ton of stuff, so I wrote a second program that should filter out everything labeled Genesis and Kohath, with variables. Once we have the data, we can reconstruct the last couple of years, see all of Rodgers's transactions. This Rodgers guy is good, he completely obscured most of it."

"Explain what you mean he's obscured most of it."

"It's all numerical," Adam said, picking

up the phone and the hotel menu. "From what I can tell, the files are coded both by company and by longitude and latitude. Which is an interesting way to do things, but it's his way of keeping his clients separate and secure."

Adam ordered prosciutto and melon with cheese, looked over at Louisa, doubled the order, and added a full Italian breakfast, with extra bacon.

Louisa got up, began pacing. "I wish Nicholas would call."

Adam hung up the phone. "While you napped — okay, I napped some, too, but for the most part, I kept an eye on the satellite, as he asked. So far, no one has left Castel Rigone." He frowned. "It's weird. Either the Kohaths have flying brooms or they're hunkered down inside that mountain.

"What really worries me is there's no movement on Kitsune's tracker, not since Nicholas set off the micro EMP. I can only assume it's been knocked offline somehow, and isn't transmitting. I don't know what else could be happening."

Louisa said, "I hate to ask this, but will the tracker continue working if Kitsune is dead?"

Adam rubbed a hand through his hair. "Yes, it would continue to work for seventy-two hours. It was originally designed for the military to keep track of their spec-ops people should they be taken or killed in the field."

"I sure hope Kitsune is all right and she's found her husband. I like her. She's tough and smart. A pity she's a career criminal and we're FBI. And that's just bizarre. I'm going to take a shower. Call me when the food gets here or Nicholas calls."

Louisa headed into the shower, and Adam sat back and watched the four quadrants on his computer screen. The satellite imagery shifted incrementally on one quadrant, the data dump from the hack into Rodgers's files on the second, a third showed data from the Genesis Group's files, and the fourth showed Kitsune's tracker, only it was blank. Adam didn't like it one bit. What he'd told Louisa was right — he had no clue what had happened to it.

Adam's feet dropped to the floor when Kitsune's tracker suddenly came online and started to move.

He sent a thank-you heavenward and shouted, "Louisa! Get in here." She dashed out, a towel wrapped around her, and her hair twisted up in a turban. "What? What?"

"Kitsune's tracker lit up. She's on the move."

"Thank goodness. Where is she heading?"

"West. Fast. Look at this."

He pulled up a green screen overlaying a map of Europe. The GPS locator representing Kitsune's location was a small, flashing dot of white. "I have no idea how they got out without my seeing the tracker. The satellite's been watching and no one's left the mountain."

"Then they have a way out of the mountain that no one can see."

"I know they absolutely did not take the road down to the lake. And they must be on a plane, no way a car could be moving that fast."

"Why do you think the tracker came back online?"

"Maybe it rebooted itself once it was free of the EMP zone? Maybe she hasn't been moving until now. Either way, go finish your shower. It's probably the last chance you'll have for a while. I'm calling Nicholas."

CHAPTER FIFTY-THREE

The Kohath Letters
Tunguska, Siberia
July 6, 1908

My dearest Genevieve,
I will try to be home before our baby is born, but I don't know that the storm will ease enough for me to leave this dacha anytime soon. Think of me with nothing but vodka and a fire as my companions.

Tesla left in the dead of night, a week ago, right after the storm hit. He was devastated by what he calls our failure. I told him over and over it was a great success, but you know Nikola, he's as big a pessimist as he is brilliant — nothing is ever right for him. It is an incredible sight — the trees were blown down for miles, the skies were as bright as day. The Coil harnessed immense energy, and the explosion was unlike anything I have ever witnessed.

Now I know — it will work. The Coil can be used to draw the earth's energy into a contained field. I must simply find a way to harness the power to send it straight into the sky and bring down the heavens with it.

I will return home as soon as the snows clear and allow me passage. You are in my thoughts and prayers.

With ardent love always,

Appleton

CHAPTER FIFTY-FOUR

Castiglione del Lago, Italy

The Italian police were suitably concerned when Nicholas debriefed them, especially at the news of Lilith Forrester-Clarke's murder. The officer he was riding with, Dr. Sienza's deputy inspector brother, Nando, explained that the homicide team had been dispatched to the mountain, and offered to allow Nicholas to tag along while they did their investigation.

But this was the last thing Nicholas wanted to do. He convinced Nando to let him off at the Škoda. His backup gear and the go-bags were in the boot, along with his spare mobile. He got it out immediately and saw four missed calls from Adam.

He called him back. "What's wrong?"

"Kitsune's tracker was off, and suddenly, it just came back on. I'd swear no one left the mountain so they must have another way out. Sorry, Nicholas, I can't think of any explanation. All I know is that somehow, undetected, they managed to get to either a helicopter or a plane."

"Bugger all. All right, keep watch. Now, back to the Kohaths' planned attack on D.C. Adam, do you see any weather system on the radar?"

"There is a storm in the Atlantic, yes. It's been on the news because it's such an early storm, out of season. Hold on, I'm pulling up the latest track — here we go. All the meteorologists are saying it's no threat to the eastern seaboard. It's supposed to move into the Gulf. But you believe the Kohaths can really change its course, strengthen it somehow into a hurricane?"

"Yes, I do, and imagine a tsunami in front of it inundating Washington, wiping out the entire city, killing thousands. They have to be stopped."

"Nicholas, I'm not sure even you and Mike can stop a hurricane once it's on course to landfall."

"We're going to have to figure out a way. If these two psychopaths can start storms, then Mike and I can stop them. And to have a prayer of doing that, we have to find out where they're going."

"With Kitsune's tracker, I've got their co-ordinates. They're moving fast — they're already out of Italian airspace."

"What's their heading?"

"West by southwest. Toward Spain."

"Keep on them. Watch it closely. How much time do we have left on Kitsune's tracker?"

"Just under twelve hours."

"There's no chance you can pick up the signal off that bug I planted on Cassandra's clothing, is there?"

"Sorry, it only broadcasts to fifty yards."

"All right. I'm going to need the plane. Get Clancy and Trident in the air and to the airport in Perugia. Tell them to gas up for a nice long trip. In the meantime, I need you to call Gray in New York, and the two of you lock down the financials. We need proof that the Kohaths have been manipulating the markets with their weather attacks."

"The plane will be ready when you are," Adam said. "Oh, Nicholas, I did some checking on Grant Thornton's employer, Blue Mountain, identified myself as FBI and reported Grant was missing. They'd already run a kidnap-and-ransom assessment on him since he hadn't checked in since his last operation. They're smart and have a lot of resources. Do you want their help?"

"Normally I'd resist, but right now, honestly, the more the merrier. Call them, tell them we're tracking Grant and his wife, and Adam, keep them in the loop. We need all the help we can get. Thankfully, we're sure they're not on the Kohaths' payroll."

"Will do. Take care of Mike, okay?"

"You can count on that. Thanks, Adam. You and Louisa hang tight, gather proof that will nail these two nutters."

He punched off, started to call Zachery and Savich but decided against it. There was simply too much to explain, and too many questions, too many uncertainties. And too many ways for them to say no, no way, he's in over his head, this is way above his pay grade. When he knew more, he'd fill them in.

Cassandra and Ajax had to know he'd be looking high and low for them, but they'd also think he'd have no way of knowing where to look.

They were in for a big surprise.

CHAPTER FIFTY-FIVE

Over the Atlantic

Kitsune opened her eyes to darkness. Her first thought was *Grant's dead.* And she couldn't bear it, couldn't accept it. Because of her, he was dead. Then she thought about killing Cassandra with her bare hands, and that made her realize she had to stay alive to do it. Oh yes, she'd get out of this, then she'd kill the crazy bitch.

She was cold, she was dying of thirst, and she had a splitting headache. Her whole body hurt and she realized she couldn't move.

She was alive, though, and she would do anything to stay that way. Where was she? *Focus, Kitsune, focus.*

She was tied tightly, arms and legs, propped against something, hard and soft, and wasn't that strange. It was a man's leg — Grant's leg. He was alive, he was right beside her. She listened to his every breath,

409

and nearly wept. Together, they had a chance. She thought about strangling Cassandra and her palms itched.

She leaned close, smelled his own unique scent. Alive, he was alive, and he was here, with her.

"Grant?"

No answer. They'd drugged him again, as they had her. She supposed they'd given her less. Why? Because she wasn't such a danger to them? Kitsune felt a moment of insult.

She was surrounded by a loud, intense roar, rhythmic and steady. They were on a plane. It wasn't entirely dark — she saw a small red light blinking on the wall and in that blinking light, she saw the pulse beating in his neck. Why had they left them alive? Because they wanted something, but what?

Then she remembered the tracker. How much longer would it last? Still, she felt a bit of relief. Nicholas and Mike would follow, she was sure of it.

Grant moaned. She rested her chin against his thigh, more to comfort herself than to comfort him. At least they were finally together.

She needed to think, to plan. And once

they'd survived this, she'd consider retiring.
Well, maybe.

CHAPTER FIFTY-SIX

The Kohath Letters
Lake Michigan
November 11, 1913

Dear Nikola,
The machine works. If only you'd stayed, you would have seen our monstrous storm rip through the Great Lakes region of the United States. Twelve ships sank, at least thirty were disabled. The damage is astronomical, the investments I made in anticipation of this will turn a pretty profit.

The problem, Nikola, is that you are too much of an idealist to understand how useful the Coil will be to us. You are too concerned with the collateral damage. I've promised you we will find ways to mitigate the risk, to stop the machine from damaging human life. It will simply take time.

I know Edison's men did a thorough job discrediting you, but you cannot give up, you cannot fall into your depressions. You must understand that what Edison says about you is unimportant, you are the brilliant one, the one whose name will live forever. You must believe me.

I know you have sworn to leave for good, to cut your ties to me and our machine. I know you've said society is not ready for this level of manipulation. But surely you understand that you can't invent without first understanding how society will be changed by your advancement. Do not be lost to me, Nikola.

You needn't worry about money, thanks to my father-in-law's generous funding. Of course we will need more money in our next stage of development, and the only way to get enough money is to set the Coil to work for us.

Think of the power we will have, how we can bring about change, good change, to help humanity. Who knows what the future holds, what we can do with this in the years to come?

Please reconsider, Nikola.

Appleton

CHAPTER FIFTY-SEVEN

Castiglione Del Lago, Italy

Nicholas found Mike asleep when he stepped into her hospital room, carrying a prosciutto panino and a Coke Light from the vending machine. Between bites, he called Ben in London.

"Tell me you have something."

"I do, more than something. You aren't going to believe what I have. I've been combing through a treasure trove here. St. Germaine has a letter from Appleton Kohath to Nikola Tesla, dating back to 1901, when he found a folio in a junk store he believed was a lost set of papers by Leonardo da Vinci."

"Da Vinci? What's that all about?"

"Give me a minute. Okay, so Kohath found this Da Vinci folio in Venice and sent it immediately to his good buddy Nikola Tesla, and the two of them married Da Vinci's ideas to Tesla's Coil and started

414

cooking up a machine to control the weather."

"You're saying the Kohaths' weather machine is originally a design from Da Vinci?"

"Yep. Didn't you tell me Savich spoke to you about Tesla and his electricity experiments?"

Nicholas chewed on his final bit of panino. "Yes. When I asked Savich to research anyone early in the century who could possibly have done groundwork on weather control, he gave me Tesla, and reminded me about the Siberian devastation. I didn't see it being any use at the time, but maybe he was on the right track. What did you learn about Tesla, Ben?"

"Since I'm not an expert on Tesla, I looked him up. Like Da Vinci, he was a man ahead of his time. He believed the earth could be used to create power, believed he could create energy from the earth's crust. And go figure this: Tesla believed he could signal other planets.

"In addition to all his electricity experimentation, he did a number of experiments with the ionosphere, traveled all over the world messing with it. That Siberian explosion in 1908 was so large it knocked down sixty million trees across eight hundred and thirty square miles. Pretty intense for a couple of twentieth-century scientists."

"But even knowing this," Nicholas said, "how does it make sense that the Kohaths can control the weather?"

"I found another letter to Tesla after the 1913 Great Lakes Storm that killed many people and caused so much damage. Kohath was basically begging Tesla not to be such a wuss and a pessimist, and leave him high and dry. But, of course, Tesla did just that. Kohath even wrote about his wife's father funding his work.

"He and Tesla never worked together again, saw each other again — but it didn't matter. Appleton Kohath had figured out how to manipulate both the weather and the markets."

Nicholas said, "So that huge 1913 storm, that's how they got more development money."

"Yes, straight-up stock buying, selling."

"Nicholas, can you imagine, back at the beginning, Kohath sending Da Vinci's papers to Tesla, saying, 'Hey, lookee here, Da Vinci created a machine to control the weather but the old dude didn't understand enough about electromagnetic energy to make it work. Between us, I'll just bet we can make our own lightning bolt.' "

Nicholas said, "And so together they developed a machine to create weather half a century before our scientists were on their way to figuring it out."

Ben said, "Yes, and the Kohath family continued to refine and perfect their storm machine to the point where they can do precision storms, like starting that horrific sandstorm in the Gobi."

Nicholas said, "Or sending a storm and tsunami to level Washington, D.C."

"What? What did you say? They want to destroy Washington?"

Nicholas told him what he'd overheard.

Ben said, "This is beyond scary. Does Zachery know?"

"Yes. Mike and I will try to pull the plug. Ben, keep going through all those papers. Be in touch with anything else you find that's relevant."

"Yes, all right. Oh, and there is one more thing you need to know."

"More? I don't know if I can handle more."

"Were you aware they're doing an inquest on Elizabeth St. Germaine?"

Nicholas set down his coffee. "No, Melinda told me it was cardiac arrest. Is that not the case?"

"Melinda said there were concerns about

the fact her mother died alone, when every-one, including her doctor, said she was in good health. Melinda said the coroner did a tox screen. Did you know there was a threatened lawsuit by the Kohaths, all to stop the completion and publication of St. Germaine's second book on the Kohaths, a book that would include all of Appleton's early letters? In other words, the cat would be out of the bag and it's possible the Ko-haths would be busted. But then Elizabeth St. Germaine died, very conveniently."

"Ben, you believe those insane twins killed her to stop publication?"

"You've met them, I haven't. But from everything I've been reading, those two would stop at nothing to protect themselves and their weather machine. Listen, you have connections, do you think you could find out about St. Germaine's tox screen? I haven't said anything to Melinda, but she knows I'm worried."

"I will do that right away, Ben, and call you back. As soon as I can get Mike out of here, we're going after the Kohaths."

Nicholas punched off and dialed a number from memory. Hamish Penderley, his old boss at the Met, answered on the first ring.

"Penderley."

"Hello, sir, it's Nicholas Drummond."

"We don't want any, or need any, Drummond. Not buying anything you're selling today. Where the devil are you?"

"I'm currently in Italy. Good to talk to you, too, sir. How are things at New Scotland Yard?"

"Never dull. Now, I know you're not remotely concerned about the state of the Met. You want something. Spit it out. But I do not want to know what you're doing in Italy, nor do I want to hear about your involvement in that shoot-out in Venice."

"No, sir, I won't say a word about Italy or any shoot-out. I'm calling about Elizabeth St. Germaine. There's an ongoing inquest into her death?"

"Did her daughter ask you to call and speed things up? Because I've told her all I know."

"No, Melinda didn't ask me to call. It pertains to a case I'm working on here involving the Kohaths, the family St. Germaine was writing about, until her untimely and very sudden death. If it wasn't a natural death, sir, I really need to know."

Penderley was silent for a moment. "You're saying we should be looking at the Kohaths for this? That's crazy, to murder someone over a bloody biography."

"Please, tell me what you've discovered."

419

Penderley sighed deeply. "Let me muck around in the file. I'll call you back."

CHAPTER FIFTY-EIGHT

Nicholas's mobile rang a few minutes later.

Penderley said immediately, "St. Germaine's death was marked down as a cardiac arrest, but the coroner thought her heart looked off and sent out a for a toxicology screen, which isn't back yet."

"What do you mean, the heart looked off?"

"Says here, 'Hemorrhagic congestion of the heart and lungs, consistent with heart failure.' But her daughter said she didn't have a heart condition, and her doctor confirmed it. It was enough to convince the coroner to send off the tox, and we went in and collected evidence from the scene. Only thing we found was a set of fingerprints on a tea tin that doesn't belong to anyone in the household. Nothing to get too excited about because the tin was part of a gift hamper from *Fortnum and Mason,* and there were partial fingerprints over everything in it, as you'd expect, but that's not what made us suspicious.

"Nicholas, the card with the gift hamper said it was from St. Germaine's editor at her publishing house, but the editor says no one sent her a gift, and *Fortnum and Mason* doesn't have a record of the publisher's credit card in the system. That's why we decided to open the inquest. Not to mention this is Melinda St. Germaine's mother, of course."

"Was the basket a hand delivery?"

"Yes, the day before she died. The maid found the hamper on the front step, all decked out with a big bow. But St. Germaine didn't have any sort of security cameras, so there's nothing to hunt there. By the maid's account, St. Germaine was delighted by the gift, had some biscuits and a cup of their tea. And that is why we ran the prints on the contents and sent them for analysis. Nothing's back yet.

"And, Drummond, don't pass this along to Melinda St. Germaine. I don't need her breathing down my neck."

"Right. Where's the gift hamper now?"

"Evidence unit. As I said, the previous tests showed it was nothing more sinister than several packets of biscuits and a few exotic tins of tea. Tracing it has been a bust as well. Do you have any idea how many of these they sell in a week?"

"I'll assume hundreds."

"Right you are. Tell me, Nicholas, have you gotten yourself into trouble with the Kohaths?"

In a manner of speaking. "Are you familiar with them at all, sir?"

"I only have a passing acquaintance with David Maynes, the husband of the late Helen Kohath, rest their souls. Maynes keeled over during a squash match a few weeks ago."

Nicholas went on red alert. "Really? Heart attack, was it?"

"That's right. Shame, he's so young. Of course, after his wife went missing, obviously dead, he went a bit loopy. Well, he was always on the loopy side, but it intensified, problems with his children and such.

"Do you remember hearing about her disappearance in the Gobi? She was in the headlines for a few weeks. They never found a trace of her. The whole crew disappeared, twelve people, I think it was. Desert swallowed them whole."

"Sir, are you certain David Maynes died of a heart attack?"

"Nothing to say otherwise, there were witnesses. As I said, he was in the middle of a

423

squash match."

"Still, what are the odds that the two people at the center of a lawsuit suddenly drop dead of heart attacks within days of each other?"

Penderley groaned. "I didn't connect that until right this minute. Do you really think there's a conspiracy afoot?"

"Maybe. You have to admit the timing's strange."

"Yes, it is. I'll check on Maynes's death. I'll let you know if we find anything."

"Thank you. And let me know about the tox screen on Elizabeth St. Germaine."

"You know, Drummond, if you'd only stuck around —"

"I know, I could do the work myself. Take care of yourself, sir."

He hung up and called Gray, not Adam. "I know you've got a lot of irons in the fire, Gray, but could you run something for me?"

"Sure."

"Lilith Forrester-Clarke's passport and credit cards for the past month."

"Easy enough. Am I looking for anything in particular?"

"Travel to England from Italy, and the purchase of a gift hamper from *Fortnum and Mason*. Make that two gift hampers for two different people."

"I'll let you know. Mike okay? Yeah, Louisa called me. You guys are butt-deep in alligators."

"Nearly to the neck. Mike's asleep. She'll be okay, I promise. Thanks, Gray."

Nicholas called Adam. "Kitsune still flying?"

"Hello to you, too, Nicholas. Yes, they're over the Atlantic now. Based on the trajectory, if I had to bet, I'd say they're heading for the Caribbean. Depending on the plane, they'll have to refuel there if they plan to go any farther. Clancy and Trident will be waiting for you in an hour, on the runway in Perugia."

"Excellent. Thank you."

His mobile buzzed. It was Gray. He said only, "Bingo."

Nicholas said, "Talk to me. What magic have you wrought?"

Gray said, "Our Lilith Forrester-Clarke was a very bad girl."

Chapter Fifty-Nine

London, England

Ben was impressed. Elizabeth St. Germaine had been thorough and organized, and every page of the manuscript held something new and interesting, sometimes shocking. But her notes were the best part. Through her eyes, he was beginning to see the Kohath family and their unrelenting obsession to find the Ark. They truly believed they were God's chosen ones, and they alone could control the power of the Ark. And the weather machine — it was ingenious, really. Deadly, but ingenious.

He was knee-deep, literally, in Elizabeth St. Germaine's material when a shadow fell over his shoulder. He looked up and smiled at Melinda St. Germaine. She wore a fitted black dress with cutout shoulders that was at once demure and shockingly sexy.

"Are you making progress?"

Ben laughed a little, gestured to all the

papers. "Yes, absolutely. I could be here for weeks. Your mother was very detailed."

"I've come to roust you for dinner. You'll need to eat if you have any hope of making it through all of this."

Ben was torn. He needed to keep pushing, but his stomach growled at the thought of food, and she heard it, punched his arm. "I guess a short break wouldn't hurt."

Melinda laughed. "Oh, no, sorry, Ben, but there's nothing short about evenings at the St. Germaines'. I suppose I should warn you that dinner will last around three hours. We don't do much halfway around here."

Well, life isn't fair, now is it? "I can't. I'd love to join you but we're on a tight time frame. I better stay here and keep working."

He was pleased to see she was really disappointed, and surprised at how good it made him feel.

"All right, I understand. I'll have something sent out to you."

"Rain check?"

Melinda grabbed a pen, and wrote something on a note card and handed it to him. "When you're in town again, you give me a ring. You can take me on a proper date."

The world brightened. Date, a proper date. Ben grinned. "I'd like that. Very much."

"Good. Maybe you can steal some of Mother's letters or notes and I'll complain to your bosses and demand that you have to return them. Here, to me, in London. That way I'll be assured you will come back."

"Oh, I'll be back. I have vacation time due. The moment we wrap this case, I'll be here."

Melinda lightly laid her hand on his shoulder. After the horror of the past weeks, she now had something to look forward to. Ben Houston, an American FBI agent, and a redhead, just like her. Who would have thought?

He rose and took her hand, said her name. "Melinda."

She leaned up, kissed his cheek. "Get back to work. Don't forget to eat."

And then she was gone, trailing the scent of roses in her wake.

He looked after her until she was gone, then sat back down and pulled the St. Germaine's notes to him, read over them again.

In 1909, Appleton founded a family-owned company called the Genesis Group, which quickly became an archaeological power-house due to a continued influx of money generated by attacks through the weather

428

machine. As revenue flowed in, the company began to fund legitimate digs all over the world. But it was finding the Ark that was Appleton's life's work. He felt his family, as direct-line descendants from the Levites, were God's designated inheritors of the Ark. Since the Ark is known to be a conduit to God, Appleton operated on a simple premise — when the Kohaths finally had the Ark in their possession, they would show the world they were the chosen ones, and would have the ultimate power, and God's blessing, to do what they would to the earth. God's blessing for evil as well as good?

Ben read through the rest, shaking his head. He'd run across genius like this before, melded with all-out craziness, but nothing on this immense a scale.

His phone beeped with a text from Nicholas.

Have you anything more for me?

Ben texted back.

The weather machine is a go. You must shut it down before it destroys Washington, D.C.

CHAPTER SIXTY

The Caribbean

The sun was high when Cassandra and Ajax landed in Cuba with their two prisoners. Both were awake, though Grant Thornton was still groggy from the drugs. Cassandra knew they were as dangerous as Nicholas Drummond, knew it would be smart to weigh them down and throw them into the ocean as quickly as possible, that if she didn't kill them now, something bad would happen.

No, she was being foolish. She needed the thief, just as she had a feeling she'd need her husband for leverage. Then she'd take great pleasure in killing them both. There was nothing they could do to stop her.

It had been nearly a year since they'd last visited Grandfather on his island, but she always recognized the smell of the water and air, sweet and tangy, a lovely combination. Always before, it was as supplicants, but not this time.

They boarded the floatplane, secured the thief and her husband to the seats, and were soon airborne. The windows were open and the sea wind blew in their faces.

She said, "Ajax, you worked more of the trip over on Grandfather's formula. Are you close? Have you figured out how to move the storm to Washington, D.C.?"

Ajax was sweating in the heat, tired and impatient. "I'm into his systems. I've learned how to intensify the storm, but that's it. Getting it to go in the right direction is what only Grandfather knows. And those instructions are in his precious vault."

"Then once we get the formula for determining directionality, you can make the storm strong enough to flatten D.C.?"

He nodded. "Without it, all I can do is force a heavy rainfall somewhere over the Atlantic. Hardly what we want or need."

Cassandra looked over at the thief. The woman seemed to be focused entirely on her husband. Thornton was getting more clearheaded with the fresh wind in his face. They'd have to watch them closely, drug him again when they landed.

Cassandra found herself wondering if the thief had been awake and listening. Did she have any idea what Cassandra would demand of her?

Ajax was saying, "Grandfather is going to see I've intensified the storm, and he's going to know I managed to get into his system."

"Who cares? Soon now, he won't matter. His last act will be to hand over the formula."

Ajax looked down at the blue ocean gliding by beneath them. "We'll be at the island soon. I hope you're prepared."

"Prepared for what?"

"Cassandra. Think. This coup has been simple so far. We've eliminated our father, the biographer, and Lilith. All of them are dead. But now we're going to kill our grandfather, the only person left on earth who even begins to understand weather control. Once he's dead, we're on our own, completely. You must prepare yourself for this. Being alone, only the two of us. Are you ready to be alone?"

"Yes, just the two of us. Nobody to tell us what to do, nobody to question us endlessly. Oh yes, Ajax, I'm ready, more than ready."

Ajax looked over at Kitsune and Grant. "Why have you bothered to keep them alive?"

She said low, "Grandfather's vault. She can get into it if he won't tell us the combination. Thornton? He'll be our leverage. Then they're dead. I think she's perfect for the job, don't you?"

He nodded. "Lilith certainly sang her praises. I sometimes thought Lilith admired her even more than she admired me."

"Doesn't matter now, does it? I never actually believed she'd be able to steal the staff from the Topkapi, but she did."

Ajax took her hand, squeezed her fingers. "Grandfather told me once he'd wired the vault with explosives. I asked him why, I mean, who would ever come close enough to break into his vault? He told me there were enemies festering all over the earth and it always paid to be prepared."

Cassandra laughed. "I do hope the old fool was thinking about us."

Ajax shrugged. "We'll soon see, but honestly, I don't think he'll give us the combination. He doesn't trust us. So we will have to use the thief. If she lives up to her reputation, if she does manage to disarm the safe, then all well and good. If not — then we'll have to find another way, perhaps another thief."

He looked out the window. "Get ready, it's time to land and make our way to the island."

She gave him a high five. "And kill that

crazy old man."

"Maybe he's had a change of heart," Ajax said.

Cassandra laughed. "Maybe his heart will give out and save us the trouble."

CHAPTER SIXTY-ONE

Castiglione del Lago, Italy

Mike heard Nicholas speaking low into his cell phone. She opened her eyes, pleased and relieved her vision was now clear and her brain was working just fine, thank you. Her body felt clearer, too, and stronger.

Nicholas punched off his mobile. He was by her bed in a moment, his hand out to touch her face.

"You're awake."

"I am. Your hand is so warm, Nicholas. I like it. Can I sit up?"

He adjusted the bed until she was upright.

"That's better. No dizziness, no weird feelings. I'm good to go."

"Good to go, are you? Right this minute?" His hand cupped her chin.

"No cough, no swimmy head. Maybe a bit of a flu feeling, but that's it. Oh, all right, lower that eyebrow. So I'm not quite one hundred percent, but I'm close. Help me up and get me to the bathroom. Did you bring my go-bag?"

He nodded, helped her to her feet, stood still, letting her rest against him for a minute.

"Okay," she said, and straightened, pulling away from him. He stuck to her side as she walked to the bathroom. When he opened the door she said, "I did it. Nope, you're not coming in. Hand me my bag, please."

He handed it through the door. "Call if you need me."

She shut the door as Dr. Sienza appeared in the doorway. "She's up?"

"She is. She walked by herself to the bathroom. No hesitation. She's going to get dressed."

Dr. Sienza put her hands on her hips. "You know she should stay another day at least, let me run one more CAT scan, make sure her head injury isn't going to cause any problems."

Mike opened the door. She'd managed to get her hair into a ponytail. She was pale but upright, now dressed in pants, her boots, a white shirt and jacket.

"Sorry, Dr. Sienza. Really, but I can't stay. Without me, he would crash and burn and the case would go sideways. He needs me."

"But —"

"Come, Doctor, what would you do in my place? Look at him. He simply can't take care of himself, not without me at his side.

"I promise to take it easy. I promise not to rush into anything. I can heal just as well on a plane or in a hotel room as I can here. Give me some pain pills, whatever you think best. Nicholas has medical training. Nothing will go wrong."

Nicholas turned to the doctor. "Is it safe?"

"At least let me do a full neurological exam now, to see if there is anything that could be a worry."

"Fine," Mike said, "then I'm out of here."

"You look as pale as the sheets on your bed." Nicholas sounded worried.

She took his hand. "Nicholas Drummond, you know I won't slow you down."

"Both of you, stop arguing, so I can examine Agent Caine."

Dr. Sienza sat Mike on the bed and began her examination. She asked her a series of questions, checked her reflexes, her pupils, her pulse. When she was through, she nodded and stood up. "I must say, Agent Caine, you have recovered nicely. You're young, you're in very good shape physically, and this has helped you bounce back much more quickly than I expected. I'm also

437

pleased to see that you are cogent, and the concussion doesn't appear to have any noticeable effects."

She paused, looked at Nicholas, then back to Mike. "To answer your question, Agent Caine, if I were in your situation, and I had to keep someone I cared about safe, I'd do exactly what you're doing." She lightly laid her palm against Mike's cheek. "Stay safe, Agent Caine, and don't let harm come to your partner."

"I won't," Mike said. "I won't ever."

"And you, Agent Drummond, you will keep her safe."

Nicholas said, "That could happen if I could only talk her out of leaping off tall buildings in a single bound."

CHAPTER SIXTY-TWO

Mike rested her head against the window as Nicholas drove and filled her in on everything he'd learned, from Ben and Penderley to Gray and his discoveries about Lilith Forrester-Clarke.

"Gray said Lilith's credit cards and passport confirm she was in London three weeks ago. She wasn't dumb enough to put the *Fortnum and Mason* gift hampers on her credit card, but Gray pulled the CCTV footage from the cameras at *F and M* and there she was, carrying two hampers. One for Elizabeth St. Germaine and the other for David Maynes, Cassandra and Ajax's father."

"So, murder, pure and simple. Those two are frightening, Nicholas. Imagine, having your own father killed."

"Evidently they believed he'd gone too far when he turned historical and private family papers to Elizabeth St. Germaine.

"I also asked Gray to send the CCTV footage to Penderley. I'm sure by now they identified Lilith's fingerprints — she was in MI5 after all — and the tox screens found poison in both St. Germaine's and Maynes's bodies."

His mobile rang. He didn't recognize the number, but answered, putting it on speaker.

An Italian voice said, "This is Deputy Inspector Nando, Agent Drummond, Dr. Sienza's brother. I wanted to update you on the situation in the Kohath palazzo, namely the tunnels in the mountain. We have found several bodies, including the female victim you spoke about. We have identified her as an employee, Lilith Forrester-Clarke, just as you said. The Carabinieri request that you come back to the palazzo for full interviews."

"I have told you everything, Inspector Nando. The dead bodies were all Kohath guards and I never knew their names, except for one — Harry. Also, I am about to get on a plane and won't be able to come back right away. Can you tell me, did you find Grant Thornton?"

"There is no one here who matches his description. But as you warned me, there is a great deal of blood, bullets, and other evidence. The maid here is insisting you stormed into the house, killed her employers, and made off with their bodies. The fact that she hadn't called us, the *polizia,* however, is telling.

"Regardless, Agent Drummond, the Carabinieri are insisting you join us and help us to understand what has happened. If you don't come willingly, I fear they will detain you."

Nicholas heard the urgent note in Nando's voice, clearly a warning.

"You should question the maid closely. She will identify all the dead guards for you. You'd do well to arrest any staff left in the palazzo, because they know more than they're letting on about the family's actions today. As for the Kohaths, her employers, they have left Italy and we, the FBI, are tracking them.

"Nando, I will do all I can to help you, but you're going to have to stall the Carabinieri for me, and wait until after we apprehend the Kohaths."

"We have frozen the scene, but I cannot control what the Carabinieri does. About the Kohath twins — be very careful, Agent Drummond. I must tell you, I have heard many rumors about the two of them, very unpleasant rumors of unpredictable and vicious behavior. Then there is the number of guards on their payroll.

"We are a small peaceful town. Why are guards even there? For what purpose? No one can or will say — again, rumors. It is all worrisome. So again, take care. Bring them back. That would be best. For me."

"I will try, Nando, thank you."

He clicked off and looked at Mike.

"The Carabinieri would like to get their hands on us, I fear. Do you think Major Russo could be involved?"

"Nothing would surprise me at this point. Let's hope they don't stop the plane before we get in the air."

Nicholas called ahead, explained the need for urgency.

They got to the airport in Perugia just as the plane finished refueling. They saw Trident making her exterior check. She waved, called out, "We know, we know, we need to get off the ground in the next ten seconds. Clancy's inside, doing his flight check as fast as he can. Get inside. I'll keep an eye out. You said the Carabinieri's not happy with you?"

"Not a bit," Nicholas said cheerfully.

Nicholas followed Mike up the stairs into the cabin. He supposed he shouldn't be surprised to see Louisa and Adam already on board.

Louisa held up her hand. "Don't start, Nicholas. No way were we going to stay in Venice and let you and Mike have all the fun. So sit down, be quiet, and suck it up."

"Sucking it up," Nicholas said, and helped Mike into a seat, fastened her seat belt, and covered her with a blanket. He looked at the two of them. "Actually, I'm really glad you're here. We need all the help we can get."

"Recognition — about time," Adam said. "Hey, Mike, you look like someone tried to drown you."

Mike cocked an eye at Adam. "Whatever gave you that impression? I suggest you don't answer that, Adam, or I'll make you eat your sneakers when this is over."

Trident said from the cockpit doorway. "Okay, guys, all buckled in? Good. We've got drinks and sandwiches for you. What is that? I do believe I hear sirens. And here I thought just maybe you were exaggerating. We're out of here!"

The plane was barely wheels up when Carabinieri cars roared onto the runway and raced after them. When they were in the air, Adam pumped his fist in the air. "Way to go, Clancy, Trident!"

"Top Gun!" came two voices over the

intercom.

Louisa stretched. "Is anyone ready for a sandwich?"

Laughter. Always food for Louisa. It felt good, Mike thought, as she snuggled into her nest. She heard Nicholas ask, "Did Lia and her father get off all right?"

"She was discharged just before we left Venice. She's good. Her father loves Venice."

Nicholas said, "I'll bet Lia won't have any fond memories."

"Actually, she wants to come back with her dad. As a tourist."

He looked from Louisa to Adam. "Listen. Mike will swear she's one hundred percent, but she's not. At least not quite. I suggest all of us get some sleep, it's going to be a long flight. You, too, Adam. I'll keep an eye on Kitsune's tracker."

"You also need to keep a watch on the storm." Adam handed Nicholas his laptop. The weather panel showed the storm, spinning slowly on the radar. "The meteorologists and their hurricane models have it strengthening, but it's still heading toward the Gulf. They expect it to become a category-three hurricane and hit Texas, but that's all based on their computer models. They don't know it might very well change course and head to D.C."

"At least the Kohaths haven't changed its direction yet," Nicholas said.

Louisa said, "I have a hard time imagining how they're going to pull this off."

"Any rational person would," Nicholas said. "Adam, Louisa, before you're off to dreamland, let me tell you what Ben's learned about the Kohath family history." He told them about Da Vinci, Tesla, and Appleton Kohath, and their weather machine.

Adam asked, "Is there some sort of formula based on electromagnetics? Lasers? Use of satellites?"

"Hopefully Ben will be able to add more explanation of the machine to us." Nicholas yawned.

Louisa said, "Nicholas, you look ready to drop. I'll take the first watch. Make it four hours? Then you can take over."

Half his brain was already in never-never land. "Thanks, Louisa. Wake me if anything changes."

And without opening her eyes, Mike said, "Put in your earplugs, people. He snores."

Nicholas gave a little smile. "Yeah? So do you."

CHAPTER SIXTY-THREE

Over the Atlantic

Nicholas woke to darkness. The plane's interior lights had been turned down, and everyone was asleep, slumped in their chairs, except for Adam, who'd taken Nicholas's turn after Louisa, staring at the multiple open screens on his laptop.

When Nicholas, rose, stretched, Adam looked up. "Good timing. You're going to want to see this."

"You got her?"

"Yes. They landed in Cuba. GPS has a ping at 20°44'03"N 075°39'26"W. There's an airport there called Preston, on the southeastern coast.

"From what I can tell, this ain't no hot spot like Havana, it's a tiny, out-of-the-way place. They've been there for about an hour. I already alerted Clancy and Trident. They're going to get permission to land there. They say about two more hours. The

Kohaths had a decent head start, but we're catching up. The longer they stay in one position, the more time we cut down."

"I doubt the Cubans will be thrilled with a planeload of FBI descending upon them, even if travel has been normalized between our countries. Oh, bugger all. Zachery is going to love this call."

"Well, before you do check in, there's some bad news. The storm hasn't changed course, but it's intensifying, rapidly. The millibars dropped by twenty since the last flyover by the National Weather Service planes. The predictions are all over the map — literally. Every model has it going a different way now, apparently the jet stream is changing and the storm could get caught up in it. They have weather watches from Texas and Louisiana to the coast of Florida, and they're discussing the storm even heading up north, all the way to New York. No one knows where it's going. It's 'wobbling,' as the meteorologists say. And it's been named. Since it's the first storm of the season, its name starts with an *A*. Want to guess?"

"Tell me."

"Athena. Nice Greek name to go along with our crazy Kohath twins."

"At least we know where it's going — to

D.C. But I'm wondering why it hasn't already plowed into the coast. Why are they waiting?"

"Maybe the twins don't know how to do it."

"That would mean another Kohath. Near Cuba."

Adam said, "Could be. Nicholas, I'll sure feel better when we find a way to stop it. It's on screen one, the tracker is screen two. If you're up now — ?"

"Yep, it's my turn. Look at Louisa, she's smiling, must be a really nice dream she's having. Go on, Adam, get some sleep."

"Yeah, like that's going to happen, not when the pot's coming to a boil. I couldn't sleep now anyway. Only two hours until we land. The financials are almost ready, too. I've been running some variables that match up the stock shorting to specific completely unexpected storms in the last five years. And yes, I'm seeing a pattern. Not enough to fry them, but still, we're on the way."

"You can tell me everything after you get some rest. At least close down your brain for five, Adam."

Adam saluted, went back to a seat, put in his earbuds. Nicholas wasn't surprised when he was out in under a minute.

Nicholas watched Kitsune's tracker.

Could there be another Kohath near Cuba? Was this the connection between Italy and Cuba? He should call Zachery, but not yet, no, not just yet.

His cell phone dinged a message from Ben.

Sending you some fascinating reading. Kohaths believed they discovered Atlantis. Stay tuned, there's more that might tie into where you're going.

When his cell dinged an incoming email, Nicholas scrolled down the pages Ben emailed him, and read:

There appears to be an underwater city off the coast of Cuba, discovered in the fifties. Alexander Kohath, that's Cassandra and Ajax's great-grandfather, was big into the Atlantis legend, was one of the world's preeminent Atlantis scholars. And naturally, because he was a Kohath, he believed the Ark could be there. According to his journal, they found this city off of Cuba on a dive and had been working on ways to get down to discover more — they actually cooked up a deal with the British government to use their military submarines for exploration. But then the Cuban Missile

449

Crisis happened in 1962 and the whole area was shut down.

Was it Atlantis? Photos they claim to have taken show large pyramids and even a sphinx. Guess what? They had a satellite Genesis Group office there for a while, so at least Cuba as a destination for the family to use as a bolt-hole makes some sense.

And this is where the weather machine comes in. The Kohaths have been creating storms to make money for over a century. It's as simple as that. I'm sure you know most of this already.

But here's what I've been able to sort out from St. Germaine's notes and David Maynes's letters he gave her. Appleton Kohath and Tesla fell out because Kohath wanted to use the weather machine to get money to fund his digs, and he saw the machine — Tesla called it "the Coil" — as an easy way to do so. In 1913, they invested in several companies — insurance, construction — then hit the Great Lakes with a storm. Horrendous damage. And here's how the scam worked — the companies Kohath had invested in were hired to repair and rebuild throughout the area, and became incredibly wealthy, thus paying out huge dividends to their investors. The Kohaths have been refining the weather machine ever since.

They make money on both ends, playing the market, owning reinsurance firms and huge construction conglomerates. Concrete, especially. When a hurricane knocks down half a city, someone has to rebuild, and there they are, ready to fill the void. They short stocks of companies in the areas there will be damage, make money on their losses. And that's just the financial side of things, the science is even freakier.

Tesla's Coil was pretty elaborate in the beginning, and Kohath spent years testing all the different ways he could monetize the Coil. As the Coil was perfected, as the science behind it got better, the ways to make money were refined as well. You already know their broker, Landry Rodgers, is a Brit living and working in Singapore. He's been on the Kohath payroll for the past twenty years, making them tons of cash, buying and selling and investing, taking advantage of the disasters they bring about. Unconscionable stuff.

Here's the Kohath family tree for five generations. I thought it would make more sense to you if you can see the actual players.

451

Appleton Kohath
- b. 1881 d. 1953
- From Richmond, England
- Married 1908 Genevieve

Their son
- b. 1917 Alexander d. 1969
- Married 1939 Babette

Their son
- b. 1941 Jason
- Married Diana

Their daughter
- b. 1965 Helen Kohath
- Married David Maynes

Their twins
- b. 1986 Cassandra and Ajax Kohath-Maynes

Nicholas sat back, closed his eyes. Five generations of Kohaths in on this scheme. No wonder Cassandra and Ajax went over the edge when their father handed over the family letters and journals to Elizabeth St. Germaine. The family secrets were worth killing for.

CHAPTER SIXTY-FOUR

Another ding on his cell phone. Nicholas looked down to see more texted information from Ben:

Jason Kohath, born in 1941, the Kohath twins' grandfather, is supposed to be some sort of über genius. He didn't go into archaeology, instead got a degree in mechanical engineering from Imperial College London, then went to MIT for grad work. The man had serious schooling. He even applied to NASA at one point but was turned down because he wasn't American. He worked for the European Space Agency for a bit, and then he disappeared. Went underground, according to the journals David Maynes gave to St. Germaine. All sorts of rumors about his having agoraphobia, but no verification. He simply disappeared.

I believe he's the one who's taken control

of the Coil and is running the storms. Since they were involved in Cuba, that would be a good guess for their center of operation.

Ben, it's all coming clear now, the connection between Cuba and Italy. The storm hasn't hit Washington, D.C. because the twins don't know how to make the Coil do it. Is Jason Kohath refusing to level the U.S. capital? They're headed to this island to talk him into it? Or is it a confrontation? We'll be in Cuba in an hour. Do you have anything useful on David Maynes?

Hold your horses, Nicholas. Let me upload my notes on him. A minute . . . Here we go. David Maynes never got along with Helen's father, Jason Kohath, who was adamantly against his daughter marrying him. After Helen's death, in the Gobi in 2006, word was Maynes went bonkers. And then his children, Cassandra and Ajax Kohath, kicked him out of the Genesis Group. He slunk back to England, pissed off, one imagines, and that's a good reason why he so joyfully gave over the Kohath papers to Elizabeth St. Germaine. Good old-fashioned revenge.

You're right, Ben, and it got him dead, about the same time as Elizabeth St. Germaine. The Kohath twins were behind it, of course, using their own private assassin, Lilith Forrester-Clarke. I sent Penderley all the info. He'll deal with it.

Nicholas looked out the window, down thirty-five thousand feet, clouds mostly, but every once in a while, a glimpse of the ocean. And he thought, *If Kitsune hadn't called, all the storms, all the decades of indiscriminate killing and destruction, would have continued indefinitely.*

Nicholas couldn't wait to learn more. Finally, he got another ding on his mobile with more text from Ben:

When Helen Kohath went missing in the Gobi Desert, the twins were already in their third year at Oxford, in the same college as their father and mother. They were very advanced, very intelligent, very driven. They were devastated by her disappearance, and by her being presumed dead. Maynes was devastated as well, by all accounts, and took a leave of absence from his job. He spiraled for a while, then pulled himself together and got back to work. He never said anything about the situation until he met recently with St. Germaine. And the biggest question St. Germaine had was: How could the Ark get in the Gobi Desert?

According to Kohath family lore, Pope Gregory X was the last known possessor of the Ark of the Covenant. The Kohaths have his secret papers in their possession, letters from the pope himself to a man named Evid Dupuy, a Templar master, and a spy for the Vatican. The letters detail how the Church came into possession of the Ark in 1060, when the Templars took back Jerusalem for the Church. The Templars brought the Ark to Rome, where it was hidden in the Vatican for two hundred years. Gregory X learned word had gotten out about the Ark being in the Vatican vaults and so he had it sent to a secret Templar stronghold, Castel Rigone, which was Dupuy's wife's family home. And yes, it is also the current home of the Kohaths. And this is why they bought the palazzo, realizing what they could have. After all, the palazzo was the perfect hiding place, what with all the Templar tunnels beneath the mountain.

Again, according to Kohath lore, Gregory was betrayed, and the Polo brothers, the father and uncle of the infamous Marco

Polo, were on their way to open relations with Genghis Khan and apparently stole the Ark from its hiding place in Castel Rigone, took it with them to China. The Kohaths believe one of the Polo brothers got the bright idea to try and open it. Apparently the Ark doesn't like to be opened by anyone but Levites, direct descendants of Moses, which the Kohaths are, and God sent a huge storm in the desert and the Ark disappeared.

Now, coming along to nearly present day: Helen Kohath found letters hidden in a secret compartment in a wall at the palazzo, letters Gregory had sent to Dupuy. She became completely convinced the Ark was still in the Gobi, lost in a biblical sandstorm that magically appeared to punish the non-Levites who tried to open it. And then she herself was lost in another sandstorm.

These people might be jacked-up crazy, particularly the twins, but it's true — everything the Kohaths have done for a century has been to find the Ark.

And that, Nicholas knew, explained exactly why Cassandra and Ajax had been focusing their weather storms in the Gobi, and after this last one, he'd bet they'd found their mother's site.

Nicholas looked over at Mike, saw she was awake. He got himself a bottle of water and orange juice for her, and sat beside her. "When you're up for it, Ben has texted me fascinating reading about the Kohaths. Explains just about everything."

She was wrapped in a blanket, snug in her seat, and she reached out her hand. "Now, I want to read it now."

He handed her the orange juice. "Drink first."

She did and he handed her his cell phone. When she finished, she said, "The reason Lilith didn't take all the papers from St. Germaine's shed or destroy them was because Cassandra and Ajax wanted everyone to believe she'd died of natural causes. To rob the place would invite suspicion. Same with their father. They should have waited a week, then burned the place down. I wonder why they didn't."

"I guess since they'd already filed the injunction to get the papers back, they assumed the moment she was dead the courts would comply and give them the material."

"Or maybe Lilith was supposed to stay in London, and after a suitable amount of time, get those papers out of there. But maybe something happened, and she had to go back to Italy when Kitsune turned up with the staff of Moses."

Nicholas said, "The exact date Lilith left England for Istanbul corresponds with Kitsune's grand theft. And then she flew to Italy."

Mike drank the rest of the orange juice, closed her eyes.

He studied her face. Her hair was in a straggly ponytail, she wore no makeup, there was a bruise on her jaw and stitches in her forehead, and she looked beautiful. He leaned in, kissed her, then, when she opened her eyes, he crossed his finger over his chest. "I solemnly swear I will never again drive a motorcycle through a wall and fly out of a tunnel over a lake." He paused. He wanted to simply say the words, but his voice shook. "I tried to grab you, but I was jerked away."

She saw the fear in his eyes, saw his hands clenching. Mike leaned into him, breathed him in. She said against his neck, "You know what? I'm grateful the lake was there, and not the ground. I don't think either of us would have survived that. We were lucky."

"That's one way of looking at it. I'm getting you more orange juice."

She'd made light of it, let him off the hook. He didn't come back until he had himself in control again. "Here, you need this, drink it down."

"You're right, I don't want to get a cold." She grinned as she drank the juice, wiped her hand over her mouth, and that made him smile. She said, "I think you and Ben are right. This frigging weather machine and Jason Kohath — they're both somewhere in or near Cuba, it only makes sense. Now, when do we land?"

"Soon, an hour at the most. What are you doing?"

"Texting Ben to tell him he's a genius."

When she'd finished, he took her hand, sat back, looked out the window. Then he looked over at Adam's laptop, saw Kitsune's tracker hadn't moved, the storm still hovered. Then he couldn't believe it.

"It's gotten stronger, Mike."

Mike said, "But it hasn't turned toward Washington yet. Nicholas, we have time, we'll stop it."

CHAPTER SIXTY-FIVE

The Caribbean, off of Cuba

After disembarking their plane at the Preston airfield, Alfredo, an airport maintenance worker, drove Cassandra, Ajax, and their prisoners the short distance to the dock to board the *Atlantis,* a sixty-six-foot motor yacht originally owned by Jason Kohath's father, Alexander, now used primarily for ferrying larger supplies to and from the island.

Old Ramos, called that since before the twins had been born, was captain of the *Atlantis.* Weather-beaten and gnarly, he was the patriarch of a huge family, and completely immoral. He welcomed them with a bow and a gap-toothed grin, nodded to three young men. "These three are family, of course, my brother's sons, and each is as tough as leather. As ordered, they will attend to your two prisoners."

Cassandra turned to the three young men,

461

none of them more than twenty years old, all trying their best to look vicious. She pointed to Kitsune and Grant, both unmoving, both silent, both, she knew, assessing their situation, planning how to escape. She said, "They might not look like much right now, but they are dangerous. Put them down in the salon, and keep a sharp eye on them."

She turned back to Ramos. "An hour to the island?"

Old Ramos patted the *Atlantis*'s wheel. "She's in top-flight shape, as always, *señorita.* One of my sons now oversees her maintenance, so no more than an hour."

Ajax nodded to Old Ramos's sailors, two of his own sons. This was a family enterprise as well as a family secret. One they were paid an enormous sum each year to keep.

Five minutes later, Old Ramos eased the *Atlantis* away from the dock and headed north.

Ramos steered, as was his wont. "It is better I take you to the island today, and not Rafael. His floatplane is too small for all of you and the supplies. I believe he flew to Havana, but he will be back soon, and available, if he is needed."

Cassandra didn't mind the extra time it took to go by boat to the island. Both she and her brother loved this lovely old yacht her great-grandfather had originally had built in Holland. She also loved the sea wind on her face.

Today the ocean was slate gray and cold, unusual for this area and this time of year. She breathed in, turned to her brother. "You said you managed to intensify the storm even more?"

"Yes, I told you. I hacked into grandfather's precious computer to intensify the storm, but who cares? I tell you, Cassandra, I've tried everything I know to make it move on Washington, but I still can't figure out how to make it go where I want it to go. Once I have Grandfather's directionality instructions, then it will be over very fast."

Cassandra said, "I can imagine how it will be when it lands — hurricane-force winds slamming into the Potomac. I can see the whole city underwater. Then we'll be home free, Ajax."

"Yes, home free." Ajax raised his face into the wind. He loved the feel of it, the power of it, as much as his twin. Soon now he would know exactly how the Coil worked from storm inception to devastation. He would be a god. He looked at his sister, standing beside him, the wind blowing her hair. She was smiling.

"With all the intensity I've added, the storm surge is going to be historic. Cassandra, the winds should reach one hundred fifty miles per hour. They'll never have a storm like it." He pumped his fist. "My first storm."

Old Ramos said, "I can have one of my nephews bring you some coffee if you're chilled. The weather is not nice today. We may hit some waves as we get closer, though your grandfather will do his best to keep them controlled. We're coming the southerly route. It won't be too bad but I'd feel better if you and the prisoners below put on life vests."

"Why? You're not going to capsize us, are you, Ramos, in this magnificent yacht?"

"Oh no, *señor,* never that, I just do not wish either of you to get tossed about."

Ajax only shook his head. Cassandra touched his billowing sleeve. "If Grandfather refuses to give you the formula, I know the thief will be able to open the vault. And then" — she snapped his fingers — "then we will finish things. Both she and her husband will feed the fishes. Isn't that what the Mafia dons say?"

He said, "In the movies, anyway. Lilith told me stories about the Fox, how she was one of the best art thieves in the world. If you needed to steal a Rembrandt from a museum or a private collection, she'd do it. Actually, she could steal anything, Lilith said."

Cassandra hugged him, shouted to the skies, "Soon this Fox will be as dead as Lilith. Ajax, look around you, it's only us in the empty sea — miles and miles of empty sea. Absolutely nothing in sight. But that doesn't mean there's nothing there." She threw back her head and laughed, and Captain Ramos looked over at her, wondering what the joke was. Whatever she was laughing about, though, he didn't want to know. He was thankful he didn't have to see these two very often, there was something about the two of them that made his blood run cold. He saw the *señorita* lean back against her brother. He clamped down on his cigar and turned all his attention back to the heaving seas.

Cassandra said to Ajax, in a dreamy voice, "When I was a child I remember Grandfather telling Mother he kept part of his formula in his vault. And I remember Mother thanking him. And I wondered, Why? For what? I asked him several times but he'd always shake his head, pat me on my head, and tell me to be patient." She snorted. "We've been more than patient.

You and I are thirty our next birthday. Soon, Ajax, we'll know if Mother left anything in the vault. I'm hoping she did, with all my heart, something for me, just for me."

"But what could it be? Certainly not treasure. Maybe papers on our great-grandfather's theories about Atlantis being in the Bermuda Triangle? He used this boat, you know, to explore this area." He shrugged and wrapped his arms around her when the boat dove from the top of a wave into a trough. He said against her cheek, "As you said, he would never tell you. I asked, too, of course, but he never told me anything, either."

"You know he always hated our father, hated that we carried his blood. I think he decided a long time ago not to trust us." She shouted into the wind, "You were right, old man! And now the end is coming for you."

She looked over at the box that held the cherubim's wing and her mother's map, both covered with a tarp and secured. "Maybe we won't need the thief — the Fox — to open the vault, maybe we can trade the cherubim's wing for the combination. You think Grandfather will agree?"

She didn't wait for him to answer. "Do you know what I'm hoping, Ajax? That there'll be proof in his vault that Mother is somehow still alive." Just saying the words aloud made her heart begin to pound faster. "That makes sense, doesn't it? Mother alive, somewhere, in hiding, with the Ark?"

"What, and the old man never told us? Could he distrust us that much?"

She turned and smiled up at her brother. "If he does distrust us that much, he certainly deserves to have us kill him. I can't wait to prove the old man right."

"We're nearly there," Old Ramos shouted over the wind. "I'm calling in." The transmitter hissed and barked. Ramos said, "This is *Atlantis* to Base One. We're approaching on the southerly route."

A British voice came back through the radio. "Roger, *Atlantis,* Base One confirming. Bear ten degrees to your northeast, we'll have the field down and ready for you in five."

Ramos turned the wheel a fraction to the right, moving the boat into position, and began to slow.

The sky ahead was clear and empty. There was nothing in front of them but water.

Absolutely nothing.

Then suddenly there it was — massive, rising out of the sea — the island. It always thrilled Cassandra to see it, magic, absolute magic, that's what they'd believed as children, and on the island dwelled the Wizard of Oz. Soon they would take his place. They would be the wizards. And they would have absolute power.

Old Ramos shook his head. "I never get used to it. One minute, blue air and endless empty sea, then the next, a massive dormant volcano reaches into the sky, is in front of you."

And it was beautiful, this island of theirs, covered in green jungle. It was their home, the heart of the Genesis Group, their greatest secret.

Soon, it would be their island. There would be no one to tell them what to do ever again.

CHAPTER SIXTY-SIX

Nicholas was putting together the gear they'd need when Adam said, "What is this? Wait, wait —" And he began banging his palm against the side of his laptop.

Nicholas was at his side in an instant. "What is it?"

"Kitsune's tracker just went down. Kaput. Nothing. I had her, it's been a great signal, nice and strong, and then it disappeared."

Nicholas looked down at Adam's laptop. "How many hours has it been since we gave it to her? Could it have expired?"

Adam looked at his watch. "We're at seventy hours and ten minutes since she ingested the tracker. We should have at least another two hours."

"Are they that accurate?"

"In testing, yes. If anything, the signal will linger on for another two to three hours after the planned seventy-two. I've never seen one stop early."

Louisa hovered over Adam. "Guys, she's been through a lot. Her adrenaline levels are probably through the roof, maybe that made her system metabolize the tracker faster than normal."

Adam chewed his lip. "It's a good theory, but the tracker shouldn't be affected by her body chemistry. The designer made allowances — Wait, give me a minute. I want to look at something. I'm playing with an idea of why right now."

"Where was the tracker's last ping?" Nicholas asked, and Adam pointed to the screen. He'd been tracking Kitsune the old-fashioned way, like a submariner tracking a whale, with small *X*s drawn on the chart to show her last known coordinates.

"You can see exactly where she went off the map. There's nothing there. It's ocean, miles and miles of empty ocean. No land, nothing."

Nicholas watched as Adam pulled up another file and started running an algorithm on the previous geo-located marks. "What are you looking for?"

"This," Adam said, pointing at his screen. They gathered around him to see he'd pulled up a map up on his tablet with Kitsune's trajectory outlined in white. "From the velocity and speed the tracker was traveling, we know they were on a plane. But" — he swiped to a new image, and enlarged the map — "when the tracker started to move again, it was at a much slower pace. They flew into Preston, then put her on a boat." He tapped his finger on the screen, which obligingly magnified the areas. "And this is where the signal abruptly stopped."

Mike leaned down and used two fingers to enlarge the map, then minimize, enlarge, minimize. She traced the edge of the tablet with her finger. No matter what she did — there was still nothing in the spot Kitsune's tracker disappeared, only miles and miles of blue water.

"It doesn't make sense," Mike said. "There's simply nothing there, nothing to account for the tracker not working. And we're sure she's still with the Kohath twins? I wonder if they dumped her off somewhere."

"Wouldn't matter," Nicholas said, "the tracker would still work. I think they're with her and Grant, somewhere. But where? Not a clue."

Adam looked at each of them, drew in a breath and said, "I've got a theory."

"A theory? Okay, Mr. Hot Shot," Louisa said. "Tell us what you've got."

"The only thing is, it's sort of out there."

Nicholas laughed. "Everything on this case is 'out there,' Adam. Launch away."

Adam said, "Remember Ben told us that way back at the beginning of the twentieth century, Appleton Kohath worked with Tesla, and they developed the Coil using all kinds of electromagnetic power, right?"

"Yes."

"And now, they've managed to push the limits, create storms that are incredibly sophisticated, probably more advanced than we can imagine, right?"

"Spit it out, Adam," Louisa said.

"Watch this." He had a video queued. It was an animation of the GPS tracker, overlaying a map of Europe.

"Okay, this is the first time we lost her signal — she's in the tunnels beneath the Kohath palazzo, then her signal magnifies, and then it simply goes silent. Remember, Nicholas, we were thinking maybe the EMP had knocked it out? And then, inexplicably, it came back on and stayed on?"

They watched the screen shift to the Caribbean. "Now we're here, over an empty expanse of water, and her tracker signal's strong. Watch this. The blip magnifies, just like the first time, and then it's gone, totally gone."

472

Adam ran the video three more times.

Louisa said, "This is seriously weird."

"I would have agreed with you until I did some research on the ingestible GPS trackers, and guess what?" He gave them a maniacal grin. "The suckers can be affected by magnets."

Nicholas said, "So if you hold a magnet near enough to the tracker, it will go offline."

Adam nodded.

Louisa said, "You take the magnet away, the tracker comes back online."

"Yep."

Mike said, "Okay, it's a glitch in the design, but who would imagine wearing a tracker next to a magnet? The designers probably didn't even consider it." She smacked Adam's shoulder. "Good thinking, Adam. But what does it mean? Kitsune is sitting near a big-ass magnet?"

"It's more than that." Nicholas and Adam said together, both smiling like loons, "We're talking about a cloaking device."

Mike's eyebrows shot up. "Come on, guys, what do you mean, a cloaking device? Like the Romulans on *Star Trek*? That sort of cloaking device?"

Adam said, "Yep, exactly that sort of cloaking device. Look here." He tapped the screen, right where Kitsune's tracker disappeared the first time. "I asked myself, if a physical magnet can make the tracker go offline, what would an electromagnetic field do to it?"

Nicholas said slowly, "You told me you never saw the Kohaths leave the mountain and you couldn't explain it except with magic flying brooms, and you were watching like a hawk."

"Right. And when they cleared their palazzo and their mountain, Kitsune's tracker suddenly came back online. Actually, it came back online when they were exactly thirty miles away from Castel Rigone. It's like they've managed to figure out how to use electromagnetic interference to hide themselves. And I'm not talking mirrors, stealth, reducing their radar signature, nothing like that. I'm thinking it's something like a portable electromagnetic jammer they use whenever they want to get out of town unseen."

Nicholas chewed this over, then said slowly, "So they drove away from their palazzo, flipped the switch, and poof — they're invisible."

Louisa said, "But that'd sure be dangerous, I mean, if you're driving, and other drivers can't see you?"

"And that's why I think they were in a helicopter," Adam said. He scrolled back on his tablet. "Look at the satellite shots. There's nothing there. Then thirty miles away from their mountain, the signal appears, flying low. It had to be a helicopter. They transferred to a plane and headed south."

Mike said, "So forget magic brooms, it's more like Harry Potter's invisibility cloak. Imagine the technology to do that. I don't know, Adam, it sounds like more than science fiction to me."

"I wish I could find another explanation," Adam said, shrugged. "But I can't. Actually, the first time her tracker stopped, I chalked it up to a malfunction with my software until —"

"Until Kitsune disappeared again," Nicholas said.

"Yeah, no explanation, same as the first time. Talk about science fiction — if the Kohaths can control the weather, why not extend their discoveries, it's all along the same line, all based on electromagnetics. I gotta say though, a portable EM cloaking device is pretty impressive. Even cooler than your micro EMP, Nicholas."

"But here in the middle of the ocean? And not a thing for miles? This isn't a portable,

Adam," Louisa said. "This is something else entirely."

Mike said, "You're telling me we could be looking right at them and not see them? They're cloaked?"

Adam nodded to Mike. "That's it. Can they see us? Of course they can. We know Appleton Kohath worked extensively with Tesla for a number of years and Jason Kohath is supposed to be an über genius with electromagnetic fields."

Louisa said, "I've always thought it kind of stupid, what Sherlock Holmes said, 'When you have eliminated the impossible, whatever remains, *however improbable, must be the truth.*' Now I'm not so sure."

Nicholas was shaking his head. "It's hard to get my brain around this, but if it's true, which it appears to be, then it's ground-breaking science. Imagine the applications — if it can be applied to moving objects as well as stationary, you could send squadrons and troops into place without anyone knowing they're coming. It's war-winning technology."

Mike looked at the screen again, where Kitsune's tracker had disappeared the second time. "So they're hiding or cloaking something really big. Right here, in the middle of the ocean."

Nicholas was looking off into the distance, past her left shoulder. She knew what that meant — he was making a big leap of logic. She grinned as she counted down in her head, *Three, two, one,* and Nicholas said, "Adam, pull up a map of the Bermuda Triangle."

CHAPTER SIXTY-SEVEN

Adam and Nicholas were bent over their laptops, maps at their elbows, their fingers typing rapidly, grunts, smiles, head shakes. Louisa and Mike were watching and listening as they cleaned their weapons, Mike's in greater need since it had gone swimming in Lake Trasimeno.

Nicholas raised his fist, "Yes, it fits, Adam. It's inside the lines. The Bermuda Triangle."

"I think our team just scored," Louisa said, and blew gently along the muzzle of her Glock. "It's fun to watch them spark off each other."

Mike called out, "What fits? What's this about the Bermuda Triangle?"

Adam said, "Nicholas thinks they might be responsible for all the planes and ships lost in the Bermuda Triangle."

"No, no, that's not what I'm saying at all," Nicholas said. "I think the Kohaths took advantage of the bizarre happenings attributed to this part of the ocean that have resulted in dozens of lost ships and planes. They knew people avoided the area. What better place than a mythical triangle of ocean to have their home base, where no one can find them or see them? But most important — they don't have to worry all that much because people don't want to come here in the first place."

Louisa called out, "But if there's something physical out there, surely people have come across them. Even if they didn't see them, sooner or later, someone would run smack into them, right?"

Adam frowned at his laptop screen. "That would mean then that they had to develop a way to steer people away if they got too close."

Mike jumped to her feet, felt a moment of dizziness, saw the sudden alarm on Nicholas's face, and said quickly, "No, no, I'm fine. Look, guys, wherever they're hiding must be near the spot Kitsune's tracker disappeared, got to be.

"Nicholas, we need to get out there and find out where they're hiding. And we need to yell for help."

"Yes, but tell them what? First we have to find the Kohaths."

Adam said, "But, dude, we don't even

know what we're looking for."

"Adam," Nicholas said, "we can't see anything from the surface, what about looking below the water? Is there any way we can do that?"

Adam lit up like a Christmas tree. "Hold on, hold on, yes, I remember reading something — yeah, here it is, I bookmarked it to look at later for a computer program I'd like to write. Ah, here it is. Bathymetric LIDAR — it's a remote sensing method that NOAA — the National Oceanic and Atmospheric Administration — uses to map seabeds. LIDAR stands for 'Light Detecting and Ranging.' They can map coastlines and seabeds to examine natural and man-made environments. If we can get our hands on the technology —"

Mike said, "That'd take too much time —"

"I'll call a friend who works at NOAA, see if she knows."

"Go, do it," Nicholas said. "But be careful what you say. We don't want anyone getting word of what we're doing, especially the Kohaths. We don't know the sophistication of their communications."

Mike reholstered her spanking-clean Glock, hoped it worked. "You're saying we now have a way to find them?"

Louisa propped her chin on her fisted hands. "So any sort of cloaking device wouldn't extend to beneath the water. And maybe that means we're looking for some sort of base they built, or —"

"An island," Mike said. "What if they found a place to live out here and have managed to keep it off the radar — literally — all these years?"

Nicholas said, "So you're thinking they found an isolated, uninhabited island and set it up as their home base? And this is where all their manufactured storms come from? Okay, that could work. Adam, is there any way to track where the storms were generated from? Are there any sort of co-ordinates that trace back to this area?"

"Nothing I can see. Sorry, Nicholas. Unless my friend has something for us to latch on to, we're going to have to go out there and take a look around. I've also been looking at pre-twentieth-century maps of this area. No sign of an island in a thirty-mile radius of where Kitsune's tracker went off. Okay, my call went through. Let's see what my friend can do. Chill out, guys, we've still got thirty minutes before we land."

Nicholas smiled, stepped away. He looked over at Mike. She was watching him as she put on her gear. She was moving slowly, but she did have some color in her face. He remembered her lying so still, not breathing — he brought himself back. No, she wasn't dead, she was here, with him, locked and loaded. She was smiling. She was fine.

"Here, let me," he said, and helped her with the Velcro panel of her bullet-proof vest. She rested her head against his shoulder for a minute, then straightened and passed her belt through the holster and settled it at the right spot on her hip. She grabbed Nicholas's hand and gave it a good squeeze. "Wipe the worry out of your brain. I'm all right, Nicholas. Quite all right. And both my Glock and my ankle pistol survived their swim. Hopefully."

He watched her fasten the small holster, then pull on her boots. She looked up at him, frowned. "The boots still feel wet. I doubt they'll ever dry out."

"Yeah, give them a decade." And he brought her up, cupped her face in his hands. "Tell me the truth, and I'll shut up. How do you feel?"

She lightly stroked her fingers over his scruffy cheek. "I'm good to go, I promise. I like the beard stubble, it's sexy."

He had to laugh. "You mean I can seduce you if I don't happen to shave?"

"Could be. Maybe. Probably."

CHAPTER SIXTY-EIGHT

Preston Airfield
Cuba

Louisa was standing on the tarmac, having a discussion in heated Spanish with the airport authorities, who were doing their best to make her and Adam get back on the plane and bugger off their tarmac. Clancy and Trident were still in the cockpit, Louisa had told them they couldn't help, they didn't speak Spanish. As for Adam and Nicholas, they were still studying maps and doing their computer magic.

Mike, who'd been listening and understood some Spanish, moseyed over. "Louisa, tell our friends here that I know the vice president of the United States personally. I'll call her, let them speak to her about letting us use their airport."

Louisa translated in rapid Spanish, and Mike had a feeling she was embroidering Mike's message. Who cared? Whatever worked.

She saw the official finally nod. He stood there, his shoulders hunched, and kicked a pebble out of his path. Another man came to join him, but he said nothing, merely looked at Louisa, and if Mike wasn't mistaken, there was admiration in his eyes. Finally, both men nodded.

"Good going, Louisa," Mike said.

Adam had come out of the plane, stood at the top of the stairs, and stared at a culture completely alien to him — ancient airport, cars from the fifties, jungle creeping onto the runway, impenetrable tangled green as far as the eye could see. He'd watched Louisa, forensics queen of the universe, spewing out fluent Spanish, throwing her weight around. It was a fine sight to see.

He saw a speck on the horizon. Within moments, it grew larger, and he could hear the whine of an engine.

"Nicholas, come here now."

Nicholas came down the stairs, shaded his eyes. "It's an old Grumman Albatross coming in for a landing. Louisa, find out where that plane's coming from."

She launched into another barrage of Spanish. The first man spoke, then shrugged, and both men hightailed it back to the ancient corrugated steel building that looked close to collapsing in on itself, and disappeared inside.

Mike asked, "What did they say?"

Louisa looked disgusted. "They claim they have no idea. For whatever reason, they're both afraid." Louisa pushed her hair off her face and waited, tapping her foot, while the pilot of the Albatross landed and taxied in to the hangar. He came closer and closer, saw them, and saw the airport manager frantically waving him off. He veered away, gunned his engines, and headed back toward the runway.

Adam yelled, "That plane — It's got the Genesis logo etched on the side — a stylized *G*! We've got to stop him!"

Louisa took off after the plane in a dead run.

"Boy, can she move," Adam said.

"I watched her in the New York City Marathon last year," Mike said. "She came in fifth. And that's why she carb-loads — fast fuel."

"What if he runs over her?"

"He won't," Nicholas said. "Too dangerous for him. And Louisa's got a gun."

They watched the old plane do a full turn to make it back to the runway. Louisa put herself in front of it, right in the line of sight of the pilot. She raised her weapon, pointed it directly at the small windshield, and shouted in Spanish even though she strongly doubted the pilot could hear her over the engines, "Turn off the engine and get out of the plane, now, or I will shoot either you or your plane dead!"

The pilot didn't stop, so Louisa pulled the trigger. She didn't shoot the pilot, she nicked a panel right above the pilot's head to show him she was serious.

The pilot stopped and killed the engine.

They watched him climb out of the Albatross with his hands up. Louisa stood facing him, her gun aimed at his chest. The airport manager and his buddies had stayed inside the hangar.

They all converged on the pilot. Nicholas asked him if he spoke English. The man looked insulted. "Of course. Everyone speaks English here. It's required, well except for those fools who work here at the airport."

"Who exactly requires you to speak English?"

"My employers."

"What is your name?"

"I am Rafael Guzman."

"Rafael, you will tell me where you flew the Kohaths."

"I came back from Havana. I don't know

what you're talking about."

Nicholas sighed. "Rafael, forgive me, but I don't have time to engage in a lively discussion with you. Your plane is owned by the Genesis Group, see the *G* on the side of your plane? And that means you are owned by the Kohaths.

"You will tell me how I can find the Kohaths or I will shoot you in the kneecap and you will never fly again." Nicholas drew his Glock, aimed it at Guzman's right knee.

Mike came up to stand beside Nicholas. Aimed her Glock at his left knee. "Now," she said, "or not only will you never fly again, you will never walk again. You've got a nice long life ahead of you. Imagine it in a wheelchair."

Rafael gulped. "Stop, please don't shoot. My wife wouldn't like it, she might kick me out, she —"

"Where are the Kohaths, Rafael?"

"Okay, sure, I fly for the Kohath twins when they visit and make other flights for *El Creador* for supplies, whatever he wishes. But not this time, this time Old Ramos took them in the *Atlantis,* it's a big old yacht. There were four passengers and supplies, and they would not fit on my plane."

"And where, exactly, do you fly?" Mike asked.

"I always fly to specific coordinates. I call Base One and soon a boat appears. I don't know any more than that."

"A boat appears? From where?"

He looked at Mike. "It comes from the —" He swallowed and froze, and both of them saw the fear. Was he more scared of the Kohaths than he was of losing both knees?

Mike said, "Three seconds, and you're crippled for life, Mr. Guzman."

Guzman splayed his hands in front of him. "Listen, listen, no one knows. It is a secret." He paused a moment, then, "It is a very *valuable* secret."

"Now you want to make us pay for what you know? Say goodbye to walking by yourself to the bathroom." She flicked off the safety and aimed her Glock.

Nicholas said, "A moment, Agent Caine. Mr. Guzman, we are not unreasonable. We will give you ten thousand dollars if you tell us everything, because we realize that once you have told us everything, there won't be any more trips for you with the Kohaths."

"And we will leave your knees intact."

"And you will get me to the United States? My daughter goes to medical school in Miami. I haven't seen her for two years."

"You've got yourself a deal. Talk."

"Listen, if I tell you everything I know, they will kill me and my family. So we could not remain here. Could my wife and I live permanently in the United States. Forever?"

"Yes," Nicholas said, and hoped Vice President Sloan would come through for him. "Yes, forever."

Rafael pulled a dirty handkerchief from his jeans pocket and mopped the sweat off his forehead. "Okay, the boat comes from the island. I've seen it only a few times. They have a way of making it disappear. I can't fly the plane all the way there, I have to land in the water, and they bring the boat to me. I fly in smaller supplies to them, supplies they need quickly, like groceries and small maintenance items, since my plane takes a shorter time than the *Atlantis.* Otherwise, Old Ramos ferries supplies from here to the island. He says he's worked for the old man for forty years, he has deliveries about three times a week, sometimes more."

"What is this crazy old man's name?" Nicholas asked.

"They call him *El Creador.*"

"Creator of what?"

"He builds things, everyone says he builds crazy things, weird things. I don't know, how could I? I'm a pilot. I fly for a living. I do know his name, though. And the names of his twin grandchildren. Jason Kohath. The twins are Cassandra and Ajax."

"What does it look like, the island?"

"It's a volcano."

"A volcano? Is it active?"

"No. Around this area there are all kinds of volcanos, on all the islands. This island, though, it isn't on any of the maps I've seen. You look on some old nautical maps, maybe you find it. I don't know. It's been hidden my whole life."

"How old are you?"

"Fifty-three."

Nicholas and Mike shared a glance. The timeline fit. The Genesis Group, namely, Alexander Kohath, had been in this area looking for Atlantis in the 1950s and '60s and that was probably when they'd come across an uncharted volcano. And Jason Kohath's father had taken it over as a testing ground for their Coil.

"How many people are out there?" Mike asked.

"Six, maybe eight — *El Creador,* a cook, anywhere from two to four guards, and an assistant — a ghoul of a fellow, very serious — and of course the Brit captain of the boat that unloads supplies from my plane, and his first mate. The pay is great, the Brit captain told me once, but he said it's tough, since they're so isolated, nothing to do except play Ping-Pong and watch movies. And his first mate said the old man sits in front of a dozen computers all the time. No one knows what he does. Except for his assistant, I guess."

"How often do his grandchildren, Cassandra and Ajax Kohath, visit?"

"Once, maybe twice a year, more often when they were younger. They don't usually show up without a lot of notice, but not this time, almost no warning at all.

"That beautiful girl, I've got to warn you, she's nuts. She didn't like something Alfredo — he's one of the mechanics who works here — said the last time they came, and she kicked him onto the ground and kept kicking him until her brother pulled her off. Alfredo was in bed for a week with broken ribs.

"Me? I'm more afraid of him, the brother, Ajax." Rafael shuddered. "He's all calm and reasonable one minute and then the next, those eyes of his are glowing, like a demon's." As if he knew how melodramatic that sounded, Rafael added, "Not really a demon, more like a volcano you thought was dormant. He'll explode without warning. Both of them, they're . . . not right in the head."

"They came without warning this time?"

Rafael nodded. "I got word to be ready only a few hours ago, in case they wanted me. But as I said, they went on the *Atlantis* to the island."

"Weapons?"

"I don't know. This time I know Old Ramos brought along three of his nephews, and they all had guns."

"Does the *Atlantis* go to the island?"

"No. Like me when I fly in supplies or people, the Brit captain brings a boat from the island. I've been ordered never to go past the drop zone, but I remember the first time, I hung around to see what would happen."

"What did you see?"

"One minute there was simply nothing but water all around, the next this island with a volcano in the middle of it. It was like magic, scary magic. I hear talk the *El Creador* is some sort of mad scientist. But of course I can't ask how he does this magic since I wasn't supposed to ever see it. You do believe me, don't you? I mean, you won't shoot out my knees?"

Mike said, "We believe you, your knees are safe from us."

Nicholas said, "One last thing. I want you to ask the airport manager if there was a

492

man and woman with the Kohaths. Prisoners."

"I was told there were four people. Does this help you?"

Nicholas said, "Go ask the airport manager to describe them to you."

Rafael trotted to the hangar and was back again in a couple of minutes. "Alfredo said the two of them were tied up. Both of them were dirty, beat-up, but you know what? Alfredo said they still looked dangerous, both of them."

Mike asked, "When are you due to fly in the next shipment?"

"Tomorrow."

"Rafael, you're going to make that delivery today. Call them up, make an excuse. You have to get it to them now. However you communicate, do it. Don't forget your knees, your ten thousand dollars, your forever in the United States with your wife, and your daughter in Miami."

"Yeah, okay, I'll call them now. I speak only to the British captain. Once I set up a drop, then what?"

"Then —" Nicholas smiled. "Then, Rafael, you will fly us out there."

CHAPTER SIXTY-NINE

The Bermuda Triangle: October 1, 2015, a 790-foot cargo ship, the SS *El Faro,* reported a tropical storm hundreds of miles away suddenly dashed toward them and circled the ship. Communications went dead. The hurricane was later reported going back from where it had originally been, once again a tropical storm. Weeks later, *El Faro* was finally located sitting upright in one piece at a depth of fifteen thousand feet. No trace of the thirty-three man crew.

The Bermuda Triangle

When Cassandra had visited Grandfather's island for the first time as a child, she'd expected tremendous heat, even brimstone, and her grandfather lighting his cigars in the burning lava, like a god, or the devil. Shortly, they would prove he was no god, or the devil, only a relic who'd outlived his usefulness, lost his courage.

Soon it would be her island. No brimming lava, no sulfurous brimstone, instead, the smell of rocks, and that made her smile.

Rocks were one of her mother's favorite things, and hers as well, of course. Earth was forever, Helen would say, and rocks marked the time.

Cassandra hadn't been able to stop thinking about her mother since they'd found the cherubim's wing and the note, about what might have happened to her, about spending the rest of her life without her. She could still listen to her mother's voice, though. Cassandra had offloaded several of her mother's voice messages. Sometimes she played them, to listen to her mother's voice, like lovely British bells.

She wouldn't think of her mother now, she couldn't afford to because she knew her mother wouldn't approve of what she and Ajax were going to do. But there was no choice, it had to be done or everything would fall apart. And after Grandfather was dead, her focus had to be finding the Ark.

Sometimes, when she opened her mind, she fancied she could feel the Ark under her fingers, she could see her hands raising the lid, she could taste the power it would bring, feel its promise, a light in the darkness. She would become one with it and then it would hit her like a bolt of lightning, and then she'd be omnipotent. And Ajax, would he be omnipotent as well? Somehow, Cassandra couldn't imagine Ajax sharing in the glory that would be hers, alone.

Cassandra walked into the perfectly camouflaged concrete structure, built, Grandfather believed, by the Russians. It was covered with ivy and vines, and gnarled bushes with huge twisted branches and birds nested there. The entrance wasn't noticeable unless you knew where to look — just in case, her grandfather had always said — just in case.

She walked through the security gate, knowing one of Grandfather's X-rays was looking at her to the bone. It came to her then, a memory from when she was nineteen, and he'd told her and Ajax about their mother being lost in the Gobi. She'd asked him then if he had her notebooks. She remembered clearly now that he'd shaken his head, said, "Your mother's notebooks are not for you."

And why not? But she hadn't asked, she was too grief-stricken. Maybe her mother's notebooks were in the vault.

Cassandra felt a spurt of excitement as she nearly danced into the inner sanctum. She wasn't at all surprised to see her grand-

496

father seated in his chair, sipping a cup of that disgusting coffee he loved so much.

Jason said without turning, "I saw you come in. Why are you here, Cassandra?" His voice sounded scratchy and old — no, ancient, unused.

She said gaily, "We haven't seen you for too long, Grandfather. We missed you." Should she hug him, kiss him? She didn't move.

Finally he turned to face her. A thick gray eyebrow went up. "You honestly expect me to believe that? Where is your brother?"

"Securing the cargo."

The old man's eyes narrowed. "Why did you bring that man and woman with you?"

Cassandra went over to look at the satellite screens in front of him. "I might need the woman, we'll see. It's nothing for you to worry about, Grandfather. Where is the storm?"

Jason smiled, showing yellow teeth from the gallons of that vile coffee he drank, and she felt revulsion. She didn't want to believe she was of his blood, that her mother was his child. He looked so ordinary, so shrunken, with his stark white hair in tufts on his head, his thick glasses magnifying his eyes, and that mean slash of a mouth. His meager shoulders were rounded from decades in front of his computers. She looked at the liver spots on his hands and arms and quickly looked away. It was past time for him to die. Long past time.

No, he wasn't a god. She imagined he clung so desperately to life because he knew the Ark would make him immortal, make him a god. *Not for you, old man, not for you.*

He pointed toward one of the screens behind him, where the storm had grown to an alarming size. "Did you truly think Ajax could intensify the storm without my noticing?"

"Of course not, Grandfather. You see everything, don't you?"

Jason felt sadness looking at her beautiful face, Helen's face. But not Helen's voice. He heard the slick sneer, the not-completely-hidden threat in Cassandra's voice. Then he felt more — soul-deep fury. "Surely your brother knows he cannot move the storm into the position he wants. Only I can do that."

Cassandra fought for control. "You must give Ajax the rest of the formula, Grandfather. We must destroy Washington, D.C. Otherwise all we have built, all we have accomplished, it will vanish in the blink of an eye, and Ajax and I will be taken or killed. So rather than New Orleans again, we destroy their very seat of power. Please, Grandfather, the American FBI is close, too close."

He said abruptly, "Show me the cherubim's wing."

He was ready to negotiate. Excellent.

"I will not only show it to you, I will give it to you. But first, you will give me the combination to the vault so we can have the formula."

Jason studied his granddaughter's face. She stood perfectly still, the box holding the cherubim's wing under her arm. So like Helen, yet nothing like her at all. Helen's innate goodness hadn't bred into her children. The girl thought to bribe him. It was amusing if it hadn't been so sad. He said quietly, "Do you remember you once asked me if I was the Wizard of Oz?"

She leaned close, studied his seamed face. "That was long before I realized what and who was behind the curtain, before I saw what you were and what you'd become — a pathetic gutless old man."

He scooted his chair away from her, studied her as she'd studied him. "A pity you only see me now as an obstacle and not as *El Creador,* as Burnley says some of the Cubans call me. No, Cassandra, I will not give you the directionality procedure. I would fear for the world's survival if I did. Why can't you realize I am only trying to do the right thing? To help find the Ark, to keep the Genesis Group financially healthy." He saw she wasn't even listening to him. He said abruptly, "You say the FBI is close behind you. Tell me what you did."

She didn't meet his eyes. "Ajax and I did only what was needful."

She wasn't going to tell him, still he tried. "You and Ajax could remain here, safe from the FBI. And together, we can continue to run the Genesis Group."

"I cannot find the Ark if I'm hiding out here."

He wanted to tell her the Ark wasn't for her, but he said, "I will not weaken the United States by destroying their capital, all because you and your brother haven't been wise in your choices.

"You know the FBI or any other country's law enforcement can't find you and your brother here. Say you will stay with me, and be safe, learn what you must learn to honor your mother's memory."

He stared at her, seeing yet again her hatred for him, her contempt, and it chilled him. Like her damnable excuse for a father, she and her brother were unstable, a kind word for it, but he couldn't bring himself to think crazy, it was too final, too scary, it meant the end of everything. Of course, he'd known it for a long time, even accepted it, but to see her now, realizing what she was, seeing this bone-deep hatred of him, in the open for the first time, it nearly broke him. And he remembered Helen's words that he would do everything he could to help them until there was nothing more he could do, and she understood, then she'd bowed her head.

Still, he was shocked when she screamed at him, "Don't you speak to me about honoring my mother's memory! Everything I do is for my mother. Enough, you profane old man. Open the vault or I will crack the cherubim's wing over your skull and watch your genius brains fly all over your computers. Give me the combination!"

CHAPTER SEVENTY

Jason knew he had to keep calm, and use reason that would make her understand even though he knew it wouldn't work. "Cassandra, what do you think you would gain if you destroyed Washington? You think they wouldn't come after you, that you would be safe?"

"Of course. The storm will be so massive it will take the U.S. years to recover. As for law enforcement, the FBI, we will be far down on their list. Think of all the looting, the anarchy, the chaos. We will be nothing to them." And she snapped her fingers.

"Now, I want the formula. It's time for Ajax to direct the storm to Washington."

"No."

"You're refusing to give us the rest of the formula?"

"Yes."

She slowly opened the box and lifted out the golden cherubim's wing. It glowed, warmed her hands. She felt the writing indenting its surface and saw the words in her mind:

Through this door lies a weapon of great power. Open it, and it will indeed kill.

Through this door —

She whispered, "The Ark is here, it's in the vault, isn't it? You've had it this entire time. You've lied to us, to me and Ajax, our entire lives. The Ark is here."

"No," he said, and felt a sudden spurt of fear. She was walking toward him, never taking her eyes off him and the look in her eyes was wild and cold and black.

"You bastard. What else have you been hiding in that ridiculous vault? My mother's whereabouts? My mother's notebooks? Tell me, you worthless old man!"

Jason simply shook his head back and forth.

She said, "The Ark belongs to the Kohaths. We are the last of the line. The Ark will be mine, not yours, never yours."

He slammed his fist onto the console. "Get a hold of yourself, Cassandra. Listen to me now. I don't have the Ark. As for the formula, I keep it here." He tapped his head. "Do you believe I would ever write it down and stash it in my vault? Yes, I see you want to kill me, but if you do, you will never be able to use the Coil again. And that means you will never find the Ark. Think carefully before you do something you will regret for the remainder of your life."

Her eyes — he saw his death in her eyes. This was the end. He knew it. He must find a way to warn the others, to warn his assistant, Burnley, but there was no way, and he felt sorrow, deep in his soul.

Cassandra knew he was lying. No, the formula wasn't in the vault, nor was it his ancient memory. He would keep it close, she knew it.

Jason spread out his arms, knew what was coming, accepted it. "Your mother knew that neither you nor your brother could be trusted, that you were both the product of your father, and she wept for a future that promised nothing but pain and loss and disaster for you."

"You're a liar! Mother left us a message with the cherubim's wing. She loved us, do you hear me? She wants Ajax and me to have the power, the immortality."

He ignored her question. "I will not give you the combination to the vault. You won't be able to enter without it."

"Of course I will. I checked it out, read everything about your precious vault."

Jason was tired, mortally tired. "If you think you are so clever, if you know so much about my vault, then try to open it, but I must warn you, you will die trying."

"Oh, I know all about the explosives you fashioned into it as well. It will not be a problem. I have a way to open it, you'll see."

There was nothing more to say.

"You miserable old man, give me the formula!"

Jason swiveled around to see Ajax coming toward him.

"No," he said. "As I told your sister, I fear for humanity were you to have it."

Ajax was on him. He sent his fist into his grandfather's head, knocking him out of his chair. Jason lay motionless facedown, unmoving, Ajax standing over him, breathing hard.

"Ajax, is he dead?"

Ajax went down on his haunches, grabbed his grandfather's arm and pulled him onto his back. His eyes were closed, his mouth slightly agape. Ajax could see his chest rising and falling rapidly. Blood was running from a cut on his forehead, running into his eyes.

"No," he said, "I didn't want to kill him. He still hasn't told us where he keeps the formula."

"Ajax, he told me the formula wasn't in the vault, that he had it memorized. He was lying. The procedures for directionality can't be all that simple, so wouldn't he keep it close? Here, by his computers?"

She ran toward and began pulling open drawers. Ajax joined her. They looked in every drawer, they lifted books off the shelves and fanned them. Nothing.

Ajax said, "When he comes to, I'll get it out of him."

"Keep looking. I know it's here, it has to be here."

He lifted the keyboard from his grandfather's main computer. "Cassandra, something's taped to the bottom."

He carefully pulled a folded piece of paper off, unfolded it. Ajax couldn't believe it. "No wonder he kept it close, it's instructions, directions, if you will. It's long and it's complicated, just like you thought, no way to remember all of it or memorize it.

"Cassandra, making the storm go in a certain direction is all based on longitude and latitude of the target, and that determines the angle of the lasers — some intersect at certain degrees, others simply align in a specific pattern. I must find the longitude and latitude of Washington." He flung himself in front of Jason's computer.

He punched some keys, laughed. "I love Google. Washington is 38 degrees, 89 minutes north longitude, 77 degrees, 3 minutes, west latitude. Now —"

"What have you done? Oh no, Dr. Kohath!" Aaron Burnley fell to his bony knees beside their grandfather, grabbing his hands, rubbing them, pulling out a handkerchief, wiping the blood from his forehead, daubing at his eyes. He stared up at Cassandra. "What have you done? Why did you hurt him? He's the greatest man who ever lived, he's your grandfather! Are you insane?"

"I'm not insane!" She kicked Burnley in the face and he fell over their grandfather. She looked toward her brother. "I never liked him. He looks like a ghoul, all skinny and pasty-skinned."

But Ajax wasn't paying any attention. "Now that I have longitude and latitude, I need to calculate the position of the lasers to determine directionality. Give me a minute and I'll get it."

She saw a glint of something shiny. She leaned down and shoved the unconscious Burnley off her grandfather. His shirt had ripped when he'd fallen, and around his neck she saw a gold chain, and hanging from that gold chain was a double-hasped director's key. "Ajax, I'd forgotten. It's impossible to get into the vault without this key, then the combination. It's a double-safe."

He was still doing calculations, didn't look at her. "We don't need to get into the vault now. Forget it."

"No, no, he's hiding something in there, something important, maybe Mother's notebooks. Who knows? Maybe even the Ark. I've got to get it open."

"Hold on, another minute." Then he was madly typing in numbers. He spun around in their grandfather's chair. "I've done it! The storm is huge and it's heading straight for Washington, D.C.

"Three hours, Cassandra, three hours! The winds will slam into the city, flatten it, and the water will rise from the Potomac and drown them all. D.C. will be gone, like that." He snapped his fingers. "And that Drummond character, he has no idea where we are. We're safe, at last we're safe. He'll go back to the U.S. to nothing at all."

"Ajax, the vault!"

He was shaking his head at her. "You think the Ark could be in the vault? Mother's notebooks? That's crazy, Cassandra. Impossible."

"Get the thief. Get her now."

A light began to flash on Jason's desk. Cassandra reached down and hit the button. "Yes?"

"Madam, this is Amos, on the dock. Rafael is on his way in. Apparently he was able to get your food shipment moved up, and he's flying it in."

"Tell Guzman to turn back. Not today."

"It's too late, Ms. Kohath. They are on their way."

Ajax said, "Hang on, Amos. How could Rafael have gotten it to us so quickly? No one knew we were coming."

Amos said, "Evidently all was ready and so Rafael believed it would please you. He will be here shortly. Captain Snelling will meet the plane and unload the supplies. You need to bring the island into view. Now."

This, at least, was something Ajax knew how to do, shown to him by their grandfather when he was still a boy. He punched in the code to lower the electromagnetic shield.

Burnley moaned.

"Oh, kill the idiot! I'll get the thief."

Ajax pulled his stiletto out of his jacket pocket, leaned down, and slid it into Burnley's heart.

A strange metallic sound rang out above them. They looked up to see the metal catwalk flex.

Ajax wiped his stiletto off on Burnley's shirt and rose, still looking up, frowning.

Cassandra jumped. "What is that?"

"I don't know, but we'd better find out."

CHAPTER SEVENTY-ONE

Kitsune got to work. Ajax Kohath was stupid, having them thrown into a room, locking the door and leaving, thinking them secure. First the handcuffs. She arched backward like a bow being strung, and brought her hands beneath her butt. She stepped through, her hands now in front of her. She pulled the gag off her mouth, dropped to her knees, and pulled off Grant's. Then she used the small pointed charm she wore on her ankle bracelet, and opened the handcuffs. She shook her hands, then opened his handcuffs. She gave him a moment to catch his breath, then kissed him.

To her relief, he kissed her back. He was shaking off the remains of the drugs. He opened his beautiful eyes and looked at her. "You're amazing," he whispered. "I would have been the biggest ass on the planet if I'd let you go. Give me a minute. And then

I'll help you get us out of here."

This was one of the benefits of being married to a spec-ops genius — no blaming her, no complaining, just instant acceptance of what was, and work toward getting them free.

She kissed him again, then rose. "Keep getting yourself oriented." She began walking around the room. "All right, they dragged us down the slope of the volcano, into a vast building, and into a small room off a well-lighted tunnel. The room looks like sterile cement, lots of electrical cables piled in the corner. I have no idea what they use it for, if anything. We're on an island, so they must have generators to run everything, or they bring in fuel for electricity. Our only light is coming through that single window."

Grant said, "I doubt they're bringing in fuel, more like they have solar and thermal power. That's how many of the Caribbean islands generate electricity. They've clearly been here for years — this architecture is Cold War era, probably this was a Soviet base back in the bad old days. What are you doing?"

"Looking for something I can use to make us some light. It's too dark in here."

"Over here," Grant said. "Behind me, there's a large geode in the wall. It looks like this room was built right into the side of the mountain."

She came back to him and saw the jagged rock edge behind him. Ran her eyes along the wall to the ceiling. "Not just a geode, look up here. An air vent. Of course. They couldn't shut us in without air. It looks rather tight. Big enough for me, but will you fit?"

"Doubtful. But I can boost you up and you can get into the vent, maybe get to the outside and unlock the door."

"Boost me up, let me see what the vent's like."

He made a bridge with his hand and raised her up.

"Oh, bugger all, Grant, it's screwed shut."

He grinned up at her. "You knew it couldn't be that easy. The screws have to be old. Work them loose."

She tried, but they held firm.

He eased her back down, then leaped up and smashed his fists into the vent. Nothing. He did it again, hitting harder. The screws sheared but didn't give way.

"Once more ought to do it." He leaped up again, and punched, hard. The screws popped out and so did the vent. They ducked as it landed on the concrete floor.

She grabbed his face, kissed him. "Okay,

shove me up and in."

He tossed her up and into the narrow vent tunnel. She called back down to him, "It's not wide enough for you, tight for me. I'll be back as soon as I can."

"Hurry," Grant said. "I think I hear footsteps. They're coming to investigate. I only remember seeing a couple of guards. I'll take them if they unlock the door to check on us. Go!"

"No, I'm coming back out, we'll take them together. You're not at your full strength yet and —"

"No! Go!"

No way would he let her stay. Whoever was coming could come in shooting. "Be careful, you hear me?" And Kitsune crawled forward on her hands and knees. She didn't hear anything from the room. So they'd looked in and she'd bet they'd see Grant lying on the floor, looking at them out of drugged eyes. Would they wonder where she was?

The vent shaft was long and dark and full of things that brushed her face. She didn't want to think about what they might be. She finally saw light, knew she was looking at another vent.

She crawled the last bit. As the shaft brightened, she heard voices. She edged to the metal slats, looked down. She could see the twins, and an old man on the floor between them. They were arguing, and the old man looked dead.

Their grandfather, Jason Kohath. And lying beside him was another man, and Ajax was leaning over him.

They'd murdered their own grandfather?

She had to get out of there. She couldn't keep going forward, they might hear her, see her. She had to go back, find another offshoot. She shifted, edging backward, and her knee hit a soft spot in the metal. The resulting twang rang out loud and clear. She froze and prayed.

But the twins both looked up, right at her, though she knew they couldn't see her in the vent.

"What was that?" Cassandra said.

Kitsune saw Ajax rise and wipe off a bloody stiletto on the dead man's shirt. Another one dead.

"I don't know, but we'd better find out."

Kitsune inched back. The old metal creaked again, louder this time, flexed and gave way.

Kitsune landed on all fours at their feet. The metal ventilation shaft sheared and gave way, flying down, and hit Cassandra on the head. As she fell, hard, Kitsune scrambled up from the floor and started running.

CHAPTER SEVENTY-TWO

Off the Coast of Cuba

The Albatross seaplane might be Korean War vintage, but Rafael kept it in excellent shape. The stylized *G* on its side was freshly painted. It held four passengers with a small area for supplies.

"You guys will stay here," Mike said to Louisa and Adam, when the arguments started. "You have to keep communications open with Zachery, and guard the plane. No way we want to wreck her on our first outing, or have the Cubans confiscate her."

Nicholas let them grouse and curse, then added, "Can you guys imagine what Zachery and Savich will say? After they fire the lot of us? So, protect our jobs, guys."

The Albatross lifted into the sky. It was loud, nothing sleek like their jet. Mike was glad not to have to talk. She'd never admit it on the pain of death to Nicholas, but her throat hurt, her head hurt, her chest hurt.

Once they were strapped in, headphones on, they skimmed the slate-gray Caribbean water, and lifted into the sky. Rafael Guzman was whistling, no longer afraid they would shoot out his kneecaps, and knowing he'd made the deal of a lifetime. He said into their headphones, "It's the same thing every time — load up, fly out, unload, fly back. I'm on-call twenty-four/seven. Even on Christmas and my wife's birthday. But now this job is going to be over because they're criminals." Slight pause. "You think I can fly in Florida?"

"Why not?" Nicholas said, then sighed. "All right, Rafael, I'll make some calls."

"That won't fly, try again," Mike whispered, watching the whitecaps under them, followed the shadow of the plane skimming over the water.

"What was that?" Nicholas asked. "What won't fly?"

She leaned in. "I'm trying to figure out a nonviolent plotline to tell Big Mike and my mom, the Gorgeous Rebecca. They know we were in Venice, in that shoot-out, no way around that since the media gave out names, but this? This they do not need to know."

"You think I'm going to fill in my parents? My grandfather would send a squadron of special ops to bring me back to England.

Now, when we land —"

"— we go in hard. Kitsune and Grant, they're both warriors. If they're able, they'll be right beside us." *If they're still alive,* but she wasn't about to say it out loud.

"Yes. We'll be fine." He leaned over and kissed her. "And I've got my own warrior to protect me."

"Don't you forget it and go cowboy on me, okay?"

He smiled, but, she realized, he didn't answer her.

"Look down, Mike. There's the boat." He fell silent, and both of them stared. Unbelievably, a beautiful, large island suddenly appeared out of nothingness. It was astounding, hard to accept.

Rafael shouted over the headphone, "This is strange, usually the island doesn't appear until I'm offloaded and ready to leave. I wonder why it's early. But there it is. Magic, that's what it is. And there's the boat. We're going to land."

"I didn't really want to believe it," she said, staring at the island. "But it's true. Still, it's hard to believe what I'm seeing."

He squeezed her hand. "True and amazing. You ready for a grand adventure?"

CHAPTER SEVENTY-THREE

The Bermuda Triangle

Rafael set them down smoothly and glided to a stop. An old cargo ship appeared, motoring quickly toward them. The waves were not gentle, and Mike suddenly tasted black, bitter lake water in her mouth.

And Nicholas knew. He grabbed her hand. "It will be okay."

"I'm fine, really." She swallowed hard. "The thing is, Nicholas, I didn't even know I was drowning. I would have died without having have realized what happened. Sorry, weird time for me to bring it up."

He closed his eyes a moment, feeling the fear, the panic, not knowing if she'd live.

Rafael said, "The boat will be here in a minute. There are two men, Captain Snelling and Aldo, his first mate. From what Captain Snelling tells me, carrying supplies is their main responsibility, otherwise, he says, they watch movies. He calls it a sabbatical from life.

"The way this works is that if Captain Snelling thinks something's not right, their orders are to leave immediately. It's good I have some supplies here. Here, help me with a couple of these boxes, so that's all they'll see."

Nicholas and Rafael pushed two large boxes labeled RICE and COCONUT MILK in full view and he and Mike crouched down behind them.

Mike heard the boat's engines, loud now and nearly to them. She risked a glance out the plane window. The boat was a cabin cruiser retrofitted to be a short-haul cargo ship.

The two men on the boat waved, and pulled up alongside the plane. The waves were making it hard to balance, and both she and Nicholas had to hang on or be thrown against the plane's hull.

They anchored the boat, tied themselves to the float, and immediately Rafael started passing over boxes.

Nicholas said, "Now," and they stood up, weapons drawn.

The two men on the boat had boxes in their hands. They froze.

"That's right, don't move, mates," he called. "Keep holding the boxes." Nicholas thought about announcing they were FBI, decided against it, at least for now.

Mike edged onto the float, careful to hold on to the edge of the door.

Rafael called out, "Relax, guys. They need to go to the island. They're after their friends. They're not going to hurt you. They're FBI agents. That's Captain Snelling and his first mate, Aldo."

Captain Snelling was a bald, tall, buff Brit, with a red goatee. A red eyebrow went up. "No harm, eh? They're pointing weapons at our heads. FBI? What's this all about, Rafael?"

Nicholas said, "Captain Snelling, Aldo, we need to get to the island. We are FBI agents and the Kohaths captured two of our people. You ferried them in, so you know. I suggest you wait here with Rafael until we come back."

Aldo grabbed the captain's sleeve. "You know if we go back, even with their guns at our heads, they'll kill us."

Mike said, "They will not kill you. We're going to shut down their operation. I strongly recommend you remain here with Rafael."

Captain Snelling said, "No, Aldo, the old man wouldn't kill us."

Rafael said, "Maybe he wouldn't, Captain,

but those twins are here now. Both of them are mean as snakes, and twice as crazy." He looked at Mike and Nicholas. "Don't get me wrong, the old man is nuttier than a fruitcake, but he's smart, and so long as you do your job well, he's kind. But the twins, they're not like him. They have something wrong, deep inside. Oh yes, they'd kill us in a flash."

Mike asked, "The two prisoners with them, a man and a woman — what shape were they in? Drugged? Beaten?"

Captain Snelling said, "She wasn't drugged, but she'd been knocked around. As for the man, he was still out of it. He could barely walk.

"Cassandra backhanded the woman for no reason I could see. I wanted to help her, but I knew the crazy witch would kill me without hesitation."

Nicholas said, "As I said, we want to rescue them, shut down this operation. Will you let us do our job? Will you stay here with Rafael?"

Snelling looked from Aldo to Rafael, back toward the island and slowly nodded. "Everything is different now that the twins are here. They were manic, I could feel a sick sort of excitement rolling off them. Listen, I'm afraid for the old man."

"We are, too," Mike said. "We've already learned firsthand how ruthless the twins are. We'll be back as soon as we can. How many other guards are there?"

"Four, all as vicious as the twins," Aldo said. "Maybe more so. We keep away from them."

Snelling said, "I know what you're thinking. You're wondering why we're giving up so easily, that we're going to screw you over. Not going to happen. I know those twins are here to do something really bad. I don't know what it is, but they need to be stopped."

Mike asked, "Do you know what Jason Kohath does here?"

"I haven't got a clue, he's always very close-mouthed, but he's the smartest man I've ever met in my life. We occasionally play chess. I'm not bad, but he can look at the chessboard and I know he's picturing twenty moves ahead with at least fifty possible variations. Once I was on his command center, that's what I call it, anyway, and there was a bank of computer screens, mostly showing the world weather." Snelling paused. "What he's doing, it's criminal, isn't it?"

Nicholas said very deliberately, "If we don't stop him, he will destroy the earth."

Snelling clearly didn't believe him. "Destroy the earth? What is he doing?"

"You saw the news a couple of days ago — the sand blizzard into Beijing from the Gobi Desert? He's responsible for that."

They still didn't believe him, and Nicholas couldn't blame them. "Listen, we have to hurry. Come on, mates, make up your minds."

Snelling nodded. "Okay, we'll stay here, wait for you. A couple of things you need to know or you will very likely die. The computer systems will reset the exterior wall once the boat's signal registers — it pings as we pass through, that way, they're sure it's us sailing in and out. If we don't ping the system, a storm unlike anything you've ever seen will roar up, and you'll go down. You can sail through the barrier, or fly over it, and if you aren't identified as a friendly, you are turned away, so to speak. The old man doesn't like surprises and he doesn't like strangers." He frowned. "But something's not right. The island shouldn't have popped up so quickly, it's something the old man never does. I think the twins have taken over. When they arrived with the man and the woman, we knew something was up. I suggest you both be very careful."

Once they were transferred, Nicholas

gunned the boat forward.

The ocean was turbulent, and Mike was having a hard time keeping her feet under her. She hung on to the railing for dear life. She forgot the headache, the hits of nausea, the nibbling of fear at being on the water, that was all for yesterday, now, today, she flung back her head, felt the wind tear her hair, make her eyes tear. "It's a trampoline! I love trampolines!"

Nicholas wanted to hug her, but instead he pushed the engines as fast as they would go. Both he and Mike stared at the gorgeous green island drawing closer and closer.

"It's amazing," she shouted over the wind. "Look at that volcano in the middle. It's Fantasy Island."

Nicholas said, "Both Rafael and Captain Snelling were surprised the island appeared so quickly. That makes me think that Jason Kohath is indeed no longer in command. This smacks of Cassandra and Ajax, and they don't know the protocols. They've taken control and are running things now."

"Do you think they'd actually murder their own grandfather?"

"To be honest, I don't think anything they could do would surprise me."

"There's a reason they brought Kitsune and Grant with them. They need them to do something for them. What is it?"

He shouted back, "We'll find out. Who do you think would come out alive if you put Cassandra and Kitsune together in the ring?"

"Kitsune," Mike said without pause.

Nicholas agreed. They saw a huge crevasse in the mountain, a natural cove that sheltered an elaborate dock. Nicholas slowed, tightened one hand on the wheel, the other on his Glock.

CHAPTER SEVENTY-FOUR

Ajax was fast. He grabbed Kitsune's hair as she scrambled away, yanked her off her feet. She landed hard on her back, right next to Cassandra, who was sitting with her palm to her forehead trying to stanch the flow of blood.

Ajax stood over her, an ancient Colt revolver in his hand, probably his grand-father's gun. Kitsune watched Cassandra tear off a piece of her knit top, make it into a bandage and press it against the cut. Only then did she turn to Kitsune. She reached out her hand and lightly stroked her hair. "You could have pulled it out, Ajax, all that beautiful hair." Without another word, she slapped Kitsune. Kitsune wanted to attack, but she heard the click of the Colt revolver and didn't move. "Now that I've got your attention, tell us how you got out of that room."

"Through the air vent."

Both twins looked up and in that instant, Kitsune leaped to her feet, stomped hard on Ajax's instep, and sent her fist into his throat.

His gun went flying out of his hand to spin across the smooth stone floor. He grabbed his throat, gagging, but she hadn't hit him hard enough, she hadn't collapsed his trachea.

Cassandra scrambled to her feet, grabbed the wooden chessboard and came at her. Before Kitsune could run, Ajax was on her again. She ducked his fist, but it landed solidly against her shoulder, spinning her around. Cassandra lifted the chessboard over her head, ready to smash it over Kitsune's skull.

Kitsune went in fast, head-butted Ajax in his stomach and knocked the air out of him, sending him stumbling backward. She saw Cassandra in her peripheral vision, blood trickling down her face from the cut on her forehead, and she was swinging the chessboard madly back and forth in front of her. Kitsune only had a second. She spun around, ducked down, even as Cassandra swung the chessboard and came up behind her. She lashed out with her foot, right into Cassandra's back, the force knocking her into her brother, sending the two of them crashing against the computer station, arms flailing as they tried to regain their balance.

Keyboards went flying. The huge screens on the walls started changing, showing numbers, equations, different land masses, merging, splitting apart, like cards shuffled by a madman.

A warning Klaxon began, quickly built to an earsplitting crescendo.

Kitsune saw a satellite turning lazily in space, then a beam of orange light shoot away into the darkness. The next screen showed the orange beam hitting the earth.

"What have you done?" Cassandra screamed at her over the siren. "Stop it, Ajax, stop it! We don't know if it's going to Washington now, it could be going anywhere. Stop it!"

Kitsune didn't wait, ran toward the hallway and stopped cold. Two men were marching Grant between them. He was barely conscious, and they had handcuffs on him again. Blood trickled down his chin from a cut on his lip.

She should have stayed. Together they could have taken these two goons. But they'd had weapons, probably came into the cell with them. Grant hadn't had a chance.

Cassandra yelled to them, "Kill the man if she moves!"

Kitsune was so angry she was vibrating, so scared for Grant she wanted to weep. She was panting hard, but she didn't move. Neither did the two men. Everyone was watching Ajax typing frantically. They knew something was wrong, very wrong.

Ajax hit a final computer key and the screens stopped shifting, the siren cut off midwail.

"Where did the laser hit?" Cassandra asked.

"Five hundred nautical miles northeast, as best I can tell. It went straight down to the seabed."

Cassandra stood mute, watching her twin move through the screens now, searching the data as it began to scroll onto the center screen. "I don't know what it will do. Depending on the strength of that blast it could shift the seabed. Someone could have seen it strike the water, alerted the Coast Guard." He swiped his hand through his head. "We need the storm in position to strike D.C., and now I think it's back on track, but I can't be certain."

"It will be all right, you'll see. You've very good, Ajax, it will hit Washington, D.C., just as we planned."

"Cassandra, if the algorithms are off a meter, or the strength isn't properly measured, the lasers aligned just so, it can cause a global catastrophe and not hit Washington, D.C. at all." He drew in a deep breath. "As close as the hit was to us, a seabed earthquake could send out a tsunami and wipe our island off the face of the earth. Then if the hurricane hits Washington, D.C., we won't care. It would have all been for nothing."

Cassandra looked over at Kitsune. "I told you, Ajax, I think the Ark is here, in the vault. Grandfather's big secret. She will open it for us and then we will have the power to control the Coil again. Trust me, Ajax. We will not only control the Coil, we will control everything."

Kitsune heard him snort, saw him studying first one computer, then another.

Cassandra had knotted a cloth around her forehead to keep the blood out of her eyes. She looked at Kitsune. "This better not leave a scar or I will take a knife and carve up your face." She nodded toward the behemoth holding Grant's left arm. "Now, you will either open the vault for me or I'll have Bantam Weight break your husband's neck."

She was calling that hulk Bantam Weight? What did she call the other one? Feather Weight? Her brain was squirreling around;

532

she had to get it together, figure out what to do. She looked over at an old man, silent, unmoving, his head bleeding on the floor, another dead man beside him. "You killed your own grandfather. And for what? You honestly believe Jason Kohath has been sitting on the Ark of the Covenant this whole time?"

Cassandra laughed. "You're stupid, you have no idea what you're talking about." She turned to the two guards. "Bring the man."

Ajax stopped typing. He was staring at one of the screens, as if willing what he wanted to happen.

"Straighten up and walk," Bantam Weight said, and kicked Grant.

It was then Kitsune saw Grant's eyes. They were clear, focused on her, and she knew he wanted them to stay together. She knew hope.

Kitsune said, "Let's open the safe."

Cassandra said to Bantam Weight, "If either of them tries anything, shoot him. Ajax, do you need to stay here or will you come with us?"

"There's nothing more I can do," he said, rising.

They walked through byzantine passages, forking left, then right, fanning off intersections. Kitsune realized these passageways had been dug out and reinforced decades earlier — probably by the Russians — they were stark, cold, well-maintained by Kohath's guards no doubt. And always, they walked deeper into the heart of the volcano itself.

They came into a large space carved into the rock, lights inset, reflecting out a gauzy red glow. The walls weren't metal, they were smooth rock, like the back of the small room where she and Grant had been locked in.

On the far wall Kitsune saw a commercial-grade vault, one similar to those she'd seen in Swiss banks in Geneva and Zurich, state-of-the-art, virtually impossible to open. She'd need special tools and several hours to have a prayer of getting into this vault.

Cassandra pointed to the round steel door in front of them. "This is one of the most secure vaults in the world. It is made of steel-reinforced concrete. The lock is a dual combination and key. I have the director's key right here, a gift from my grandfather. You need to figure out the combination.

"It is a class-three lock, and it's set into an explosive charge. Get it wrong, and you will be vaporized. Once inside, there will be another door, but you won't have to worry about that one, it's a special climate-control door." She twirled the combination lock. "You have twenty-two minutes."

"Listen to me, Cassandra, you know well enough I can't have the combination miraculously appear. I need a thermal lance to cut through the rods, even with a class-three, it will take me an hour, if I'm lucky."

She tossed Kitsune a stethoscope. "You have this. And I'm not kidding about the time, this door is set to self-destruct if the dial is moved and no one puts in the combination. When I spun that lock, the timer started inside. Twenty-one minutes, now. Get going and open that vault, or I will slit your husband's throat."

"You want me to use the stethoscope to listen to it open?"

"Bring her man. And a knife."

"Be reasonable, there's over a million possible combinations. It would take a computerized crack system three days to run that many."

"You're speeding down to twenty minutes."

Kitsune looked at Grant. And in his eyes she saw certainty. That she could open the vault? Well, yes, okay, she could open the bloody vault, she was the best, after all. Kitsune grabbed the stethoscope, said over her shoulder, "I need complete silence, and your breathing sounds like cannons in my ears. You want it open? Leave me."

Cassandra gave her a long look. "We'll be in the corridor. Do not even think, for one second, I won't hesitate to kill your husband, should you not get it open."

Kitsune laid her hands on the metal and felt the earth move under her feet.

CHAPTER SEVENTY-FIVE

"Mike, take the wheel. I'll get the rope to tie us to the dock."

Mike steered the boat toward the dock and stared at the green jungle. It looked impenetrable, so thick it crowded against the white sand that covered a beach at least twenty feet wide. Off to her left were spectacular bare rock cliffs that had shifted over the years, spilling boulders onto the beach. This could have been a paradise, not a hideaway for a mad genius.

As they motored into the natural harbor, the air grew cooler. She continued to search the beach, and saw a narrow path that led to a door.

"There's no one here."

"In the jungle, perhaps, but there are cameras on every pylon, and one farther in, above that metal fire door. If anyone is watching, we've certainly been spotted by now. No hope for it. Cut the engine."

Nicholas threw a rope to the nearest pylon, anchoring the boat to the dock.

As their feet hit the sand beach, Mike felt a tremor, then another and another, gentle, like rolling waves. She instinctively reached out and grabbed Nicholas's arm. The ground they were standing on shook harder, and she braced her feet wide. Then nothing.

She saw Nicholas's face had gone white.

She ran her tongue over her dry lips. "This isn't okay, Nicholas. It's tremors. You know volcanos are almost always related to a fault."

"I'm thinking it's related to the Coil, maybe a malfunction. But whatever it is, we have to hurry, Mike."

When they reached the fire door, Nicholas turned the handle. "Luck is with us, it's unlocked."

"I don't like this, Nicholas. No guards? And Captain Snelling told us a man named Amos would be here, he's the one who controls entry and exit, but I'm not seeing anyone."

A man's deep voice came from behind the door. "Don't open that door or an explosive will blow you to bits. That door is a dead end. I have to bring you in. If you look to your left —"

Hidden in a vine-covered wall was a door

with a window. The voice said on a chuckle, "Pretty good camouflage, don't you think? Not that we've ever needed it. I'm going to open the door now, and don't worry, I don't have a weapon."

Nicholas hoped the man wasn't lying. The door opened a crack and they saw a small bald man with bushy white eyebrows step quickly back and stick his hands in the air.

"Get back, into the room. You're Amos?"

Amos's eyes never left Nicholas's as he inched himself back against the wall, his hands still up. It was a security office, and it was empty except for the three of them.

Nicholas looked over at a control board, but didn't recognize much.

Amos said, "This is where we run the dock. I developed all the protocols. If someone unwanted bypasses the other security measures and gets too close, I can trip them up here. It's only happened three times since I've been here, fifteen years now."

Mike asked, "Why didn't you let us open the door and blow ourselves up?"

"Let me show you instead. May I put my hands down?"

Nicholas held his Glock at his side. "Go ahead."

Amos went to the console, typed in a command, and what looked like security footage began to play. "This happened twelve minutes ago. I'm sorry, there's no sound, never has been. My boss didn't want it."

Nicholas and Mike leaned in close. It looked like NASA's Houston command center.

Mike said, "There's Cassandra. She's arguing with that old man — is that Jason Kohath?"

"Yes, he's my boss and friend, the twins' grandfather. Watch." And he flinched when Ajax punched his grandfather in the head, knocking him to the floor.

Amos said, "I don't know if he's dead. I have medical training, but I'm afraid to go in alone. She and Ajax might kill me, too."

They watched another man come in, saw that Cassandra was yelling, and then Ajax stuck his stiletto into the man's chest. They saw him collapse over Kohath. Then Kitsune crashed through the ceiling vent, and they saw the vent hit Cassandra. They saw the fight, then the two guards marched in dragging Grant Thornton.

"After fifteen years without sound, I've learned to lip read. I didn't understand everything, but Cassandra wants the other woman to open the vault, and she said something about the Ark being inside, which is foolishness. The Ark of the Covenant isn't here, never was."

"Then what's in the vault?" Mike asked.

Amos said simply, "Secrets, but only Jason can tell you what they are. I cannot. We must hurry. If you come with me, I'll take you to the control room. I can see how badly Jason is injured."

Nicholas hesitated. It was simply too easy. "You could lead us right to Cassandra and Ajax."

"I could have let you blow yourself up, but I didn't. Listen, Captain Snelling alerted me, told me you were here to shut things down and rescue that man and woman.

"I know what those kids are — they'd dance in the world's ashes after they blew it up. And it's very possible they've killed a man I greatly respect. Please. I'll take you there. I've got to help him."

Mike raised her Glock when Amos reached beneath a counter. "What are you doing?"

He straightened quickly. "I have to get my medical kit."

Nicholas opened the bag. Medical supplies, and handed it back.

Amos closed the bag and threw it on his shoulder. "I know I don't need to tell you this, but be careful if you come face-to-face with those two. As for the guards, they're well trained and will shoot first."

They followed Amos into the heart of the volcano. It was quiet, eerily so. It took only a minute or two before they stepped into a large room, its walls covered with computerized screens. Amos hurried away to the man they saw lying on his back beside a huge desk.

Nicholas said, "Would you look at this, Mike, three hundred and sixty degrees of screens. Computer programs running, and there's a satellite in space." He cursed. "Mike, see the hurricane spinning toward Washington? And all that data running down the side? And on the next screen it shows an earthquake and tsunami warning."

"There's our earthquake," Mike said, pointing. "Says here it measured six point six on the Richter scale, and was centered around five hundred miles northwest of here. There's a tsunami warning for the Eastern Caribbean."

"We've got to warn them."

"Nicholas," she said, pointing at the screen, where the warnings were running lightning quick. "They already know. Can you shut down the hurricane? Maybe disperse the tsunami?"

He gave her a crooked grin. "Why not?"

"Then we'll find Kitsune and Grant and get out of here."

Amos said, "Sir, I don't know how you possibly think you can stop the hurricane and the tsunami but —" He shook his head, said to Mike, "Could you help me here?"

Mike went down on her knees beside Amos. He was holding Jason Kohath's head in his lap, rocking him. "It's really bad. I can't do anything for him. Ajax hit him hard, most likely a bad bleed going on. We need to get him out of here, to a hospital. Poor Burnley is dead, God rest his soul."

Nicholas was bent over the keyboard of the main computer. He yelled, "I'm sorry, Amos, you've got to hold tight."

"Please, hurry."

"Try to stabilize him, Amos. Mike, come here."

Nicholas pointed to another computer screen. "Look, it's the security feed. There's Kitsune trying to open the vault."

"But where are the twins?"

"Right behind you."

CHAPTER SEVENTY-SIX

Ajax Kohath stood in the entrance to the control center, aiming the ancient Colt revolver at them. "What do you think you're doing? Get away from there, now."

Nicholas said, "I'm undoing your work, mate. No hurricane for Washington today."

Ajax laughed. "Go ahead, do your best, but you can't stop it. You can't stop anything, you don't know how. I was worried there for a minute, but I see I fixed it — the hurricane is still headed where I set it to go. There's no stopping it now, particularly by a stupid cop like you." He pointed at the screen, where the huge storm spun, gathering more and more force. "The outer bands will hit the coast in a little over an hour. Two hours and Washington, D.C., will be leveled by the hurricane, your government will cease to exist, all your people will be killed. And you think you can stop it? You can't, all you can do is watch it happen.

How does that make you feel, Agent Drummond?"

Mike laughed. "You don't realize who you're taunting, Ajax. Nicholas is as much a computer expert as your grandfather. He can do anything."

Nicholas wanted to smile at her incredible show of confidence in him, or bravado, he didn't know which, but he didn't, he kept eye contact with Ajax. Ajax was coming closer, and he let him. When Ajax was ten feet away, Nicholas knew he couldn't let him get any closer. Even with that old Colt, it was possible he'd shoot him dead. He turned and slammed his hands down onto the main computer keyboard. The lights went out and the screens went blank and Nicholas was typing as fast as he could, shutting down the generator.

But the darkness only lasted another second. The lights came sputtering back on. Yeah, he was a real computer expert.

Cassandra came running into the control center as Ajax charged toward Nicholas, firing wildly. "No!"

Mike shot once, twice, at Ajax, missed him. Cassandra yelled and Mike turned and shot at her, but Cassandra ducked away. Nicholas yelled to Mike, "I've got this, get her."

Before she ran after Cassandra, Mike turned and very deliberately aimed her Glock and caressed the trigger. Ajax's Colt went flying out of his hand, hitting against a computer screen and spinning across the floor, nearly to Amos's side. "I've got it!" Amos shouted.

Ajax cursed in English, then in Italian, and he was running toward Nicholas. Nicholas jumped to his left as Ajax came at him, beyond himself now with rage. Nicholas saw blood dripping from his hand. Mike had gotten more than the Colt.

Nicholas ducked and weaved and got himself to the other side of the main computer station and into the open room. Ajax drew up and grinned. "I won boxing matches, I could have gone pro. You think you're so big and strong — you're nothing to me." He ran toward Nicholas, fists up, swerving, dancing lightly on his feet. Nicholas ducked a sharp punch.

"Sorry, mate, there are no Queensbury rules here." Nicholas was on him, hit him with a left, a right, two forearm blocks, and a hard kick to the leg just above Ajax's knee, then he spun to the left, his hands a blur as he rained blows upon Ajax's face and neck. Ajax stumbled but he didn't give up. He grabbed Jason's chair, threw it at Nicholas.

Nicholas moved quickly to his left, and the chair spun away, crashed into the bank of computer consoles.

"You'll have to do better than that." Nicholas wiggled his fingers at him. "Well, come on, you puking little nutter, let's get this over with."

Ajax moved fast, and Nicholas saw a glint of silver. He had a knife and wasn't that a nice surprise? Nicholas hated knives, nearly impossible to come away uncut.

He let Ajax come closer, closer, let him jab out with the knife, and once, twice, three times, he managed to jump back at the last second. When Ajax stabbed out again, his arm fully extended, Nicholas leaped forward, caught his wrist between his hands, and twisted, hard. Ajax's forearm snapped, the knife clattered to the floor. Nicholas kicked it away, then landed a hard right to Ajax's face, splitting his cheek open. Then a spinning kick to the broken forearm. Ajax went down, hard, and hit his shoulder on the computer console. Nicholas kicked him in the head as he fell. The younger man's head snapped back, his neck at an odd angle, and when he landed on his back, his eyes stared unseeing up at Nicholas. The fight had lasted only a minute or two, and he'd managed not to get cut. Nicholas straightened. "Amos, he's dead. How is Kohath?"

Amos was staring at him. "I've never seen anyone fight like that outside of a movie."

"Yes, well. You'd be surprised what you can do when your life's threatened. How's he doing?"

"Holding on, but we need to get him out of here soon."

"I'll be back as soon as I can." And he ran toward the hall where he'd seen Mike disappear after Cassandra just as Grant Thornton came running into the control center. Nicholas recognized him instantly.

Grant took in Ajax's dead body on the floor. "You're Drummond. Follow me, we have to hurry. It's Kitsune. Oh, yes, I'm Grant Thornton, and I know who you are, Nicholas Drummond." He turned and ran back into the dark passageway, Nicholas on his heels. He saw Grant helping Mike back onto her feet.

Nicholas grabbed her arms, shook her. "Mike, are you okay? What happened?"

"I'm okay, really. Cassandra was hidden around a corner with a big block of wood in her hand. She clocked me when I got into range. Are we secure? Did you stop the hurricane?"

"I did all I could, but I don't know. Ajax

is dead. Grant, where's Kitsune?"

"Up ahead. She's still trying to open the vault. Cassandra will be nearby. I took out the guards and followed the fight. Thanks for coming for us. I was worried no one would ever find us, but Kitsune never doubted you'd come to us in time."

Mike said, "We'll pray we're in time. Now we have to stop Cassandra."

"The vault, it's lined with explosives and Kitsune is trying to get it open with a bloody stethoscope. If she doesn't open it" — he stared down at his watch — "in four and a half minutes, she'll be dead. I'm going to kill that crazy bitch, then we'll get Kitsune and get out of this death trap."

Grant took off down the passageway, Nicholas and Mike behind him. Mike called out, "Why didn't Kitsune run? Cassandra and Ajax were both in the control room."

Grant shouted over his shoulder, "Cassandra told her she'd kill me if Kitsune didn't get the vault open. Kitsune believed her. You know Cassandra will be in there, probably with a gun on my wife.

"Before I clocked my guards, I overheard Kitsune shouting out she'd already dialed in the first two numbers. There's four to the combination, she's halfway there."

Nicholas said with absolute conviction,

549

"She'll do it."

Grant turned then, grinned widely. "She told me about you two, told me how you managed to bring her down. And it's obvious you know how talented she is. I don't think there's a vault in the world that can keep her out."

Grant slowed. "The vault is around that corner, maybe twenty feet farther. We must go quietly now."

Mike leaned down and pulled out her ankle piece, handed it to Grant. "It belongs to my father. Keep it safe."

CHAPTER SEVENTY-SEVEN

Cassandra had struck the woman agent as hard as she could, and she'd gone down. But for how long?

She needed to move, and fast. Her guards were both dead, necks broken by the thief's husband. She'd left Drummond back there with Ajax, but she was worried. They'd somehow traced them here to the island. But how? She had to get to the vault before the thief realized no one was in the corridor guarding her.

She looked at her watch. Three and a half minutes for her to get the vault open, or they'd all be dead.

What had happened between Ajax and Drummond? Ajax was an amazing boxer, surely he could take down one FBI agent. She knew she should have stayed, but she couldn't, she had to get back to the vault.

She leaned down and grabbed the guards' guns and as many magazines as she could shove into her pants pockets and ran full out to the vault. If the thief got it open, then she wouldn't need the guns. She knew the Ark was waiting for her to come, only her. It would open for her, the last of the Kohaths. It would surround her with power and flow into her and then she would rule the world, Ajax at her side.

Cassandra stopped, saw the thief's face was glued to the vault door. She knew combination dial locks were straightforward, knew that when Kitsune hit the right number, the rotation of the internal wheel pack would line up and the gap would open, ready to be filled with the nose of the bar. Simple. The trick was to get all the wheels lined up, four times running. She wanted to yell at her to hurry but she forced herself to stay perfectly still.

Kitsune held the stethoscope inverted to the bell side, knew she was listening for the lower frequency clicks that would indicate the nose of the bar had slid into the wheel pack, and that number the dial was resting on was a part of the combination.

Kitsune had memorized the first two numbers — eighty-seven and twenty-eight — and now she was listening for the third. How much time did she have left, did Grant have left? No, she couldn't think about that,

she had to focus. She knew she was close —
a gentle click started up and she knew she
was nearly there, and she heard it, *tick, tick,
tick, tick, tick,* slight and tiny in the background, then suddenly a metallic *slap*
indicated she had the third number. Her
breath came out in a loud whoosh as she
said aloud "forty-two," wiped her sweating
hands on her pants, then put her ear back
to the stethoscope. She couldn't have more
than two minutes before the world exploded.

Cassandra knew time was nearly up. She
ran toward Kitsune, screaming, "Get it
open, get it open now!"

Kitsune didn't move. "I'm nearly there.
Stand quietly."

"You have two minutes and ten seconds.
If you don't get it open, then we'll all bloody
die!"

"Be quiet." Kitsune shut it all out, the
possibility of dying, of Grant dying. She'd
felt the earthquake and wondered what
those insane twins were doing. Then she
emptied her mind and lost herself back in
the lock.

She could hear other noises now, but she
was close, the fourth number was near to
the last one, she turned the dial one minute
step at a time, bringing the dial back to zero,

just past the ninety-eight, and then it *thunked,* loudly, and she was in.

"Get out of the way," Cassandra screamed at her, and she shoved Kitsune to the ground, grabbed the massive titanium spindle wheel, pulled with all her strength, and finally the heavy door opened. She ran inside.

Kitsune stumbled to her feet, heard voices, Grant's frantic voice. And Nicholas and Mike. They were here. She knew they'd come. Another kiss for Adam, this time for the tracker. She ran full speed away from the vault.

CHAPTER SEVENTY-EIGHT

Cassandra stood in a small antechamber. It wasn't dark, lights burned in low lamps on the walls, turned on automatically when the door was opened. She went to the inner door and drew up short. There, carved into the metal, was the warning, the same warning on the cherubim's wing. She knew, at last, her grandfather had lied, had been lying for years. He had the Ark and now Cassandra had found it.

Through this door lies a weapon of great power. Open it, and it will indeed kill.

There was a bar and she lifted it easily. The door swung open. It had been cold outside, but as she stepped into the small inner room, it was warmer, the air dry, to keep the Ark safe, that was the reason.

She closed her eyes, expecting a light of great brightness to appear, bathe her face, fill her mind and her heart. But there was no intense white light. Slowly, she opened her eyes. There was nothing at all. The room was more dimly lit than the outer room, and it was empty.

She stood dumbly, unable to believe the Ark wasn't here. Had her grandfather managed to cloak it somehow, as he did the island and their palazzo in Italy?

She walked slowly around the room, hoping to feel it, and tripped. She looked down and saw a small Moleskine notebook, old, black, worn, but there wasn't a speck of dust or mold on it.

Cassandra leaned down and picked up the book, and stilled. It was one of her mother's notebooks, her mother's name inscribed inside the cover. She brought it to her chest and held it there. She wanted to weep.

The light in the small room begin to dim, and the air grew even warmer. She turned slowly and looked back at the entrance. And there in the open doorway stood her mother, smiling at her, gesturing for her to come.

"Mama?"

And then she spoke, her beautiful voice so clear in Cassandra's mind. "Quickly now, Cassandra, I need you and your brother to hurry, we're going to be late for our flight. We're going to the Gobi, we're going to follow the trail Marco Polo went down when he took the Ark to Genghis Khan, and you and Ajax will be at my side. Isn't this exciting? Hurry now, little dove. We need to gather up your brother and go."

"Will I be able to ride a camel, Mama?"

Helen laughed, the sound like the ringing of bells in a cathedral, deep and beautiful, and Cassandra's chest swelled. She'd made Mother laugh.

"Yes, you and Ajax, too. I will get you one with two humps so you can ride together."

Cassandra wanted to ride a camel by herself, but she said nothing. She knew her mother never liked her excluding her twin.

Her mother walked forward, gently cupped Cassandra's face in her hands. Cassandra could feel her warm, soft palms on her flesh, see her mother's boundless love for her in her brilliant blue eyes. "I must caution you. Where we are going, it will be dangerous. You must promise me, Cassandra, that you will listen to me, to every word and obey me."

"Are bad men coming for us, Mama?"

"There are always bad men, but we are Kohaths, we are the chosen ones. We alone can protect the Ark, and you and your brother, as twins, are the most powerful of any Kohath who's lived in the past two centuries. When we find the Ark, I want you and Ajax to open it together."

"I want to open it myself."

She saw a flash of concern in her mother's eyes, but she said calmly, sweetly, "No. You must work with your brother. You must share. It is never more true than with the Ark. Now, hurry, grab your bag, let us go find your brother. Our adventures are only beginning."

And Helen stepped back into the doorway. The air began to chill, the light became brighter, and her mother slowly faded away. Cassandra felt tears running down her cheeks, mixing with blood from the wound on her forehead. She was alone, she'd always been alone, even when she'd had to share with her twin, but not like this, no, not like this.

She remembered that trip, hot and boring and they dug in the sand all day, until that morning she and Ajax had wandered off and fallen into a partially dug well and had to be rescued. Helen had sent them back to England.

A small light appeared, and Helen was back, in the far corner of the vault. Cassandra ran to her.

"Mama! Where did you go?"

But Helen didn't appear to hear her, didn't look at her or acknowledge her. She was there, yet she wasn't. Suddenly, Cassandra saw her standing on the edge of a mighty cliff, its granite sides flat and smooth. She was wearing a flowing robe and she looked young and incredibly beautiful. She was shading her eyes, looking into the distance. Once again she faded away.

She appeared again, this time near the door, and Cassandra didn't understand. "Mama, why are you playing like this? I'm here, I finally found you."

Helen wasn't alone. She was arguing with their father. Then David Maynes slowly turned empty eyes toward Cassandra. "You killed me, my own daughter killed me, and she knows, oh yes, your mother knows." When he reached out his hand to her, she couldn't move, could barely breathe. She saw the flesh fall from his arm and his skeletal hand locked hard around her throat. "My only daughter, my favorite child, you know I always loved you more than Ajax, my second Helen. But you didn't love me, did you? It was always your mother and only your mother, only the damned Kohaths. And then you had me poisoned. Your own father. It is time you answered for your sins."

Cassandra felt those skeletal fingers begin to tighten around her neck. Still she couldn't move. But then she realized she was alone, her father's hand wasn't choking her to death, her father was gone.

Her mother's notebook, it was putting these visions into her mind. She threw it against the far wall, watched it bounce off onto the floor. But the visions wouldn't stop.

She saw her grandfather sit up from his grave, burial earth falling off his body, and he was holding the cherubim's wing. "I gave you and your brother everything I had, yet Ajax murdered me. I knew you carried insanity from your father's line, yet I hoped and prayed, as did your mother.

"You have murdered wantonly, even my poor Burnley, devoted, loyal to me, a better person than either of you. You and your brother are damned, Cassandra. I denounce you. You do not deserve to be Kohaths."

She wanted to scream it wasn't so, she wanted to explain, but the words choked in her throat. She saw all of them then, standing in the doorway, shaking their heads at her — from Appleton Kohath to her brother — and there was Lilith and that bitch, Elizabeth St. Germaine, who would have exposed them all if Cassandra hadn't stopped her. She screamed, "You failed, Lilith, you deserved to die! Mother, it wasn't me, it was Ajax. Not me, really, not me!"

There were so many of them, faces she was sure she'd never seen before, and they were advancing on her and she knew they would kill her. She yelled, "Mama, help me!"

But Helen stayed in the doorway and watched them drag her down to her knees.

"I am sorry," she heard her mother's sad voice, "We tried so hard to teach you, to show you what you must do. You and your brother are so very smart, so focused, but you were twisted, I saw it, as did your grandfather, yet we continued to pray, to hope. Until I had to face the truth. Your grandfather tried and tried to help you, until you came to kill him.

"Your grandfather was forced to kill so many thousands of innocent lives in Beijing for you to find my camp and the cherubim's wing and the misleading map of the Ark I created for you. And I saw clearly that neither of you looked upon the wing or the map as the path to learn and understand and embrace your calling. You wanted the Ark for the power it would give you.

"I am sorry, Cassandra. Your brother is dead, lost forever, and you will join him shortly."

"But where is the Ark? Please, Mama, tell me, I want to see it, I have to open the Ark, feel its power filling me. You'll see, it wants me, it will recognize me. I will become one

561

with it. You have to believe me, I swear I will use the power only for the good of the world. I swear it!"

Tears ran down Helen's face. "It breaks my heart, even though I knew this would come to pass. The Ark will always be safe, now and forever."

Her mother was gone and Cassandra was alone. The room was chill again, the air dry. The dead were no longer there to kill her. She rose slowly to her feet. The notebook, where was it? She had to find it, it had to be here, the ghost of her mother couldn't have taken it.

She looked wildly around, then ran into the antechamber. She saw her enemies standing there, staring at her. Nicholas Drummond held her mother's notebook in his hands. How had he gotten it without her seeing him?

Grant was yelling, "The clock that's tied to the explosives, it hasn't stopped! We've only got one minute and ten seconds."

Cassandra knew it was a lie, another vision, and Grant Thornton was dead, he had to be, the guards would have killed him. But hadn't she seen the guards were both dead? None of this was real. But her mother's notebook? She saw it in Drummond's hands, but no, that couldn't be right.

It was a vision, like the others, but —
Cassandra screamed and charged at them.

CHAPTER SEVENTY-NINE

Mike yelled, "Grab her! We can't just leave her here. Hurry."

Kitsune grabbed Cassandra, slapped her hard, once, twice. "Snap out of it!"

Cassandra stopped struggling. She stood still. She raised her hand to her face and rubbed where Kitsune had struck her. She said in a singsong voice, "Are you here to arrest me? Because I've committed murder? But not all of them, I swear not all of them." She rounded on Nicholas. "Give me my mother's notebook."

"I don't know anything about your mother's notebook."

"You have it! I saw it, you have it!"

"We don't have time for this." Nicholas cuffed the screaming Cassandra and threw her over his shoulder. "Let's get out of here. Go, go!"

Grant slammed the steel vault door shut, and they ran.

Moments later, the explosion knocked Nicholas forward, and he lost his hold on Cassandra as he fell into darkness.

He didn't know how long he was out, but he came to when he felt Mike shaking his arm. "Nicholas, are you all right? Come on, come on! Come back to me."

He shook his head, focused his eyes on Mike's face above him. "Mike?"

"Yes, I'm here. Are you all right?"

"I'm okay. Where's Cassandra?"

"I don't know. The explosion, there's so much dust. Grant was trying to find Kitsune, and I was looking for you."

Cassandra was gone.

They ran back to the control center. Nicholas grabbed Mike's arms. "I don't know where Kitsune and Grant are, but they can take care of themselves. Mike, you go on, get out of here. I see the storm's going to hit Washington very soon. I've got to try to shut it down."

"Agent Drummond," Amos shouted. He was still on the floor holding Jason Kohath in his arms.

"Hang on, Amos." He said to Mike, "Get everyone out, now. I'll follow."

"You swear?"

Amos shouted. "The vault blew?"

"Yes. Cassandra got loose. Do you know

where she is, where she might go?"

Amos shook his head.

"You and Mr. Kohath are going with Mike."

"Not yet. Jason is trying to say something, come quickly."

Mike and Nicholas came down on their knees on each side of him. Amos was leaning close. "It sounds like — yes, he's saying 'palm, eye, command X.' I don't know what that means."

"I do." Nicholas leaned down, now face-to-face with Kohath. "Must you do this yourself?"

Jason blinked.

Nicholas lifted Jason in his arms and carried him to the console. "Mike, Amos, go. Hurry. Find Kitsune and Grant, all of you get to the boat. Watch out for Cassandra. I'll be right behind you."

Amos didn't want to leave Jason, but Mike grabbed him by the collar and dragged him out.

Nicholas eased the old man down in the chair, gently laid his hand on the biometric reader. He saw it was designed specifically to measure a heartbeat beneath the palm. A dead man's hand wouldn't work.

He pressed his own hand over Jason's, helped him flatten his palm on the reader.

The screen in front of them whirred to life, and a protocol began running that Nicholas could barely follow. The language was incredibly complex, the coding sophisticated beyond anything Nicholas had ever seen, had ever even conceived of. Nicholas gently laid Jason's fingers on the keyboard, helped him press two keys, a *J* and a *G*, no more, only two keys.

He watched in astonishment as the giant spinning cloud hovering near Washington, D.C., grew smaller and slower until it broke apart and gradually faded away, disappeared into nothingness. It was incredible, unbelievable, and he knew he would never understand how it worked. The storm that would have destroyed Washington had simply vanished, as if it had been sucked up in a vacuum and all with two key strokes. And he realized that was it exactly, the storm had been funneled away. There would be no incredible winds, no massive storm surge. Without the energy to keep it running, it would slow and dissipate as well.

Nicholas pulled a thumb drive from his key ring and showed it to Kohath. "It would be a travesty to lose all your work. May I have this coding?"

Kohath blinked his eyes again, then whispered, "Not the twins, never the twins."

He didn't tell Kohath that he'd killed his grandson, that his granddaughter was insane and he didn't know where she was. "No, don't worry, the twins won't get it." Nicholas slid the thumb drive into a slot. It only took a moment to transfer, and that was amazing. He'd never seen code work so fast. He slipped the thumb drive back onto his key ring.

Jason's hand slipped from the console and Nicholas caught it, pressed his palm back onto the pad.

"Help me destroy this." He flipped open the second stage reader, and leaned Jason forward. He held Jason's head still, and with a great effort, Jason opened his eyes. He rested his head against the plastic, waited for the biometric reader to take full measure of his iris.

There was a click. The two forms of identification were registered, accepted. Jason Kohath's head slumped forward, and Nicholas knew he was dead. Still, Nicholas checked for a pulse, found nothing. He felt both anger and loss for this man he would never know, a genius responsible for great destruction and death and greater sacrifice.

Nicholas hit Command X on the computer keyboard.

The room began to shake.

CHAPTER EIGHTY

The huge wall screens began to crack one after the other, shattering glass flying everywhere. The floor was suddenly moving, thick slabs roiling upward at crazy angles. Nicholas tried to leap over the steepening slabs, but it was too late. He lost his footing and went down, rolling toward a huge chasm that split open the floor. He grabbed a corner of the console, managed to drag himself upward. The floor shuddered again and swelled and heaved and split apart. There was nowhere to go, every direction blocked by metal and glass and huge chasms in the floor.

The temperature spiked and he saw lava begin to bubble up through the cracks and widening crevasses. The room was steaming, thick jets of hot air rising all around him and he couldn't see, could only go by the faint sound he heard over the eruption. Was it Mike? He didn't know.

He had to get out of this inferno or he would die.

He staggered to another shattered console, hoping to get out that way, but a huge jagged rock cut through the control center itself. He realized this wasn't a dormant volcano magically come to life, no, Jason Kohath had built his control center on top of an active volcano and he'd managed to contain it, but no longer. Now it was free and it would destroy the island.

He tried to get around a huge shaft of boiling hot rock, but a table blocked him. It fell into one of the huge splits in the floor.

He was stuck in the center of the room, Jason Kohath's body on fire at his feet, his grandson stretched out ten feet away, the body sliding toward a canyon of glass and molten rock, clothes burning.

Nicholas didn't want to die with the Kohaths, but he was choking, the steam from the lava burning his hands, his skin —

And then Mike was there, in the room, he could hear her now shouting at him above the din and through the steam and the billowing lava. Where was she?

"Up," she was screaming. "Nicholas, look up!"

And he saw Kitsune on the catwalk twenty feet above his head, the lava making her hair glow red.

A catwalk he hadn't noticed before. He couldn't go across, but he could go up.

Without hesitation he leaped up on the table that was sliding inexorably toward a gaping hole in the center of the room, gathered himself and leaped as high as he could. His hand grabbed around the bottom rung of the railing just as the desk slid into the pit and sank out of sight. The floor around it disappeared into the widening pit, lava bubbling high, swallowing everything. The whole room was shaking now, shuddering, and the railing swung wildly and he knew he was losing his grip. He tried to catch the railing with his right hand, but his hand slipped. He looked down to see the control center disappear into the red gaping mouth to be burned away by the molten fire. No way was he going to fall in that pit. He hung there for a second, legs dangling over bubbling lava, and the metal railing was heating up, his hands burning. He couldn't die, he couldn't leave Mike.

Then he heard Kitsune's voice, yelling, "Give me your hand, Nicholas! Hurry!"

He stuck out his right hand and she grabbed it, pulling, her legs wrapped around a metal pylon so she wouldn't lose her balance and be jerked forward. She was strong.

Finally, he got his leg up and over the railing and she hauled him up onto the metal mesh floor of the catwalk.

He was on his feet in an instant. "Kitsune, get out of here. Go! I'm right behind you."

She turned and ran down the catwalk, yelling over her shoulder, "Mike's at the intersection, about forty feet ahead."

No time to catch his breath, the metal would melt next. He ran.

He couldn't believe it. He saw Cassandra, twenty feet ahead of him, not moving, staring down at the devastation, and she was smiling. She'd made no move to stop Kitsune as she'd run past. "There they go, Ajax and Grandfather, into hell where they belong." She repeated it again, standing there, and Nicholas would swear she was happy.

He tried to grab her arm. "Come on, we have to get out of here."

His hands were blistered, and he couldn't hold her. She pulled away. Oddly, she smiled at him and he saw the emptying madness in her eyes, the complete loss of self. She still had the handcuffs around her wrists. And in her arms she held a golden wing. "Mother wouldn't save me. Perhaps this will." And she leaped from the railing into the lava below.

He saw her and the cherubim's wing disappear into the fire, the wing still clutched to her chest.

Nothing he could do, nothing. He ran. The catwalk ended at the doorway to the dock. Mike was there screaming at him to hurry. He put on a burst of speed and jumped from the catwalk toward the open door. He landed in a heap, and she yanked him to his feet.

"Hurry, hurry," and they ran down the hallway, the lava swelling, beginning to flow behind them.

He felt the unbelievable heat, saw the floor turning red, and he didn't know if they were going to make it.

But they burst through the door and the boat was on the dock waiting for them, the engine running. Amos and Grant were on board, screaming, waving. Kitsune was in front of them, she leaped onto the boat. He grabbed Mike's hand and poured on the speed.

They jumped from the dock onto the deck and Grant slammed the boat into gear and it shot away from the dock just as the lava reached the water and steam gushed up, making the water hiss and roil.

They motored into the open water away from the devastation. Nicholas was on his hands and knees, Mike running her hands all over him. She was yelling at him, and he thought he heard, "Lamebrain," and then she was kissing him all over his face, hugging him, kissing him more, and he smiled and knew he was alive. Both of them were alive.

When he opened his eyes, Mike was staring at him. She sounded like she was in a bottle, something about she couldn't get to him, but Kitsune could, and was he okay, but he couldn't quite make out the words, but he nodded. He moved, sitting up, and his ears popped, and he could hear clearly again. He saw Kitsune and Grant, both of them huddled over the wheel, the throttle fully open, the boat at its maximum speed. Amos was hanging on to the boat rail, water splashing the tears from his face.

Mike was pointing and he turned to look back toward the island. The volcano, unfettered, had roared to life, sending huge spumes of lava high into the air and with it an immense ash cloud, and then the lava began sliding down the side.

Grant dropped to the deck in front of them. "What's the right heading?"

Amos said, "Straight on, then maybe angle ten degrees south."

They slowed when they were far enough

away, and all of them looked back to watch the volcano's show. The electromagnetic field had been knocked out for good. What would the volcano do? How much damage? Nicholas knew ash clouds were bad. But there was miles and miles of open sea around the island.

He said to Mike, "Jason Kohath saved us. I couldn't do anything without his palm and his iris — he stayed alive long enough for me to get the storm stopped." He paused. "I've never seen anything so crazy in my life. It was a huge storm cloud and it was so close to the coastline and then suddenly, it broke up and was gone. I accessed Jason Kohath's files, he gave me permission.

"One more thing." He called out, "Kitsune, thank you for saving my life."

She looked at him, held close to Mike, and gave him a huge smile.

Once back at the Albatross, Rafael looked at the crowd and shook his head. "I've already got Captain Snelling and Aldo inside. I can't fit the rest of you, we'll go down."

They heard a huge roar coming from the island.

"You woke up *El Diablo,*" he said.

Mike threw back her head and shouted, "Isn't it a good thing that the devil doesn't have long arms? We're safe."

Nicholas said to Rafael, "Can you take five?"

"I can try, if they're skinny enough."

"They are," Nicholas said.

He watched Mike hug Amos, whisper to him, hug him again.

"What?"

"Amos is from Horton, Nebraska, close to Omaha. I told him to call my dad, he'll see he gets a good job."

They shook Grant's hand. Then Nicholas turned to Kitsune and took her red blistered hands in his, leaned in close. "Thank you for my life. Again. And, Kitsune? Next time you want to steal a biblical artifact, think long and hard." And he handed her up to her husband.

"Go, Rafael. Mike and I will wait here for you to come back for us." Because he and Mike were Rafael's meal ticket, he knew he'd come back, and be sharp about it. They stood together in the boat, waving as Rafael skimmed over the waves, gained speed, and lifted into the air, heading back to Cuba.

Nicholas looked back at the ash cloud rising high into the air. His shirt was nearly ripped off, his pants were torn and filthy, and everything hurt, his head, his hands, even his hair. He didn't even think he'd have energy for a shower; sleeping for a week was what he wanted most in the world.

As for Mike, her hair was straggling around her face, streaked with ash, her face as dirty as his, her clothes just as torn and filthy. She looked beautiful. She was smiling up at him and how could she smile? After all this, and yet she was smiling. She lightly touched her fingertips to his cheek. "How long do you think Rafael will take to get back here?"

"An hour, maybe less."

"Nicholas, did you see James Bond movies when you were a kid?"

"Never missed one. But my favorites were the old Sean Connery ones. Why?"

"Did you see the one where James and the heroine are alone in a boat waiting to be rescued?"

"Oh, yes, I think they were supposed to be in the Sea of Japan, but I found out it was filmed off Bermuda. Unfortunately, I also remember a submarine came up under their Zodiac, and they were busted."

Mike shaded her eyes, did a complete 360. "I don't see any submarines."

Nicholas thought about all the unexpected twists his life had taken, how his life was now intertwined with people he hadn't known the year before, good people, people who would fight until they had no more breath. He realized he cherished life more this moment than he ever had. Both he and Mike were alive, they'd made it. He grinned. "Well, then."

CHAPTER EIGHTY-ONE

Mysore Base
Gobi Desert
2006

Helen Kohath shielded her eyes from the setting sun. She stood over a large pit, being shored up by her foreman, Dr. Thomas Zahn.

"Thomas, how much longer?"

"I'm going as fast as I can, Helen. We don't dare move quicker, the whole desert could collapse in on us."

"I know it's here. I can feel it."

And she could. Her ears buzzed with it. She hadn't needed the spectrometer, she was able to stand right over the spot where the Ark was resting and sense the energy flowing up through her feet into her body, flooding her brain with light and flashes of long-ago memories, memories that weren't hers, but maybe those of long-ago ancestors whose blood she carried. She saw a mass of people walking, pulling carts, carrying children — the flash was gone, but she knew to her soul it was an original memory. When she was one with the Ark, she would see everything, understand everything.

She felt incredibly blessed, and impatient. So many years she'd waited for this moment, prayed for this moment. She stood motionless, watching, saying over and over under her breath: *Come on, come on, come on.*

It was hot, small, biting flies buzzed around her head, the sand kept falling back into the pit, but finally, *finally,* they had the sands moved away and the pit reinforced.

Thomas whispered, "It's here, Helen. It's here. There's a crate, it's marked with a simple cross, just a cross, nothing else. Come see."

She closed her eyes in a silent prayer, then walked to the edge of the pit. The buzzing grew stronger. "Do any of you hear that?"

Blank faces stared at her. So it was only her. The Ark of the Covenant was hers alone.

"Bring it out." Saying the words aloud made her tremble.

They'd long perfected the rope pulley system and the crate was quickly brought up. Brown and orange scorpions fell from the wood and scrambled away. They set the crate gently on the ground.

She heard her crews' excited voices and the deepening roar of the approaching storm. Then all eyes turned to her as she waved away the crowbar Thomas held out to her. She lightly laid her palm on the lid. And it came up with barely a sound, only a slight crack of the wood. The buzzing was growing louder, nearly a high whine now. She smoothed her hands over the rest of the wood and it simply fell away. She knew all her crew believed the wood was rotted, and simply touching was all that was necessary. But the wood wasn't rotted at all. Helen saw gold flash in the sunlight and her heart nearly stopped beating.

Two golden cherubim, wings outstretched, hovered protectively over the top of the Ark, almost as if they were crying. She reached out her hand to touch them, perhaps to comfort them, to let them know she was here.

"I've found you at last," she whispered. "You're with me as it was meant to be."

Thomas whispered at her elbow, "It's beautiful."

The crew broke into spontaneous applause, calling and cheering. "You've done it, madam. You've found the Ark!"

Helen held up a hand for silence. She shouldn't do this here, she shouldn't do this now, not in front of these people who shouldn't even be seeing this blessed gift God had preserved for millennia, but the Ark was calling her from deep inside, low, vibrant, insistent. *Helen, Helen. Helen.*

Thomas leaned forward to help her, but she waved him back. He believed the lid was heavy? She smiled as she laid her hand on it, felt it pulse, felt it breathe. She pushed at the lid with her finger. It slid off as if she'd struck it, and crashed to the sands. A piece of a cherubim's wing broke off.

She'd heard their surprise when she'd lifted the lid so easily, heard their gasps when the cherubim's wing broke off. She saw fear in their eyes, of some possible biblical curse? Of her? Thomas bent down to pick up the wing.

"No! Don't touch it, Thomas."

He straightened slowly, his eyes never leaving her face. Her friend for many years, her occasional lover, Thomas Zahn, brilliant, dedicated, had always been at her side. He'd been her confidant and she saw he was upset because she was shutting him out.

She raised her hand. "No, don't worry. The lid flew off because gases had built up, nothing more." A lie, but how were they to know? "We'll repair the wing. It's okay." Some of them looked away from her. The others, did they believe her? It didn't matter.

She knelt in front of the box and looked inside. The Ark sat on the golden shell. It was small, smaller than she'd believed it would be, even though she'd long ago memorized the biblical measures.

She saw the lid closed with strings of rope. With a finger, she traced the old ropes and they sprung free at her touch. The lid of the Ark lifted, and a glow as bright as the desert sun wreathed her face. Its warmth was like a soft caress against her flesh. It grew more intense, a burning bright light, but she didn't have to close her eyes against it, no, she leaned closer, breathed it in, thousands of years of an ancient life force, flowing into her. She bathed in it, let it fill her, let it settle.

A voice filled her, neither male nor female, human or beast, it was a thousand voices at once, but only one, and it reverberated like echoes of chimes through her entire body.

Helen Kohath. Your family was chosen at the beginning, the blessed ones, the only ones to guard me, but still I was lost. You found me and now you must protect me, keep me safe. Not your children, for they would use my power against the earth. No one but you can ever see me. Only you are worthy to guard me.

Take me away where none will find me. Those here cannot be allowed to tell the world of my existence. Do it.

She closed her eyes, the words flowing through her, and she said with no hesitation, "Like the Kohaths before me, I was ordained to watch over you and I will, I swear it."

"Helen? Helen!" Thomas was shouting in her ear, pulling on her arm.

The thousand-single-voice commanded, *Do it, Helen. Do it now.* The voice stilled, the brilliant light faded, the lid slapped shut. She was suddenly back in the Gobi Desert, facing her crew, all of them gaping at her, fear and awe on their faces. And Thomas, dear Thomas, now a stranger to her.

She rose, and brushed the sand off her pants. She was Helen Kohath, the leader of this group. "Thomas, load the Ark on the truck. Fashion a new crate for it, this old wood is rotted through. Find the piece of wing, it slipped into the pit. Good job, everyone." She paused only an instant, before smiling at them all. "Thank you for all your hard work, the world will be at our feet when we return." She looked over

Thomas's shoulder. "We must hurry. We have less than two hours before the sandstorm is on us."

Her voice sounded entirely normal, slightly excited, appropriate to the situation. Thomas continued studying her face. "What was inside the Ark, Helen?"

She smiled. "A great sweetness, Thomas, a great welcoming. Don't let anyone try to open it again. Let's get it packed up and on the truck before the storm hits."

She stepped away, watched her crew follow her orders, everyone excited, moving quickly.

It took less than an hour to pack the Ark into a newly built crate and get it into the bed of the truck. She memorized all their faces, she never wanted to forget them and knew she wouldn't. They would become part of her.

Thomas brought her the wing fragment. She held it in her arms and saw the small lettering along the edge, and read the warning.

Through this door lies a weapon of great power. Open it, and it will indeed kill.

She looked at Thomas's dear face, at all their faces, so happy, so excited, some of them staring at her, obviously worried, filled with questions, and she simply knew she couldn't do it, she couldn't kill these people whose lives were so close entwined with hers, even with the voice telling her to, commanding her to, even with the knowledge that one word from any of them and the precious Ark could once again be in danger, and lost for millennia yet again.

Still, she couldn't do it.

She stood silently. The babble of voices grew louder in her head, so many, yet only one, and it was neither male nor female, and it was so very calm, mesmerizing and reassuring, saying words, strange words she didn't understand, over and over, but not to her. No, these words were not meant for her.

Her people didn't hesitate. One by one, she watched them kneel down in a long straight line. Thomas smiled at her even as he knelt beside them, and bowed his head as all the others had. And she watched them simply fall forward on their faces.

She felt for a pulse in each throat. They were all dead. She closed her eyes, said a prayer, but knew in her soul that the Ark would somehow enfold them and cherish them for their sacrifice.

Helen secured the site. She took the broken cherubim's wing, and a map she'd drawn inside a soil core, and dropped them into the pit for Cassandra and Ajax to find sometime in the future, as she now knew they would, as it was meant for them to. And they would act on what was deep inside them, what drove them to be what and who they were, and she knew what would happen. No way to escape that. A great lie, all a great lie, she knew, although she now couldn't remember what her hand had written on the map. Perhaps the words would foster goodness and truth in her children, even as she despaired. *Please,* she prayed, *please.* She looked back at her dead team, wiped the tears from her face, and drove off, alone, toward her destiny.

The sandstorm whipped the desert into a frenzy, but the flying sands never touched the truck.

CHAPTER EIGHTY-TWO

Cuba
Present Day
When Rafael made his second landing at the Preston airfield and taxied toward the FBI Gulfstream, Nicholas and Mike saw that Clancy, Trident, Adam, and Louisa were standing by the stairs, clapping and cheering.

The Albatross rolled to a smooth stop and a beaming Rafael dashed out, waved, then waited for Mike and Nicholas. Everyone was on an obvious high, yelling questions, telling them what they already knew, but from the other's perspectives. And now it was their turn, and on and on it went, Nicholas and Mike smiling and laughing.

Adam said, "Mr. Zachery will never believe this."

"Sure he will," Nicholas said, "I kept him up to date on everything that was going on, well, most of it —"

"Some of it — when he had to," Mike said, "but we have yet to make the last call, assure him the world will survive another day."

Finally, everyone was running down. Adam was shaking his head. "I still can't believe it. Even from here we knew when the volcano blew, only now is the ash beginning to dissipate and the winds are carrying it out into the Atlantic."

Nicholas said, "Where are Captain Snelling and Aldo?"

Adam said, "Captain Snelling and Aldo paid one of the workers to drive them to Havana. As for Kitsune and Grant, a Blue Mountain Gulfstream landed about a half hour ago. You told me to keep Grant's people informed and I did. They took Grant and Kitsune, lifted back off within a few minutes. We don't know where they went. At least we got to say goodbye."

"I can't believe they just left," Mike said.

Nicholas shook his head at her. "You really didn't expect to see them here waiting for us, now did you, Mike?"

No, she hadn't, but that wasn't the point. She got in his face. "You knew she and Grant would be gone when we got back, didn't you? If Blue Mountain hadn't come, they'd still be gone. And you already said goodbye to her."

"Yes, I did. I'm sorry, I didn't realize you'd want to say goodbye to her, too. Did you?"

It was hard to be pissed at him when he smiled at her like that, when she still felt so mellow and yet remarkably energized. But the fact was, she owed Kitsune, she owed her more than she could ever repay, and she'd wanted to tell her that, tell her she owed her big-time, forever.

She cocked her head to one side. "The thing is, Nicholas, I really would have liked to have said goodbye to Grant. He's incredible, isn't he? All rough and tough and don't-mess-with-me." She gave a little shake. "Imagine, having him sharing some of his adventures with me —"

She got him, she saw it, even though the *let me kill him* look was gone in an instant. He said, all bonhomie, "You know, Mike, I wish I could have talked to him more, too."

She gave him a little bow and turned to Adam, eyebrow raised. "I don't suppose you'll ever tell us where Kitsune and Grant live?"

Adam said, "You'd have to make me an offer I couldn't refuse."

No, Mike knew Adam would never talk.

Louisa said, "I expected you two to look

like crap, ripped clothes, all banged up, some burns here and there, split lips, and that's all true —" She paused, frowning at them. "But you both look so happy and so relaxed . . ."

Then her eyes popped, and she started to laugh. She walked over to Adam and said something to him. He shot Mike and Nicholas a look, nodded. "Oh yeah, I bet that isn't going in their report to Zachery."

Nicholas clapped his hands. "All right, that's quite enough. All of you, get on the plane. I'll be right with you after I've conducted some business with our pilot."

Nicholas set into motion all the promises they'd made to Rafael Guzman.

Rafael didn't leave until he watched them fly out of his sight in their new Gulfstream before he pulled out his cell phone and called his wife to tell her to pack for Miami, they wouldn't be coming back to Cuba.

Once they were airborne, everyone fed, watered, and snuggled in with blankets and pillows, Mike pulled Helen Kohath's notebook out of her jacket pocket.

Nicholas stared from her to the notebook. "I thought it went into the lava. How did you get hold of it?"

"It was lying on the grate at the end of the catwalk. I thought it had fallen out of your pocket."

"I never had it. Cassandra, she must have dropped it."

"I only saw her carrying the cherubim's wing. Well, in any case, I grabbed it up on our race to the boat."

Louisa called out, "Kitsune said something about Helen Kohath's notebook being in the vault, said she didn't know what happened to it. What's in it, Mike? Adam, wake up, it's from Helen Kohath, you want to hear this."

Adam's head appeared from beneath his blanket. "Okay, okay, don't rip my arm out. Yeah, I want to hear about this notebook."

Mike said, "As we all know, the Kohaths liked to keep journals, Appleton Kohath's was the fodder for Elizabeth St. Germaine's biography of him. But in this notebook, there's no journaling, no entries at all. There is only a letter from Helen to her father, written a few days after she went missing in the Gobi in 2006.

"*After* she went missing, not *before.*

"And that means, of course, that Jason Kohath knew she was still alive and he never told Cassandra and Ajax. I'll read it to you."

My dearest father,
I found the Ark. I am now its guardian.

592

It is up to me to protect it forever. The power of the Ark, it is overwhelming, Father, it fills my head, my body, my soul, it imbues me with life.

I belong to it now, only me. I'm sorry I cannot come home, but it simply wasn't ever intended to be, the Ark made that very clear to me. My greatest pain to bear is the loss of Cassandra and Ajax and what will happen to them. But neither you nor I can change the future for them, though I know you will continue to try until the time comes when you are no longer able to.

I must leave now, so this is my goodbye. I love you, I have always admired you, and been astounded by your genius. Please believe I am happier than I have ever been in my life. The Ark — we will be well. No one will ever find us.

All my love,
Helen

CHAPTER EIGHTY-THREE

Over the Atlantic

Only Mike and Nicholas still had their eyes open, but just barely. Nicholas was massaging her shoulders, and telling her they could visit his parents at Farrow-on-Gray, or maybe take a trip to see her parents in Omaha.

The button at Nicholas's elbow beeped.

It was Clancy. "Nicholas, I've received a secure email from the Metropolitan Police of London. Gareth Scott?"

"Thank you, Clancy. Send it to my mobile. You remember my old second at Scotland Yard, right, Mike?"

At her nod, he added, "Penderley promoted him when I left to join the FBI. Let's see what Gareth has to say."

Nicholas, update on St. Germaine and Maynes cases. Coroner's court confirms both were poisoned with high doses of digitalis — foxglove — present in the tea tins from Fortnum & Mason. Caused cardiac arrest in both victims. Believe Lilith Forrester-Clarke is responsible, but seeing as she's dead, I doubt we'll ever know the complete truth. If you want details, give a shout. Do try not to get killed in the meantime. Oh, yes, your ex-wife, Pamela, is in London. We had dinner.

Nicholas texted back, Thank you. Watch yourself with Pamela, Gareth.

He paused, then texted, Really. And he pressed send.

Mike touched her fingers to his face, then yawned again.

"Gareth is right, we'll never know the whole truth, about Cassandra and Ajax and all the things they did. You know what? I don't think I really do want to know."

Nicholas said, "Hopefully the Genesis Group will continue their legitimate work with honest people at the helm."

"Time to hang it up, Nicholas, time to sleep."

But he couldn't. Finally, he pulled out the thumb drive and plugged it into his laptop.

"From Jason Kohath's computer?"

"You're awake, too, are you? Yes, this is from Jason's computer." He began to scroll down, then stopped. "We're going to need a team of astrophysicists to figure all this out and translate it for us so we have a prayer of understanding it." He sat back, pulled her close. "Imagine, Mike, to be able to create lightning, to be able to create a thunderstorm, to whip up a sandstorm, to blow in a hurricane. We know the basic ingredients are moisture to form clouds and rain, then unstable air and lift. And we know unstable air has to be relatively warm to rise rapidly. But with the Coil and the lasers — it's all quite remarkable and I don't understand it."

"Will the astrophysicists?"

He grinned at her. "We'll see."

Mike said, "What if one of the astrophysicists could replicate it, Nicholas? And become another Jason Kohath?"

"I believe we're going to have to let our superiors decide. They knew what to do with the micro nukes Havelock created, they'll know what to do with this information as well."

"And exactly what did our superiors do with the micro nukes?"

He frowned. "I don't know."

"There you go. Maybe some criminal or a spy got hold of the micro nukes and sold them to an enemy."

He studied the thumb drive lying on his palm, then slipped it back on its key ring and put it in his pocket.

Mike smiled at him through another yawn. "We have one more task to perform before we can nap."

He raised a dark brow. "You're calling it a task? Again? Aren't you too tired? And on the boat, Mike, didn't we already perform —"

"Yes, yes, be quiet. Let's call Zachery. I'd rather have him screaming at us at thirty-five thousand feet than in our faces."

Zachery didn't yell at them, he was frankly too relieved. He'd gotten a call, he told them, from Kitsune — the Fox — and she'd told him everything, answered his questions, at least those she could. "She said you were both heroes and the world owes you a big debt. And then she blew me a kiss over the phone and said she doubted she'd ever be speaking to me again and have a good life and enjoy my doubtless stimulating future with you guys."

Kitsune had called their boss? Called them heroes?

"Sir, did Kitsune also bother to tell you she saved my life — twice?"

"Remember, the Venice ambush," Mike called out. "She showed up there, too."

There was a pause, then Zachery said, "No, she didn't tell me about saving your life, Nicholas. Is that why you let her go?"

"She didn't need either Mike or me to let her go, sir, she and her husband were gone, destination unknown, when Mike and I flew back to Cuba. Grant Thornton's security firm, Blue Mountain, showed up in Cuba and flew them out."

Zachery sighed. "I hate to say this about a major international crook, but I like her, can't help it. When she called you guys heroes, I heard a man laugh in the background. Her husband?"

"Yes, a very brave man," Mike said, "who appears to understand her very well."

Zachery sighed. "Why can't things be black or white? Forget I said that, that'd be boring. Savich called me before Kitsune did, told me how you guys must have managed to stop the storm because the mammoth hurricane off Washington, D.C., simply up and disappeared. He said the meteorologists are flummoxed, no explanation, nothing, and that was nice to see. It will remain a mystery, needless to say.

"Now, come home, rest a couple of days, then you have to go back to Italy, check in with the local police as well as the Carabinieri in Castel Rigone. Evidently you left bodies in tunnels and more bodies in wrecked cars off the highway.

"Oh, one other thing. A local cop, Deputy Inspector Nando, said to tell you Major Russo of the Carabinieri was arrested. I don't know for what exactly, but this Nando said you'd understand."

That was very fine news indeed. It was good to occasionally see some justice in the world.

Nicholas said, "Sir, rather than fly home, Adam, Louisa, Mike, and I would like to chat up the police in Castel Rigone immediately, then drive over to Venice for a couple of days."

Zachery laughed, told them not to fall into the Grand Canal, punched off.

"Venice, Nicholas? Really?"

"Agent Caine, I promised you a night out in Venice. Adam and Louisa are all for it. I've already made a reservation."

"Where?"

"You'll see."

CHAPTER EIGHTY-FOUR

Harry's Bar, Calle Vallaresso
Venice, Italy
Saturday Night

Harry's Bar was a hole-in-the-wall that had proudly sat right on the Grand Canal since 1931. It was arguably the most famous establishment in all of Venice, best known for its Bellinis — prosecco with white peach puree. Mike couldn't wait.

Nicholas was wearing a gorgeous gray cashmere jacket, slacks, and a crisp white shirt with a black tie, sinfully soft black Italian loafers on his feet, all purchased that afternoon from Armani in the Marzaria near the Rialto Bridge, close to Harry's Bar and to their hotel. He'd had to admit his go-bag had let him down. To make matters worse, there was no Barney's in Venice, so what was he to do?

After he'd been outfitted, he and the salesman had talked Mike into a new little black dress. She'd put her foot down when the salesman had presented her with four-inch stilettos to go with the dress. She held firm, nope, it was her biker boots. Didn't Nicholas agree?

He agreed, laughing. If the biker boots were good enough for the president of the United States, they were good enough for Venice.

The moment they stepped through the door of Harry's Bar, the hostess was at his side, greeting him like she would a movie star, and Mike couldn't blame her for that. She even waved away the maître d' and led them herself to a prized table, right in the center of the room. She whisked away the RESERVED sign. She kept sneaking looks at Nicholas, probably trying to figure out who he was.

Mike realized she was surrounded by beautiful people and some not so beautiful, but all were dressed to the hilt, diamonds flashing. Mike counted three celebrities she recognized, walking nonchalantly across the small room to head upstairs. One of the men paused, looked directly at her, and smiled, gave her a small salute.

"Isn't that Mark Ruffalo?"

"Yes, I think it is. And Stanley Tucci was behind him. They just did a movie together."

She fiddled with the napkin. "I should have bought those mile-high killer stilettos, not been stubborn and worn my biker boots."

"Nah, those boots nearly brought Ruffalo over here to slaver on you."

Mike hated to wave that lovely image away. "I wonder what he would do if my mom — the Gorgeous Rebecca — was sitting here. He'd probably crawl over and pant like a puppy at her feet."

Nicholas thought Ruffalo had looked at Mike as if he wanted to sling her over his shoulder and take her to bed, but he kept his mouth shut. Her hair wasn't in a ponytail this evening, no it was shining and loose around her shoulders, one side hooked back with a gold clip. He took her hand and kissed her fingers. His eyes never left hers. "Actually, now that I think about it, that hour we spent in the boat waiting for Rafael to come back to fetch us — the clothes you were wearing then were stunning as well."

She spurted out a laugh just as a waiter delivered their Bellinis.

They toasted each other and sipped. It tasted like ambrosia and Mike wanted to drink it straight down and order another one, fast. She suspected that after a couple of these, she could fly over the Grand

Canal, swoop down and kiss Louisa and Adam in their gondola.

"I called Nigel, confessed to him I had to shop at Armani, but all he wanted to talk about was how you and I saved Washington, D.C. He said the news was blaring out how an apocalyptic storm slated to hit the city had people panicked, trying to drive inland, resulting in horrific traffic. And then it was simply gone, disappeared. And no one could explain it. I asked him why he thought you and I were responsible, and he laughed at me."

"And you'll tell him all about our adventures when we get home, won't you?"

"I don't plan to, but Nigel has his ways of learning anything he wants to know. Then I'll have to bribe him not to tell my parents or my grandfather."

"Well, I'm going to tell my folks, not all of it, but the parts that make us look good and not like idiots. My dad will be impressed, and my mother will wonder what shape my nails are in."

Nicholas ordered them another round of Bellinis.

"I wish Adam and Louisa were here. Do you think they'd give Adam a Bellini since he isn't twenty-one?"

"It's Italy, Mike. Besides, when I asked

him and Louisa to join us, they both shook their heads. Turns out Louisa had made him a deal: he'd go running with her and she'd pay extra for a long gondola in the moonlight, and sing him arias. I think Louisa even talked him into leaving his cell phone in the room."

It was nearly midnight when they left Harry's Bar and walked hand in hand back to their hotel beside the Grand Canal, a half-moon lighting their way, sparkling off the water. The night was warm, the air soft. They were both on the tipsy side, and it felt wonderful. There were very few people out this late and it was quiet, except for the gentle splashing of the water against the pylons. They'd forgotten their burned hands, their bruises, even forgotten the horror on that island in the Devil's Triangle, Louisa's new name for it.

Nicholas pulled her to a stop.

She cocked her head up at him as he reached into his pants pocket and pulled the thumb drive with Jason Kohath's formula off his key ring. "You made me think about this some more. Who knows if Jason's ideas, his formulas, his instructions, wouldn't end up in the wrong hands? The world is rife with greedy, immoral people. It could easily happen." He drew a deep breath. "So what do you think?"

Mike never looked away from his face. "Throw it as far as you can into the canal."

He did. The thumb drive didn't make a sound, simply slid beneath the surface of the dark water. They both hoped it would sit in the bottom silt until someday the city itself finally collapsed on top of it.

They stood quietly. Then, "Listen, Mike."

Mike cocked her head. "What?"

Nicholas said, "I think I heard Louisa singing the aria from *Madame Butterfly.*"

EPILOGUE

Somewhere Near Greece
May 2, 2040
The catch was good today. The hold of
Christos's boat was full of red mullet. His
young son Alexio was resting on the pile of
nets in the prow of the boat. Unlike his
brother, Alexio wasn't afraid of the Guardian.

Before Christos steered the boat another
mile into the bay below the promontory of
their little island, he slowed his boat to look
to the sheer granite cliffs, as he always did.
His day never ended without seeing her,
without saying his short prayer: *Please keep
my family safe and keep safe what you watch
over, my lady.*

There had been many changes in the
world since Christos was a boy, but the
Guardian had never changed. She was
always there, every night, silhouetted against
the sunset, her hand to her forehead, shad-

ing her eyes as she looked out to sea. He wondered what she did, this woman, this amazing being, who was woven into the very fabric of his life. Like young Alexio, Christos had fished with his own father, and they'd seen her daily. Though the Guardian was far away, he could tell that in all these years she had never changed — her long white gown blowing gently against her legs, her golden hair braided in thick plaits atop her head, her skin smooth and white. He remembered her from his youngest years, remembered his father saying:

I remember when she first appeared, Christos, and it was magic. I felt her goodness and I knew she was here to watch over us. I knew she was holy. She is holy. I knew she would never leave us.

It was Christos, at five years old, who had waved madly at her from his father's boat, now his boat, and he remembered so clearly how she had looked down at him, how she had nodded, recognizing the small boy, and he'd felt such warmth and deep sense of wonder and happiness. And he'd whispered, *Guardian.*

Over the years, he'd listened to many stories about her, who she was, what she was, and what she was guarding, for all knew there was something that kept her there, year after year, decade after decade, but he'd never said anything. And no one spoke of her, no one tried to climb those cliffs to reach her.

Christos bowed to her as he always did, and knew that she saw him, recognized him, blessed him. As a child, he'd felt warmth and wonder. Now he felt a deep sense of reverence, and awe. He looked to the prow of the boat to see Alexio waving at her. And she nodded at his small son.

ABOUT THE AUTHORS

Catherine Coulter is the author of over 70 novels, most of them *New York Times* bestsellers. Coulter grew up on a horse ranch in Texas, and graduated from the University of Texas, receiving her graduate degree from Boston College. She lives with her physician husband and three cats in Marin County, California.

New York Times bestselling author *J.T. Ellison* writes dark psychological thrillers starring Nashville Homicide Lt. Taylor Jackson and medical examiner Dr. Samantha Owens, and pens the Nicholas Drummond series with #1 *New York Times* bestselling author Catherine Coulter. Cohost of the premier literary television show, *A Word on Words*, Ellison lives in Nashville with her husband and twin kittens. Follow J.T. on Facebook or Twitter @thrillerchick for more insight into her wicked imagination.